THE PROBLEM OF
THE MISSING MISS

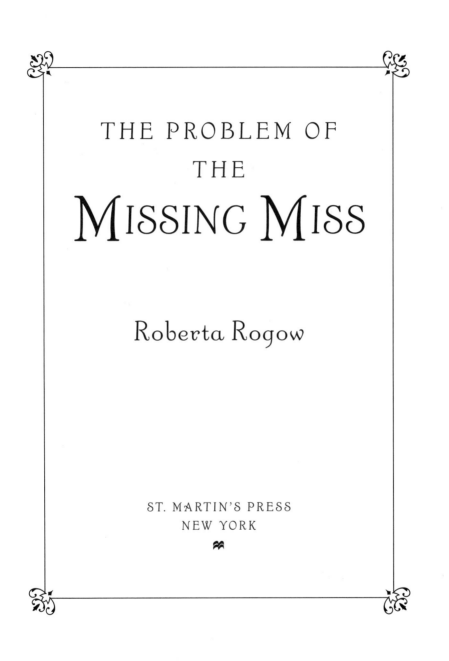

THE PROBLEM OF
THE
MISSING MISS

Roberta Rogow

ST. MARTIN'S PRESS
NEW YORK

Design by Nancy Resnick

Library of Congress Cataloging-in-Publication Data

Rogow, Roberta.
    The problem of the missing miss / by Roberta Rogow.—1st ed.
        p.   cm.
    ISBN 0-312-18553-7
    1. Carroll, Lewis, 1832–1898—Fiction. 2. Doyle, Arthur
Conan, Sir, 1859–1930—Fiction. I. Title.
PS3568.0492P7   1998
813'.54—dc21   98-5329
                                                            CIP

First Edition: May 1998

10   9   8   7   6   5   4   3   2

ACKNOWLEDGMENTS

This novel would not have been written without the encouragement of many people. Especially important to me were:

Keith Kahla, my editor, who made a suggestion at a Convention;

Marvin Kaye, my mentor and friend, who asked me to write a story;

Cherry Weiner, my agent, who took a chance on a voice over the telephone;

and always . . .

Murray Rogow, my husband, who has always been with me when I needed him.

To my grandfathers,
Harry Heller and Irving Weinstein,
who introduced me to
Mr. Dodgson and Dr. Doyle.

THE PROBLEM OF
THE MISSING MISS

CHAPTER 1

No one expected to find murder in Brighton. London, that great metropolis, was well-known as a sinkhole of vice, where murder was part of the ambiance, as it were. The grim manufacturing towns like Manchester and Birmingham had their share of grim crimes committed by grim men (and a few women) and even the sanctified towers of York Cathedral looked over bloody deeds in a past that included Viking raids and the Wars of the Roses. But no one would have any reason to believe that a holiday in Brighton would lead to murder, abduction, and general skulduggery.

After all, Brighton was a holiday spot, a place dedicated to recreation and entertainment, although this had not always been so. For centuries, the village known as Brightelmstone had been a haven for fishermen and the occasional smuggler. Then it had been "discovered" by no less a person than His Royal Highness, George, the Prince of Wales, soon to be the Prince Regent. The town was now fashionable, and became more so as the eighteenth century eased into the nineteenth.

By the time the Prince of Wales had become the Prince Regent, Brighton was being rebuilt, from the sea inland. As the Prince's vast

Pavilion took shape, rows of elegant houses were erected to accommodate the visitors that followed royalty. The seafront was enhanced by a Promenade, so that the bucks could ogle the charming ladies and the ladies could more modestly eye their prospective mates. Brighton was, indeed, the place to be in July and August, when London was no place for the fashionable.

When the Prince Regent finally assumed the throne as George IV, he retired to Brighton to finish his reign in his ornate palace, surrounded by memories of past frolics. His brother, the seagoing William, enjoyed Brighton's opulence, and brought his considerable (and illegitimate) offspring there to take the sea air.

Time passed, and so did "Sailor Billy," to be succeeded by his prim niece, Victoria. Victoria shuddered at the thought of residing in the incredibly ornate and Oriental Pavilion, where she and her thoroughly legitimate offspring could be ogled by the mob. Her thrifty Prince Consort sold the structure to the borough of Brighton, and the town itself lost a good deal of its fashionable cachet as society followed the Crown to the Isle of Wight or to Scotland to escape the summer stink.

Though the fashionable left, the unfashionable continued to flock to Brighton, which was delighted to accommodate them. Regency town houses became lodgings. The Pavilion was refurbished and used for public events, concerts, and lectures. A grand pier was built, jutting into the English Channel, so that the visitor might have the experience of being on the sea without the discomfort of mal-de-mer.

With the railroads came an even greater influx of visitors. Brighton was now a resort for the many instead of the few. Anyone with the railway fare could come to Brighton for a day, to paddle in the sea, gawk at the street buskers, eat whelks and chips, and get as much of a sunburn as the English summer can give. In Brighton, a holidaymaker could have a decent meal, see a Punch and Judy show, or lose a few bob on a penny dip, and still be home in time for work on Monday morning.

On this particular August Friday, in the year of Her Majesty's reign 1885, the vast vault of Brighton Railway Station was overflowing with humanity. Everyone in England seemed to have but one goal: to get as far away from hot flats, cottages, houses in cities, towns, and villages as they possibly could. To this end, a vast multitude of men, women, and children descended upon Brighton, armed with valises and carpetbags filled with summer linens and cottons, determined to enjoy themselves or die trying.

Train after train, from as far away as darkest Yorkshire, bore visitors to the once-fashionable (now rather blowsy) summer terminus. Whistles echoed and re-echoed as each train announced its arrival. Porters scrambled to accost prospective patrons. Fathers in black alpaca coats and mothers in striped calico (with or without the requisite bustle) counted and re-counted their broods. Unattached young men in red and white–striped shirts and buff blazers ogled unattached young women in flowered chintz dresses, who giggled back. Sailors on leave from Portsmouth and soldiers from the Encampment beyond the town added touches of Navy blue and bright red to the shifting scene. The sounds of transportation and incipient revelry bounced off the glass and iron roof of the terminus, making normal conversation almost impossible.

In the middle of all this hullabaloo stood a stooping, middle-aged man with a curiously unlined face, surmounted by artistically long iron-gray hair topped by a slightly out-of-date tall black silk hat, his hands encased in gray cotton gloves, his black coat as conspicuous as a crow in a flowerbed among the dainty cotton prints and white linens of the holidaymakers on the platform. Oblivious to the throng, he fussed along the platform, peering into first one car and then another, growing more and more agitated with each compartment he searched. Over and over again he checked the paper in his hand, even going so far as to refer to the large overhead sign that announced each incoming train.

Finally, he sought help from the stationmaster, that august personage enthroned in the glass-enclosed booth at the furthest end of the station. The stationmaster, one McNaughton, a large and mustachioed functionary whose dark blue uniform fairly gleamed in the light that filtered through the station, ignored the frantic tapping on the walls of his *sanctum sanctorum*.

3

The elderly gentleman persisted. "Sir! Sir! I must inform you . . . " The rest of the message was lost in the noise of the crowd, the shriek of a whistle, and the sudden hubbub that indicated some disaster in the offing.

The stationmaster stared at the ostensible lunatic who was waving at him on the other side of the glass. What manner of man was it who interrupted a stationmaster on this, the busiest time of the day, in the middle of August, the sacred time of the holidays?

The intruder staggered suddenly and seemed to collapse. The stationmaster emerged from his glass coccoon to find a hearty-looking young man in tweeds, with neatly brushed reddish hair and a not so neatly trimmed reddish mustache, attending to the stricken one, while a fresh-faced, plump young woman in a tartan traveling dress hovered anxiously behind.

"Here, here, what's all this?" The stationmaster relied on the terms used by his brothers-in-arms of the Brighton Constabulary.

"Hello! It's all right, I'm a doctor. I noticed this old chap having some kind of a fit." The young man turned to his putative patient. "Are you all right, sir?"

"I b-beg your pardon? I didn't understand." The older man looked up at his rescuers in some confusion, putting a gray-gloved hand to one ear.

The young woman behind the doctor peered over his shoulder. "Arthur? The porter is ready with our baggage . . . "

"In a minute, Touie. Just thought I could lend a hand, you know." The doctor's Edinburgh burr was noticeable even through the noise of the station, and McNaughton decided that here was a fellow Scot, a practical fellow capable of dealing with madmen who interrupted busy stationmasters by having fits in front of their offices.

"Better have him in my office, then," the stationmaster conceded. "Can't hear yourself think out here."

The group filed into the glass-enclosed hub of the Brighton railway station, an office already crowded with two rolltop desks, a carved chair, three high stools, several piles of Bradshaw's *Railway Guides*, and the reams of paper that seem to follow officialdom wherever it may lurk. Charts covered the walls, announcing everything

4

from the Firemen's Outing to the excursion rates for Parliamentary trains. The office, somewhat cramped before, seemed filled to the bursting point once Touie in her traveling dress (and its bustle) was added to the three men.

Having closed the door and shut out the roar of the crowd, Mc-Naughton straightened his cap, adjusted his uniform, stroked his mustache, and asked again, "What's all this about? Are you quite well, sir?"

"I am quite all right, thank you." The victim straightened himself and patted his coat into place. "Stationmaster, I must speak with you. I fear a child is missing!"

"Eh?" The stationmaster's eyebrows nearly met over his well-developed nose. There were persons whose whole business it was to deal with misplaced children: guards and porters. Busy stationmasters had better things to do.

"I was to meet her when she arrived on the four-thirty train from London. I have searched the station, but she is not here." The older man spoke with the shrill tones of the deaf, emphasizing each plosive consonant.

"Well, sir, the train from London was a mite late, but not all that much. It arrived at four-twenty-two. I have it noted here in my log." The stationmaster produced a complex chart, with times neatly entered.

"Are you certain?" The older man frowned.

"Oh, yes, sir. The train was due at four-twenty and came in at four-twenty-two."

The elderly gentleman looked about him, as if to locate a safe place to collapse. The doctor caught him as he was falling and eased him into the nearest seat, the stationmaster's own, sacred chair.

"This is quite imp-p-possible," the older man stammered. "See here, I have the letter with instructions. I was to meet Miss Alicia Marbury on the platform of the train arriving from London at four-thirty. She was to visit me at Eastbourne," he explained, his stammer becoming more and more pronounced. "I had arranged for us to stay with my friends, the Rv-Reverend and M-Mrs. Barclay, Rector of St. Peter's Church?" He looked to McNaughton as if for approbation but received a cold stare. In agitation, he searched for his precious letter in the pocket of his coat.

Out came the contents: a piece of string, a selection of colored scarves, a pair of small dolls, a bag of spice drops, and a folded piece of paper. Arthur took it and unfolded it as his putative patient restored the rest of the debris to its hiding place.

"Interesting. Your correspondent uses the new typewriting machine," the doctor observed. "Ah, I see your problem. The two has been overstruck with a three. Hence your dilemma: do you meet the four-twenty train or the four-thirty?" The older man snatched the letter back.

"I supposed that the three was correct, since it had been struck over the two," he said testily. "What I want to know is, where is Miss Marbury?"

"I assume you know the young lady by sight," the stationmaster said.

"Er . . . no. Her father is an acquaintance by s-sight . . . " the older man stammered.

The stationmaster frowned. "Related, are you, then?"

"Er, not precisely . . . "

"Then I suppose someone else met the girl," the stationmaster said abruptly. The colloquy was interrupted by one of the underlings, a guard in a blue uniform who tapped urgently on the window of the glass booth.

"There seems to be some other difficulty, sir. Good-day!" McNaughton glared at the underling, who approached him in a highly agitated state.

"Mr. McNaughton, may I have a word?" That most ominous of phrases.

"What is it, Payton?"

"There seems to have been an unfortunate occurrence—" The guard glanced over his shoulder. "I have summoned the police, but I believe you should take charge, sir."

McNaughton settled his cap on his head, glared at his uninvited guests, and marched out of his booth. "I suggest you take yourselves elsewhere. Good-day!"

"But . . . "

"Thank you for your assistance, sir. I think we will look for the child ourselves." The doctor took the older man by the arm and firmly walked him out of the glass office, followed by the faithful Touie. Once back on the platform, the older man pulled away from his would-be rescuer.

"Sir, that was not necessary. I am quite capable of dealing with persons like that."

"Undoubtedly, sir, but I could tell that he was about to be extremely rude, and I couldn't have that, especially not in front of my wife." The young doctor glanced at the love of his life, who smiled prettily.

"Very well, but I am sure I can manage . . . "

"Please, sir, permit me to help you find your missing child."

The older man glared at the younger one. "Are you always this—determined?" he asked querulously.

Touie followed them as they walked toward the baggage platform. "Indeed he is, sir. Why, when my poor brother was ill, he tried everything in and out of his power to cure him."

Her husband laughed heartily. "Aye, that's it. I cannot walk away now. I must see this through to the end. I would die of curiosity if I did not solve this mystery."

"Mystery indeed!" huffed the older man. At the baggage platform large men in striped shirts were heaving huge trunks onto waiting wagons, and grimy urchins with handcarts shouted for customers.

" 'Ere! You're back!" one of the largest of the porters accosted the trio.

"Back? I just arrived," the older man protested.

"You was 'ere not ten minutes since," insisted the porter. "Tile 'at, gray gloves, black coat . . . "

"With a little girl?" the doctor asked.

"Ah! Pretty little thing, with all that red 'air down 'er back," the porter observed. "Didn't even stop fer 'er trunks, wot the nursery-maid said wos to be sent on." He indicated a well-made traveling trunk, securely lashed, neatly labeled. "And wot's to be done with it, eh?"

7

"You may send it on, by carrier, to this address," the elderly gentleman said, producing a card, which the porter took with a nod. He turned to the young doctor. "Miss Marbury is supposed to have auburn hair," he added, consulting his letter.

The doctor frowned. "This becomes more and more tangled," he complained. "Presumably the domestic was told they would be met, and by whom . . . or at least, was given a description of the person who was to meet them, namely, you, sir."

"The—the ch-cheek of it!" The older man looked as if he might have another fit.

"This is all quite mysterious," Touie said. "But perhaps we had better find somewhere less public to discuss it. Arthur, where is our lodging?"

"Just off the Queen's Road, my dear, near Duke Street. Porter, can one of these lads bring our valises to this address?"

"As you say, sir." At a wave of the porter's hand, one of the larger boys trotted up with his handcart.

"If you insist on pursuing this acquaintance, I had better introduce myself. I am Mr. Dodgson," the elderly man said. "The Reverend Mr. Dodgson, of Christ Church, Oxford." He bowed and extended a gray-gloved hand.

"Aye, and I am Dr. Arthur Conan Doyle, practicing in Southsea, and this is my wife, Louisa." They solemnly shook hands and followed the handcart down the hill, around a corner, through the cobbled streets and into the summer sunlight.

CHAPTER 2

B righton had changed considerably in the seventy years since the Prince Regent brought his glittering friends to take the air and show off their splendid equipages to the gaping yokels, fisher-folk, and other low persons who inhabited the village of Brighthelm-stone. Now, instead of Regency bucks and demure debutantes, stout provincial shopkeepers and their wives filled the Steine, while their daughters shopped at the quaint stalls along the King's Road. There was even talk of using some of the less sinister portions of The Lanes for commercial purposes, and the merchants of Brighton made their financial hay while the July and August sun tried to shine.

Along the steep and cobbled streets that led down to the Es-planade, anyone with a room to spare set a sign in the window and took in lodgers. Rooms were let by the day, week, or month. The hordes of pleasure-bent Britons could find accommodations for any pocketbook, from a back alley for a few shillings a night to the grand hotels facing the sea, where a suite might be had for a month at a sum that equaled a laborer's yearly wages.

Young Dr. Doyle and his wife were in neither the back alley nor the seafront category. They followed their guide down the Queen's

Road with Mr. Dodgson locked between them, past houses where women called out raucously from upper-story windows (Touie pretended she did not hear them), and down the cobbled street toward the Esplanade. They could just catch a glimpse of the Channel between the rows of buildings, which grew larger and more ornate as they approached the strip of blue sea visible at the end of the road. The Doyles eagerly sniffed the salt-tinged air as they marched along with Mr. Dodgson. The tang of the sea breeze mixed with the less wholesome scents drifting out of the taverns and fish-and-chips stalls: stale beer, frying fish, and cheap tobacco.

The rest of the holiday crowd pressed on to the sea, and through it the urchin with the handcart wove his way, with Dr. Doyle and Mrs. Doyle and Mr. Dodgson close behind him. There was no time for conversation, even if one could be heard above the roar of humanity and the snatches of music from the Esplanade, where the band was playing the popular airs of Dr. Sullivan. At last, the boy made a sharp turn and angled his cart into a side street lined with three-story houses, jammed together to form a row, each adorned with the universal placard: ROOMS TO LET.

Touie paid off the boy, while Dr. Doyle mounted the steps and rang the bell. A stout woman, swathed in the prerequisite black bombazine demanded by all landladies, loomed behind the maid who answered the bell.

"Dr. Doyle, and Mrs. Doyle," the Scottish doctor introduced himself.

"Ah," the landlady said. "I'd fair given up on you, you're that late." She gave Mr. Dodgson a sharp-eyed stare. "The booking was for two, was it not?"

Dr. Doyle laughed. "This is Mr. Dodgson. He's staying elsewhere, but—"

"I really must be going on," Mr. Dodgson said, disentangling himself from Dr. Doyle's enthusiastic grasp. "I m-must find Miss Marbury! There is no t-time to be lost!"

He turned as if to move off.

Touie took him by the arm. "You cannot go off without some refreshment, Mr. Dodgson. Wherever the child is, your starving will not bring her back any quicker."

"Touie's right," Dr. Doyle said. "Mrs. Keene, could we have some tea?"

"Tea's extra," the landlady reminded him.

"Hang the expense! We're on our honeymoon!" Doyle exclaimed.

Mrs. Keene smiled suddenly, revealing a set of well-manufactured dentures. "Honeymoon, is it? Well, then, you just step into the parlor, and I'll bring you tea. And I'll have your things brought in, then. Hi, Jemmy! Look sharp!"

Jemmy, a large youth in a striped shirt, leather waistcoat, and velveteen trousers, wrestled with the Doyle's modest portmanteaus, while the guests were shown into the front parlor, a hermetically sealed room crammed with furniture. A carved and stuffed red-upholstered sofa and matching chairs jostled a whatnot filled with figurines, cup-and-saucer sets, and carefully painted shells. A carved table was placed before the sofa, adorned with several tinted engravings of the Queen and the late Prince Consort. Two more chairs, draped with crocheted antimacassars, were placed under the windows, flanked by large urns filled with dried reeds. The window itself was framed with purple velvet draperies over lace curtains.

"Here is the front room," the landlady stated unnecessarily. "You may use it for your visitor, if you like."

"Thank you so much, Mrs. Keene? It is Mrs. Keene?" Touie asked.

"It is. Keene was my husband, but not as keen as all that!" The landlady chuckled at her own wit.

"I really cannot stay to tea," Mr. Dodgson fussed. "My friend Barclay and his good wife are expecting me for dinner, with Miss Marbury. Whatever am I to tell them? How can I face her father? Lord Richard Marbury, you know, one of Mr. Gladstone's most devoted and useful backbenchers."

"Indeed!" Doyle broke in. "I am the secretary of the Portsmouth Liberal Unionist Club. I will do anything in my power to assist Mr. Gladstone, in or out of office."

11

"Quite kind of you, I am sure," Mr. Dodgson said, his voice growing shriller, "but quite unnecessary. Thank you for your assistance, Dr. Doyle." He suddenly stopped. "How odd. I knew a man named Doyle. Dicky Doyle, of *Punch*. I called on him when I was in London. He died, you know. I thought of him to do the illustrations for *Alice* but Tenniel was so much better—"

"If you mean Richard Doyle, he was my uncle," Dr. Doyle said. "My father's brother, actually. I was saddened to hear of his death. He was rather kind to me when I was a boy."

"Indeed. Fancy that! If you are Dicky Doyle's nephew, I will take tea with you after all."

Mr. Dodgson settled back into his chair just as Mrs. Keene arrived with a tray containing the teapot, cups, cream and sugar, and a plate of suspiciously pink cakes, all of which she placed ceremoniously on the table in front of Touie.

"You just pour out, my dear. First time, eh?" With a vast chuckle, Mrs. Keene surveyed the honeymoon couple and their guest.

"Thank you, Mrs. Keene, that will be all." With the aplomb of a seasoned hostess, Touie poured the tea and dealt with cream and sugar. Mrs. Keene sighed sentimentally and left the couple to entertain their elderly guest.

Mr. Dodgson stirred his tea. "As I was saying, Miss Marbury was meant to come to me for two weeks in my lodgings in Eastbourne while her father is occupied with a Bill before Parliament. All this is quite mysterious. I do not understand why she was abducted; I am not even sure why her father sent her to me in the first place."

Dr. Doyle frowned over his tea. "Then, when the stationmaster quizzed you back there . . . ?"

Mr. Dodgson looked from one young face to the other in bewilderment. "I received a letter from Lord Richard Marbury two weeks ago asking if I could take his daughter Alicia to stay with me, as I often do have young ladies to stay with me, at Eastbourne. My landlady would be able to attend the young lady, as she often does. The domestic who traveled with her was to return to London on the next train."

"Of course," Doyle said.

"And now this! Someone impersonating me, removing the child from Brighton Station. I tell you, Dr. Doyle, I do not know what to make of it."

The Doyles exchanged knowing glances over the teapot. The young doctor cleared his throat and said carefully, "It is possible, you know, that the child was removed to one of those, um, establishments of the sort one reads about in the articles in the *Pall Mall Gazette*."

Mr. Dodgson exploded: "Do not mention that filthy, scandal-ridden publication to me! Most assuredly, do not mention it in the presence of your wife! Never have I read such an atrocious, disgusting account of perversity as those articles, which are polluting the eyes and ears of everyone capable of reading them. I have written to Lord Salisbury on the subject. My letter was published last week in the *St. James' Gazette*, under my own name!" He set down his teacup in his agitation.

Dr. Doyle's eyebrows rose. "As to the subject of the articles, sir, I can assure you that as a medical man, they come as no shock to me. When I was a student in Edinburgh, the charity wards were filled with such pathetic cases, children used brutally for the pleasures of those who should have been succoring the poor. Touie is as one with me on this subject, isn't that right, my dear? We abhor the filthy trade, but we must admit that it exists. If those articles can alleviate some of that misery by exposing the procurers and their customers . . . "

Mr. Dodgson shook his head violently. "No, no, Dr. Doyle. It is not that I doubt the veracity of the claims. That there are such villains, I am quite certain. That such things must be stopped is the business of the police, and the courts. In fact, Lord Richard Marbury is at this very moment leading the fight for the Bill that will extend the age of consent to sixteen, and force criminal penalties on those who indulge in such abominations. No, sir, it is the tone of the revelations that is so repugnant to me. The gloating, if you will. That, and the fact that the writer of the articles, the editor of the newspaper, and the proprietor of the publication are doing it, not to improve the lot of those unfortunate children, but to make money. There, sir, is the true villainy!" Mr. Dodgson looked fiercely about him, as if to find one of the offending persons in the parlor.

Touie sipped at her tea thoughtfully. "I see you care very much for children, Mr. Dodgson," she said softly.

"I love children—except for boys," Mr. Dodgson replied. "I have had many happy hours in the company of young girls. In fact, on one occasion . . . " He stopped suddenly, and put his lips together, as if a wayward word might escape.

Touie blinked suddenly. "Did you say Alice?" she asked, just as her husband shouted, "Dodgson! I knew I was familiar with the name!"

"Oh dear," Mr. Dodgson murmured, shifting in his chair. He shuffled his feet as he tried to rise, but the plush upholstery held him fast.

Dr. Doyle spoke first. "Are you *the* Mr. Dodgson of Oxford?"

"I am certainly a scholar of Christ Church, Oxford," Mr. Dodgson admitted.

"Then, sir, I must congratulate you on your work. I found it most enlightening."

"Enlightening is not the adjective generally used to describe my writings," Mr. Dodgson said wryly.

"I know of no other phrase to describe *Euclid and His Modern Rivals*," Dr. Doyle said enthusiastically. "I am the secretary of the Portsmouth Literary and Scientific Society. We all read your work on mathematics with great interest. It made clear a great deal that was obscure."

Mr. Dodgson looked severely at his admirer. "It was written as a text for Oxford undergraduates."

Dr. Doyle grinned infectiously. "Surely, sir, you must permit a few of us who have not had the opportunity to attend your lectures to absorb your knowledge at second hand, as it were?"

Touie had been busy with the teapot while her husband ws enthusing. Now she said, "I don't know about Euclid, but I do know about Alice. Mr. Dodgson," her voice lowered conspiratorially, "I have heard that you are really Lewis Carroll, who wrote my favorite book. I read *Alice's Adventures in Wonderland* over and over when I was a girl. I always felt so sorry for the Dormouse, being put into the teapot. And I never did learn 'Why is a raven like a writing-desk?' "

Her husband looked at her. "Touie, this is Mr. Dodgson, of Oxford, the mathematician, not someone who writes fairy stories."

Mr. Dodgson began to release himself from the grip of the chair. "Mrs. Doyle, I admit to you, but only to you, because your husband's uncle was a friend, that I am Lewis Carroll. However, this is in the strictest of confidence. I do not wish it to be generally known."

Touie leaned over and said, with a glance at her husband, "You know, Arthur writes, too."

"Indeed?" Mr. Dodgson had found his balance and risen to his feet.

"Only a few stories, in *Cornhill* magazine," Doyle said modestly. " 'Habakuk Jepson's Statement,' now that was a good tale."

"Did you write that story? *Cornhill* does not usually find its way into the House, but that particular tale was considered especially interesting. The *Marie Celeste* case, wasn't it?" Mr. Dodgson looked around him for his hat.

"It was, thinly disguised, of course," Dr. Doyle said proudly. "I fancy I came up with a more interesting solution to the mystery than some, eh?"

"Quite. Well, now, I must take my leave of you. I thank you for the tea, Mrs. Doyle, and now feel quite refreshed and capable of dealing with this mystery. I must notify the police of Miss Marbury's disappearance at once." Mr. Dodgson moved toward the door. Dr. Doyle sprang to his feet and followed him.

"You had better allow me to help you, sir," he said. "I have some acquaintance with the local constabulary, if only on the playing field."

Mr. Dodgson's face was a mask of loathing. "I assume you mean cricket."

"A grand game," Dr. Doyle enthused. "Keeps one fit. And I just remembered, one of my friends is acting as pathologist for the Brighton Constabulary, so I have some acquaintance there, too. Now,

Touie, you can get us settled in here, and I shall accompany Mr. Dodgson to the police station. And then, sir, I will see you to the Rectory, to your friend Barclay's door."

Mr. Dodgson looked helplessly about him, caught up in his new friend's enthusiasm. There was no polite way for him to refuse. Touie smiled sweetly at the pair of them.

"You might as well let Arthur help you, Mr. Dodgson," she said. "He will do it anyway. Arthur is a remarkable man, sir. He will surprise the world someday."

Dr. Doyle had found his hat and took his new partner by the arm. "We'll find your missing Miss," he consoled the agitated Mr. Dodgson.

"Oh, I do hope she is safe, and unharmed," Mr. Dodgson murmured, as they sallied forth once more.

CHAPTER 3

At that moment, Alicia Maybury was extremely put out.

She had accepted, with a minimum of pouting, the news
that Cousin Bertram had come home from Eton with measles, and
therefore, she could not take her usual holiday at Waltham Castle in
Derbyshire. Instead, she had been promised two weeks at the seaside
with her father's old tutor, Mr. Dodgson, who was supposed to love
little girls very much. She would have preferred to spend her summer
with her Waltham cousins, roaming the park, playing exciting games
of Robin Hood and Crusaders up and down the castle stairs, and
generally getting into as much trouble as a ten-year-old child can, but
Brighton sounded exciting, even with Papa's tutor in charge. Alicia
knew ways of getting around elderly gentlemen, most of whom, in
her limited experience, were not really familiar with little girls.

Alicia's life had been centered around the house in Grosvenor
Square, where she stayed in the schoolroom with Miss Quiggley or
the nursery with Nanny Marsh. From her vantagepoint at the top of
the house, Alicia could observe the comings and goings in the hallway, where she could learn much that her governess, Miss Quiggley,
either could not or would not teach her. She knew that Papa was a

Very Important Man, and that Mama was Very Important in helping him, and that the best thing for a little girl to do was to obey Miss Quiggley and grow up as fast as possible, so as to make a good marriage and become the wife of a Very Important Man like Papa. All this was part of her life, and she accepted most of it, although she was not too sure why she could not be a soldier, like her mama's father, Grandpapa Kinsale.

It had been explained to her that she would go by rail to Brighton, with her nurserymaid, Mary Ann, who would put her into Mr. Dodgson's hands, and then return to London. Mr. Dodgson would take her to see Brighton, and then they would go to Eastbourne while Papa and Mama stayed in London. It sounded like fun, and Alicia was ready for an Adventure.

She had enjoyed the train trip, with Mary Ann. She preferred Mary Ann to Miss Quiggley as a traveling companion. Mary Ann was ready to gawk at the passing scenery without instructing her on the history of the localities they were passing, or commenting on their agricultural products. Mary Ann was a source of information on those aspects of life about which Alicia was curious, and never told her (as Nanny Marsh did) that "such things is no business of young ladies." Alicia had begun to feel that perhaps this odd change of plan might be for the best after all. And then it had all gone wrong.

They had arrived at Brighton Station, and Mary Ann had looked around for a porter to tend to their trunks. An old gentleman had approached them and shown Mary Ann the crest on a letter (since Mary Ann did not read very well) and Mary Ann had handed Alicia and her traveling bag over to him without a murmur. Then Mary Ann had gone to send the trunks on to Eastbourne. The old gentleman had not waited for Mary Ann to come back, but had taken Alicia by the hand and had led her out to the baggage men, and without a howd'y'do, had hauled her off through the streets, on foot, to a poky house in the middle of the town on a street full of shops.

Alicia had not seen much more than a hall and a parlor before she was bundled up a flight of stairs, down a hallway lined with what looked like bedrooms, and up another flight of stairs and into an attic room, furnished with an iron bedstead, a chamberpot, and a set of hooks on the wall. There was a very small circular window set into the wall that did *not* look out on the sea, as she had been promised. When Alicia went to protest, she found that the door was locked. Clearly, she had been kidnapped!

Alicia sat on the bed and considered her position. She was a delicate-looking girl of ten, with a heart-shaped face surrounded by auburn curls, which were carefully brushed every day by Nanny Marsh. Few who looked at her recognized the gleam of intelligence behind her angelic blue eyes. Alicia Marbury was not going to remain a prisoner for long, not if she had anything to say about it.

She sighed deeply. Her Waltham cousins had smuggled her copies of *The Boy's Own Paper* when they visited London at Christmastime, and she had greedily read the forbidden literature, relishing the tales of derring-do and adventurous escapes. Most of them were about clever boys who got out of the most amazing predicaments. Well, she, Alicia Marbury, could show them a thing or two!

The door opened. Alicia jumped up, ready to run. Her way was blocked by two adult women and a scrawny girl of her own age.

"Alicia," said the elegant-looking young woman in the flowered gown. "This is Kitty. She will attend you while you are here." She sounded much like Miss Quiggley, Alicia decided, although Miss Quiggley would never have been seen in a gown cut so low in the bosom, nor would Miss Quiggley have used such a cloying scent. Nor, Alicia decided, would Miss Quiggley have hair of such an aggressive shade of red.

"Where is Mr. Dodgson?" Alicia demanded.

"He had to leave—on private business," the other, older woman, dressed in sober brown silk, stated.

"Who are you?" Alicia asked. "And where is this place? Why is my door locked? If you hurt me, my papa will call out the Army and put you in the Tower!"

"Who we are is not important," said the younger woman. "You may call me Miss, and this is Madam," she indicated the older woman. "What is important is that you obey us. You have our word that you will not be hurt, as long as you remain quiet. Now, take off your dress."

"Why should I?" Alicia's chin went up.

"Because, if you don't, we'll take it off for ya," rasped out Madam, in a coarse accent that betrayed her London origins. Madam was short, stout, and strong, with a broad red face, small dark eyes, and three chins. Alicia disliked her immediately.

Miss stepped forward and took Alicia by the chin. "You are a clever child," she pronounced. "If you behave, you will be rewarded. You will be fed, and you will not be beaten. If you do not behave yourself, then we will assume that you are a naughty child. Naughty children are punished. Do you understand what I am saying to you?"

Alicia jerked her head away. "I understand that I am not where I am supposed to be. My papa said that Mr. Dodgson would take me to his lodgings in Eastbourne after we went to see the Rector and Mrs. Barclay for tea. If you are Mrs. Barclay, where is the Rector? Rectors live near a church, and this house isn't near a church. If that's so, then the man who came for me is not Mr. Dodgson. And therefore, I do not think I have to do what you say."

Miss slapped her, suddenly. Alicia gasped in shock as much as in pain.

"You are a very clever little girl," Miss said. "Now understand this: clever little girls come to a bad end. You will now take off your dress, as I asked you, or you will find out what punishment really is."

Alicia lifted the hair off the back of her neck and stood, waiting.

"What d'ya expect us to do about that?" asked Madam.

"I can't do the back buttons," Alicia pointed out. "And Mary Ann usually helps Nanny dress me."

"Well, missy, ye'll learn to do for yourself here, that you will!"

Miss pushed Kitty forward. "Assist Miss Alicia," she told the scrawny girl. "And then get back downstairs."

Alicia let Kitty fumble with the buttons of her white lace dress. "You've got to help me!" she whispered through the veil of her hair. "I can't!"

"No talking there!" Miss ordered. "Kitty, take Miss Alicia's dress with you. Perhaps one of our other young ladies can fit into it."

"That's *my* dress!" Alicia shouted, but the two women and the girl were out of the room before she could think of anything to do about it. Once again she was alone, clad only in her camisole and drawers, which, considering the stuffiness of the room, was something of an improvement.

Alicia wanted very much to cry. She was frightened and alone, and she wanted to howl . . . but what would Cousin Edmund and Cousin Bertram and Cousin Harold say to that? She bit back the tears. No, she told herself, I am a Marbury of Waltham. Marburys never howl. Great-grandpapa Waltham didn't howl at Waterloo, did he? Nor did Grandpapa Kinsale, Mama's father, at Sebastopol, where he got his interesting scar. Well, she, Alicia Marbury, was a Waltham and a Kinsale, and she wouldn't howl. She would find a way out of this prison, and make them all sorry they ever tried to kidnap her.

She searched the cramped attic room. The bed consisted of a wrought-iron frame, with a thin mattress over steel spring-strung slats. There were no sheets or blankets to make a rope ladder (that mainstay of *The Boy's Own Paper*). She stood on tiptoe to reach the window. The glass was fixed fast, and she was too high to be heard if she shouted.

Alicia frowned. Sooner or later, she would be missed. Her papa would ask of Mr. Dodgson where his Alicia was, and they would come looking for her when Mr. Dodgson (if that really was Mr. Dodgson) did not produce her. Or, perhaps, she was being held for ransom! Then Papa would pay the kidnappers, and she would be set free.

Alicia didn't like that idea. Kidnappers ought not to be paid, she decided. They would find out that she, Alicia Marbury, could rescue herself. Then wouldn't Harold and Bertram and Edmund be sorry they left her out of their games!

Alicia watched the sun through the grimy window as it set, while the sky turned a flamingo pink and then darkened. Sooner or later, she would be rescued, but she hoped it would be sooner. She wondered whether the real Mr. Dodgson was as nice as Papa said, and whether they were already looking for her . . . and whether she was going to get supper or be starved. For the time being, she could do nothing but wait, and that she did.

*   *   *

21

Two floors below her, the inhabitants of the house stirred, preparing themselves for the night's activities. The very young women who worked for Miss Julia Harmon put on their light silk chemises and fine linen underdrawers, and went down to the dining room for tea. Miss Harmon presided at the table while Kitty served. The atmosphere was that of a very peculiar girls' school: much giggling, some pouting. No one seemed to know or care that there was an extra girl in the building.

In the kitchen, below the dining room, Madam Madge Gurney and an old actor, Will Keeble, sat over their tea (or in Keeble's case, gin).

"The Guv'nor'll be pleased," Keeble said. "It went like clock-work."

"The Guv'nor's not the only one calling the tune," Madam warned.

Kitty slid into the kitchen. "Miss Harmon wants to see yer," she said breathlessly to Keeble. She turned to Madam. "Do I give the new 'un her tea now?"

Madam laughed. "Let 'er wait for it. Do 'er good ter go 'ungry fer a change. I'll tell yer when ter feed 'er. And yer not ter let the others know she's there. She's bein' kep' as a surprise, fer a very special customer."

Keeble finished the last of the gin and made his way to the kitchen door, up the stairs, and down the hall to Miss Harmon's private sanctuary. As he entered her tiny office, little more than a niche at the end of the long front hall on the ground floor, Miss Harmon frowned.

"You've been drinking again, Keeble," she reproved him. "This won't do. You have one more task, and then your work here is finished. Here is ten pounds. I suggest you try to get employment elsewhere, perhaps Margate or Torquay. I do not think it wise for you to be seen here in Brighton again."

Keeble took the ten sovereigns and bowed ironically. "As you say, ma'am. What more can I do to further the illustrious career of . . . "

"You take this note, meet the Guv'nor on the Chain Pier at eight o'clock tonight, and give it to him. Then you remove yourself from Brighton as quickly and quietly as possible. Am I understood?"

Miss Harmon handed Keeble a folded piece of paper. Keeble bowed again. "I take my leave of you, my dear young woman, and this establishment. I trust your various enterprises succeed. Good evening."

Miss Harmon permitted herself to breathe once more as Keeble let himself out the front door. So far, so good; the child was in her hands, and the Guv'nor would see to the rest. She stared at an engraving clipped from the London Evening *Standard* that she had placed over her writing desk.

"Well, Lord Richard," she said bitterly. "Let us see just how much your daughter is really worth to you!"

CHAPTER 4

B righton by day was gleaming with fresh paint over old buildings, full of obviously respectable holidaymakers of what might
be called the "lower orders." Brighton by evening became gaslit, with
young men of dubious antecedents emerging from their lairs like fer-
rets, bowler hats perched at jaunty angles over their eyebrows, or
cloth caps tilted pugnaciously forward. Their female equivalents
were highly painted young (and not-so-young) creatures in gaudy
finery, who promenaded on the Esplanade, eyes promising much.
The lamplighters were already on their rounds, although the summer dusk was just beginning to paint the western sky with vivid
pinks.

Dr. Doyle led his older companion back along North Street, past
rows of cheap eating houses and taverns, where the enticing smells of
greasy fish and frying potatoes mingled with the tang of salt air blowing off the Channel. They turned east, where North Street ended at
the Old Steine, with its elegant buildings erected by the Prince Regent's pet architects to house the hangers-on of the Court. Up the hill
they went, past the Pavilion and its small surrounding park, where
the gaslights flickered in the twilight; then across the Grand Parade,

where carriages were already depositing the better-heeled visitors to Brighton at the Albemarle Hotel. Edward Street was tucked behind the law courts, and John Street was little more than a passage, where the police station lurked.

Like much of Brighton, the police station had been built only recently, replacing the quasi-medieval dungeon that had served Brighton's local population as headquarters for the constabulary for nearly fifty years. With its current prosperity, the borough of Brighton could provide a properly monumental edifice of sturdy brick, faced with stone, from which the Brighton Police could operate. Within its walls were holding cells for malefactors temporarily awaiting judgment; private offices for the Chief Inspector and the Superintendent; a less private room where the lesser inspectors could keep their records; a set of interviewing rooms for the questioning of suspects; a proper dressing room for off-duty constables; and a small, but adequate morgue. One felt that Brighton's inhabitants, both transient and permanent, could feel safe with such a police station, and such a police department to guard them against petty thievery and vice.

Mr. Dodgson entered this edifice with proper diffidence, and looked about for the sergeant on duty. He found him behind the counter in the lobby, his supper spread out before him on several pieces of waxed paper. Sergeant Barrow was tall and rotund, with a spectacular mustache, a policeman who looked to be more than a match for any belligerent drunkard or overconfident pickpocket, though at the moment he was devoting himself to the consumption of fish and chips.

"Ahem!" Mr. Dodgson finally got the sergeant's attention. "If you are quite finished with your supper, Sergeant, we wish to report a crime."

Barrow put down his mug and observed the two men before him with the look of one who has heard more lies than truth in a misspent life. With an audible sigh, he pulled a sheet of paper out of a drawer behind the counter, took up the stub of a pencil, and looked expectantly at Mr. Dodgson. "What sort of crime are you reporting?" Barrow asked.

"A young girl is missing," Mr. Dodgson said sharply. "She was supposed to meet me at the Brighton railway station. Someone representing me seems to have removed her . . . "

Barrow put down his pencil. "Any witnesses, sir?"

"One of the porters claims to have seen me with her, but since I did not meet the girl, it could not have been I. One cannot occupy two places at the same time," Mr. Dodgson told him.

"Ah." Barrow frowned. "We've got a young girl here, just brought in. From the railway station. Sad, that. Run over by the train."

Dr. Doyle turned to Mr. Dodgson. "That disturbance at the station. Could it be—an accident?"

Mr. Dodgson gasped, "But not Miss Marbury, for she was observed by the porter after the guard summoned the stationmaster."

Dr. Doyle frowned. "But there was to be someone with her. Perhaps this is she?" He looked at Dodgson's stricken expression. "We must look at her, Mr. Dodgson."

"You can identify this gal?" Barrow asked hopefully. "No one else seems to know her. Down for the day, seemingly. And there ain't much left to go by."

Mr. Dodgson closed his eyes for a moment, then opened them resolutely. "Dr. Doyle, I rely on you. I do not think I can look at a dead child. She has auburn hair. . . . "

"But it is your duty, sir," Dr. Doyle reminded him.

Mr. Dodgson nodded. "If I must, then I must. Lead on, Sergeant."

"Surely you know what she looks like," Barrow interjected.

"I have never met the young lady," Mr. Dodgson said.

Barrow turned his cynical stare on the elderly gentleman before him.

Doyle frowned. "Who's on duty, Sergeant? I'm Dr. Doyle, from over Portsmouth way. If Baxter's about, he can vouch for me. I don't want to step on any toes, mind."

Barrow shrugged. "Dr. Baxter's down with her now. If you can tell us who she is, more power to ye." He opened the gate of the counter, and let the two men through to the stairs that led down to the basement room.

There a scrawny man not much older than Dr. Doyle was leaning over a collection of remains. In the flickering gaslight, all that could be made out at first glance was a dark blue dress and white apron. Mr. Dodgson gasped again, in horror. The remains were not connected to each other. The girl had been torn apart by the force of several tons of steel crushing her brief life out of her.

Mr. Dodgson took one look and immediately announced, "That is not Miss Marbury. That is not a girl. That is a young woman!"

"Aye, that it is." Dr. Baxter looked up from his work, revealing a face full of freckles topped with sandy hair, surmounting a vividly striped shirt, a tattersall waistcoat, and a coarse apron spattered with dried blood.

"Hello, Arthur," he carolled, in accents reminiscent of Liverpool. "Care to join me? This one's a corker, I tell you! Poor thing must have caught her cloak on the fly-rod of the London train as it was pulling into the station. Got pulled into the big wheel; little wheels did the rest. Engineer's in a taking, but the police are assured it was all a dreadful accident."

"Dreadful indeed," quavered Mr. Dodgson, retreating to a corner.

Doyle, on the other hand, stripped off his tweed jacket and rolled up his sleeves with professional aplomb. He peered at the various bits and pieces before him, reminding himself that he was, after all, a medical man, and such sights should not make him queasy. "I can't put a name to her, of course, but I can tell you something about her, Sandy. Will that help your inquiries?"

Behind them, Sergeant Barrow grunted assent. Baxter shook his head in pity. "The usual thing, I suppose," he said. "Can't tell by what's left, but I've seen her like before. Got herself in the family way, took the easy way out. Happens all the time."

Barrow's voice rang out in heavy disapproval. "Not on my patch and not in my watch."

As he spoke, Dr. Doyle looked at the limp arms and examined the dead girl's hands carefully, then turned his attention to what was left of her feet. He looked for the head.

"Thought you might want this," Baxter said. "Skull was found halfway down the station. Dreadful sight for the punters to see. Puts a damper on the holiday!"

Doyle swallowed hard, then peered into her mouth, nodded, and stood straight.

"Not a suicide, Sandy. If a girl were to commit suicide, she would hardly tip herself backwards. The marks of the wheels of the train are clearly on her chest and face, indicating she fell face-up. No, I suspect foul play here, Sergeant. And I am sure your Coroner will concur, eh, Sandy?"

Baxter made noncommittal sounds. Sergeant Barrow snapped out, "And what else can you be sure of, Dr. Doyle?"

"Without a full examination, and without the rest of the, um, torso, I couldn't say whether or not the poor thing was, as you put it, in the family way, but I would go bail she wasn't. I'd put her age at seventeen or eighteen, certainly not over twenty. A healthy girl, too; sturdy teeth and bones, not your town-bred sort; country girl, in good service, possibly as a nurserymaid, in a prosperous household; employers of a liberal, reforming bent, I should say. Probably came down with a family. You might begin your investigations by checking at the better hotels and seeing if anyone's missing a servant."

Dr. Doyle rolled down his sleeves regretfully and replaced his jacket. "Carry on, Sandy," he told his old school chum. "Remember what Dr. Bell said."

Sandy Baxter gave him a grin. "Just like you, Doyle, leaving me alone here. What're you doing here, anyway? I thought I saw you off to be married?"

Doyle rubbed a hand through his hair in embarrassment. "I was. I am. I just happened upon this gentleman here," he indicated Mr. Dodgson (now edging his way towards the door, the stairs, and possible escape from the scene of horror), "and thought I could help him find a missing child. I never thought it would come to this!"

"This is not the child we seek," Mr. Dodgson said. "It is a very great pity, but it is not Miss Marbury. May we get on with our business, Dr. Doyle?"

Sergeant Barrow led them back up the stairs to the common room.

"Now, about your missing young lady," he said, once Dr. Doyle and Mr. Dodgson were on the "civilian" side of the counter once again.

"Her name is Alicia Marbury. She is ten years old, has auburn hair . . . " Mr. Dodgson looked helplessly at Sergeant Barrow.

"What was she wearing when last seen?" The sergeant took pencil in hand.

"I . . . I d-do not know." Mr. Dodgson's stammer began to manifest itself.

"Was she carrying anything? Reticule? Some kind of toy?"

"I . . . I d-do not know."

"Just what sort of relation is she to you, sir?" Sergeant Barrow's look was now glacial.

"I am—was—an acquaintance of her father . . . "

"And what was she doing when last seen?"

"Presumably, going up the street with someone who resembled me!" Mr. Dodgson's voice grew shriller.

"And why was you supposed to be meeting her?" Barrow glared at the outraged scholar.

"Because her father requested it!"

"This being Lord Richard Marbury, what makes speeches in the Commons?" Barrow said, with heavy sarcasm.

"The same. I am delighted to learn that the constabulary keep up with current events." Mr. Dodgson's sarcasm matched Barrow's.

"And what proof have you got that she was ever here?" Barrow put down his pencil.

"Do you doubt my word, sir?" Mr. Dodgson's voice grew even louder and shriller as his anger rose.

"There's all sorts come to Brighton," Barrow said meaningfully. "Some folks even think it's a lark to give false reports to the police."

Mr. Dodgson's face took on a crimson hue. "Are you linking me with the sort of person who would—Are you calling me a liar?"

Dr. Doyle took Mr. Dodgson's arm gently. "Mr. Dodgson, may I speak for you?"

Mr. Dodgson nodded wrathfully.

"Sergeant, Mr. Dodgson is a noted scholar, who occasionally enjoys the company of young children . . . "

"Ho!" Barrow said, his eyebrows beetling over his nose in a ferocious scowl. "I know *his* sort! Missing girl, indeed! You want that kind of thing, you go to Church Street for it! Be off!"

"But—" Mr. Dodgson looked helplessly about him for support. He found none in the eyes of the constables who had been attracted to the noise of the dispute.

"Perhaps we should leave the sergeant to his interrupted dinner," Dr. Doyle said.

Barrow glared at the two men before him with the look of one who had been far too lenient with rank outsiders. Mr. Dodgson's protests were stilled as Dr. Doyle led him out of the police station and back into the now-darkened streets.

"He actually thought . . . I cannot believe . . . !" Mr. Dodgson was incoherent with rage.

"He is, after all, a policeman," Dr. Doyle explained. "The question is, what do we do now?"

Mr. Dodgson stiffened. "You may escort me to the Rectory of St. Peter's Church," he told Dr. Doyle. "It is at the upper end of the Grand Parade. They are expecting me to dinner and will be quite worried if I do not appear. And then I am going to find that child, sir, and bring the ones who abducted her to justice!"

"At least let me help you," Dr. Doyle pleaded.

Mr. Dodgson's long legs were already eating up the distance between John Street and St. Peter's Church. Dr. Doyle had to trot hard to keep up with him.

"I thank you, but I believe you have done all that is required of you. You really do not have to put yourself out, sir. Think of your wife."

"Oh, Touie will understand, sir. I am like the sleuth-hound; once the game is afoot, I must pursue it to the end!"

They had reached the venerable church, and the charming residence provided for its clergy. Mr. Dodgson turned to face his companion.

"In that case, Dr. Doyle, I intend to take the very first train tomorrow to London. I suspect that poor young creature in John Street is the domestic who was accompanying Miss Marbury . . . although how you were able to tell so much about her, I do not understand."

Dr. Doyle shrugged modestly. "Oh, that I learned from my old mentor, Dr. Bell, up in Edinburgh. He always said, examine the hands first. The hands can tell you everything. That girl's hands were red, but clean, showing she did plenty of washing up. Her shoes were new and of good quality, and fitted well, which indicated that whoever her employers were, they were able to supply their staff with proper clothing, not cast-off finery, as so many young persons in service are given. Anyone who took care to see that their servants were well-shod would probably be of a liberal and reforming temper. I had reached your conclusion, sir. Lord Richard Marbury is a Liberal stalwart, and his interest in social reform is well known in the Party. I would be happy to accompany you to London tomorrow, sir."

The figures of the Reverend and Mrs. Barclay emerged from the gloom of the churchyard.

"Mr. Dodgson, is that you? We were so worried—where is the child? We have prepared a cozy room for her." Mrs. Barclay, tall and lean, peered at her guest.

"It is a very long and unpleasant tale," Mr. Dodgson said. "Dr. Doyle, will you call for me tomorrow morning? If you insist on taking part in this adventure, you must keep my hours."

"Good evening, then. And I'll be here at first light!" Dr. Doyle strode away down the street, whistling happily. Mr. Dodgson turned to his hosts.

"That is a most extraordinary young man," he decided. "Now, Henry, I greatly fear our young guest is not coming tonight. I shall find her tomorrow."

"Charles!" The Reverend Henry Barclay bustled forward to lead his friend into the house.

"We have had dinner put back," Mrs. Barclay announced. "You must tidy yourself, and then you must tell us all about it."

CHAPTER 5

⁂

Friday night in Brighton! The first day of the weekend, the first chance for visitors to sample the delights on the Esplanade and the piers, to stroll on the Marine Parade, and to examine (from a discreet distance) the bizarre charms of the Royal Pavilion. Friday was the perfect time for holidaymakers to make their plans over platters of turbot and sole in grim lodgings or well-appointed dining rooms. What to do next was the question. Should they drive out to Arundel and look at the castle? Risk life and limb on Volk's Electric Railway? Or just pray that the next day would be suitable for sea bathing?

The sea breeze whipped around Brighton, ruffling the waves on the Channel, fluttering the fringes on the paisley shawls of the women on the Esplanade and the Chain Pier, and making the gas lamps on the streets not yet electrified flicker. Brighton by day was gaudy; Brighton by dusk slightly sinister; Brighton by night was a glittering (if slightly tawdry) fairyland.

At the heart of the merrymaking were the two piers: the Chain Pier, and the newly built West Pier, jutting out into the English Channel, its rails and columns outlined by the new electrical lamps, visible for miles out to sea on a clear night. To this beacon came the holidaymakers, seeking refreshment in the fish-and-chips stalls, hokey-pokey wagons, and taverns, and entertainment from the buskers, those wandering entertainers who could carol a popular ditty, dance a few steps, and pass the hat for pocket change. The Pierrot troupe was there, performing the same basic play that had kept the crowds pleased for four hundred years. Punch and Judy knocked each other about on the puppet stage; Columbine flirted with Harlequin; the singers led the choruses, and no one noticed the tough-looking men who lurked in the few dark corners of the pier while their furtive partners' eager fingers felt for wallets, watches, and whatever else might be loose.

None of this attracted Mr. Dodgson tonight. He sat in the back parlor of the Rectory, on a sofa covered with Mrs. Barclay's carefully worked antimacassar doilies, under the watchful eyes of past rectors of St. Peter's Church, and worried. He had planned to show Miss Alicia the wonders of the new pier, while protecting her from its less enchanting aspects. Now she was taken, possibly removed from Brighton altogether.

The Rector, rotund and genial, his scalp barely covered by a few strands of graying hair, and his taller, severely dressed wife, whose lean figure led the more frivolous of their congregants to compare the couple to Jack Sprat and his lady in reverse, sat on their well-stuffed chairs and listened to their guest unburden himself.

" . . . and that young man has insisted on accompanying me to London tomorrow," Mr. Dodgson complained. "He is most extraordinarily persistent. Dicky Doyle's nephew, of all things. He sounds like a Scot. I believe the Scots are known to be persistent."

"You know, Charles," the Rector said thoughtfully, "it might not be a bad thing to have a young man of his stamp about you while you pursue this business. One does not like to think about such things, but these people are, um, prone to violence."

Mr. Dodgson turned his accusing gaze on his host. "Henry! You have not been reading the *Pall Mall Gazette*! I thought better of you."

His friend turned bright purple with embarrassment. "Well, Charles, a pretty fool I should look if I did not keep pace with my parishioners. One cannot get away from those articles. I tell you, sir, there will be a reckoning. I understand that there have been mass meetings in Birmingham and Manchester, demanding action at the Parliamentary level. In fact, I have been requested to organize such a meeting myself, right here in Brighton."

Mr. Dodgson looked grave. "That is not for you to do, Henry. Your duties are to the Church. You should not be involved in political maneuverings."

Henry shook his head, setting his plump jowls wobbling. "Here we must disagree, Charles. In matters of morality, the Church should take the lead. I quite agree with my parishioners that something should be done. I read this morning that a Bill is before the House of Commons, and a vote is being called for. I shall most certainly lead the fight to get it passed." The little cleric looked positively militant.

Mrs. Barclay nodded her approval of her husband's statement. "Henry is quite right," she stated. "As a rule, I do not approve of such matters being discussed in the public forum, but if half of what these articles say is true, something must be done!" She emphasized her statement with a curt nod.

Mr. Dodgson disagreed. "I am all too aware of this Bill," he complained. "It has been read at least two times, and twice it has failed of passage. There is no reason to expect any better now. Mr. Stead has overreached himself with these articles."

"On the contrary," the Rector argued, "by publishing these facts, Mr. Stead has brought them to the attention of the people, and the people will be heard!"

Mrs. Barclay closed the discussion. "Henry, that will do. Charles has had a dreadful experience, first losing that child, and then the police. Charles, you must go to your room and change for dinner. You will be able to think more clearly with some sustenance."

Mr. Dodgson rose and allowed himself to be led away. "You are undoubtedly right. I must have my dinner, and then I shall think about this. There are dark forces at work here, Henry. I do not like it at all."

* * *

34

Down the hill, Dr. Doyle and his bride had sallied forth to enjoy the splendors of the Esplanade. Touie had changed from her traveling tartan to a flowered chintz dress, buttoned up to the neck, and covered with a warm woolen shawl. Dr. Doyle had added a deerstalker cap to his traveling suit by way of marking the transition from day to night. Together they walked happily to Muttons, that venerable establishment where a signboard announced: TURTLE SOUP AVAILABLE AT ALL HOURS. Under the famous glass dome, the honeymooners enjoyed the turtle soup and each other's company, while Dr. Doyle told his wife of their reception at the John Street Police Station.

" . . . So you see, Touie," he finished, "there's nothing for it. I feel it is my duty to assist Mr. Dodgson in any way I can. Scholar he may be, but he is no match for any ruffians or villains that may be after him. And Marbury! Think of it, Touie, the daughter of a Member of Parliament, the Marquis of Waltham's brother! If those fiends can abduct her, then no child is safe."

Touie placidly spooned up the dregs of her turtle soup. "Of course, Arthur. Mr. Dodgson needs you, and afterwards, once you have found the child, you may be able to use his name as a reference. It would be too much to expect him to be a regular patient, if he lives in Oxford, but one never can tell when he might be called on to recommend someone in Portsmouth. After all, you and I have the rest of our lives together."

Dr. Doyle smiled fondly at his bride. "Touie, you are a woman in a million! Most new brides would have their husbands dancing attendance on them day and night . . . "

Touie interrupted him. "Arthur, dear, I know how much you want to be part of this adventure. You needn't worry that I will be bored or mope. Mrs. Keene has told me of several quaint shops where I may purchase a few things for our establishment, and Mother has asked that I get her some small things as well. Then I shall sit on the beach and watch the bathers, and perhaps even go for an ice. Now, I want you to tell me everything, as soon as you can, and you must bring the child to me as soon as she is found, poor little thing."

Dr. Doyle reached across the table and squeezed Touie's hand. "I knew you would understand. You are the best wife in the world, and we are going to be very happy!"

Together they smiled into a future that they were sure would lead to fame and fortune, either in medicine or literature, or both.

Outside, on the Chain Pier, the crowds jostled each other in joyful camaraderie. Below the pier, the Jolly Jokers lined up for their performance, clad in mismatched checked and striped trousers and spotted shirts, topped with battered hats. The leader, Joker Jim, flourished his trumpet, while the others pranced about him, waiting for the signal to begin their well-rehearsed banter. The only problem was that the feed, the person who began the routine with a well-timed quip, was unaccountably absent.

"Where's Keeble?" the trumpeter hissed.

"Dunno," said the lanky fellow with the concertina. "Went off before tea, said 'e 'ad summat to do. 'Aven't seen 'im since."

"I thought I saw him in the boozer," piped up the youngest member of the troupe, a wiry youth with a mop of dark curls topped by an outrageous striped cap, who answered to the name of Bouncing Billy. "He was with some toff."

The trumpeter cursed. "Damn the old souse! Well, Billy, you'll take his lines. The crowd's picking up, and we've got to make our nut somehow. Here we go!"

The trumpeter stepped out of the shadow of the pier and onto the pebbled beach, into the pool of light thrown down by the electric bulbs on the pier above him. His trumpet fanfare drew the audience, while the rest of the group cavorted to the gay strains of the concertina. No one noticed the two men at the very back of the pier, where only a railing separated the crowds from the tumbling surf below, and the lights cast deep shadows.

Keeble, the old actor, had used his riches to fortify himself with gin. Now he faced "the Guv'nor" and breathed alcoholic courage into the other man's face.

"Miss Harmon employed me to abduct a child," he wheezed. "Well, I did. However, I did not reckon on the child belonging to a Member of Parliament, and one related to the Marquis of Waltham at that. Ah yes, Guv'nor, I recognized the young lady for who and what she is, and ten pounds is not enough payment for that, Guv'nor. Not by a long chalk."

The other man tried to step backwards, but found himself braced at the railings that separated the pier from the lapping waves below. "You've been paid once. That was all that was agreed to."

"Ah, but that was before I got a good look at you," Keeble said with a boozy grin. "I have seen you before, Guv'nor, and under very different circumstances, with very different companions, on more than one occasion. You would not like your noble employer to be aware of your, um, secondary interests?"

"If this is an attempt to get more money from me—" The other man began to shift around. Keeble persisted. The two men were now leaning against the railings, while the water beneath them lapped at the exposed struts of the pier.

"Ten pounds? Did you think that I, Keeble, who trod the boards with Forrest, would be bought off with a mere ten pounds?" The old actor drew himself up with dignity bolstered by gin. "Oh, no, Guv'nor. You shall pay me ten pounds a week, until I say nay!"

"I don't have that kind of money!" The other man tried to get away from the insistent drunkard.

Keeble grabbed at him. "Don't you turn away from me!" One trembling hand closed around the man's waistcoat, wrenching the top button from its moorings.

"Get your filthy hands off me!" The Guv'nor seized Keeble's fist. The actor clutched tighter at the natty waistcoat that matched the suit worn by his victim.

"You will pay me, or I will go to . . . "

"You may go to the Devil!"

The Guv'nor grabbed Keeble's wrist with a surprisingly strong grip, and threw him off. The other hand reached for Keeble's throat. Keeble feebly tried to pull the man's hands away, but the Guv'nor's chokehold grew tighter. Only the actor's stiff, old-fashioned collar saved his neck from being broken. In a reflex action, he brought up a knee to try to break away from the throttling. The Guv'nor grunted in pain and rage; the choking stopped.

37

Keeble tried to dodge away, but the Guv'nor was upon him again. The two men struggled in the shadows cast by the electric lights. Keeble reeled forwards, bending the Guv'nor over the rails. Together they staggered back and forth, while the crowd shouted encouragement to the Jolly Jokers on the other side of the pier.

With one last effort, driven by fear and rage, the Guv'nor turned Keeble around, lifted him by the tails of his frock coat, and heaved him over the rails. There was a cry, a splash, and a heavy thud. The waves lapped at the pier, daring those cast-iron struts to give way under the relentless pressure. For this night, at least, they did not.

The man on the pier joined the rest of the merrymakers. He was breathing hard. This was the second accident he had seen in the space of twenty-four hours, and he had to keep telling himself it was not his fault. Keeble was still alive when he went over the side. He must have been, for he had cried out. The girl had cried out. . . .

The Guv'nor took a deep breath. "It's not my fault," he repeated to himself. "It had to be done." He straightened his hair, pulled his waistcoat down, and found his hat, which had been knocked off in the fight. He must get on with the business at hand, he told himself sternly, as he caressed his bowler hat, the symbol of his respectability. The Plan must be followed. Tonight he would go back to his lodgings; tomorrow he would go to London and see Marbury, and everything would be all right. To this end, he joined the crowd again, one more punter in Brighton.

Somewhere below him, Keeble floated in on the tide.

CHAPTER 6

Dr. Doyle appeared at the door of the Barclay house before breakfast, as promised. Mr. Dodgson and his hosts were still ingesting tea, kippers, and muffins when the young doctor was shown into the breakfast room by a flustered butler.

"You did say you wanted to take the earliest train to London," Dr. Doyle explained. "I took the liberty of consulting my Bradshaw. There is a train at eight-forty-six. We can just catch it, and be in London in an hour. One of the miracles of modern transportation!"

"Will you sit down and have some tea?" Mrs. Barclay asked, ever mindful of her duty as a hostess.

"No, thank you, I have had my breakfast. Mr. Dodgson, are you ready for this, sir? I can go myself . . ."

Mr. Dodgson carefully wiped butter off his chin and set his napkin down. "Dr. Doyle, I am quite capable of finding my way to London. I have done it for more years than you are alive. However, since you have invited yourself on this expedition, I suppose we had best be off. Henry, I thank you for your hospitality. I will return as soon as I can, with Miss Marbury!" He glared at Dr. Doyle, who appeared totally oblivious to sarcasm. The butler handed Mr. Dodgson his hat at the door, while the scholar felt about him, mumbling to himself.

"Fare for the train, for the cab to Grosvenor Square, back to Victoria, back to Brighton."

"Are you quite ready, Mr. Dodgson?" Dr. Doyle asked sharply.

"I keep my various monies in different pockets. It foils thieves." Once more farewells were exchanged, and once more Mr. Dodgson headed for the door.

"And one more thing . . . " he began. Dr. Doyle's patience had worn thin.

"I can see why you missed the child," he said sharply. "Mr. Dodgson, with respect, all this fussing about does no good. We have a train to catch!" Mr. Dodgson found himself being bustled out the door, down the steps, through the garden and into the street before he could tell the Barclays that he would bring the child directly to them as soon as she was found.

"That was quite unnecessary!" Mr. Dodgson huffed, as he and Dr. Doyle strode across the town and into Brighton Station. At that hour of the morning, most of the platforms were clear of holiday crowds; the early trains had not yet arrived, and the merrymakers would try to extend their time in Brighton as long as possible.

Dr. Doyle led Mr. Dodgson to the first-class carriages, where they were properly ticketed in by the conductor, and carefully bought return tickets. They found seats in one of the well-upholstered carriages, with Mr. Dodgson facing the front of the carriage and Dr. Doyle next to him. The whistle shrieked its warning; the train began to inch forward.

A man came scrambling along the platform, coattails flying, bag in hand, waving wildly to stop the train. Neither the engineer nor the conductor had any intention of heeding one passenger who had not the common sense to consult his watch as to the time.

"Stop!" The man redoubled his efforts as the train began to ease along the platform.

Dr. Doyle opened the carriage door. One tweed-clad arm reached out and practically scooped the latecomer into the carriage, where he collapsed into the seat opposite the other two men.

"Thank you so much," gasped the late arrival, as the train picked up speed and steamed out of the station. "I would have been in quite a pickle if I'd missed this train." He spoke carefully, as if watching his "aitches." Once he had settled back, he proved to be a lanky individual with thinning, mousy hair, in a suit of brown "dittoes," more suited to London than Brighton, topped by a bowler hat.

"Business?" Dr. Doyle inquired, with a quirk of his eyebrows.

"In a manner of speaking. My name's Upshaw, Geoffrey Upshaw. I'm Lord Richard Marbury's confidential secretary, you see, and we are embarked upon a matter of the utmost importance to the nation!" The man spoke as if the nation depended on him, personally, for its salvation.

Dr. Doyle glanced at Mr. Dodgson, who frowned at the newcomer as if trying to place him in his memory.

"You were not with Lord Richard when I met him in July," Mr. Dodgson said querulously.

"I have been in Lord Richard's employ these last two years. He relies on me for information. 'Upshaw,' he says, 'find out.' And I do, sir!" Upshaw tapped his long nose with a bony finger. "I find out! And then—I assist Lord Richard in whatever must be done." He folded his arms and looked at the other two passengers triumphantly.

Dr. Doyle leaned forward. "And what have you found out about this dreadful business in the *Pall Mall Gazette*?" he asked.

Upshaw removed his hat, brushed it carefully before setting it on the seat beside him, and began to run his fingers through his stringy hair by way of putting himself to rights. "A nasty business, gentlemen. Very nasty. Lord Richard is most distressed that such things exist. He has sent me to inform the members that action must be taken. The people demand it!"

"But Parliament is not in recess," Mr. Dodgson noted.

"Not officially," Mr. Upshaw stated. "However, it is summer, and many members are visiting their constituents, or on holiday." He sighed. "It is not easy, gentlemen, getting a man to give up his holiday. I have been from Penzance to Ullapool to Torquay and back to London, and all for the Cause! I have not seen my own rooms for nearly a week."

41

"Lord Richard must value your services greatly," Mr. Dodgson said. "You have even lost your waistcoat button in your attempts."

Mr. Upshaw smiled weakly and tried to cover the gap in his attire. "I do what I can. Lord Richard is a rising man, sir." He looked at his traveling companions again. "Do I know you, sir? You seem somewhat familiar?"

"I am Mr. Dodgson. Of Oxford. Lord Richard and I spoke when he visited Oxford in July, for the Regatta."

Mr. Upshaw looked stricken. "Mr. Dodgson! Lord Richard mentioned that he and you had conversed, but I thought . . . that is . . . Lord Richard told me that you would be in Eastbourne . . . " His voice trailed off in confusion.

"Then you are aware that Miss Marbury was supposed to come to me?" Mr. Dodgson asked sharply.

"Lord Richard had mentioned that he was sending Miss Alicia to his old tutor, yes," Upshaw said weakly. "But I had no idea . . . " He turned to Dr. Doyle in confusion. "You, sir, are you traveling to London, too?"

"I am assisting Mr. Dodgson with his inquiries into Miss Marbury's disappearance," Dr. Doyle said.

"But if you are here . . . where is Miss Alicia?" Upshaw looked confused.

"A very good question, which I intend to have answered," Mr. Dodgson said. "I must speak to Lord Richard myself, before any more is said on this matter."

"Lord Richard has no secrets from me!" Upshaw protested.

"Oh, I fancy he must have some. For instance, he did not introduce you to me when we met in July."

"I meant to ask, Mr. Dodgson, how you came to know Lord Richard Marbury," Dr. Doyle ventured.

"My old student," Mr. Dodgson said. "One of the few who actually listened to my lectures. He was meant for orders, you know, until that unhappy business with the stationer's daughter." Mr. Dodgson closed his eyes, apparently in contemplation of a happier past.

Dr. Doyle's curiosity got the better of his sense of discretion. "Stationer's daughter?" he hinted.

"Oh dear me, yes. I had quite forgotten about that until just now. Unfortunate, but young men will fall in love with the most inappropriate young females. Although, now that I recall, she was a rather pretty child. Red hair, yes, and green eyes. Quite pretty, but there is always something slightly coarse about tradesmen's children. What was his name? Yes, Harmon, that was it. A very respectable man, and I was rather upset when he had to leave Oxford. The man who came in never really suited. Harmon kept the best quality drawing paper, and the pen nibs I liked, and he was quite knowledgeable about book bindings. A pity about the girl, but there it was, and the consequences were all too clear."

Upshaw's eyes were wide as he drank all this in. Dr. Doyle coughed, as if to remind Mr. Dodgson of his audience.

Mr. Dodgson opened his eyes, looked about, and said, "After that, Lord Richard was sent down for a term, and finished without taking orders. A most serious young man; he even suggested that he, as he put it, 'do right' by the girl. Naturally, that would never have done. The son of the Marquis of Waltham and a stationer's daughter? Oh dear, no."

"And the girl?" Dr. Doyle could not resist asking.

Mr. Dodgson said, "I really don't know. Harmon removed from Oxford, and no more was said. I assume the, um, consequences, were taken care of by the girl's family. Lord Richard was sent on a tour of Europe, and returned with the intention of standing for Parliament as soon as he could. I believe he spent some time with Mr. Gladstone's more radical reformers. A most serious young man. Even stodgy; I recall the other undergraduates used to call him the Young Fogey. Very careful, always thinking of the future. The sort who'd take his umbrella if there was a cloud in the sky."

"Quite so," Upshaw said.

Mr. Dodgson suddenly realized that he had been gossiping about a man in front of his subordinate. "Of course, all this is in the category of Ancient History," he said.

"Of course," Upshaw agreed.

"And you must not breathe any of this to Lady Marbury," Dodgson added. "Lord Richard was kind enough to invite me to his wedding, although I was not able to attend. Let me see . . . oh, yes, of course. He married General Kinsale's daughter. I believe they called him 'The Terror of the Crimea.' Quite dreadful, the things written in the Press; even a Board of Inquiry looking into his conduct regarding prisoners of war, and some orders that the troops might have misconstrued. Patricia? Yes, that was her name. She was with Lord Richard at the boat races this summer. How odd that she should have red hair, too."

"That would account for the child's having auburn hair," Dr. Doyle put in.

"Yes, indeed." Mr. Dodgson glanced at Mr. Upshaw, who was trying to organize the sheaf of papers he had set aside to take care of his personal appearance.

Dr. Doyle glanced at Upshaw and whispered to Mr. Dodgson, "Could I have a look at that letter Lord Richard sent you?"

"Eh?" Mr. Dodgson turned and glared at him. "Don't hiss in my ear like that, young man. I may have trouble hearing every word that is said to me, but I can understand well enough if people speak clearly. I do not think this is a good time for such things. Besides, we are nearly in London. We can discuss the matter in privacy, later."

Dr. Doyle shrugged and turned his attention to the scenery, which was becoming more and more urban as the train approached its London terminus.

Victoria Station was considerably busier than Brighton. Even on a Saturday, the trains pulled in and out with remarkable frequency. Mr. Dodgson and Dr. Doyle emerged from the station and looked about for a hansom, one of those remarkable cabs that had become a major factor in London's transportation system. However, on this particular Saturday morning the cabstand was deserted.

"That is unusual," Mr. Upshaw remarked. "There should be a cab somewhere."

A decrepit vehicle drawn by the sorriest excuse for a cab horse plodded its way down the ramp to the cab stand. Mr. Dodgson looked at Mr. Upshaw and Dr. Doyle.

"I assume that we are all bound for the same establishment? Lord Richard Marbury's house in Grosvenor Square?" There didn't seem to be any doubt about it. "Then I suggest that we share this cab, since it is unlikely that there will be another very soon, and all of us have urgent business with Lord Richard."

"Hi! Cabby!" Dr. Doyle's curiosity had to be satisfied. "Where is everybody? Not a cab today? All on holiday?"

The cab driver, a wizened gnome of a man swathed in an oversized and outmoded greatcoat, grunted. "All gone to watch Mrs. Jeffries let out of Newgate! What ain't been took is out there on their own."

"Mrs. Jeffries? And who is she?" Mr. Dodgson shrilled out.

Dr. Doyle's mustache twitched as he tried to hide a grin. Mr. Upshaw was more outspoken.

"She is the owner of a number of, um, establishments of ill repute," he said primly. "She was sentenced to a term in jail and a fine. The fine was paid by an extremely prominent peer, who is one of her most fervent patrons."

Mr. Dodgson's face twisted in revulsion. "And this person has called up every cab in London?"

"I believe it is in the nature of a victory parade," Mr. Upshaw said apologetically. "It must be said, Mr. Dodgson, that disgraceful as Mrs. Jeffries's establishments are, they are supported by a certain portion of the population. She has her influential backers, sir. It is said," Upshaw's voice dropped to conspiratorial level, "that Mr. Gladstone himself has been seen in one of her, um, houses."

Dr. Doyle's mustache quivered again, but not with amusement. "Mr. Gladstone's interest in the unfortunate females of a certain profession is that of a reformer and humanitarian," he declared. "Well, gentlemen, I believe that we must take this cab, since there will be no other. Grosvenor Square!" he ordered, as the other two squeezed into the seat next to him.

The cab inched through the streets of London, past the shops and the strollers who were eager enough to venture out on a Saturday morning in August, when the temperature was reaching eighty degrees Fahrenheit, around the squares and parks, and into Mayfair, enclave of the rich and powerful. Mr. Dodgson fretted as the ancient steed plodded past elegant houses built by the great Whig aristocrats for their London residences. Dr. Doyle tried to appear unaffected by his proximity to the seat of wealth and power, while Mr. Upshaw, to whom this was familiar territory, merely fussed with his papers all the more.

"There she is!" crowed the cab driver. "Dang me, but she's got the brass! She's come to Mayfair, she 'as!"

Mrs. Jeffries's victory parade was heard before it was actually seen. A raucous howl of male voices, mixed with the shriller shrieks of female laughter, split the Saturday silence of Mayfair. The noble families whose great houses lined the streets of that exclusive district had left for greener pastures in Scotland or the Shires; only servants remained to witness the procession of cabs mixed with sporting carriages bearing the coats of arms of the most noble families of Britain. Scantily dressed young women waved at the astonished maids, housekeepers, and butlers. Young men (and a few who looked old enough to know better) pranced along on their high-stepping horses.

In the lead was a coach-and-four, driven by no less a personage than a ducal coachman, disgust mingling with amusement on his face as he led the throng. Inside the coach was the famous (or infamous) Mrs. Jeffries herself, an imposing figure of a woman in violet velvet, rubies twinkling in her ears, diamonds on her fingers, and plumes nodding over her bonnet, reveling in the limelight.

The parade had wound its way through Regent Street, up Bond Street, and now into Grosvenor Square, where Mrs. Jeffries had her coach stop in front of a modest house (by Mayfair standards).

She leaned out of the coach and gave tongue: "Ho! You up there! Let me out!"

The powdered footman at the back of the coach hopped forwards. Mrs. Jeffries majestically stood on the coach step and stared at the closed door of the house in front of her.

"You—Marbury! I know you're in there!"

The door remained obstinately closed. Only a twitching window curtain gave any hint that there was a soul within.

"You won't win, Marbury! I'll still be in my house long after you've been thrown out of yours!"

Dr. Doyle, Mr. Dodgson, and Mr. Upshaw watched as the wild panoply moved on. Only one man remained: a tall, youngish gentleman in a disreputable-looking check suit, with his collar undone, his cravat under one ear, and his waistcoat buttoned wrong. He had carroty-red hair and eyebrows and an infectious grin, with which he favored the three gentlemen approaching the Marbury residence.

He mounted the front stairs as the trio paid off the cab and joined him. All four were waiting when the venerable butler finally opened the door. The butler peered around to be certain none of the revelers were left in the street before permitting the four visitors to enter the House of Marbury.

CHAPTER 7

The south side of Grosvenor Square marked the boundary between fashionable Mayfair and the lesser portions of London. A row of attached houses, each with its areaway and kitchen entrance, formed a barrier beyond which the unfashionable were merely tolerated. The houses themselves had been built a mere thirty years before, and were therefore considered quite modern, fitted out with such amenities as Mr. Crapper's porcelain fixtures and gas lighting.

Marbury House was one of these: a narrow, five-story slot in the south face of Grosvenor Square, its windows shielded from the gaze of passersby by red-velvet draperies and lace undercurtains, its front door at the top of a short flight of steps. On the top step, now, stood the four men upon whom the butler gazed with hauteur, mixed with healthy curiosity.

"Good morning, Mr. Kinsale, Mr. Upshaw." The butler gazed inquiringly at Mr. Dodgson and Dr. Doyle. "Are you two gentlemen expected?"

The new addition to the group looked around at the others and laughed. "I don't know who these two are, Farnham, but you might tell Lady Pat that I'm here. Any chance of breakfast?"

"Lord Richard and Lady Richard have already breakfasted," the butler informed him loftily.

"Farnham, I must speak with Lord Richard at once!" Upshaw shoved through the crowd to bark at the butler, who was not impressed.

"I shall see if Lord Richard is available." Farnham held his ground against all comers. Clearly, ten-thirty on a Saturday morning was not the correct hour for either business or social calls.

"And you may send in my card," Mr. Dodgson added, fumbling in his waistcoat pocket. "It is quite urgent that I speak with Lord Richard Marbury."

"Lord Richard is . . . "

"Damme, Farnham, you can't leave us all on the doorstep," Kinsale said breezily. "Upshaw's all right, and I suppose these gentlemen have good reason to burst in on a man at the crack of dawn of a Saturday morning. Be a good chap, now, and move yourself!"

To Farnham's dismay, the unruly Kinsale shoved him aside and marched into the house, with Upshaw, Dodgson, and Doyle close behind. Once inside, they were left to contemplate a long, dark hall, hung with funereal green wallpaper and decorated with murky portraits of former Marburys, while the butler went in search of Lord Richard.

Lord Richard saved a great deal of time by emerging from the inner recesses of the house. He was already a prime target for caricaturists, with his long nose, wisp of a mustache drooping over his thin-lipped mouth, and aggressive chin. Lank, fair hair hung down about his collar and one lock draped itself invitingly over one eyebrow. He had apparently been dressing, since he had not put on his morning coat, but was clad in shirt, waistcoat, and trousers, with his cravat yet untied. He gazed at the crowd in the hall and lighted on the one face he had not expected to see at any time, let alone ten-thirty on a Saturday morning in August.

"Mr. Dodgson!" he exclaimed, sweeping back his fair hair from his forehead in what would soon become a practiced gesture. "I thought you were in Brighton!"

"I was," Mr. Dodgson began.

49

Mr. Upshaw interrupted. "Lord Richard," he stated, "I must inform you that we are up against it! I've tried, sir, but I cannot guarantee that we shall have a majority, not even of our own Party!"

"Hello, Ricky!" Mr. Kinsale greeted Lord Richard in a ripe brogue. "I just thought I'd drop by, on the chance you might be in."

"I thought you were with that disgraceful crowd," Dr. Doyle put in.

"Och, they were just in high spirits," Kinsale shrugged.

"High spirits, indeed!" sniffed Upshaw. "At that hour of the morning? Pah!"

Lord Richard waved his brother-in-law away. "Ned, I have no time for your difficulties now. If you've got gambling debts, neither Pat nor I will pay them again." Lord Richard turned to his secretary, who thrust the bundle of papers under his nose.

"Lord Richard, the best I could do was to get a few promissory notes from those members I could track down," Upshaw said apologetically. "This is the most inopportune time to press for a Bill—and this particular Bill is most unpopular, sir. There is a certain portion of the population who consider the terms of the Bill, well, an imposition on their liberties . . . "

"To debauch young children!" Dr. Doyle burst out. "Is this the Criminal Amendment Bill before Parliament? The one being agitated for in the *Pall Mall Gazette*? I'm a doctor, sir, and it makes my blood boil to think that Englishmen consider it their God-given right to take their pleasure at the expense of young girls!"

Mr. Dodgson stepped forward. "Lord Richard, this is Dr. Doyle. Dicky Doyle's nephew, you know."

"I didn't know, and I still don't know what you are doing here, instead of keeping my daughter safe for me in Eastbourne until all this is over." Lord Richard sounded exasperated.

"If you will permit me to explain," Mr. Dodgson began.

Yet another voice was added to the hubbub in the front hall. Lady Pat, as Lady Richard Marbury preferred to be called, descended the stairs, drawn down from her boudoir on the upper floors by the sound of argument below. She had not yet dressed for the day and was still in her morning gown of pale green lawn, looking like a sea nymph with her pale skin, delicate features, and coppery hair.

"Ned!" she called out. "Whatever are you doing up at this hour?"

Ned grinned mischievously at his sister. "Haven't been to bed yet, darlin'. I happened to be about . . . "

"Really, Ned!" His sister clucked over him. "Just look at you! You must get a manservant to look after you. How could you be seen in that suit, after dark? And with a button off your waistcoat."

"Give over, Pat," Kinsale shook her off. "You've seen me in worse state. And where I was, I could hardly wear evening dress."

Lady Pat turned to her husband. "Oh, Richard! I heard all those people outside. You didn't answer that dreadful, vulgar woman, did you?" Lady Pat's wide green eyes rested on her husband for a moment, then went on to take in the rest of the group. "Mr. Upshaw, we were expecting you last night. Where were you?"

"Ah. I was about Lord Richard's business, ma'am. But it is kind of you to take notice."

"Lady Richard, I must speak with Lord Richard, privately!" Mr. Dodgson's shrill voice cut through the rest of the babble.

"But why are you all here in the hall?" Lady Pat asked, confused. "Richard, you must take them all into your study, and Farnham, bring some refreshment. Coffee, I think, not sherry at this hour of the morning. And some biscuits." Lady Pat took over as hostess, herding the lot of them down the hall and into Lord Richard's private study, a paneled room on the ground floor toward the back of the house, with French windows that were opened in the August heat to reveal a small back garden that consisted mostly of shrubs in terracotta urns.

Lord Richard's personal domain contained a large carved desk and leather-covered chair in one corner, a rolltop desk and plain wooden chair in another, both covered with manila folders, scribbled sheets of paper, and newspapers. In the niche between the rolltop desk and a glass-fronted bookcase lurked the pedestal on which rested the typewriter, with a small stool set before it for the operator of the infamous machine. Dr. Doyle made for it with a gleam in his eyes, while the rest of the group arranged themselves as best they might. Lord Richard sat in the leather chair behind the desk, while his brother-in-law perched irreverently on a corner of that same carved repository of enough paper to fill the British Museum. Upshaw dumped his sheaf of papers on the rolltop desk, and Mr. Dodgson looked about for somewhere to sit down.

"Mr. Dodgson, you must take my chair," Mr. Upshaw offered, turning the wooden chair around so that the scholar could sit properly.

"Thank you." Mr. Dodgson looked earnestly at Lord Richard. "I do not know how to tell you this, Lord Richard. . . . "

"As quickly as possible, Mr. Dodgson. My time is limited. I am needed in the House this afternoon," Lord Richard said testily.

"But why you, Ricky?" Ned asked. "I mean, there are others . . . "

"No, there are not. Mr. Gladstone is out of office, after that disastrous vote in May, and he accepted the offer of a cruise on the Norwegian fjords. For all the use he is to us now, he might as well be down a crevasse in a glacier. Lord Salisbury is in the country and cannot be found. Lord Randolph Churchill . . . I do believe only the Lord knows where Lord Randolph is. Lady Randolph is canvassing for him, but that won't help us in the House of Commons. A pity that women don't stand for Parliament."

"Surely, Ricky, you don't mean to give women the vote!" Ned exclaimed in real alarm.

"I sometimes think that would not be such a dreadful idea, considering some of the men I have to deal with," Lord Richard snapped. "After all, you got in."

Kinsale grinned. "Aye, that's a laugh, eh? 'Roaring Ned,' M.P. But I stood, and I got the votes, and here I am."

"And well I know it!" Lord Richard leaned forward. "Ned, where do you stand? I should like to think I had at least one vote in my pocket on this matter."

Ned shook his head. "Ah, Ricky, you're asking an Irishman to vote for a Bill that would make whoring and procuring a criminal offense, punishable by prison sentences?"

"Mr. Kinsale!" Mr. Upshaw nodded at the door, where Lady Pat stood. "Moderate your language, sir!"

"Pat's used to it," Kinsale said breezily.

"And don't try to play the Irishman with me, Ned," Lord Richard said testily. "It may go over well enough in your constituency, but you and I both know that the Kinsales are latecomers, by Irish standards, brought in by King William to keep an eye on the rebellious tenantry."

"But Mama was an O'Connell, and never let us forget it," Lady Pat countered. "Ned, is Richard trying to corner your vote?"

"Of course he is, darlin', but whether he gets it or not depends on whether he's willin' to help me—when the time comes." Ned grinned again.

"If you mean that Irish Self-Rule Bill, that comes up in November. The Criminal Amendment Bill is now, Ned!" Richard leaned forward. "I need your vote, and I am asking for it on Party grounds and as a Christian gentleman."

Ned unhitched himself from the desk. The amiable grin was replaced by a look of grim determination. "Then, Ricky, you'll have a hard time getting it. Your Bill goes too far, my lad. Oh, I agree with raising the age of consent from twelve to sixteen for girls, but all the rest of it? That's no business for gentlemen or anyone else. Let the police deal with the wh—that is, the Soiled Doves. What goes on in a bedroom is no concern of anyone's but those inside it. I beg pardon, Pat, but you're a married woman and know what I mean."

Lady Pat looked from her brother to her husband. "This is not the time or the place to debate this matter. Richard, Nanny Marsh is quite upset. Something seems to have happened to Mary Ann. She did not return last night as she was supposed to."

"Probably took advantage of the opportunity to kick up her heels in Brighton," was Kinsale's opinion. Lady Pat disagreed.

"Oh, no, Ned. Mary Ann is usually quite reliable. Nanny Marsh speaks well of her, and Alicia likes her."

"Mary Ann?" Mr. Dodgson rose from his place. "The domestic sent with Miss Marbury to Brighton?"

53

Lord Richard stared at his old tutor, as if suddenly remembering that he was in the room. "Yes. Mr. Dodgson, why are you here?" he repeated.

"Lord Richard, Miss Marbury did not meet me at Brighton Station," Mr. Dodgson quavered out. "She seems to have been abducted. A most ingenious plot, sir; I was sent this letter," he fumbled in his pockets for the document, "that left the time of her arrival ambiguous. I must have missed her by minutes. Have you received any communications, sir? Any ransom demands?"

"Ransom!" Lord Richard leaped from his chair. "Farnham!" he called out.

The butler appeared, almost as if he had been waiting in the hall to be summoned.

"Is there anything in the letterbox?" Lord Richard demanded.

"Wait!" Upshaw patted his pockets. "I thought someone in that crowd outside brushed up against me. Good Heavens!" He held up a folded piece of paper. "Someone must have thrust this into my pocket!" He began to unfold the paper.

Lord Richard snatched it away, read it, then groaned. Dr. Doyle stepped forward and picked the offensive message up.

" 'Stop what you are doing or say adieu to your daughter. She will be returned to you when we read of your resignation in the *Pall Mall Gazette*,' " Dr. Doyle read aloud. "I think, sir, it must refer to the Criminal Amendment Bill. I cannot think of anything else in which you are involved that would elicit such a response."

Lord Richard sat down heavily in his chair. "Then that was what Mrs. Jeffries meant. Somehow, she's got Alicia. We've got to get her back!"

"But how would they know . . . " Mr. Dodgson began.

"The newspapers, of course," Mr. Upshaw said. "I can draft a response, and you can send it out this afternoon. You can announce that you are accepting the Chiltern Hundreds and are resigning your seat, for reasons of health. Without your support, Lord Richard, the Bill will undoubtedly fail in its third reading, and so will be heard of no more." He placed himself in front of the typewriter and inserted a sheet of paper from the pile that lay next to the dreaded machine. "Such sensational news will surely make the Sunday editions."

"No!" Lord Richard snapped out. "Never! I will never give in to such tactics. If that woman thinks she can bludgeon me into withdrawing my support for a cause I truly believe in . . . "

"Richard!" Lady Pat exclaimed. "We are talking about your only child! You must do anything they ask."

"I shall call in the police," Lord Richard said firmly. "I know the Home Secretary, and the Commissioner."

"I have already been to the Brighton Police," Mr. Dodgson said, in tones of deepest disgust. "They do not wish to pursue the matter."

"The Brighton Police! Hah!" With the air of one who is about to do something totally daring, Lord Richard approached the typewriter himself, ousted Upshaw from his seat, and pecked away furiously for several minutes. He looked the result over, and handed the paper to Upshaw.

"Take this to Scotland Yard, Upshaw. I want their best man, do you understand? Their very best man. And don't come back without him!"

Upshaw stood upright and nearly saluted. Then he asked, "May I just pop around to my lodgings, sir? I fear I have disarranged my clothing in my efforts on your behalf, and I would like to change my shirt. The Albany is not all that far."

"Of course, Upshaw. But be quick about it."

"I shall be back, Lord Richard. You know you can count on me."

"I always do," Lord Richard said.

Upshaw grabbed the note and departed, just as Farnham appeared with a tray laden with coffeepot, cups, creamer and sugar bowl, and a plate of cakes and biscuits. Lady Pat smiled brightly at the rest of the group.

"Coffee?" she suggested.

CHAPTER 8

Mr. Upshaw's departure seemed to be the signal for a general relaxation in Lord Richard's study, as if something not quite pleasant had been removed from the atmosphere. Lady Pat availed herself of the secretary's place, while the butler ceremoniously deposited the tray on Lord Richard's desk with the air of one who was doing his duty, however distasteful it might be. Clearly, Farnham disapproved of Lord Richard's habit of taking refreshment anywhere he chose. He left with a sigh, as if to indicate that the proper place for partaking of food was the dining room, the breakfast room, or, in a pinch, the private parlor at teatime.

Dr. Doyle took several biscuits while Lady Pat poured coffee and handed cups to her brother and husband. Mr. Dodgson refused refreshment until pressed.

"I do not take food during the morning," he said finally. "It impedes the mental processes, and what is needed here, Lord Richard, is logical thought. This is clearly not a random act of abduction. Quite a bit of planning must have gone into it. For instance, the man who impersonated me would have to be found, and either bribed or otherwise suborned; then, the letter would have to be typed." He fumbled in his pockets to find the fatal letter. "There, you see?" Mr. Dodgson tapped the offending numerals with a gray-gloved finger. "The overstrike makes the time of Miss Marbury's arrival ambiguous, leading me to miss the train, and giving the miscreants time to take her away."

Lord Richard turned his gaze on the doctor for the first time. Mr. Dodgson performed the necessary introductions: "This is Dr. Doyle, of Portsmouth, I believe. He has been good enough to assist me in this matter. Dicky Doyle's nephew, you know," he added, as if this explained everything.

It did not explain much to Lord Richard. "Do you think my daughter will need the services of a physician?" he asked, in real alarm.

"I sincerely hope not!" Mr. Dodgson replied, shocked.

Dr. Doyle had produced a small magnifying glass from his jacket pocket and had been examining first the original letter, and then the papers on Lord Richard's desk. Now he spoke up. "Lord Richard," he asked, in a voice of suppressed excitement, "have these notes been typed on this machine?"

"They have," Lord Richard said.

"And there is no other machine in this house?"

"No. In fact, this one is the very first of its model to be installed in a private home," Lord Richard said proudly. "I believe in progress. In fact, I am seriously considering having the telephone put in, so that I may be in contact with my constituents day and night. This matter proves it to me. Why, you could have used the telephone in Brighton and spoken to me from there, and saved yourself the time and expense of the journey to London."

"I don't think I would like having the telephone," Lady Pat murmured. "Jangling away at all hours, no privacy."

"Oh, very well, but I think it might be a good idea. Think it over. Meanwhile"—Lord Richard began to sort his documents out— "there is this matter of Alicia. It is obvious why she was taken. That ransom note proves it. They want me to stop my efforts on behalf of the Special Bill. Well, I won't do it."

Lady Pat stared at her husband. "Richard!"

Lord Richard refused to look at his wife. "I cannot, Pat. Too many people are depending on me to finish what they have started. Mr. Gladstone would never forgive me if I did not see this through."

"And I may never forgive you if anything happens to Alicia!" Lady Pat's voice throbbed with pain. "How can you? She must be kept safe, isn't that what you told me? Well, your little scheme has gone awry, and where is she? Where is my baby?" She looked about her dress for a handkerchief. Dr. Doyle, ever alert, produced one. She wiped her eyes and smiled her thanks.

Ned Kinsale spoke up: "Remember, Ricky, I told you the idea was a bad one. Sending the chit out of London made no sense at all."

"Then you knew she was not here?" Mr. Dodgson asked. "I wondered who was aware of the plan to send her to me. How was the scheme hatched, may I ask?"

Lord Richard glanced at his wife and brother-in-law. "Well, it must have been as soon as those articles began appearing in the *Pall Mall Gazette*. I saw which way the wind was blowing."

Mr. Dodgson nodded. "Ah, yes, Lord Richard, you always did."

"Um, yes. Well, it occurred to me that Alicia might be in some danger. Mrs. Jeffries and her ilk are quite ruthless and will stop at nothing to protect their livelihoods, however repugnant they may be."

"As we have seen," Dr. Doyle agreed.

"Yes." Lord Richard glanced at the doctor, as if in reproof for interrupting a Member of Parliament in full oration. "Therefore," he resumed his narrative, "after the Oxford-Cambridge Regatta, when you were kind enough to recall our brief years together," he nodded toward Mr. Dodgson, "I was told that you were going to spend your holidays at Eastbourne, with a young female friend. I cannot remember who put it into my mind—Pat?"

He turned to his wife, who smiled winsomely and shrugged.

"Ned?"

Kinsale frowned. "Not I, Ricky. I wasn't even at the Oxford-Cambridge races. I'm a Trinity man. No reason for me to be in Oxford. When was this? Beginning of July? I was with my father, back in Ireland. The old gentleman's got it into his head that I've been running with a crowd that will get me hanged . . . or worse."

Lady Pat sighed. "Ned, dear, why do you do it?"

"Gambling? It's in the blood!" Kinsale laughed.

"That's not what I mean, and you know it," Pat said sternly. "Ned, those people . . . "

"Are my constituents, Pat. Our mother would have approved, I'm sure."

"Not of those."

Mr. Dodgson brought the fraternal nagging to a halt. "If Mr. Kinsale did not suggest that Miss Alicia be sent to me, who did?"

Lord Richard looked puzzled. "You know, I'm not really sure. We were all here when the first of the articles came out, Ned and Pat, and Upshaw, of course, and somehow we got to wondering about Alicia's safety, since she could not go to my brother in Derbyshire. Measles," he explained. "The boys came back from school with them."

Mr. Dodgson's frown deepened. "Then this plan, I take it, was hastily conceived?"

"It was the best I could do, considering the circumstances," Lord Richard said defensively. For a moment, they were tutor and student again.

"Which makes it more and more obvious that the abductors had a spy in this household," Dr. Doyle said. "Lord Richard, may I examine the ransom note?"

Lord Richard handed it across the desk. Dr. Doyle frowned as he looked it over, sniffed at it, and handed it to Mr. Dodgson. "What do you make of it, sir?" he asked the scholar.

"Unusual. The paper is of good quality. The letters are printed, but even so, they are well-formed. Not an illiterate hand, I should think. There is a scent"—Mr. Dodgson sniffed at the letter—"a most penetrating and peculiar scent. I have smelled this scent on certain young persons in Brighton. And most unusually, all the words are correctly spelled, even 'daughter' and 'adieu.' A literate abductor, then. Most remarkable."

"I suppose they will consult the *Pall Mall Gazette* tomorrow to see if I have, indeed, withdrawn my support for the Bill," Lord Richard said moodily.

"That seems to be their *modus operandi*," Mr. Dodgson mused. "Until then, they will undoubtedly keep Miss Marbury under guard but near at hand. We may therefore assume that she has not been removed from Brighton."

"But what if the information is not in the newspapers?" Lady Pat quavered.

"Then the alternative is for them to retain possession of your daughter until the Bill either does or does not pass in the House." Mr. Dodgson frowned. "That could take some time."

While Mr. Dodgson contemplated the slow processes of British legislation, Dr. Doyle was examining the original letter to Mr. Dodgson.

"This note reinforces my belief that the perpetrators of the abduction of your daughter are members of this household," Doyle pronounced. "You see, every typewriting machine is unique. It may seem that the typeface of each model is identical to every other, but under a lens, each machine leaves an impression that is quite particular, depending on the user's touch, wear and tear on the machine, and so on. I intend to write an article about it and present it to the Portsmouth Literary and Scientific Society."

"Where is all this leading?" Kinsale asked.

"To the conclusion that the letter sent to Mr. Dodgson was typed on this very machine," Dr. Doyle said triumphantly. "See? The 'e' is slightly worn, which is natural, since 'e' is the most used letter in the English language. Lord Richard, who uses this machine?"

Lord Richard cleared his throat. "I do," he admitted. "None of the maids will touch it, even to dust it. Upshaw, of course; I had him instructed in its use when we purchased it. I understand that young women are being taught to use the typewriter, since their hands are smaller and their fingers more nimble. It seems to me to be an excellent idea; certainly an alternative to the life of shame on the streets. I shall have to look into it, Pat."

"Mr. Kinsale, have you attempted to use this machine?" Dr. Doyle asked.

Ned shrugged. "My own handwriting's a scrawl, I admit it. Ricky insisted I try out his new toy to write out my maiden speech to the Commons. Bad enough to have 'Roaring Ned Kinsale' in Parliament, he said; don't shame us all by not being able to read your own speech. So I tried my hand."

"Then you can use the machine?" Dr. Doyle persisted.

"Oh, I can use it, but if you think I'd kidnap my own niece, you're far out! I like little Alicia, in spite of her temper. She's a clever little puss, and she's going to be almost as pretty as her mama one of these days." He winked at his sister, who shook her head as if to reproach him for his impudence.

"Then who else knew of Miss Marbury's whereabouts?" Mr. Dodgson asked again. "The servants?"

Lady Pat looked troubled. "Her governess, Miss Quiggley, usually takes Alicia to Waltham with her for her holiday. Miss Quiggley is our vicar's wife's sister, a most respectable and well-educated woman. This year, we told her that she could have her holiday, and Mary Ann Parry would accompany Miss Alicia to Eastbourne. Oh, dear, where is Mary Ann? She was supposed to return last night. Nanny Marsh, Alicia's old nurse," she explained to Mr. Dodgson, "tends to grumble a bit about the nurserymaids, but we thought it better to send a young person with Alicia to Eastbourne. Alicia can sometimes be a trifle fractious with nurserymaids, and she got on well with Mary Ann."

Dr. Doyle glanced at Mr. Dodgson. Then he said, "I fear I have sad news, Lady Richard. Can you describe this Mary Ann for me?"

Lady Pat looked puzzled. "I don't understand . . . oh, no! Has something happened to Mary Ann?"

"We saw the body of a young woman at the headquarters of the Brighton Constabulary. She had apparently fallen or been pushed under a train," Dr. Doyle said bluntly. "I particularly noticed that she was wearing new shoes."

Lady Pat closed her eyes in pain. "The poor, poor child," she whispered. "She was so proud of those new shoes. The ones she had were quite worn out, and we bought her a new pair."

Dr. Doyle shot a triumphant glance at Mr. Dodgson. Lord Richard's face was like marble.

Ned Kinsale looked thoughtful. "Why get rid of the nurserymaid?" he asked.

"Possibly because she recognized someone at Brighton Station, someone who was not supposed to be there," Mr. Dodgson stated. "Possibly because she was simply in the way, and was therefore removed. These people are quite ruthless, as you have noted, Lord Richard, and the Brighton Police have done nothing. Dr. Doyle and I traveled up to London to discover what we could, and to inform you, sir, of the misfortune that has befallen your daughter. Now I am going to return to Brighton to find where she is being held, and to urge the police to do their duty!"

"How do you know she's still in Brighton?" Ned asked. "She could be anywhere by now."

Mr. Dodgson picked up the ransom note and held it with two fingers distastefully. "That paper is sold in a particular stationer's shop in Brighton," Mr. Dodgson said. "I know it well. I use that shop myself. It is logical, therefore, that the child has been taken by persons residing in Brighton, and is still there." He turned to his eager companion. "Dr. Doyle, you have been most kind and helpful, but you really should get back to your young wife."

Dr. Doyle was at Mr. Dodgson's elbow, helping him to stand. "I can't leave the chase now, sir. Besides, these people have already proven themselves to be desperate. I would never forgive myself if they made you a target. No, Mr. Dodgson, I am with you to the end."

"I thought you might be," Mr. Dodgson murmured.

The older man adjusted his gloves. A tap at the door broke the silence.

"Inspector MacRae, from Scotland Yard," Farnham announced.

Lord Richard nodded. "Good. Now we shall have some action! Show the Inspector in, Farnham, and bring some more coffee. We may need it."

CHAPTER 9

Farnham marched into the study with a stately tread, his lofty frown indicating his opinion of the person behind him.

"I did not know whether to place the policeman in the hall or show him into your particular study," Farnham said, as he collected the remains of the coffee and cakes. He was far too well trained to reveal his intentions of handing in his notice at the first opportunity. Policemen did not come to the houses of the best people, and Farnham had his own career to look out for. Member of Parliament or not, Lord Richard Marbury had had very strange visitors of late, and this Inspector MacRae was of a piece with the rest.

Inspector MacRae did not fit the picture of the sturdy policeman that Lord Richard expected. He was a short, narrow-faced man, with thinning dark hair and a pair of wire-rimmed spectacles incongruously perched on his sharp nose. He clutched a straw hat, indicative of the season, but otherwise was dressed in a set of small-checked "dittoes." Behind him, Upshaw loomed like a wraith, in a freshly cleaned gray suit, clean shirt and collar, and the inevitable bowler hat.

"I beg pardon, sir," Upshaw said breathlessly. "I was detained, but I shall be on my way to Scotland yard." He looked at MacRae, who stared back.

"As you see, Upshaw, the police are here," Lord Peter said. "Good morning, Inspector. I want to consult you in this matter of my daughter."

Inspector MacRae glanced around the room, dismissing the elderly gentleman in black and his younger tweed-clad companion, and settling on the man behind the desk as the leader of the pack.

"Your daughter, sir? I was not informed that the young person in question was any relation of yours."

"But why else would you be here? I sent my man, Upshaw, to Scotland Yard . . ."

"I tried to tell you, Lord Richard," Upshaw said apologetically. "I did not get to Scotland Yard. I was on my way there, when I saw this person," he indicated MacRae, "mounting the steps, so I took the liberty of returning here."

Lord Richard turned his gaze to MacRae, who returned the look without a trace of deference, and more than a little truculence.

"I have been sent to this house, by my superiors, at the request of the Brighton Constabulary," Inspector MacRae stated.

"Have you found her, then?" Lady Pat darted forward. "Where is she? Is she all right?"

The Scotland Yard man frowned. "She's dead!"

Lady Pat shrieked and dropped against her brother. Dr. Doyle was at her side in an instant, chafing her wrists and looking around for female servants.

"What a thing to say!" he scolded the Inspector. "Where is her maid? Lady Patricia, please!" He looked about for the smelling salts usually carried by ladies. Lord Richard sat, stunned, while Ned Kinsale and Dr. Doyle brought his wife back to consciousness and eased her onto Mr. Dodgson's vacated chair.

Mr. Dodgson glared at MacRae. "That was quite unnecessarily brutal, Inspector. Whatever can you have been thinking of?"

MacRae blinked behind his spectacles. "I beg your pardon, but I thought . . ." He began again. "I did not know that your servants were so dear to your heart, Lord Richard. In my experience, most noble households don't pay much heed to those below stairs."

Now it was Lord Richard's turn to be confused. "Servant? I sent Upshaw to Scotland Yard because my *daughter* has been abducted."

"I don't know any Upshaw, and I had no idea that your daughter was concerned in the matter. I've been sent because we received this wire from Brighton." MacRae flourished a familiar slip of flimsy yellow paper.

Dr. Doyle saw the light first. "Lord Richard, it is possible this has something to do with that poor girl I saw, the missing Mary Ann."

MacRae consulted the telegram. "A young woman, age seventeen or thereabouts. Fell, or was pushed under a train in Brighton Station. A small reticule was discovered near the body, which, when searched, contained a letter with the Marbury crest, which led the Brighton authorities to suspect that the victim was employed in this household."

Lady Pat had revived under Dr. Doyle's ministrations. "It's all right, Pat," Ned told her. "The Inspector here got his girls mixed. Dr. Doyle's idea about poor Mary Ann was right, it seems, and the good Inspector here is on the case."

"But what about Alicia?" Lady Pat moaned.

"Alicia?" MacRae's eyes narrowed behind his spectacles.

"My daughter," Lord Richard explained. "She was removed from Brighton Station . . . "

"By someone masquerading as me," Mr. Dodgson interrupted. "And those blundering fools in Brighton . . . "

"I'm sure the Brighton Constabulary did what they thought was correct," Dr. Doyle put in.

MacRae listened to all of this with tight-lipped annoyance. "Was this Mary Ann of yours with the little girl?"

"Of course. I'd hardly send my daughter off without an attendant," Lord Richard said testily.

"Why send her at all?" MacRae asked.

"That is none of your concern, Inspector. What is important is that she be found, and found quickly," Lord Richard snapped.

"That's your business, sir. Mine is murder," MacRae said. "Which is what this matter of Mary Ann may be. My colleagues," he emphasized the word slightly, with a sharp look at Dr. Doyle, "in Brighton have asked me to come down and consult with them. As for the matter of your daughter, that will be attended to in due course. Have you received any ransom note, or other communication?"

"What do you make of this?" Lord Richard handed Inspector MacRae the much-fingered ransom note.

"No envelope? No seal?" Inspector MacRae looked skeptically at Lord Richard. "How'd it come to you, then?"

"It was in my pocket," Upshaw confessed. "It must have been thrust there by someone in the crowd, during that disgraceful scene with Mrs. Jeffries this morning."

"Eh?" Inspector MacRae's eyebrows worked up and down.

"The woman had the audacity to parade herself and her, um, entourage, in front of my door this morning," Lord Richard said. "They created a public disturbance, and the police were nowhere in sight!"

"No law against an Englishman, or woman for that matter, exercising the right of assembly," MacRae rumbled. "Now, tell me again, how did the young lady come to be taken?"

"She was supposed to meet me, at Brighton Railway Station," Mr. Dodgson explained wearily. "But I was given false information, and she met someone else instead."

"Ah." MacRae appeared to digest this information with bovine indifference. "And who are you?"

"I am Mr. Dodgson, of Oxford. Miss Marbury was to be my guest while the debate over the Special Bill goes on."

"Only she never arrived," Dr. Doyle put in. "And while we are chattering here, she may be in dreadful danger."

"And who are *you*?" MacRae asked, with a withering glance.

Dr. Doyle was not to be withered. "I am Dr. Arthur Conan Doyle of Portsmouth, and I am assisting Mr. Dodgson with his inquiries into this matter."

"He's Dicky Doyle's nephew, you know," Mr. Dodgson put in.

"Who's Dicky Doyle?" MacRae asked.

Mr. Dodgson looked offended. "The comic artist, from *Punch*."

MacRae was not impressed by these credentials. "Well, Mr. Dodgson of Oxford and Dr. Doyle of Portsmouth, you had best go about your own business and leave this to the professionals."

"I have already been to the Brighton Police," Mr. Dodgson sputtered. "They have done nothing. And the young person sent with Miss Marbury has been found dead—perhaps murdered!"

"That's for the Coroner's jury to decide," MacRae said. "They don't meet until Tuesday. In the meanwhile, I've been sent here to find out what I can about the girl."

Lord Richard leaned forward over his desk. "Inspector MacRae, I am a Member of Parliament and a good friend of the Home Secretary. You have been summoned to Brighton to assist with the death of my daughter's nurserymaid. Now I strongly suggest that you combine that investigation with the search for my daughter's abductors."

Inspector MacRae was not to be hurried. "I always do my duty, sir. And I've often fancied a trip to the seaside, but I never thought it would be at the expense of the department."

"Send any bills incurred in your investigations to me," Lord Richard said with a wave of his hand.

"I shall submit my expenses to the department, as per regulation," MacRae said. "Now, then"—he produced a shaggy notebook and the stub of a pencil—"I have to take statements from all of you. The girl was killed . . . " Lady Pat gasped. "Begging your pardon, ma'am. The, um, death was placed at approximately four o'clock yesterday afternoon. The occurrence was witnessed by several travelers . . . "

"But did any of them recognize anyone in particular?" Dr. Doyle asked sharply.

"If by that you mean that someone has come forward with information, no, they have not," MacRae said. "The driver of the engine was not aware of anything untoward until he heard cries from the guards, who signaled for him to stop. Those who witnessed the, um, accident . . . "

"If it was an accident," grumbled Dr. Doyle.

"As far as the Brighton Police can tell, it was an accident. Only someone," he glared in the direction of Dr. Doyle, "pointed out that the girl fell backwards, not forwards. In this case, the question of intent comes into play. No one is calling it a murder, not yet, but—for my notes, sir, ma'am—where were you at four o'clock yesterday afternoon?"

"I was paying calls," Lady Pat said. "What does this have to do with . . . ?"

Ned Kinsale had been kneeling beside his sister. Now he stood up and grinned at the Inspector.

"Taking alibis? Well, you'll have to take my word as a gentleman and a Member of Parliament that I was in London all day and all night. Unfortunately, I cannot say precisely where."

"Cannot or will not?" MacRae snapped out.

Kinsale shrugged expressively. "Either one, as you wish, Inspector. These two gentlemen can tell you that I met them this morning, right here upon these very steps. From teatime on, yesterday, I was in the company of . . . friends."

"What friends?" MacRae's eyes glittered behind his spectacles.

Kinsale's grin broadened. "Particular friends. I don't choose to name them, although I suppose if I did they'd vouch for me."

Lady Pat regarded her brother soulfully. "Oh, Ned, you weren't out gambling again?"

Kinsale's only answer was another grin and a shrug. "Ricky, take my advice. Drop this Bill. Make the announcement to the Press, take the Chiltern Hundreds, and let everyone go home to their families, or shooting in Scotland, or taking the waters in Scarborough or wherever they care to spend their summer holidays. As for the scribblers in the *Pall Mall Gazette*, they can write their dirty little tales for the great unwashed to gloat over. No doubt Alicia will be returned to you by teatime, as soon as the first Sunday editions are on the newsstands."

Lord Richard's pale blue eyes looked like chips of ice in his white face. "Ned, you go too far! I have committed myself to see this Bill through. My constituents demand it. I should consider myself a coward if I gave in to this . . . this bludgeoning! As for my handing in my resignation and stepping down, that is for the electorate to decide in

November. If I were to withdraw now, I should deserve to be beaten!"

"Bravo!" applauded Dr. Doyle.

Ned Kinsale sneered, "Save it for the hustings, Ricky."

Lady Pat's soulful look turned to outrage. "Ned! How can you be so . . . so . . ."

"Callous? Cruel? Pat, me girl, such are the times we live in." Ned dropped a kiss on his sister's head and waved at her husband. "If that's all, Inspector, I've spent over much time here. There are a few people I have to see."

"You'll keep us informed if you decide to leave London." It was a statement, not a question.

"My movements are no concern of Scotland Yard, Inspector." Ned Kinsale bowed mockingly and sauntered out. "Don't bother to see me out, Farnham," he called, as he slammed the door behind him.

Inspector MacRae turned to the distraught parents. "If I'm to consult with the Brighton Constabulary, sir, I will have to take the next train down."

Upshaw produced a time table from the shelf of books over his desk and consulted his watch. "There are trains from Victoria Station every hour," he declared. "Lord Richard, with your permission, I would like to accompany Mr. Dodgson and Dr. Doyle, and Inspector MacRae to Brighton. Perhaps I may be of assistance in tracking down the culprits who have stolen Miss Marbury."

Lord Richard swept his hand through his hair. "No, no, Upshaw. Your sentiments are appreciated, but I need you here. With this Bill coming up, I must have my notes in order."

Upshaw's long face became even longer with anguish. "If nothing else, I could, perhaps identify the . . . the deceased."

Lady Pat sat up and looked at Upshaw. "Mr. Upshaw," she said severely, "I was not aware that you even knew Mary Ann. The nursery staff do not usually mix with the rest of the servants."

Upshaw's pale cheeks were slightly stained with red. "I . . . occasionally met Mary Ann when she went walking with Miss Alicia," he confessed. "Under the circumstances, I could not pursue the acquaintance, but I always considered her a . . . an attractive young person."

"A positive identification would be useful," MacRae admitted.

Lord Richard swept his hands through his hair again and looked helplessly at the papers on his desk. "But my speech . . . the Bill . . ."

Upshaw shuffled papers around on Lord Richard's desk. "These are the cuttings from the *Pall Mall Gazette*. These are the statements of the witnesses in the Magistrate's Court. These are your notes from our discussion last week."

Lord Richard nodded. "Good, Upshaw. Now, while you are in Brighton, you must look in at the hotels, and find out if any of the members have checked into the Old Ship or the Crown. And if they have, you must speak to them, and get them up here in time for the vote."

"And if—when—we find Miss Marbury?" Mr. Dodgson asked.

"Keep her safe, that's all that I ask," Lord Richard said.

"Very well, Lord Richard." Inspector MacRae touched his hat in salute. Dr. Doyle followed Upshaw into the hall.

Mr. Dodgson remained behind for a moment. "Lord Richard," he said, his voice trembling in agony, "I cannot help but think that this is all my fault. If I had been more prompt . . . if I had not misread the letter . . ."

Lady Pat reached over and patted his hand. He shyly withdrew from her touch.

Lord Richard got up and walked around to pat his old tutor's shoulder. "No one could have foreseen this," he told him miserably.

"Someone arranged that I should be involved in the business," Mr. Dodgson said. "Undoubtedly, they thought that I would retreat to Eastbourne when I could not find the child. They were wrong. I promise you, Lord Richard, that I shall do all in my power to see that your daughter is returned to you safely."

"You must wire me as soon as she is found," Lord Richard insisted.

"Of course." Farnham had appeared to escort the three men to the door. Outside, Grosvenor Square had returned to its normal drowsy aspect. The cab that had brought Inspector MacRae to Mayfair had long since departed.

"Victoria Station, gentlemen," Mr. Dodgson said, striding toward the rumble of traffic on Regent Street. "We must find Miss Marbury before it is too late!"

CHAPTER 10

Alicia Marbury had spent a restless and disturbing night. The room, while hot and stuffy during the daylight hours, lost heat with astonishing rapidity once the sun set, and her camisole and drawers were no protection against the chill. She had been fed a platter of bread and cheese and a cup of very milky tea, brought to her by Kitty, while the Madam looked on. There had been no time for more than a quick smile between the girls. "No talking there!" ordered the Madam, and that was that.

Alicia had been left alone, in the dark, in this very strange house, sitting on the bare mattress in her drawers and camisole, listening to the noises outside and in. From the street came a faint rumbling, as if heavy carts were being hauled over the cobblestones. Then there were strains of far-off laughter that seemed to come through the bare floorboards. Alicia struggled against the call of nature, but eventually used the chamberpot provided for her comfort. The result added an overpowering aroma to the stuffy room. She could not sleep but fell into a sort of doze, from which she was jolted into consciousness when she heard a slam, as if a door had been shut.

Morning brought little relief. When she could see clearly again,

Alicia decided to examine her prison more carefully, for any means of escape. The bed could be moved, she decided, but not by her; it was far too heavy. The doorjamb was lined with strips of carpeting, a sinister thought: Was it to muffle the screams of terror emanating from this room? The hooks on the wall were even more suggestive. They were just shoulder-high to Alicia; what, or *who*, were they meant to hold?

Alicia shouted: "Hey! Someone come up and take this pot away!"

No one answered. For the first time in her life, no one responded when she called. Even at Waltham someone answered her, although it might well be to tell her to stop bawling.

"I know someone's there!" Alicia shouted again.

From the door came a stifled snort. "I hears you," whispered the unseen friend behind the door.

"Kitty? Is that you? Where is everyone?" Alicia ran to the door and tried to see through the keyhole.

"I've got to lay the breakfast and scrub up after, then get the pots," Kitty said.

"What about mine?" Alicia complained. "I had to use it and it smells awful!"

"Dunno," Kitty whispered. " 'Ere comes the Madam."

A heavy tread announced the arrival of Madge Gurney. Alicia heard the sound of a slap, a muffled "Ow!" from Kitty, and a patter of scampering feet.

"You'll stay put!" the Madam grunted. Alicia heard her stamping down the stairs, and a fierce resolve grew within her. Somehow, some way, she was going to get away from here! Her only difficulty seemed to be in finding a workable plan of attack.

Attack! That was what Grandpapa Kinsale had said when he came to visit them in London, to hear Uncle Ned's speech in the House. He had told her all about the Crimea, and how he had led the charge. "Attack! That's what we did at Balaclava. Attack and damn the consequences!"

Uncle Ned had said something about the consequences being a whole regiment destroyed, but Alicia could still see the fierce look on her grandpapa's face and the light of battle in his eyes. Grandpapa

Kinsale had attacked! So would she, as soon as they opened the door again.

Downstairs, the table had been set for the six young women (aged eleven to fifteen) residing in Miss Harmon's establishment. One by one they straggled downstairs, weary with their previous night's labors. One by one they took their seats, waited patiently as Miss Harmon took hers, and, at her signal, began to spoon up their porridge.

Miss Harmon glanced at Mrs. Gurney and raised an eyebrow. The older woman jerked her head in silent call for a conference. Miss Harmon set aside her spoon and joined her partner in crime at the door to the pantry.

"She's awake," the older woman informed her. "Does she get breakfast?"

"We don't want her to think herself ill used," Miss Harmon murmured. "But just enough to keep her quiet. Porridge, milk."

"Any word from Mrs. J.?"

"The message should have reached him by now," Miss Harmon said, a slight smile curling her lips. "We'll know by tonight. According to the Guv'nor, the *Gazette* writes what Marbury tells them. If he sends his resignation letter in by noon, it'll just make the Sunday editions."

"You think he will?"

Miss Harmon stared over the heads of her charges. "I don't know," she said slowly. "He loves the girl, no doubt, but he's a man of principle. He won't give up so easily."

"The Guv'nor thinks he will."

"The Guv'nor doesn't know him as well . . . "

"Ahh!" Madge breathed, a sly leer of understanding forming in her eyes. "So *'e's* the one . . . "

"That's none of your concern," Miss Harmon snapped out. "If Marbury doesn't comply with our wishes, then . . . "

"Then—what do we do?"

"There's always Monsieur LeBrun. An English girl, red hair, guaranteed virgin, and a peer's niece? She'll go for five hundred pounds at least."

Madge sniggered, then a thought overtook her and she looked worried. "What if Marbury calls in the coppers?"

Miss Harmon's smile deepened. "Then he will wish he had not." She looked at her little charges again. They had finished their porridge and were staring back at their teacher, their mentor, their employer.

"Young ladies," she said. "Go upstairs and get dressed. We will go walking this morning, on the Esplanade."

"Now?" whined the tallest, the dark beauty who liked to call herself Victoria, because she said she was the Queen of the House.

"Now," Miss Harmon ordered. "Gentlemen do not like fat, lazy girls. Besides, you must be seen in the right places. Wear proper shoes. Stockings with no holes. Clean linens. Wash your faces and necks." Each order brought another groan.

"The gentlemen like me already," plump Gertie said, shaking her blond ringlets. "Why do I have to go walking out in the hot sun?"

"Because I wish the gentlemen to know we are here," Miss Harmon said flatly. As the girls grumbled their way upstairs back to their bedrooms, Miss Harmon nodded to her confederate. "What if he does call in the police? This is a modest house; we don't have rough trade, and gentlemen of quality find their little satisfactions here. We have a working relationship with the Council. Mr. Carstairs assured Mrs. J. that he has made arrangements with the local constabulary. No, Madge, I don't think we'll be bothered by the police. Just wait until I've got the rest of the girls out of here. They talk, and I don't want anyone to know about our latest arrival—at least, not yet."

It took the better part of an hour before the six young women of Miss Harmon's establishment were dressed to their mentor's satisfaction.

"Susanne, you must not permit your underchemise to show. Helen, you have a ladder in your stocking. Gentlemen do not like young ladies who are not properly dressed."

"Me sister don't spiff up like this," Helen said sulkily.

"Your sister's on the streets," Victoria snapped back. "She only gets a shilling a time. I get a pound," she added with great satisfaction.

"And you will get more, if you do as I tell you," Miss Harmon said. "I shall give you each half a crown to spend when we get to the Esplanada. Remember, the gentlemen are always watching."

The line of well-dressed young women marched down King Street, pretending not to hear the admiring cries and catcalls that followed them until they turned the corner into North Street and were gone.

Madge shrugged and went back to the kitchen, where Kitty was hauling a bucket of water from the outside pump. With a grunt of exasperation, the Madam dumped a ladleful of porridge into a bowl, and poured milk into a mug. The truncated breakfast was shoved at Kitty, who put it on one of the trays that usually went up to the dining room.

"Get this up to the new 'un," the Madam ordered.

"Door's locked," Kitty reminded her.

"I'll be right behind yer."

With the bowl of porridge and the mug of lukewarm milk on the tray, Kitty climbed the stairs from the kitchen to the front hall, then slogged up the front stairs to the upper story, trudged down the hall to the back of the house, and approached the concealed door in the back wall. As far as anyone could see, that wall ended in a decorated panel, depicting a plump cupid floating above a rustic couple. Only a small keyhole betrayed the existence of something behind the panel: a final flight of stairs that led to the attic room kept for Very Special Girls. Kitty waited for Madam to produce her key and open the secret door, then inched up the steep stairs, conscious of Madge Gurney's heavy hand behind her.

The Madam turned the key in the lock. The door flew in, and a howling banshee flew out.

The tray flew out of Kitty's hands. The milk spilled onto the bare wooden stairs. The Madam, thrown offbalance, braced herself against the wall of the stairwell with one hand and caught Alicia by her camisole with the other.

Alicia thrashed around wildly, yelling, scratching and clawing whatever she could find. Kitty shrank back, unsure of which combatant to assist. Madge found her footing, grabbed Alicia, and twined one hand into the girl's flying red curls.

Alicia shrieked again, this time in pain, and she was thrown back into the bedroom. Madge's little eyes glittered with malice.

"Feisty, are we? Well, we have ways of taking care of feisty little girls here, missy!" She gasped and coughed, conscious of the line of scratches on her cheeks where Alicia had left her mark.

"You don't dare harm me," Alicia retorted. "If you do, my papa won't pay any ransom."

"Your pa's going to do exactly as he's told!" the Madam shot back at her. "And you just spilled good porridge on the floor. Now you get to eat it, off the floor!"

"I won't!" Alicia shouted.

"You won't get nought else!" Mrs. Gurney loomed over her.

Kitty crept into the room. "I'll help clean it up," she offered.

"That you will not," the Madam declared. "You take the pots and do 'em right this time. Missy here can 'elp yer, and earn 'er porridge like everyone else in this world!"

She stamped downstairs, hauling Kitty and Alicia with her. Alicia waited for the moment when that tight grip on her arm would be relaxed. Then she could bolt out. The Madam shook her fiercely and said,

"Don't even think it, missy. Where d'ye think you'll go, in your drawers?"

Alicia's face reddened. Of course, she had to get some clothes! Her pretty new dress had been taken away by that hateful Miss Harmon. She had to get it back.

"You two can just wash them pots," the Madam said. "And don't think you can talk, because I'll be watchin' yer all the time!"

Alicia watched as Kitty went about her chores: emptying the reeking potties into a vile-smelling pit in the yard, then dipping each into one bucket, scrubbing them out with a wad of straw, and dipping them into a second bucket.

"You do these," Kitty said, pointing to the scrubbed receptacles.

"I heard that!" Madge roared out behind them. "No talking!"

"She'll get her gin soon," Kitty whispered. "She'll be asleep, and we can talk then."

"I heard that!"

Alicia had never been so quiet for so long, not even in church. Only when a series of heavy snores could be heard behind them did Kitty speak again, in a hoarse whisper.

"You must be summat special. I never know 'er to hold back 'er 'and. And yer marked 'er, too!" Kitty said, admiringly.

"Did I?" Alicia asked.

"I saw scratches on 'er face." Kitty giggled. "But yer mustn't do that no more. It's bad for the 'ouse."

"What is this place?" Alicia whispered.

"It's Miss 'Armon's," Kitty explained, as if that was sufficient. "Lots of gentlemen come 'ere for their pleasures," she added, reciting the motto announced by Miss Harmon to new recruits.

"Oh." Alicia digested this information. "What sort of pleasures?"

"Wif the girls, you know."

"Games and such?" Alicia had been allowed to participate in adult parlor games at Christmas. The sight of grownups indulging in such antics as Charades, Blind-Man's-Buff, and Sardines could be amusing, but she didn't see why they had to do it here in Brighton, or why someone should lock her in an upstairs room while they did.

Kitty, on the other hand, regarded Alicia with scorn based on superior knowledge. "No, silly. They goes upstairs and does *it*."

"What?"

"*It!*"

Alicia was totally confused. "What do they do upstairs?" she persisted.

Kitty tried to explain. "Like wot me mum does. The gentlemen puts it into 'em."

Alicia decided to pursue this at another time. Whatever *it* was, if it was done here, she decided, she wanted no part of it. "You have to get me out of here," she told Kitty fiercely.

"Why d'ye want to leave?" Kitty asked. "Grub's good. There's 'eat, and the old bitch don't 'it 'alf as 'ard as me mum."

"In my house no one gets hit," Alicia said stoutly. "My papa won't permit it. And all the servants get new shoes and new dresses at Christmas, and a . . . a . . . living wage." She tried to remember what her papa had said when he practiced his speech for the House of Commons. "If you help me," Alicia smiled winningly, "I'll take you to my house and you can be my maid. Mary Ann will show you how to go on. Then you won't get hit at all. And you won't have to wash these horrid pots because we have a proper water closet," she added.

Kitty glanced over her shoulder. " 'Ow am I supposed to get you out?" she protested. "The Madam watches me like a 'awk, and Miss 'Armon . . . "

Alicia tried to remember the last chapter of the exciting story she had been reading in *The Boy's Own Paper* before her incarceration. She felt under her camisole. "Here," she said. "When you took my dress off, you forgot to take this. It's my grandmama Waltham's own locket, that she left me because my uncle only has boys." She unhooked the delicate chain from around her neck and pressed it into Kitty's hand. "What you must do is take this, and see that the policeman on the corner gets it."

"Wot policeman?"

"The one on the corner, of course!" In Alicia's world, there was always a policeman on the corner: a blue-coated guardian of little girls, who smiled at the nurserymaid (in the case of Mary Ann, he sometimes added a polite greeting) and touched his helmet to Papa. "He'll see it and know that I'm somewhere nearby, and then the police—"

"Police!" Kitty was horrified. "*Me?* Go to the coppers? I couldn't do it! Not for all the tea in China, not for . . . "

"For a whole half-crown a week, all yours? And a half-day off, every other week? And living in London?" Alicia tried to think of every inducement that Mary Ann had relished.

"But . . . "

"Ssssh!"

"I heard that!" Madge Gurney was awake again. "Are them pots finished?"

"Yes, Madam," Alicia said. Miss Quiggley would have known that voice of sweet compliance, but Madam Gurney was not Miss Quiggley.

79

"Then take one of 'em up them stairs, and this time, you stay put!" The Madam grabbed Alicia by the right arm and dragged her back up to the attic. In the light from the areaway, Alicia could see the scratches that she herself had inflicted upon her jailer. She smiled secretly to herself. Not even top-lofty Cousin Edmund, fresh from his triumphs at Eton, could boast that he had injured his torturer!

Alicia allowed herself to be locked up again. She was hungry, she was bruised, but she felt that she had done as much as she could toward earning her freedom. Now it was up to Kitty.

CHAPTER 11

Saturday trains to Brighton ran every hour from Victoria Station, and in the summer holidays they were crammed to capacity. Every one of the first-class carriages was filled. Mr. Dodgson and Dr. Doyle took advantage of their first-class return tickets to insert themselves into the last two seats on the 1:00 P.M. train, while Inspector MacRae and Mr. Upshaw had to be jammed into the second-class coach with the rest of the populace.

Mr. Dodgson removed his hat as he and Dr. Doyle settled themselves into their carriage, across from a stout man in a striped jacket and straw hat, and two ladies of middle years dressed in severely cut écru linen summer traveling dresses.

"I am not displeased that Inspector MacRae and Mr. Upshaw are elsewhere," Mr. Dodgson commented, as the engine began its rhythmical puffing, preparatory to leaving London. "I cannot be easy in the company of Mr. Upshaw. I dare say I am being too particular. It is not logical to take a dislike to a man because he appears too ingratiating. I wonder that Lord Richard Marbury would take on such a common person as his secretary."

"I imagine he finds him useful," Dr. Doyle said. "For my part, I find Inspector MacRae overbearing. I suppose it's that Glasgow accent of his. As for Upshaw, he seems a good sort. Fawns on Lord Richard, of course; it can't be easy for him, being in a subordinate position, and having such expensive tastes."

"Oh, you noticed that, did you?"

Dr. Doyle stroked his mustache smugly. "Hard to miss it. His suit, for instance; the material is quite good. He's finicky about his dress, too; why change one's suit and shave before going to Scotland Yard? And his boots are of the best."

"And he keeps rooms at the Albany," Mr. Dodgson mused. "Not an economical address."

"He doesn't have his own room in Lord Richard's house?" Dr. Doyle frowned slightly. "So he is not precisely a confidential secretary."

"Apparently not. In fact, he appears to be more of a general dogsbody, being sent on errands here and there. Dear me, this is becoming quite tangled. I do not understand the logic of it."

"Logic?" Dr. Doyle shot the mathematician a quick look.

"Yes, logic. Whatever can these people hope to gain by holding Miss Marbury? Lord Richard will never recant, and he cannot draw back from his campaign at this date."

"Perhaps they intend to keep her until the vote is taken," Dr. Doyle suggested.

"But that might not be for months," Mr. Dodgson pointed out. "With most of the members of both Houses on their holidays, the Bill may be debated well into next year. Given the glacial rate at which legislation passes in our government, what is there that makes these people so desperate at this time?"

"Apparently, the articles in the *Pall Mall Gazette*," Dr. Doyle commented. "Mr. Stead and his friends have caused quite a commotion. Large protestation meetings are being held all over England this weekend, according to the leaders in the newspapers. And I noticed a band of Salvationists in the second-class carriages, complete with their instruments, on their way south. I assume Lord Richard is finding more supporters this time than he did the last."

Mr. Dodgson was on a different train of thought by now. "In that case, why do these people retain the child? How can they be certain that Lord Richard would not, as he already has, seek help from Scotland Yard?"

The two ladies opposite them had been listening avidly. At the mention of Scotland Yard, the stouter of the two lifted her head from the red-backed copy of *A Guide to Brighton* and nudged her taller, fairer companion.

Mr. Dodgson went on, his voice becoming louder and shriller. "Logically, the person responsible for Miss Marbury's disappearance would have to be familiar not only with the household and its routines but also with me, and my appearance and habits. I find that most disturbing."

Dr. Doyle nodded. "I can only conclude that someone is not only trying to get Lord Richard to remove his support for the Bill before the House but is also trying to harm you, Mr. Dodgson. And that, if you don't mind my saying so, seems quite impossible. Your reputation is unsullied, your literary output is."

"Literary output? Dr. Doyle, I am a mathematician. I have no literary output except for some articles and letters, and a few entertaining puzzles." Mr. Dodgson shook his head vigorously.

"But my wife said . . . " Dr. Doyle began to protest.

"She was mistaken. She thought I was Mr. Lewis Carroll. Mr. Lewis Carroll does not exist."

Dr. Doyle laughed heartily. "You may say so, sir, but the children of England . . . nay, of the world! They know better."

Mr. Dodgson shook his head again. "I assure you, Dr. Doyle, that if I were Lewis Carroll, my life would be made miserable by sensation seekers, literary lion-hunters."

The taller of the two ladies sharing their carriage stared at the man opposite her. "Oh, dear me! *Are* you Mr. Lewis Carroll? I am Miss Drusilla Griggs, of the Thrush Grange School. My girls have all read the 'Alice' books, and they love them dearly. Are you going to write another? Do say you will, Mr. Carroll, for we will all read it, won't we, Miss Belfridge?"

The stout woman next to her nodded so fiercely that her chins wobbled. "I do wish the girls were here right now," she gushed.

"This is quite the best adventure, Drusilla. I feel justified in having accepted your offer, instead of taking the walking tour of the Lakes."

"Imagine! Sharing a railway carriage with Mr. Lewis Carroll!" Miss Griggs beamed at her idol, who responded with a weak smile of his own, and a look directed at Dr. Doyle that said, Look what you just got me into. "What are you writing now, Mr. Carroll?"

"Actually," he said, "I am working on a new story, to be called 'Sylvie and Bruno.' Some of it is in verse," he added.

"And I suppose you are also a writer?" Miss Belfridge surveyed Dr. Doyle through her spectacles.

"On occasion," Dr. Doyle admitted.

"There! I knew it when I set eyes on you!" The two ladies nodded to each other as if to agree on their mutual findings.

"Is this your first trip to Brighton?" Dr. Doyle asked politely.

Miss Belfridge nodded. "I have a connection who lets rooms," she confessed. "And when she asked if I could come, I decided to do it."

"On the spur of the moment," giggled Miss Griggs.

"Brighton is very pleasant at this time of year," Mr. Dodgson offered, "but rather crowded. I trust you will have a pleasant stay." He seemed to fold into himself.

Dr. Doyle smiled at the two ladies, and privately wished them elsewhere. He wanted to talk about the Case, but now that would be impossible. He glanced over at the stout man in the corner, who snored loudly.

What an adventure! How odd that it should be wasted on a gentle old duffer like Dodgson! He felt the older man shrinking into his seat next to him, and wondered what the poor old fellow made of it all. Kidnapped children, houses of ill repute, mysterious deaths . . . what fodder for the writer! Dr. Doyle glanced at his companion and wondered if, perhaps, he could get Mr. Dodgson to read some of his unpublished stories. The opinion of a published writer, even one like Mr. Dodgson, would always be of value. Dr. Doyle gazed out the window and dreamed dreams of glory.

Mr. Dodgson's thoughts were far from glorious. He wished that he had never accepted Lord Richard Marbury's offer of a child companion. He wished Dr. Doyle would not be so ebullient. He wished the train would get to Brighton so that he could get on with his self-imposed task of finding Miss Alicia Marbury. Most of all, he wished that the two women opposite were not so lavishly scented with some floral odor that permeated the stuffy carriage. It teased at his nostrils. He had smelled something similar, and quite recently, too . . .

He went over the situation in his mind. The logic of it escaped him. How could the abductors think that Lord Richard, who had staked his reputation on Reform, would give way now? Unless . . . Mr. Dodgson cogitated as the train rumbled through the countryside to the seashore.

Dr. Doyle glanced at his traveling companion with a kind of exasperated pity. I can use this, he thought to himself. I can write the whole thing up, with suitable changes of name, of course. *Cornhill* is usually good for a tenner, and the extra money comes in handy, now that I'm a man with a family to support. He thought of Touie, faithfully waiting for him at Mrs. Keene's lodgings, and hoped that she had found amusement while he was pursuing these dastardly criminals.

Touie, at that moment, was on the Esplanade, contemplating the crowd. She had spent the morning happily pottering about in those shops particularly recommended to her by Mrs. Keene, who seemed to have friends and relations up and down the Steine. She had daringly entered a teashop, all on her own, and had had a luncheon of egg sandwiches, cakes, and tea. She had watched the Punch and Judy, and was sitting on one of the benches, observing the scenery and wondering when Arthur would get back from London, when her eye was caught by a procession (there was no other word for it) of girls strolling down the Esplanade, led by a tall young woman with astounding red hair, visible under her straw hat.

Touie tried to assimilate what she was seeing. The girls themselves were well-dressed and good-looking—rather remarkably so, Touie concluded, given that most children between twelve and fifteen were in the podgy, spotty stage. They seemed to walk with a kind of brazen confidence, as if they knew just how good-looking they were; not a trait fostered in most homes of Touie's experience. She picked up her packages and drew closer.

There was something wrong about this. If only Arthur were here, she thought. He's so clever! But I shall tell him, as soon as he returns from London. He told me to watch for anything unusual. I think this may be it.

As Touie watched, a cry came up from the stony beach below the pier. "Help! There's a man down here!"

A fisherman in a damp jersey and trousers joined the growing crowd. A large young man in the familiar blue tunic and helmet of the police leaned over the railing of the Esplanade and added his voice to the din.

"Looks like he had an accident!" someone shouted up.

"I'll get the ambulance," the policeman offered.

"Too late for that," the fisherman declared. "He's long gone."

As Touie watched, the policeman shouldered through the crowd to examine the body that had been left by the outgoing tide.

"Must have fallen in at the neaps," offered the fisherman sagely. "High tide was an hour ago."

"Anyone recognize him?" asked the constable, looking about the beach.

The silence was deafening.

"I'll have him taken up to the station," the policeman decided. "If you hear anything of someone gone missing, let us know, hey?"

The fisherman nodded. The horribly limp body was dragged onto a fishing net, bundled up, and brought up to the roadway, where a cart was commandeered to take it elsewhere.

What a dreadful thing! Touie thought. Poor old man; he must have taken too much to drink and fallen into the sea and drowned . . . although that didn't seem quite right. The railings were quite stout on the piers, and the Esplanade was nowhere near enough to the sea for any danger of drowning. I do wish Arthur were here. I will have to tell him about this when he gets back from London.

* * *

In his carriage, Dr. Doyle was mentally embroidering the adventure to relate to his friends in Portsmouth. Meeting with Lord Richard Marbury himself . . . bringing a gang of filthy ruffians to justice! What a tale for the Portsmouth Literary and Scientific Society! The only thing missing was the ending . . . and that, Dr. Doyle decided, he would not forego. Whatever happened, he would stick with Mr. Dodgson until he learned what had happened to little Miss Marbury, and the kidnappers had been properly punished.

The train wheezed and whistled preparatory to arrival in its terminus. Miss Belfridge and Miss Griggs looked about them for their various bundles and handbags. The stout man, who had snored straight through the ride, miraculously woke up, just in time to open the door to the carriage and disappear into the crowd. It was up to Dr. Doyle to assist Miss Griggs and Miss Belfridge off the train. The two ladies thanked their acquaintances profusely and apparently set off on further adventures.

Dr. Doyle and Mr. Dodgson were left to look for Mr. Upshaw and Inspector MacRae in the mass of humanity pouring toward them.

"I suspect they will wish to see the last of us," Mr. Dodgson said, when he spotted them. "Dr. Doyle, you have been of invaluable service, but you really must go back to your wife."

Dr. Doyle grinned boyishly. "I shall accompany you back to the police station," he said firmly. "Scotland Yard or no Scotland Yard, I want to find out what my colleague thinks of that girl's body. And I do want to hear Upshaw make the positive identification. Then I shall have dinner with Touie. Will you join us, Mr. Dodgson?"

"Oh, I really . . . "

"It would give both of us great pleasure to have you to dinner," Dr. Doyle said firmly. "We can dine at Old Ship, which is considered quite good, I believe."

"I suspect my friends, the Barclays, will wish me to dine with them," Mr. Dodgson said desperately. He looked about him for some source of rescue from his rescuer. With an odd sense of relief he hailed the two men walking toward him: "Inspector MacRae? Mr.

Upshaw? Dr. Doyle and I would like to accompany you to the police station, to make a final and positive identification of the young person, and to give the particulars of Miss Marbury's abduction." "Yet again" was unspoken, but hung in the air nonetheless.

Behind them, the two women in severely cut linen dresses watched with narrowed eyes. Three large men in grimy, collarless shirts and leather waistcoats worn open over heavy corduroy trousers emerged from the crowd.

"You from Lunnon?" the largest of the three bruisers addressed Miss Belfridge.

"Mrs. J. wants them two followed." Miss Belfridge pointed out the dark coat of Mr. Dodgson and his tweed-clad companion.

"And warned off," added her friend.

There was a brief exchange of coins; then the two putative schoolmistresses boarded the next train back to London, while their companions followed Mr. Dodgson and Dr. Doyle out of Brighton Station and into the crowded streets.

CHAPTER 12

If anything, the crowds in Brighton on this Saturday in August were even more intense than those of Friday. Early Closing meant that the local population could join the transients on the pebbled beach, where they could observe the visitors making fools of themselves, sauntering on the beaches or experimenting on Volk's Electric Railway. Children ran screaming to their parents with scraps of seaweed washed in by the tide. Older folk sat on the benches along the Esplanade, or observed the passing show on the Marine Parade, while flashier persons of both sexes displayed their prowess on horseback by taking the perilous hill at a moderate trot.

The indigenous population was not entirely free of the cares of the week. The fishermen had pulled in their boats and were hawking their wares at one end of the beach, while the robust proprietors of bathing machines were ensuring that modesty prevailed among those intrepid enough to try sea bathing.

The sounds of music mingled with the roar of the crowd, as street buskers vied for the attention of the strollers on the Esplanade. At the entrance to the West Pier, the Brighton City Band played the airs from Dr. Sullivan's clever operettas, while further down the strand a lone violinist solicited pennies from the few who could appreciate Mendelssohn. Below the Esplanade, ragged boys called "happy-jacks" capered about, turning somersaults and shouting encouragement to those who threw coins down at them. A few brazen girls even walked on their hands, displaying scarlet drawers and striped stockings to the delight of the onlookers above them.

At the railway station, cabs jostled each other to snare the new arrivals, the cabbies all too aware of the swift passage of time. The influx would come to a boil by teatime, and then fall off, as the visitors sought entertainment further down the hill.

Into this hurly-burly shoved Inspector MacRae, with Upshaw close behind him. It was all Dr. Doyle and Mr. Dodgson could do to keep up with them.

"You'd think they were trying to lose us," Mr. Dodgson puffed.

Dr. Doyle's ineffable spirits refused to be dampened. "They may try, sir, but they will not succeed."

MacRae shoved Upshaw into the nearest cab. "John Street," he ordered.

Dr. Doyle chortled happily. "John Street is their destination, and to John Street you and I shall go. Follow me!"

He grabbed the protesting Mr. Dodgson by the arm and started east on Trafalgar Street, past rows of houses, all built to the same pattern.

"But"—the scholar shook off his protector—"would we not be better suited in a cab?"

Dr. Doyle gestured at the line of horse-drawn vehicles, all crammed into the Queen's Road. "I know a better way." He ducked into a side street and led Mr. Dodgson away from the crowds, unaware of the three burly men behind them.

"Where are we going?" Mr. Dodgson asked.

Dr. Doyle explained: "This street runs across the town and comes out just behind the Pavilion, quite near the Grand Parade. From there we may cross the road to the law courts, and meet Inspector MacRae on the doorstep."

Mr. Dodgson looked about him at the four-story buildings, jammed neatly into square rows, each with its own cornices and areaway. The shops were being closed by their proprietors, shutters being fastened, giving the streets a closed, almost hushed look.

"Just around this corner, we come out into North Street" Dr. Doyle promised. He led the way back and forth, across newly laid brick-paved streets, each of which looked exactly the same as the last, with only the signboards on the shops to give any indication that they had progressed any closer to John Street Police Station than they had before.

Mr. Dodgson looked up, surveyed the scene, and declared, "We are back where we began. I suppose we must go in the opposite direction to where we wish to go, in order to arrive at our proper destination."

"That's nonsense," Dr. Doyle said.

"Of course it is," Mr. Dodgson countered. "And so is my conviction that we are getting nowhere."

Dr. Doyle grimly pressed on. Once the shopkeepers had closed, the customers drifted off, leaving only a few desultory strollers to examine the wares in those windows that were not covered by wooden barriers.

Behind them, the three large men in leather waistcoats moved closer.

"Dr. Doyle, I do believe we are being followed," Mr. Dodgson said sharply. "I strongly suggest that we remove ourselves from this locality as quickly as possible. I do not like the look of this at all!"

They went around yet another corner. The three men moved closer. Mr. Dodgson laid his hand on Dr. Doyle's arm.

"I sincerely hope you know something of self-defense," the older man said. "I am not a timid person, but I do not think those three men behind us wish us well."

"Just one more turn . . . " They took it, and came back into the daylight world of Brighton as they knew it. Before them was the Pavilion, that quasi-Oriental fantasy wrought by the Prince Regent and his various architects. Beyond it, John Street and the police station. When they looked behind them, the three men had vanished.

With a shrug, Dr. Doyle crossed the road and led his mentor around to the back of the law courts, where they mounted the steps

91

to the police station, just as Inspector MacRae and Mr. Upshaw arrived in their cab. The Scotland Yard man glowered at them as they welcomed him cheerfully. Upshaw looked faintly puzzled.

"Still with us, are you?" MacRae grunted.

"As you see," Dr. Doyle said with a boyish smile. Mr. Dodgson nodded in agreement, being too winded for speech.

MacRae marched into the station, followed by Upshaw, Dodgson, and Doyle. Sergeant Barrow was back on duty, this time drinking tea from a china mug. The good sergeant rose to his feet at the sight of the delegation.

"MacRae, of Scotland Yard," barked the Inspector. "I'm expected."

"I'll tell Inspector Wright," the sergeant said.

"And be quick about it," added MacRae. "All I want is to take a look at this body of yours, and get her identified."

"And to find Miss Marbury," added Mr. Dodgson.

Sergeant Barrow recognized his visitors of the previous evening. "Oh, it's you again," he sniffed. "Dr. Doyle of Portsmouth? And Mr. . . . . "

"Dodgson. We reported Miss Marbury as missing. You have had twenty-four hours, and where is she?" The scholar's shrill voice cut through the buzz of conversation in the dressing room beyond the public offices.

Inspector Wright chose to emerge from his private sanctum at this point. He was the perfect policeman for Brighton: tall and fair, mild-mannered with visitors; blunt to the point of crudity with local malefactors. He had shaved his unfashionable beard, but retained a fine mustache, which he stroked carefully to emphasize a point. He preferred the seaside wear of summer whites to the darker shades affected by city dwellers. He looked the four men over.

"Inspector MacRae?" Wright moved forward, extending his hand to the two men in "city" suits. The old duffer he had heard of; the young fellow must be that meddler, Doyle, the bane of the Portsmouth Constabulary. "But why did you bring reinforcements?"

"I didn't bring 'em. They came," MacRae said. "This one," indicating Upshaw, "thinks he can make a positive identification of the young woman."

"What about the other one?" Wright asked.

"Eh?" MacRae shot the other man a sharp look through his spectacles.

"The poor fellow who was just brought in this morning."

"What? Lively place, Brighton is! Two bodies in one weekend! And they say we have it rough at the Yard."

Inspector Wright shrugged. "We have our share, Inspector. Not that there's too much doubt as to this one. Just an old fellow, too much drink taken, no doubt." He led the way back down the grim stairs to the morgue, where the mangled remains of the serving girl had been joined by those of the late Keeble.

The young Dr. Baxter looked up from his work. "Well, if it isn't Arthur!" he called out. "Can't you keep away from this place? If I'd just been married, I'd be with my bride, not haunting this place. It's like the old joke, y'know, about the chap who comes home and sees his best friend and his missus going at it, and says, 'I have to, but you?' " He laughed heartily, while Mr. Dodgson pretended not to hear, and Mr. Upshaw edged around the two policemen, his face growing paler by the minute.

"We've brought someone to take a look at the girl from the railway accident," Dr. Doyle explained. "What's this about another death?"

Dr. Baxter waved a gore-spattered arm at his colleague. "A nice puzzle, Arthur. Come and take a look, and tell me what you make of this."

To the evident distress of Mr. Dodgson, and the disapproval of the police in charge, Dr. Doyle removed his coat, rolled up his sleeves, and cheerfully joined his fellow doctor at the plank table, where the body of an elderly man lay.

Mr. Dodgson peered at the body, then exclaimed, "Oh, my goodness! Oh, dear me! It—oh!" He gasped. Upshaw caught him before he fainted dead away and propped him up against a wall.

"Get him upstairs," Wright ordered Barrow. "Put him in my office and give the old . . . gentleman a stiff brandy."

"No, no, that is not necessary," Mr. Dodgson said. "It is just . . . that man . . . he could be me!"

Dr. Doyle looked at the gin-ravaged features of the old man in front of him and then at the ascetic profile of the scholar. "He's certainly taken pains to dress like you," he remarked.

"He's wearing my gloves!" Mr. Dodgson pointed to the man's hands. "And his hair—he wears it long, like mine."

"Gray cotton. Unusual," Dr. Baxter agreed. "What's more, he's got something in his hand. This is what's got me puzzled, Doyle."

The two doctors worked the fingers loose. A small, round object came into view.

"A button?" Inspector MacRae asked.

"What's a man doing with a button clenched in his fist?" Inspector Wright spoke up.

"Exactly what I want to know," Baxter echoed.

"When was he found?" MacRae wanted to know.

"Just brought in this afternoon," Baxter said. "Charming sight for a man to find on a Saturday afternoon."

"Where did they find him?" Dr. Doyle asked.

"Under the Chain Pier, apparently," Baxter said.

"Then we may assume that he drowned?" Inspector Wright said. "I shall so inform the Coroner."

"Not so fast, Inspector," Dr. Doyle said suddenly. "I'm of the opinion that this man did not merely stumble on the beach, to be washed up by the tide."

Inspector Wright glared at the upstart. "Indeed? And what right have you to intrude in this matter?"

"I am a licensed practitioner," Dr. Doyle stated. "I have been called in by my colleague. Sandy, I want to take a better look at this poor old chap. Meanwhile, Mr. Upshaw, will you please look at this young woman?"

Baxter stepped over to the other plank table. A canvas sheet had been laid over what was left of the girl. As he pulled it back, Inspector MacRae made a noise that might have been a cough or a gasp.

Upshaw gagged and retched, then turned away. "That is—it's her," he said faintly. "Mary Ann. I hadn't realized . . . "

94

"Not a pretty sight," Inspector Wright said. "Cover her up, Dr. Doyle."

"Lord Richard will make the . . . the arrangements," Upshaw said faintly. "I shall go now and telegraph him. She will be taken back to her village, of course." He stumbled up the stairs, clearly shaken by the grim scene.

"So, that takes care of Mary Ann," Dr. Doyle said.

"Was that her name?" Baxter asked. "Well, that fellow will do better in the air. Arthur, what's on your mind, eh? What would Joe Bell have to say about this old geezer?"

Dr. Doyle sniffed, and prodded the late Keeble. "For a start, he was probably a heavy drinker—notice the veins in the nose. And quite possibly worked on the pier or on the beach. Sand in the shoes," he threw back to Inspectors Wright and MacRae. "Not a mechanic, not a man who worked with his hands."

"He was a performer," Mr. Dodgson said suddenly. "I have seen him myself. I believe his name was Keeble."

"And he resembles you, superficially," Doyle pointed out. "Longish gray hair, about your height and age. And your gloves." He straightened up. "Mr. Dodgson, I believe we have just found the man who impersonated you," he said somberly. "Someone is trying to cover his tracks."

"Someone missing a brown waistcoat button," Mr. Dodgson agreed.

"That said, could we get out of here?" Inspector MacRae asked gruffly.

"Not yet," Dr. Doyle said. "Sandy, look here." He pointed to two dents on the old man's stiff collar.

"Old-fashioned sort," Dr. Baxter said. "Straightening his collar."

"But when you put your hands to your throat, your thumbs point down," Dr. Doyle. "These thumbprints point upward. Someone tried to throttle our Mr. Keeble."

"What?" Inspector Wright stepped forward for a better look.

Dr. Baxter sighed. "Arthur, why do you have to make things more difficult? The man drowned. Froth on the lips, fluid in the lungs . . . "

"And bruises on the throat? Perhaps he did not fall into the water, but was pushed from the pier. We may have a murder here, Inspector. I strongly suggest you look into it."

Dr. Doyle glared at Inspector Wright, who returned the look. Dr. Baxter shook his head.

"Easy enough for you to say, Arthur," he muttered. "You've got your little bride to console you. I'm supposed to be on my way to the Lakes!"

"You'll come visit us in Southsea," Dr. Doyle consoled him. "Touie's mother is a capital cook."

Inspector Wright led the way back up the stairs. Once out of the stultifying atmosphere of the morgue, both Wright and MacRae gained their composure and turned to Dr. Doyle and Mr. Dodgson.

Wright dismissed the two men with a casual nod. "Thank you for your assistance, Dr. Doyle. We can continue from here."

"But . . ." Doyle started to protest.

"Best leave it to us, young sir. We are professionals, and we know what we're about," MacRae patted his arm, not unkindly.

Mr. Dodgson was not to be put off so easily. "Inspector," he said, "what will you do now?"

Wright smiled indulgently, as if to say, Keep the visitors happy. "We shall pursue our inquiries," he said.

"But how? Where shall you begin?" Dodgson persisted.

"That's our business, and we know it quite well," Wright said.

"You have done nothing for twenty-four hours," Dodgson retorted shrilly. "In that time, anything might have happened to that child!"

"If it had, I'm sure we would have heard of it by now," Wright said soothingly. "Mr. Dodgson, if you please . . ."

"You know who I am?" Mr. Dodgson asked.

"Indeed, sir, you are well-known in this part of the world. My friends in the Eastbourne Constabulary have told me all about you. How much you like to befriend little girls, how you have them to stay with you."

"Known to the . . . *police?*" Mr. Dodgson looked appalled. Dr. Doyle came to his rescue.

"Mr. Dodgson, I will escort you back to the Rector and Mrs. Barclay. You have had a rather busy day—and we can let the police do their work."

This time, Mr. Dodgson allowed himself to be led away, around the corner and back onto the Grand Parade, that splendid boulevard that cut through the center of Brighton, from the Esplanade up to St. Peter's Church. As soon as they were out of the police station, Mr. Dodgson turned on his companion.

"Dr. Doyle, I have permitted you to accompany me to London, and I have taken tea with you, but perhaps it is time for you and I to part company and for you to return to your young wife. You are being far too persistent; sir, you are close to being pestilent! And furthermore . . . "

No one ever knew what furthermore would be. The three large men who had followed them through the streets emerged from the crowd and moved purposefully upon them. Dr. Doyle spotted them first.

"I think, sir, that you should come with me," he said, grabbing the older man's elbow and steering him into the thick of the crowd.

"Why?"

"Because we are getting very close to someone who has gone to a great deal of trouble to involve you in this case, and those three men behind us are not there to ask you to autograph a copy of one of your books!" Dr. Doyle looked behind him. Two of the men were visible. Where was the third?

Mr. Dodgson tried to wrench himself away from his would-be protector. Instead, he ran into the third of the three large men in leather waistcoats who had followed them from Brighton Station. The bruiser grabbed him away from Dr. Doyle and held him by the lapels of his coat.

"What . . . what do you want?" Mr. Dodgson quavered.

"You should've left well enough alone," growled the bruiser. "Now, you stay out of it." He gave Mr. Dodgson a shake to emphasize the point.

"I am in it, as you see." Mr. Dodgson tried to pull away.

"Leave him be!" Dr. Doyle shoved the tough away from the elderly scholar.

"Come on, then!" The bruiser beckoned, ready for a fight. Dr. Doyle took up the approved stance for boxing. The bruiser didn't wait, but swung at him, assuming that a young man in tweeds would be an easy mark.

The crowd parted at the sounds of a battle. Mr. Dodgson looked wildly about for assistance.

Dr. Doyle whirled about and landed a quick jab in his opponent's belly. The fighter went "Ooof!" at the sudden attack, and bent sharply at the waist. Bruiser number two joined the fight, aiming at Doyle's chin. The agile Scot dodged, and landed a blow on his opponent's chest. Number three swung around and started a roundhouse blow meant to leave Doyle unconscious. Instead, Doyle jabbed again at the bruiser and caught him in the throat.

By this time a blue-coated figure had noticed the commotion. Mr. Dodgson waved frantically to attract attention. The constable marched across the street and took up the regulation stance, arms akimbo, fists on hips, truculent stare meant to cow any hooligan who dared to disrupt the Saturday festivities.

"What's all this?" he demanded.

"These three men—" Mr. Dodgson began.

"What three men?" the constable asked.

"The ones who attacked us," Mr. Dodgson said. "If it were not for Dr. Doyle—"

By this time the three bruisers had decided that their message had been delivered, and had vanished into the crowd.

"I don't see no attackers," the constable said. "What I see is a pair of gentlemen who should know better, and at four in the afternoon, too!"

"We are not inebriated," Mr. Dodgson assured him. "But we were followed from the railway station."

"By three men. Yes, sir—Oh, it's you, Mr. Dodgson." The constable touched his helmet respectfully.

"You know me?" Mr. Dodgson peered at the constable.

"Oh, indeed, sir. I've a brother-in-law out Eastbourne way. And aren't you Doyle? Portsmouth Cricket Club?"

Dr. Doyle smiled suddenly. "Of course! You're Towson, batsman for Brighton. Gave us a good walloping last time."

Bona fides having been established, Constable Towson waved his baton at the pair. "I'll let you go with a warning, Doyle. Just don't start any more ruckuses in the middle of the street!"

The constable continued on his way. Mr. Dodgson regarded Dr. Doyle more favorably as the crowd surged about them.

"Perhaps I have been hasty in my judgment, Dr. Doyle. Your skills are many and various, as they say. The question is, what shall we do next?"

"I suggest we go to my lodgings, since they are close by, and consider our next move," Dr. Doyle said. "I want to make sure Touie is all right. Then we can get on with finding Miss Marbury, since the police are not making much progress."

"In that, sir," Mr. Dodgson said, "we are agreed."

CHAPTER 13

In the house on King Street, Kitty watched as the Madam shoved Alicia back into the attic room, turned the key in the lock, and pocketed it with a derisive snort.

"Wot you gawkin' at? Git on downstairs to the kitchen!" the Madam bellowed. "Think yer made a friend? Think again! Them sort don't care for the likes of you, girl. Besides, she'll be out of 'ere, one way or another, by the end of next week. Now, get that fire built up. The young ladies'll be back from their walk, and they'll want their luncheon."

"Yes'm." Kitty scampered back down the stairs to her own private cubby, a niche under the front steps where she could examine her new treasure. A locket, on a chain. Perhaps it really was gold?

Kitty's thought processes were careful and slow, usually involving food. This time, she had more to consider. This new girl didn't seem to have much sense, giving her the locket like that. In Kitty's limited experience, nobody gave anything away without first getting payment (or promise of payment) in advance. And this girl really expected her to approach a policeman? The police were the Enemy. A girl did not approach them; they approached girls, usually to chase them off the streets. This new girl was clearly not the usual sort that came to Miss Harmon's. The more Kitty thought about it, the more she was convinced that the new 'un just might be telling the truth when she said her pa was a Nob. Look at her clothes! Kitty had taken a good look at that little frock of hers when she took it off, and that was real lace on it, not something made in Manchester on a machine. Only Nobs had that kind of dress.

Kitty now considered what she knew about Nobs. From her post in the kitchen she could see the Nobs coming to Miss Harmon's in their carriages. Nobs did not patronize the other shops in King Street. Miss Harmon's was something special, and Kitty had gained a certain amount of prestige just by working there, even in her menial capacity. Her friends in The Lanes had begged for some of the scraps that Kitty could filch from the well-stocked kitchen. Miss Harmon kept such goodies for Nobs: chocolate biscuits, and oranges and peppermint drops. Nobs liked sweets, Kitty decided.

If this new 'un was a Nob, being held to ransom (as she said), then there just might be something to what she promised. Kitty tucked the locket into the waistband of her skirt, well under her apron, and set about her chores. The locket would keep for now; Miss Harmon's return was imminent, and the care and feeding of the other girls was more important than the possible friendship of one little girl up in the attic.

The girls straggled in, pulling their hats off. Miss Harmon looked worried, but refrained from talking until her young charges had been sent upstairs to their respective rooms to wash for their afternoon meal. Then she sat down in her tiny office and rang for Mrs. Gurney.

The Madam heaved herself out of her comfortable chair in the kitchen and waddled upstairs to confront her putative employer.

"Wot's amiss?" Madam demanded.

"Something dreadful has happened. Those girls insisted on watching some old man being brought in, drowned, off the beach, from under the Chain Pier. Madge, it was Keeble!"

Madge grunted, "Drunk, no doubt, and fell over. Just as well; 'e was a danger to us. Wot news from Lunnon?"

Miss Harmon shook her head. "Too soon to hear from Mrs. J.," she reminded her confederate. "The Guv'nor's letter would be delivered by now. Lord R. will read it, and then . . . "

" 'E'll pull out," the Madam said with satisfaction. "It'll be in the papers tomorrer."

"I don't know," Miss Harmon said slowly. "I warned the Guv'nor this might not work to our advantage. I have had dealings with Lord Richard Marbury in the past."

"So? Either 'e'll quit or 'e won't. Either way, 'is daughter's a 'ore."

"Be quiet, you old cow!" Miss Harmon spat out. "What about our little prize upstairs? How has she been?" For the first time she noticed the scratches on the Madam's face and hands. "What on earth happened to you?" Miss Harmon demanded.

"That little firecat tried to get out when I opened the door to give 'er 'er breakfast," Madge snarled. "I put 'er to scrubbing out the chamberpots. That quieted 'er down!"

Miss Harmon stiffened. "You let her out of the attic? When I told you she was to be strictly kept?"

Madge blustered, "I was right there every minute! She couldn't get away, not without 'er clothes, she couldn't!"

"You may have been there, but you were at the gin again," Miss Harmon hissed. "If she and Kitty . . . Kitty!"

The scrawny little slavey was dolefully scrubbing potatoes. At the urgent summons of the bell, she scrambled to her feet and ran up the stairs to stand before her employer. "Yes, Miss Harmon?"

"Come over here." Miss Harmon's eyes were like chips of green glass in her white face. "Did you talk to that new girl?"

" 'Ow could I, Miss Harmon, wif Madam right there?" Kitty sniveled. "All I done was show 'er 'ow to clean 'em pots. She don't know nuffin', that 'un!"

Miss Harmon caught Kitty by the chin and glared down at her. "If you are lying to me, you will regret it," she said softly. "Now, get on with your work. And do not talk to that new girl again."

Madge watched until Kitty was out of sight. Then she said, "Wot's to be done?"

"Quiet. I have to think," Miss Harmon said. "Mrs. J. doesn't want the little girl harmed."

"Tender-'earted of 'er," Madam sniffed.

"Practical," Miss Harmon countered. "All the child knows now is that she's in some house in Brighton. She doesn't know what goes on here, or who we are. Unless Kitty's been talking—in which case, she knows far too much. I have to go out," she said suddenly. "I have to send some telegrams."

The Madam looked alarmed. " 'Ere now! Yer know what Mrs. J. said! You was to 'ave free rein 'ere, but no more than that!"

"Mrs. J. doesn't know the half of it," Miss Harmon said. She opened a drawer in her desk and took out several banknotes. "I may be gone for a while. Give those lazy girls their luncheon and see that Kitty stays in the kitchen. Don't go near that attic."

"Don't Missy get fed?"

"Bread and cheese, and you make sure she doesn't get out again. I have an idea." Miss Harmon smiled, not pleasantly. "According to my sources, our godly Rector, Mr. Barclay, is planning some kind of meeting."

"About wot?"

"About us," Miss Harmon said, snapping her reticule shut. "Mrs. J. should know about it. And then we can make our own plans. As for the girl . . . there's always Monsieur LeBrun."

"You mean you're not goin' ter. . . ?"

"Let her go?" Miss Harmon sneered. "Not now. I know Lord Richard. Mrs. J. thinks she can bully him, but she's wrong about him. He was bullied once; he won't be bullied again. And since we have the girl, we might as well get some use out of her. Monsieur LeBrun can be here in two days, and little Alicia will be on her way to France by Wednesday."

"Mrs. J. don't like it when 'er orders ain't carried out," Madam said stubbornly. "And seemingly, the kid's to be let go."

"Mrs. J. isn't in charge here, I am." Miss Harmon adjusted her hat and gloves.

"It's Mrs. J. as is payin' fer all this," Madam reminded her. "It's Mrs. J. as found Mr. Carstairs to let the house."

"And it was my idea in the first place to take a house here in Brighton for the season," Miss Harmon retorted. "I've put plenty into Mrs. J.'s pocket this summer. If Lord Richard's Bill goes through, we all stand to lose a great deal more than money."

"All the more reason to keep the kid safe," the Madam said. "And if 'e calls in the Yard?"

"He wouldn't dare," Miss Harmon said. "That minx he married won't let him."

"You never can tell with Nobs," the Madam said with a shrug.

"Then he must call them off," Miss Harmon decided. "Keep that girl quiet, and out of sight. And stay off the gin!"

Miss Harmon swept down the hall and out the door, down the three stairs and out onto King Street. Kitty watched from her post in the area yard as Miss Harmon stepped daintily into the street, only to be accosted by a man in a gray suit.

From her place under the steps, Kitty saw only the legs of the man and Miss Harmon's figured cotton skirt. Their voices, however, were low but clear.

"You!" Miss Harmon sounded upset. "What are you doing here? You're supposed to be in London!"

"I was," the man told her. "Something's gone wrong. That old fool Dodgson turned up at Marbury's door with some quack in tow, and Marbury's sent for Scotland Yard."

Miss Harmon hissed a word that Kitty did not even think she knew. "What about the note?"

"Oh, it was delivered. And rejected out of hand."

"This changes everything. Go away, you can't be seen here! Find somewhere else to be."

"But, Julia?" The man's voice sounded even more upset than Miss Harmon's.

"Now is not the time, or the place. Let me think."

"What are you going to do?"

Miss Harmon's voice was firm. "I am going to change our plans."

"Mrs. J. won't like it."

"That's too bad. Have you notified her?"

"Of course, before I left London. She's already taken some steps to call off our friends. I just had to see you before—"

"All right, you've seen me. Now get away, before someone sees you!"

The man's legs moved off, as Miss Harmon's voice called crisply after him, "Yes, sir, the Grand Parade is at the end of North Street, right 'round the corner."

Then Kitty heard Miss Harmon's heels tap-tapping on the pavement as she walked down the street in the opposite direction.

So the new 'un really *was* the daughter of some Nob! Perhaps she really could get Kitty out of the kitchen and into a nice position as an upstairs maid, where she could wear a nice dress and not have to scrub chamberpots. Kitty had no illusions as to her place in life: she could never work for Miss Harmon in the parlor, not with her snaggly teeth and red hands. Besides, she didn't fancy having to do *it* all night, not with those fat gentlemen she'd seen from her place under the stairs.

She peeped out of the scullery. The Madam was busy at the stove, stirring the soup pot.

Carefully, she eased the locket out of her waistband and examined it. It was real, she decided: a gold chain with a gold pendant with a picture of a shield engraved on it, three birds in a row. Kitty could not read, but the carriages that stopped in front of the house sometimes had pictures on them, and Miss Harmon had said they were crests and the gentlemen who stepped out of them were Nobs. So: a crest meant a Nob, and a Nob was someone very important and very rich.

Kitty thought hard. Miss Harmon had captured some Nob's little girl, and was holding her to make the Nob do something. If Kitty told the coppers where the Nob's little girl was, they might even pay her a reward for it. Then, even if the little girl didn't do what she promised, Kitty would have the reward.

The only sticking point was the copper. There was one, Kitty knew, who came by every afternoon around teatime, to check the doors of the shops on either side of the house. Saturday was Early Closing Day, so he'd come 'round earlier. If she got the locket to him, Kitty reasoned to herself, then the bargain with Alicia would be satisfied, and she could claim her rewards, both from the coppers and the little girl.

That decided, Kitty was jolted out of her reverie by the Madam's harsh voice: "Get in 'ere wi' them taters, yer good-fer-nothin'. Think yer in Lunnon already, do yer?"

"What, mum?"

Madge's hand fell on Kitty's shoulder. "Promised yer Lunnon if yer helped 'er? Well, she's goin' ter France, where she'll do yer no good. Now, git upstairs and make up them beds. The gentlemen'll be by this afternoon, and the rooms ain't been swept out, nor the linens changed. Miss Harmon don't like it when the rooms ain't tidied."

"Yes, mum." Kitty bowed her head over the brooms and dust-pans. She would have to wait until after the girls had settled down in the parlor for their afternoon customers. She only hoped that the young copper would stop by for a chat with the maid next door, and that she could get to the areaway when he did.

For the next two hours, Kitty swept, dusted, and polished, ever conscious of the tiny locket tucked into her waistband. She was at the dustbins in the areaway when the stalwart young policeman, Constable Kenneth Corrigan, came striding down King Street. He knew he looked very spruce in his new blue tunic and helmet, and he practically bounced down the street, carefully nodding to each of the proprietors of the shops to show that the Brighton Constabulary was on the job. He almost passed by the narrow house between the stationers and the greengrocer. As far as he knew, this was Miss Harmon's establishment. He had seen young ladies going in and out. He had been informed (loftily) that it was no business of his who or what lived there, so long as it remained quiet during the daytime. Therefore, Constable Corrigan was not prepared to hear a hissing noise from below his feet in the areaway.

He looked down to find the source of the noise. A scrawny servant girl in a dirty brownish dress covered with a coarse gingham apron hissed at him again.

"She's 'ere!" she whispered, and tossed something at him.

At that moment, Miss Harmon turned the corner. She saw the policeman bending down at the areaway and hastened to see what was happening.

Constable Corrigan straightened up and saluted the lady smartly. "Good afternoon, ma'am."

"Is there something wrong, Constable?" Miss Harmon asked sweetly, peering over his shoulder.

"Not at all, ma'am. I thought I heard a noise, but it was only a cat," Corrigan improvised.

"Really?" Miss Harmon's eyes were hard, but her smile was as sweet as ever.

"Sorry to trouble you, ma'am." Corrigan saluted again, and strode off. Tucked into the palm of the hand that clutched his baton was the gold locket that the slavey had dropped at his feet.

Miss Harmon looked into the areaway again. No one was there. The constable had been polite, there was no sign of anyone else about . . . a large yellow cat emerged from the nearest dustbin, as if to prove the constable's story.

Miss Harmon took a deep breath. It was going to work, she told herself. She had sent telegrams to certain persons and set certain things in motion. Lord Richard Marbury was going to find out what humiliation really was, just as Julia Harmon had learned so many years before, when he had promised her everything and given her . . . nothing.

CHAPTER 14

Saturday afternoon, and the rain had held off for nearly three days. Brighton was at the height of its season, and while the shops selling assorted mundane wares in the inner streets might be shut, the stalls where refreshment could be had were doing a booming business. Winkles, chips, and pickles for those whose appetites were whetted by the salt-laden air and the sight of so much femininity on the beach displaying shapely ankles and sunburned arms; ices, boiled sweets, and biscuits for those who were in the mood for something less substantial. Teashops were spaced invitingly along the Esplanade, where a lady could sit without fear of being accosted by some masher, while taverns for the stronger sex were tucked into the odd corners between the grand hotels.

On the pebbled beach, children dashed about, while their distracted mamas and nannies called after them in pleading tones. Young men, whose usual habitat was a dark office or a crowded shop, removed their jackets to display shirts of dazzling whiteness or vivid stripes, while their companions in the working world, those young women who were timidly stepping into otherwise male preserves, watched on admiringly. Brawnier specimens of manhood, farmers and village craftsmen on their holidays, laughed at the pretensions of the rising middle classes, and joked good-naturedly with their friends as they ate their home-baked bread and cheese sandwiches, and filled their eyes with images of the passing scene, to be related to those less fortunate over the next few months at the local pub.

Dr. Doyle led Mr. Dodgson through this throng, away from John Street and back down to the Esplanade, stopping only to buy the *Pall Mall Gazette* at one of the news vendors' stands, much to Mr. Dodgson's disgust. He carried the offensive publication down to the Esplanade, where he found a space on one of the benches and sat down to examine his purchase. Mr. Dodgson sat down with him, but refused to watch him read.

"How can you read that dreadful thing?" he fussed. "Now is no time to indulge in salacious gossip and innuendo. We must find that child!"

"It never hurts to know what the enemy is up to," Dr. Doyle pronounced. "Look at this! There must have been some of the Fourth Estate present this morning; there's a vivid description of Mrs. Jeffries's triumphal march, including her challenge to Lord Richard Marbury."

Mr. Dodgson snatched the newspaper from his companion's hand and peered at it intently.

"To the very letter," he agreed, when he had carefully read the paragraphs. "But not a word about Miss Marbury's abduction. And, may I add, there is no announcement that Lord Richard Marbury is resigning his seat in Parliament."

"Then Lord Richard has not obeyed the kidnappers," Dr. Doyle stated.

"Apparently not," Mr. Dodgson agreed. He trotted back to the news vendor. "Have you the London newspapers?" he demanded.

"Got all of 'em," the man replied genially, indicating a well-stocked stand behind him. "Name your city and I 'ave your paper. London, Manchester, York, Edinburgh, Liverpool, Dublin."

"The London newspapers, if you please," Mr. Dodgson ordered, fumbling for his money. Once supplied, he carried them back to Dr. Doyle and said, "We must examine these for any indication of Lord Richard's intentions."

"But not here," Dr. Doyle told him, wrestling with the *Pall Mall Gazette*, which had taken on a life of its own, and was about to fly away into the clear blue sky. "We must get back to Duke Street, Mr. Dodgson, where Touie will be waiting for us at Mrs. Keene's. Then we can decide what to do next."

Without waiting for the older man to acquiesce to this plan, Dr. Doyle gathered up the newspapers and marched off.

"It would appear," Mr. Dodgson commented, as they loped through the streets, now encumbered with newspapers. "That the abductors are using the Press as their medium of communication, rather than the post."

"True," Dr. Doyle agreed. "And most suggestive. There must be some link between these articles in the *Pall Mall Gazette* and Lord Richard Marbury."

They had, by now, reached the Queen's Road. There they turned and went up the hill, reserving all breath for the effort, until they saw Touie sunning herself on the front steps, eagerly waiting for her returning hero.

"Hello! Here's Touie!" Dr. Doyle bounded ahead of Mr. Dodgson. "Touie, we've been to London and back! I must tell you about—oh, Mr. Dodgson, I beg your pardon, but I really must speak to my wife," Dr. Doyle said, with a boyish grin.

"Quite so, quite so," muttered Mr. Dodgson. "I shall avail myself of your good landlady's parlor once again, and inspect these newspapers." He coughed shyly, and glanced at the loving couple. "I hope you will forgive my earlier outburst, Dr. Doyle. I grow testy sometimes. I was grateful for your aid when those ruffians attacked me. Fisticuffs were never my sport."

Dr. Doyle waved the apology away. "I was glad to be there, sir. Never let it be said that a Doyle did not know his duty, and my duty in this case is to see that Miss Marbury is found and her abductors brought to justice."

While the Doyles had their fond reunion, Mr. Dodgson settled down on the very sofa on which he had been imprisoned the day before. Dr. Doyle recited to his wife the gist of what had occurred in London.

Touie was suitably impressed. "Oh, Arthur!" she cooed. "Think of having coffee and biscuits with Lord Richard Marbury and his wife!"

"And assisting Baxter with his investigations," Dr. Doyle added. "A good start, Touie. Baxter will call me in for more consultations after this, and I can bring my experience forward the next time there's an opening in Portsmouth."

Mr. Dodgson had scanned the London newspapers, which he now laid aside in a tidy pile, and he had information to impart. "This is quite interesting," he commented. "I have carefully read the *Times*, the *Standard*, and the *Globe*, and in none of these do I find any but the briefest of notices of Mrs. Jeffries's excursion into Mayfair this morning. However, the *Pall Mall Gazette* does have a detailed account, embellished with editorial comments. Remarkable. They must have had a man at the scene, in that disgraceful crowd."

Dr. Doyle frowned. "In that case, the announcement of Lord Richard's abandonment of his Bill should have been placed in the *Pall Mall Gazette.*"

"It will be looked for in the *Pall Mall Gazette*," Mr. Dodgson corrected him. "But it will not be found. In spite of Mr. Upshaw's efforts, Lord Richard is adamant. He will pursue this Bill until it is resolved, one way or another."

Touie frowned at her husband. "You really should let the police do their work," she chided the two men. "I'm sure they know what they are about."

"They would not listen to us," Mr. Dodgson said. "They have it in their heads that both the death of that poor old man and the death of that young woman were unconnected to the disappearance of Miss Marbury."

Dr. Doyle's frown deepened. "The problem is that they have to work slowly," he said. "After all, they need to be sure of their facts be-

fore they can get a warrant to search a house, even one of, um, ill repute."

"Are there such in Brighton?" Mr. Dodgson asked innocently.

Dr. Doyle glanced at his wife. "Alas, Mr. Dodgson, vice rears its
ugly head even in a seaside Eden like Brighton."

"I saw the most extraordinary procession this morning," Touie
broke in. "A string of girls, quite young, dressed in the height of
fashion, led by a woman with the most vivid red hair!"

"Girls?" Mr. Dodgson lifted his head from his newspaper. "Girls,
you say?"

"Yes. But there was something strange about them. I could not
quite put my finger on it. They were well-mannered, well-dressed
girls."

"Just walking?" Dr. Doyle asked sharply.

"Strolling on the Esplanade," Touie said. "I had been shopping,
Arthur. I got some darling seashells to place in the parlor at our
villa, and a set of teacups for Mother, and I could not help but
watch this . . . well, procession, you might say. They marched down
Queen's Road, and walked on the Esplanade, from the Chain Pier to
the West Pier and back."

"Could it have been some sort of school for young ladies?" Dr.
Doyle asked.

Mr. Dodgson shook his head. "Not in August," he declared, on
firm ground this time. He might not know about illegal establishments, but he knew about schools. "The term ends in June, and no
school will start again until mid-September."

"In that case," Dr. Doyle said slowly, "we may assume that there
is an establishment in Brighton that specializes in very young, um,
persons, and that these young persons were, um, advertising themselves."

Mr. Dodgson paled. "I cannot believe that the borough would tol-
erate such a . . . a . . . "

Dr. Doyle was more cynical. "If the *Pall Mall Gazette* is correct,
many of Mrs. Jeffries's favored clients belong to the very stratum of
society who spend their holidays in Brighton. It is just possible that
she has set up a . . . a branch office, as it were, here for the season.

And if that is so," he continued, warming to his subject, "it is also possible that Miss Marbury is being kept there."

"Or if she is not," Touie put in, "then the people there will surely know where she is."

Mr. Dodgson digested this information and nodded. "There is only one difficulty," he said. "You postulate the existence of this, um, establishment. One cannot go about asking for such a . . . a place. One does not find its direction from a guidebook. In that case, how does one discover it? In fact, that is the aspect of this business that puzzles me the most. How does one go about discovering such, um, establishments? Assuming, of course, that one is of such a depraved character as to do so when on holiday?"

"According to the *Pall Mall Gazette*," Dr. Doyle said, "Mrs. Jeffries has agents stationed at the hotels and clubs in London, who act as, er, touts, for her activities. In today's installment," he picked up the offending journal and thumbed through it, "this reporter claims that her people have penetrated the highest ranks of society, and may even be found in the hallowed halls of Westminster."

Touie gasped. "I cannot believe—in Parliament? Surely not!" She snatched the paper from her husband's hands, to read for herself.

Mr. Dodgson gently removed the newspaper from her grip. "This is not proper reading for a lady," he chided her. "Indeed, Dr. Doyle, this whole conversation is most improper."

Dr. Doyle laughed. "Touie is a doctor's wife, Mr. Dodgson. She's far more conversant with the darker side of life than you might think. She's even gone into some of the worst places, good soul that she is, for charity's sake." He smiled fondly at his bride, who flushed prettily. Then his voice lowered. "But you are quite right, my dear. The procession you saw must have been the girls spoken of in these articles."

"Assuming there is such a place, of which there is yet no concrete proof," Mr. Dodgson said severely.

"I think we may take it as a given that there is," argued the younger man. "And as for the existence of such poor creatures, in Edinburgh, I had my share of such encounters. You can't avoid it. And the charity wards gave me a sympathy for these women—mere children, some of them—who must earn their scrap of bread in this manner. I do not blame them, sir, for they are often the sole support of their families."

"The girls I saw looked well-fed, clean, quite healthy," Touie commented. "Do you know, Arthur, I think they may be considered quite fortunate by their neighbors to work under those conditions, considering what other women must go through," she added.

Dr. Doyle glanced at Mr. Dodgson. "In that case," he said, "I may have a plan. We shall have to ask some of the touts on the streets where to go for, um, pleasure."

"Dr. Doyle! Your wife is present!" Mr. Dodgson was incensed.

Touie smiled sweetly at her husband. "Arthur is quite right," she said. "It is the most direct approach to the matter. No doubt the police are questioning those same men."

"Then we shall have to question the little girls," Dr. Doyle said firmly. "Mr. Dodgson, you get on well with girls. Can you find out which house it is that is a haven for them? I realize it is a great deal to ask."

Mr. Dodgson sat up very straight. "Those street children are not young," he said. "They have seen far too much vice in their short lives to be young. But if it will assist us in finding Miss Marbury . . . "

"I can think of no other way," Dr. Doyle said.

"Then I will do it. Now, Mrs. Doyle, Dr. Doyle, you must accompany me to my friend, Mr. Barclay. He is the Rector of St. Peter's Church, and a most conscientious churchman. I believe that he even has contact with some of the more forceful members of the Evangelical community who work with the poor, and through them, we will be able to begin our search. I only hope that we are not too late, and that Miss Marbury will be returned to her family before the Sunday editions come out. Now, if you permit me, I believe that Mrs. Doyle will prefer traveling by cab. Let us go to the Queen's Road and take one, and pray that Miss Marbury has not been removed from her hiding place before we find her."

CHAPTER 15

T he cab that brought the Doyles and Mr. Dodgson to the door of the Rectory of St. Peter's was instantly claimed by a party threading its way through the front gate. Saturday was Mrs. Barclay's At Home, when any ecclesiastical visitors to Brighton might call and partake of tea, biscuits, and parochial gossip. As the cab trotted down the hill on the Grand Parade, another carriage took its place, disgorging three more ladies and a gentleman in the black suit and collar of the Church of England.

The butler, whose demeanor rivaled that of his master in ecclesiastical dignity, showed them all into the parlor, and announced, "Mr. Dodgson, Dr. Doyle, Mrs. Doyle, The Reverend Mr. Falwell, Mrs. Falwell, and the two Miss Falwells."

Mr. Barclay and his wife welcomed the arrival of Mr. Dodgson and his guests with modified joy. The Rector had been in the throes of creation in his study, a book-lined cubbyhole under the eaves of the old house, when he had been summoned downstairs by his wife to attend to his duties as host. Mrs. Barclay was already serving tea to Lady Grenfell, Mrs. Wynne, and Miss Dulcie Wynne, all of whom stared at the modestly dressed Mrs. Doyle with undisguised curiosity. The addition of the Falwell family filled the parlor with females, and their attendant draperies made the Reverend Mr. Falwell fade into insignificance (a state of affairs quite common in the Falwell household).

"Charles!" Mrs. Barclay exclaimed, as the trio was led into the parlor by the supercilious butler. "We were worried about you. Why did you not remain in London?"

"Because my business is here," Mr. Dodgson said. "You recall Dr. Doyle? Dicky Doyle's nephew, you know," he added, to give his new friend some credence in society.

"Yes, of course. How do you do, Dr. Doyle?" Mrs. Barclay smiled briefly.

"And Mrs. Doyle," Mr. Dodgson completed the introductions. "Where is Henry? I must consult with him about . . . "

"Charles!" This time it was the Rector's turn to interrupt. He had obviously been writing; his fingers were stained with ink, and his hair was all on end.

"Mr. Barclay!" Mrs. Barclay warned him. "You are not properly dressed!"

The rotund churchman realized that he was in his shirtsleeves and shrugged. "No time for all that now, my dear," he said, seizing Mr. Dodgson by the arm and leading him to the parlor door. "Charles, you must help me. I am rewriting my sermon for tomorrow, on the text of 'Suffer the little children.' That should put them in the mood for the rally and protestation meeting!"

"Eh?" Mr. Dodgson eased out of his friend's grasp. "I thought . . . that is, you said . . . "

"I know, I know, we were considering such a meeting, but nothing was firm. Well, we have received permission from the borough to hold it on Monday, so as not to desecrate the Sabbath. Moreover, we may hold it on the grounds of the Royal Pavilion!" Mr. Barclay fairly radiated civic pride and righteous indignation in equal portions.

"How . . . how apt," Dr. Doyle choked out, suddenly realizing the impact of the ornate palace, and the image of its previous tenants.

"And Lord Richard Marbury has agreed to speak," the Rector added.

"Indeed! And when did this happen?" Mr. Dodgson asked.

"I received a message from him this afternoon."

"Ah, Mr. Upshaw's been busy," Dr. Doyle observed.

"Who?" Mr. Barclay fairly shoved the other two men toward the stairs to his study, leaving Mr. Falwell to drink tea in the parlor. "Charles, as a literary man you have a facility with words that I lack. I can preach a good, sound doctrine, but you, my old friend, can be of great assistance to me."

"I am a mathematician," Mr. Dodgson protested. He turned to Dr. Doyle. "Actually, my young friend here is the one with a taste for literature. Besides, he is the, er, secretary of the Liberal Unionist Club of Portsmouth. Do I have that correct?"

"Indeed, Mr. Dodgson, I didn't know you'd remembered." Dr. Doyle looked troubled. "The thing of it is—I am not a member of your church."

"Oh, of course," Mr. Dodgson said, after a moment's thought. "Doyle is an Irish name. I should have deduced that you might be a Romanist. Well, no matter. Your thoughts on the subject are as worthy as anyone's."

"I am not precisely a member of the Roman Church," Dr. Doyle began, but Mr. Dodgson was ahead of him on the stairs. He flashed a smile to Touie, and followed the other men up to the Rector's private study, an attic cubicle filled with books, paper, a desk, chair, and ottoman. By the time Dr. Doyle arrived at this aerie, the Rector had lifted several piles of books off the chair and ottoman, and settled his visitors down for a chat.

Mr. Dodgson would not be settled. "Henry," he said earnestly, "we have come to consult you on a matter of the gravest urgency. In fact, it is somewhat connected to this business of yours. We feel that Miss Alicia Marbury is being held somewhere in Brighton, perhaps in a—pardon my saying so—a . . . "

Dr. Doyle was more blunt. "To be frank, sir, a brothel."

Mr. Barclay looked blank. "I can assure you, Charles, I have no idea where such places may be, in Brighton or anywhere else," he protested. "Such persons are not part of my congregation. However," he admitted, "it is all too possible that some of my congregation may, perhaps, have some acquaintance with them. It is for this reason that I am lending my support to the rally and protestation meeting."

"Really, Henry, it is beneath the dignity of the Church to meddle in these matters," Mr. Dodgson sputtered.

The Rector drew himself up to his full five feet six inches. "This is a matter of morality!" he pronounced. "I admit that Mr. Branwell, of the Methodist Chapel, and I have had our disagreements, on theological grounds. I do not approve of his doctrine, nor he of mine. In addition, I find General Booth's Salvation Army somewhat vulgar in its militaristic organization, although I applaud his efforts on behalf of the unfortunate victims of society. Nor am I usually on speaking terms with the representatives of the Church of Rome. However, on this matter we are all as one, and I have agreed to lend my support to theirs in an appeal to our members to cast aside Party lines and vote their consciences—assuming they have any!—on the Bill now before the House."

Dr. Doyle had picked up one of the pages of Mr. Barclay's sermon and was reading it avidly. "Warm, sir. Very warm," he commented.

"I hope so," was the reply. "If these articles in the *Pall Mall Gazette* are even half true, there are dreadful things being done to young girls, and it is the business of the Church to stop them. Evil is evil, Charles, and as a churchman I am sworn to fight evil, even when it wears the robes of state!"

"Hear, hear!" Dr. Doyle applauded.

"Rather a good line, that?" Mr. Barclay scribbled it down, before it got away from him.

"Henry, do concentrate on my problem for a few minutes," pleaded Mr. Dodgson. "I don't mean to imply that you are personally acquainted with these creatures, or that you frequent their haunts, but surely you must have heard some gossip, some clue as to where they may be encountered?"

Mr. Barclay thought deeply. "The neighborhood of Church Street, just off the Queen's Road, behind the Music Hall, is not a good one," he said at last. "My wife considers it her duty to visit the poor, and even she avoids that particular street. If one were to look for a . . . a dubious establishment, one might begin there."

118

He looked at his friend. Mr. Dodgson seemed to be in a trance, listening to some inner muse.

"Mr. Dodgson?" Dr. Doyle's voice broke through the fog of thought.

"I was trying to make sense of this ridiculous farrago," Mr. Dodgson said. "If Mr. Upshaw did not inform my friend Barclay of Lord Richard's movements, then who did?"

"I received a telegram," the Rector explained.

"Ah. Then no one named Upshaw has called here? No one by that name has left a message, on behalf of Lord Richard?" Mr. Dodgson pursued the thought.

"I can call Peters, my butler, and ascertain who, if anyone, has called," Mr. Barclay said, puzzled.

"Please do," Mr. Dodgson urged.

"You suspect this Upshaw, then?" Dr. Doyle asked.

"I do not like him, but not liking a man is no reason to accuse him of either abduction or murder. However, he is not telling the truth, or at least, the entire truth, about his movements, and clearly, Lord Richard has made a decision to act without consulting our ubiquitous Mr. Upshaw."

The butler's ponderous footsteps sounded on the stairs. "Peters, has anyone calling himself Upshaw come to the house today?" the Rector demanded.

"No, sir. Mrs. Barclay's callers have been coming all afternoon. Then, there was the Saturday post; the person from the telegraph office with a message, and these gentlemen here."

"No one else?" Mr. Dodgson asked.

"Except for the persons delivering bread and fish for the cook, no one." The butler withdrew, mightily confused.

No less confused were Mr. Dodgson and Dr. Doyle. "Curiouser and curiouser," murmured Mr. Dodgson. "Are you sure this telegram came from Lord Richard Marbury?"

"I will look a pretty fool if it did not," replied his friend. "I have already alerted our constabulary about the protestation meeting, and told them to have extra constables on duty to keep order. I have booked the rooms at the Old Ship for Lord Richard and Lady Patricia Marbury, for Monday night. And if he does not come, a large number of people will feel they have been cheated, and will undoubtedly vent their anger on me!"

"Do you happen to have the telegram to hand?" Dr. Doyle asked. Mr. Barclay sorted through the heap of papers on his desk and emerged with a familiar slip of yellow paper. Dr. Doyle examined it carefully.

"Mr. Barclay," he said at last, "this telegram was not sent from London. Observe, the origin of the telegram is encoded here." He indicated a line of type, with cryptic letters and numerals. "This telegram was sent from Brighton!"

"From Brighton? But why—why would anyone—"

"To do just as you said, make you look like a fool," Mr. Dodgson said. "Henry, this is dreadful!"

"Just to be on the safe side," Dr. Doyle suggested, "perhaps you had better wire for confirmation of Lord Richard's plans. The people behind this campaign are clever and devious."

"Or frightened and clumsy," Mr. Dodgson protested. "Otherwise, why remove the servant girl and the wretched old man who impersonated me?"

"Remove?" Mr. Barclay's voice rose to a squeak.

"We identified them at the police station this afternoon," Mr. Dodgson said, with a visible shudder.

"It is possible," said Dr. Doyle slowly, "that we are dealing with two people. One, who is clever, formulates the plans; the other, clumsy and frightened, must be the instrument."

"Both are guilty, in the eyes of the law," Mr. Dodgson declared.

"And of the Lord," said the Rector piously.

"And both of them are holding Miss Marbury," Dr. Doyle reminded them. "Well, Mr. Dodgson, now that we know where to look, we can make further plans. Mr. Barclay, shall we join the ladies for tea?"

Downstairs, Mrs. Doyle sat, scrutinized from head to foot by the sharp eyes of Mrs. Barclay and her guests. She was conscious of the condescension of Mrs. Barclay in having a mere physician's wife to tea at all, let alone one who was totally unknown to her, and not even of her parish. She was dressed in her tartan traveling dress, which was modest and serviceable, but not nearly as fashionable as the tea gowns worn by the other ladies. She sat very straight on the chair allotted to her, determined to further her husband's career socially as well as professionally.

"So," Mrs. Barclay began, while the maid handed round a plate of biscuits. "Are you a very old friend of Mr. Dodgson?"

"Actually, my husband met him just yesterday," Touie said, accepting the biscuit. "He is such a dear, sweet old gentleman."

"Mr. Dodgson is a scholar of great repute," Mrs. Barclay said icily. "He and the Rector were up together at Christ Church."

"And is this your first visit to Brighton?" asked Mrs. Wynne, a delicate-looking matron, draped in a mauve dress.

"I have lived near Portsmouth nearly all my life," Touie confessed. "Arthur—that is, my husband, Dr. Doyle—promised me a few days in Brighton before we settle down like Darby and Joan."

"Indeed?" Lady Grenfell, a faded-looking blonde in pale yellow with darker yellow flowers on her bodice, raised her eyebrows.

"We were only married last week," Touie added, with a faint blush of pride.

"A bride!" Mrs. Barclay smiled suddenly. "What an odd honeymoon for you, to be sure. Your husband seems to spend a good deal of time with Mr. Dodgson."

"I am sure Arthur has a very good reason for his actions," Touie said with spirit. "And Mr. Dodgson himself was very glad to have him near, when three dreadful ruffians set upon him! Arthur said they must have been sent by some villains he and Mr. Dodgson are pursuing."

"Mr. Dodgson set upon!" Miss Dulcie, all ingenue pink frills and rosebuds, exclaimed.

"I do not think he would make up such a story," Touie insisted.

"He does make up stories," said one of the very young Miss Falwells. "He told me such a pretty story once, about two fairies in his garden. Of course, that was when I was quite a little girl," she added.

"Mr. Dodgson may tell stories about fairies, and odd things in Wonderland, but not about brigands, or being set upon," Touie said. "My Arthur does that. He has been published in *Cornhill!*"

Mrs. Barclay's attitude grew cold again. A bride could be smiled upon; the wife of a provincial practitioner who wrote stories for the popular Press could not.

The social impasse was broken when the husband himself arrived to rescue his bride from her persecutors, followed by the two clerical gentlemen. Mr. Barclay had resumed his black coat and clerical collar, and now looked every inch the proper representative of the Church of England. Dr. Doyle looked over the tea tray and approached his wife with a grin.

"Had a good tea, Touie?" he asked breezily.

"Mrs. Barclay has been most kind," Touie said diplomatically.

Mrs. Barclay appraised Dr. Doyle and decided that she approved of him. His boyish smile and air of brisk authority made up for his deplorable taste in dress: tweeds were not quite the thing for Brighton. "Dr. Doyle, your wife has been most forthcoming about your adventures. You have been most active today. To London and back, and then saving our friend Mr. Dodgson from ruffians!"

Dr. Doyle tried to look modest. Behind him, Mr. Dodgson slipped into the room, while Mr. Barclay accepted a cup of tea from his wife and a biscuit from the tray.

"You have been most helpful, Dr. Doyle, but you must not let my affairs keep you from your honeymoon," Mr. Dodgson said. "I shall remain here to assist with Mr. Barclay's sermon, and after dinner, I shall attempt to put our plan into action."

"But—" Dr. Doyle looked crestfallen. "I had hoped to be able to see the thing through, to the bitter end!"

"I am perfectly capable of conducting my own affairs," Mr. Dodgson muttered testily.

Mrs. Barclay assessed the situation. Apparently, there was only one way to be rid of Dr. Doyle, at least for a short time. She made the decision and announced, "Anyone who saves our old friend, Mr. Dodgson, from ruffians, must dine with us. You will, of course, wish to return to your lodgings and dress."

"That is quite kind of you, ma'am, but . . . "

"No buts about it. You will be expected at seven o'clock. And please, leave Mr. Dodgson to take some rest here with us. You have been running him all over the countryside!"

Dr. Doyle looked baffled, but the butler was behind him, and he could not withstand such a monumental force. Touie and her husband were outside the Rectory door before either of them could protest.

Mr. Dodgson sat down in the chair recently vacated by Touie.

"What a very odd person that Doyle is, to be sure," Mrs. Falwell commented. "Mrs. Barclay, you are kindness itself, having him and his wife to tea. And dinner as well? Are you sure?" Her eyebrows arched delicately, indicating the unspoken question of social status.

"Any friend of Mr. Dodgson must be acceptable to us," Mrs. Barclay pronounced.

The Reverend Mr. Falwell edged forward. "Have you heard anything further, Henry? About the protestation meeting?"

Mr. Barclay frowned. "I must confirm the information, but I was told that Lord Richard Marbury would speak. And Mr. Branwell has asked General Booth . . . "

The Falwell ladies made noises of distaste. Lady Grenfell frowned her disapproval.

"General Booth is undoubtedly a Godly man," Mr. Falwell ventured, in the face of so much female disapprobation.

"And he is a most forceful speaker," Mr. Barclay added. "His presence will draw attention to our Cause."

"Of course," Mrs. Barclay soothed him.

Lady Grenfell set down her cup. Mrs. Wynne beckoned her daughter to her side. Good manners demanded that they end their visit, no matter how fascinating the subject of conversation might be.

"Perhaps we should take advantage of the good weather," Mrs. Falwell pronounced.

"Of course, my dear," her husband said. He turned to his host. "We shall return, and dine with you. There is much to be done before the protestation meeting."

"Thank you, sir, for your support."

Peters showed them out, to Mr. Dodgson's evident relief.

"Now, Charles," Mrs. Barclay said, "you must sit down and have some tea. That energetic young doctor has nearly worn you down."

"What is wearing me down, Margaret, is worry. Where is Miss Alicia, and who has her?"

"Really, Charles, you take too much upon yourself. I am sure the police are quite capable of finding her."

"But will they do it?" Mr. Dodgson fretted. "Will they? And will they find her before . . . ?" He left the young lady's fate hanging before the horrified imaginations of his friends.

"It is the child's parents who have my prayers," Mrs. Barclay said piously. "They must be beside themselves with worry."

"Lord Richard has done what he feels is right," Mr. Dodgson said. "I only hope that he has not made matters worse!"

CHAPTER 16

Four o'clock—the sacred hour of teatime! All over Brighton the urns were bubbling as holidaymakers repaired to their lodgings to ingest scones, crumpets, biscuits, and, of course, tea. Sunburned children were slicked and scrubbed, changed into white frocks or pseudo-naval outfits, and brought into the back parlors for their meal, while on the verandas of the Old Ship and the Grand Hotel, elegant ladies and gentlemen consumed exotic pastries while they inhaled the fragrance of oolong.

In London, the furious Parliamentary conferences were disbanded, while those members who had been summoned so hastily by Lord Richard Marbury went back to their own abodes for their ritual, cursing at having had to leave the hills of Scotland or the bracing breezes of the Isle of Wight to be forced back into the town houses that had been draped in linen covers for the summer.

Lord Richard himself arrived in Grosvenor Square to find his wife in the hall, obviously just having come in from paying calls, puzzling over a sheaf of telegrams on the tray handed to her by the supercilious Farnham.

Lord Richard allowed his butler to relieve him of his hat and stick as he strode back toward his *sanctum sanctorum* at the end of the hallway.

"Richard!" Lady Pat called after him. "Shall I tell Jennings to lay out your traveling kit?"

"Whatever for? I'm needed here in London," Lord Richard said testily. "Where is Upshaw?"

"This telegram is from the Reverend Mr. Barclay, in Brighton," Lady Pat followed him to his study, waving the paper at him. "He seems to think you have agreed to come down and speak at some sort of protestation rally, in support of your Bill."

"Did I?" Lord Richard asked absently.

"I'm sure I don't know. Your Mr. Upshaw is in charge of your political schedule." A thought struck her. "Do you suppose this has something to do with that extraordinary business of Alicia and Mr. Dodgson?"

"When is this meeting to be held?" Lord Richard asked.

"Monday evening," Lady Pat said, consulting the telegram once again. "Mr. Barclay has bespoken rooms for us for Monday night at the Old Ship Hotel."

"We shall go," Lord Richard decided. "If Alicia has not been found by then, I shall have to take steps myself."

He marched militantly into his study and approached the typewriter. With the same air of determination that his grandfather had assumed at Waterloo, he sat down to compose his missive. "Farnham!"

The butler appeared at the door to the study. "Yes, my lord?"

Lord Richard was pecking enthusiastically away at his typewriter. "Have this telegram sent immediately to Mr. Barclay in Brighton. Lady Pat and I will go to Brighton on Sunday afternoon, before the protestation meeting, to complete the program. Our rooms must be booked for Sunday as well as Monday evening. Where's Upshaw? He usually makes these arrangements."

"Mr. Upshaw is still in Brighton," Farnham said. "If you wish, I shall see to the tickets. I will also bespeak the rooms for you and Lady Richard."

Lady Pat appeared at the door to the study and gazed at her husband. "Richard, all this is very sudden, Of course you must attend this . . . this protestation rally, and I very much want to be in Brighton when Alicia is found, but must I attend the meeting as well?"

"I . . . certainly. I would very much like you to support me in this. Mrs. Gladstone attends her husband's meetings."

"Mrs. Gladstone is made of sterner stuff than I," Lady Pat said. "Oh, Richard, promise me one thing. Promise me that you will not . . . use . . . Alicia."

Lord Richard's outrage reverberated through the house. "Pat! What do you think of me!"

"I think you are a political animal," she said. "If it would help your Cause, you would sacrifice our daughter's reputation. Well, Richard, I won't have it. Those jackals of the Press are waiting out there, to make her life a misery. You have no idea how dreadful they can be. I remember, after the Inquiry, when Papa's conduct was in question . . . and later, when Ned had his difficulties. . . . " Her eyes filled with tears. "Richard, you will not let Alicia's name get into the Press, will you?"

Lord Richard's long face grew longer. "I will do my best. Perhaps you should not come with me after all."

"But I must," Lady Pat told him. "If . . . when they find Alicia, she will need Nanny Marsh, and Nanny will not go to Brighton alone. Besides, dear, it will sit well with your constituents." She dropped a kiss on her husband's brow. "And don't forget, we are dining with the Northrops at eight."

"Should we . . . I mean . . . ?"

"You wonder that I should continue my social obligations when my child is in danger? Oh, Richard, I only wish I could go to her immediately, but I cannot, and Lord Northrop is in town for your Bill. We dare not cry off, not at the last minute. Those reporters will think something is wrong, and we don't want that. No, dear, we will dine at the Northrops and then go down to Brighton tomorrow night."

With that, Lady Pat removed herself to her boudoir, and Lord Richard sent more telegrams and wondered where Upshaw was.

127

* * *

Teatime meant the change of shift at the John Street Police Station. Constables who had spent the day strolling up and down the Esplanade or meandering through the shops on King Street or standing at the entrance to the pier could relieve themselves of their heavy woolen tunics and cumbersome helmets and become private citizens once again, free to take themselves back to their own hearths, where they could have their suppers of fried fish or steak and kidney pie. The day's crop of petty thieves and pickpockets would be stored in the cells on the second story of the station, awaiting the ministrations of the magistrate on Monday morning.

In the dressing room, the evening shift was coming on as the day shift was leaving. It was Sergeant Barrow of the evening shift who found young Constable Corrigan staring at something in his hand.

"Eh, what's that you've got there, lad?"

"I found it in King Street," Corrigan said. He had not been on the force very long, but he had already learned that Sergeant Barrow was not a man to cross. When he asked a question, it was best to answer it, briefly.

"King Street?" Barrow's face creased in a frown. "A fine piece of work like that? No jewelers' shops in King Street, not on your beat, Corrigan."

"It was in front of that green house."

Barrow's face began to darken, like the beginnings of a thunderstorm. "You've no need to question anyone in that house," he rumbled.

"I didn't," Corrigan protested. "It was some servant girl, a maid, I think. She threw it at me. Sergeant, could this have anything to do with that old gentleman what was looking for a girl? I saw him leaving just as I was going off last night, and today he's back again, with that chap with the red mustache . . ." Corrigan's voice trailed off.

"Young coppers should mind their own business," Barrow roared out. "Don't you go a-borrowing trouble, Corrigan! You leave this matter to me."

"But I think . . ."

"You're not paid to think!" Barrow's scorn could wither a tree in full bloom.

Corrigan held on to his prize. "With respect, sir, I want to tell Inspector Wright about this."

"What's amiss?" It was the day sergeant, Hartley, come up behind them.

Corrigan stood up straight. "I wish to report, as per orders, an occurrence in King Street," he recited. He showed the locket and chain once again.

Hartley and Barrow exchanged stares. Then Hartley said softly, "Barrow, if Corrigan has something, and that man from the Yard finds out you've kept it from him, I wouldn't give tuppence for your hide. All your fine friends on the Council won't back you, not this time. There's murder involved, Barrow. Think on it."

Barrow thought on it. Then he told Corrigan, "Follow me, lad. Show your little trinket. And hold your tongue about aught else!"

Inspectors Wright and MacRae had retired to Wright's private offices where the two could size each other up, like two players before the Big Game. Wright had the height and gloss; MacRae was pugnacious and determined. They eyed each other carefully, neither quite trusting the other's abilities.

Inspector Wright, with the home field advantage, began the polite hostilities. "A nasty business, these deaths," he commented. "Not the sort of thing we go in for here in Brighton."

"The young girl could have been an accident," MacRae pointed out. "Crowds, railway trains, cloak blowing. But young Doyle may be right about the old man—is it a murder, do you think?" MacRae looked about for a chair, and found none, since Wright had appropriated the one behind the desk.

"He certainly seems to think so." Wright sniffed.

"He and that professor friend of his seem to believe that both deaths are connected to the Marbury child's disappearance," MacRae said. "There's no evidence that they are."

"And none that they are not," Wright said slowly. "What would you do at the Yard, eh?"

MacRae stiffened. "We go by the book: question the known suspects."

"We haven't any," Wright pointed out. "Oh, I'm not saying we don't have whores in Brighton; we do. But we keep 'em in their place, which is Church Street, and Queen's Road. Girls found off their patch get a fine. We leave the prize-hunting to the ladies, Gawd bless 'em!"

MacRae's eyes glittered behind his spectacles, but he said nothing. Wright nodded wisely. "Y'see, MacRae, in a place like Brighton, the rule is, the punters come first. The Council and the Mayor don't like to have the visitors disturbed by riffraff. They want Brighton to be kept safe. Which is why we aren't about to let those hounds of the Press know what's down in our little morgue, at least not until we can catch the one who did 'em in."

"And what have you done to catch him?" MacRae demanded.

"I've had my men out, on their beats, looking for anything funny."

"And . . . " MacRae leaned over Wright's desk.

"So far, nothing to report," Wright admitted. "Someone's being clever."

"Or someone's being diddled!" MacRae shot out. "You should have called us in as soon as the girl was brought in."

Wright stood up. "Now see here," he protested. "That girl wasn't brought in until five o'clock last night. She isn't cold but a day! It's Saturday! You saw the kind of help we get, with everyone on holiday."

His attention was distracted by a deferential knock at the door. Sergeant Barrow's broad face appeared, with young Constable Corrigan behind him.

"Begging your pardon, sir," the sergeant rumbled. "This young sprig thinks 'e 'as sommat of importance."

Wright glanced at MacRae and settled down into his chair again. "Yes, Constable?"

Young Corrigan stepped forward, horribly conscious of his impertinence in approaching the higher-ups directly instead of through the proper intermediaries.

"I was walking my beat, which is King Street," he said, his eyes fixed on the portrait of the Queen placed directly above Inspector

Wright's head. "I had been checking the shops which was closed, to ascertain if all was well . . . "

"Get on with it," muttered Barrow.

MacRae had had more experience with nervous underlings. "And was all well?"

"In the shops? Nothing to report there, sir."

"Then why come to me?" Wright snapped.

"It was the green house—that is, the building in King Street, which, as I understand it, is let for the season to a Miss Harmon," Corrigan said.

MacRae's eyes took on a new light. "Harmon?" he repeated.

"You know the name?" Wright pounced on him.

"It has come to my attention," MacRae admitted. "Go on, Constable. What about this green house in King Street."

Corrigan was horribly conscious of Sergeant Barrow's eyes boring into his back. He licked his lips nervously and began again. "I know that house is none of my business—that is, Sergeant Barrow said, so long as it's quiet and respectable, it's no affair of mine who goes in or out . . . " He stopped, miserably.

Wright and MacRae were glaring at the burly sergeant, who was rapidly turning maroon with embarrassment.

"My orders was . . . that is, Mr. Carstairs, of the Council, said . . . " the sergeant sputtered.

Wright's voice was glacial. "I can imagine what Mr. Carstairs said. He said as much to me. Well, Corrigan? What singular matter made you break this pact of silence concerning the green house on King Street?"

"This, sir." Corrigan thrust his hand out. From it dangled the fine gold chain and locket tossed at his feet by a very small and frightened slavey named Kitty.

MacRae grabbed for the locket before either Wright or Barrow could get it. "Very fine," he pronounced. "Aha? What have we here? The Marbury crest, as I live and breathe! And how do you suppose this got into the green house on King Street that you're not supposed to know about?"

Corrigan cleared his throat. "The servant what . . . that tossed it to

131

me said, 'She's in here,' and ran away before I could speak further with her."

"Which would indicate that Miss Marbury is being held in that house," Inspector MacRae stated.

"Not so fast," Wright countered. "What happened then?"

"Nothing," Corrigan said. "That is, nothing out of the ordinary. Miss Harmon came down the street and asked if all was well, and I told her that I had heard a cat."

Barrow snorted in the background. Corrigan stood his ground. "And there was a cat on the dustbins."

"How providential," Wright murmured. "Was there anything about the house that might lead you to suspect foul play within?"

Corrigan reddened. "No, sir. All quiet, sir. Just the young ladies."

"Young ladies?" MacRae asked sharply.

Corrigan turned to the man from Scotland Yard. "Yes, sir. The house is let to Miss Harmon for the season, her and her young ladies. I've seen them from time to time. Very nice young ladies, too, sir," he added, growing more expansive under MacRae's approving stare and disregarding the growing volcano behind him.

"You're day shift," Barrow hissed. "When did you see Miss Harmon's young ladies?"

"I've met them when they take their morning walks," Corrigan said. "I was told Miss Harmon keeps a school or some such, and that I wasn't to take no . . . any notice if a carriage should appear and stay in front of that house for over-long, since it might well be someone visiting a relation in that house."

MacRae's eyes were positively glittering behind his spectacles. "Very observant, my lad. You'll go far!"

"He's already gone too far," muttered Barrow.

Wright read the omens correctly. Young Corrigan had better be seconded away from Barrow's vindictive reach as soon as possible. Meanwhile, there was the matter of the green house in King Street to be dealt with.

"Thank you, Corrigan," Inspector Wright said. "You are dismissed."

"That's all?" Corrigan looked baffled.

"We will act on your information," Wright promised him.

With that, Corrigan had to be satisfied. Barrow, on the other hand, was ready to take further action. Wright forestalled him.

"Sergeant Barrow," he called, "will you remain for a moment?"

Barrow watched balefully as Corrigan made his escape. Then he turned to his superiors. "Yes, sir?" he asked warily.

"What do you know of this house in King Street?" MacRae snapped out.

"What young Corrigan said. Let for the season to Miss Harmon. Quiet during the day."

"And no one in King Street is to make complaints at night," Wright finished for him. "An odd location for a girls' school, isn't it?"

Barrow stared stonily at the Queen's portrait. "I couldn't say, sir."

"And yet you are considered to be the authority on such matters," Wright said silkily. "Very well, Barrow. You may return to your post at the desk."

Barrow trudged out, leaving his superiors gloating at each other.

Inspector Wright turned to his London visitor. "According to *A Guide to Brighton*, 'King Street contains small shops, of no interest to any but residents'."

MacRae took off his spectacles in an excess of emotion and wiped them off on his handkerchief, extracted from his jacket pocket. Once they were affixed back on his nose, he regarded Inspector Wright with gleeful anticipation. "Inspector Wright, I think an expedition is called for."

Wright frowned. "Getting a warrant at this time of night, on a Saturday . . . "

"Oh, I wasn't planning anything more than a fishing expedition," MacRae said. "A respectable gentleman, out for some, um, pleasure? Heard of Miss Harmon's by way of a friend?"

Wright nodded. "No one here knew you were coming," he mused. "You've not been seen on the streets in the company of the police. You know, MacRae, it just might work. I will station some reliable men outside, in case you find the chit, and we can close this case by the time that wretched protestation rally begins on Monday night."

133

"Eh?" MacRae's eyebrows quirked in interrogation.

Wright sighed. "It's those articles in the *Pall Mall Gazette*. They've got the civilians so worked up that they're staging some sort of gathering for Monday night, a protestation rally, with Lord Richard Marbury himself as principal speaker, if you can believe the notification I was handed this afternoon. I'm to provide extra constables to control the crowds they expect."

MacRae smiled. For the first time he felt a kinship with his fellow officer. "Cheer up," he counseled. "With any luck, it'll rain, and the whole matter will be done with. Now, where can I get a decent plate of fish and chips in this town? As long as I'm in Brighton, I might as well enjoy myself."

"How long do you plan to stay?" Wright asked, as they descended the stairs.

"As long as it takes, sir," MacRae said. "I've got lodgings waiting, in case I have to remain for your protestation meeting."

"In that case, Inspector, I think you'd better go there. We'll keep your presence here as quiet as possible. I don't like to think it of my men, but there's always the chap who talks in his pub."

"And keep an eye on Barrow," MacRae added. "Not that I'd accuse any officer of neglecting his duty," he said hastily, before Wright could utter the reproof that was obviously trembling on his lips, "but this Harmon woman's been linked to Mrs. Jeffries, and that one's got fingers in every pie in England—and a few across the Channel, if my information's right."

Inspector Wright nodded. "Have your tea, and meet me at, say, eight o'clock, in King Street. I think Miss Harmon's going to have a busy night."

CHAPTER 17

Saturday night in Brighton marked the height of the week's festivities. By eight o'clock, the dining room of the Old Ship was full of ladies and gentlemen (or so their attire proclaimed them) in full evening dress: the gentlemen's black coats and white shirtfronts gleaming in the gaslight, while their female partners glittered with jewels on necks, ears, wrists, and fingers, dining on quail in aspic, or lobster Thermidore, washed down with champagne. In more modest establishments, lodgers were served local fish, boiled, broiled, or baked, accompanied by potatoes fried, boiled, or mashed, washed down with beer, ale, or local cider.

On the piers, the aroma of frying fish overpowered that of the seaweed left by the tide. Under the gaslight, shopgirls out for the day giggled as brash young office clerks sought their acquaintance. Sailors off their ships and soldiers away from camp vied with the would-be gentlemen for the attentions of the young women.

The Pavilion had been requisitioned by the visiting Philharmonic Orchestra, for a Concert featuring the ultra-modern symphony by Herr Doktor Brahms, as well as the more familiar strains of Mozart and Mendelssohn. There sat the resolutely chaperoned young ladies, whose eagle-eyed mamas were all too willing to sum up the approaching young gentlemen as either eligible marriage fodder or ineligible bounders.

All over Brighton, people were dining, or preparing to be entertained, or both. At St. Peter's Rectory, the Reverend Mr. Barclay and his wife had requested the honor of the presence of Mr. and Mrs. Falwell and their charming daughters; Mr. Dodgson; the Reverend Mr. Youghall (of Hampshire, visiting Brighton); Mr. Donaldson (of St. Margaret's Church, Brighton) and his wife; and, to round out the table, Dr. Doyle and Mrs. Doyle, whose last-minute invitation had nearly sent the cook into a conniption fit.

The young couple were sensible of the great honor being done them, and had dressed accordingly. Dr. Doyle wore the dress suit in which he had so recently exchanged vows with his beloved, while she was clad in her peach-colored wedding dress, garnished with a wreath of artificial roses. Their presence lightened the atmosphere immensely. Apparently, the Rector had invited as many of his vacationing colleagues as he could find to partake of his baked cod, summer vegetables, new strawberries, and appropriate wines (since Mr. Barclay had no qualms about alcohol). The conversation initially tended to the parochial, and the scholarly, but Dr. Doyle's lively Scottish wit soon had the gentlemen smiling, even if the more censorious ladies restrained themselves.

Mr. Dodgson partook of dinner silently, while Dr. Doyle enlivened the conversation with accounts of his adventures as a seafarer. " . . . And since I was so desperately homesick, I returned," he concluded.

"Fascinating!" Mr. Barclay said. "I suppose your love of the sea led you to Portsmouth, then?"

The young doctor shook his head in mock embarrassment. "I must confess, sir, I was not led to Portsmouth, I was mis-led." He laughed at his own wit. "A friend of mine was in practice here, and he invited me to join him. It was not a particularly happy idea. He left the town and the practice, and I got—" He looked at his wife, who blushed becomingly.

"Indeed."

Mrs. Barclay glanced over at Touie, who was suddenly aware of her social duty. As the new bride, it was up to her to lead the ladies out. She smiled at Mrs. Barclay and carefully rose to her feet. Mrs. Barclay and the other ladies followed her lead, while the gentlemen shifted in their seats. Touie cast a beseeching look over her shoulder at her husband, as if to urge him to finish his port and cigar and come to her rescue as quickly as possible. Dr. Doyle, on the other hand, was in no particular hurry to leave.

"Now that the ladies are out of the room," Mr. Barclay said, as the butler set the port on the table, "we may discuss the matter that brings us together."

"The protestation meeting," said Mr. Falwell, with great satisfaction.

"Precisely. It is, I agree, a most delicate subject, but one that we must face. Presently, Mr. Branwell, of the Methodist Chapel . . . "

There was a noise from Mr. Youghall. Mr. Barclay ignored it.

"There will be some who decry the participation of Dissenters, but, gentlemen, it is they who are at the forefront of this campaign, and we must not allow them to steal a march on us, to use the military term."

"Considering that Mr. Booth is planning on attending, the military term may be appropriate," Mr. Falwell said, with a brief laugh. "He may call himself a General if he chooses, but that does not give him a commission."

Mr. Barclay waved General Booth's credentials away as being of no importance. "He is collecting signatures for a petition to be presented to Parliament," Mr. Barclay stated. "He and his good wife have asked that we allow them to set up a booth at our meeting, and I am of the opinion that we should do so."

"And where is this meeting to be held?" Mr. Youghall asked.

"Ah, yes. Mr. Carstairs, representing the Borough Council, will look in on us later this evening. I have obtained permission from the borough to use the grounds of the Royal Pavilion, if it is fair, or the Grand Saloon inside the Pavilion if it rains."

"Quite sporting of them," Dr. Doyle commented. "And who else, besides General Booth and his Salvationists, will be present?"

"I have received confirmation that Lord Richard Marbury will, indeed, address the meeting," the Rector said with pride. "That, alone, should bring out a crowd. Now, gentlemen, what I would like you to do is to inform your congregants of the meeting during your various services tomorrow, and join with me in support of the Criminal Amendment Bill."

Mr. Youghall frowned at his colleague. "That is a great deal to ask, sir," he said. "I have already written my sermon for tomorrow. Besides, I am not at all certain that the Church has any business meddling in political affairs."

"This is not political!" Mr. Barclay was on his feet. "This is a matter of morality, young man! If you will not preach, at least lend your countenance to our efforts by sitting on the platform in support."

"That, sir, I will consider." Young Mr. Youghall helped himself to port. Mr. Barclay turned to his old friend.

"Charles, you will sit on the platform, will you not?"

Mr. Dodgson had sipped at his port, his thoughts adrift. Now he seemed to wake up from a nap. "Eh?"

"I asked, Charles, if you will appear at the protestation meeting on Monday evening," the Rector repeated.

"I? Oh, no, certainly not. I am not a clergyman. I could not feel worthy of Orders."

"But you are a noted literary figure," Dr. Doyle urged him.

"I am a mathematician and professor of logic," Mr. Dodgson corrected him. "I never speak in public."

"But you have delivered a sermon," Mr. Barclay reminded him.

"To a very small group of young ladies," Mr. Dodgson said.

"And you will read the lesson at the eleven o'clock service tomorrow," Mr. Barclay added.

"In my capacity as Deacon," Mr. Dodgson agreed. "But, Henry, much as I approve of the terms of this Bill, I cannot sit on your platform. Besides, you will have far better speakers than I, what with General Booth and Lord Richard Marbury to hand."

"I sincerely hope you have the cooperation of the police," Mr. Falwell said. "There is an element—" He shook his head broodingly.
"When we arrived in Brighton, my wife and I and our daughters
were forced to pass certain unfortunate creatures on the Queen's
Road, whose very existence is a disgrace to womankind."

"Precisely the sort of thing this Bill is trying to stop," Mr. Barclay
told him.

"On the Queen's Road, did you say?" Mr. Dodgson asked.

The mournful-looking clergyman regarded him with suspicious
eyes. "Is that of importance, sir?"

Dr. Doyle took over. "Only as a curiosity, sir. When I was a medical student in Edinburgh, I noticed that certain streets seem to be set
aside for such, um, activities. No doubt it is easier for the police to
keep an eye on those women, and their, um . . . "

"Yes," Mr. Barclay harumphed. "I have heard that the area behind
the Music Hall is used for immoral purposes, but of course, I would
have no knowledge at first hand of such matters."

"Of course not," Dr. Doyle said.

"Then we may join the ladies," Mr. Barclay said, leaving the port
for the butler to remove.

The situation in the parlor had become distinctly cool. Mrs. Barclay and Mrs. Falwell were deep in a discussion of parish charities.
The two Miss Falwells were trying to play the piano. Touie was left
alone on a chair, with neither music nor conversation to divert her.
Only Mrs. Donaldson, a motherly soul of vast kindness and vaster
proportions, tried to initiate some sort of rapport.

"Is this your first visit to Brighton?" Mrs. Donaldson asked, as if
she were the first to do so,

"I have spent most of my life in Portsmouth," Touie answered.
"My brother and I . . . " Her eyes filled with tears.

"Oh dear." Mrs. Donaldson produced a fine handkerchief.

Touie used it, then said, "I'm sorry. It's only been a year since we
lost him. Arthur—that is, Dr. Doyle—was the attending physician
in the case."

"How romantic!" squeaked the eldest Miss Falwell from the
piano.

"And so you are on your honeymoon," gushed the younger Miss Falwell.

"It seems you are spending very little time with your bridegroom," Mrs. Barclay put in censoriously.

"Arthur is assisting Mr. Dodgson," Touie said loyally. Before anyone could ask what her husband was assisting Mr. Dodgson with, he appeared at the parlor door, with the rest of the gentlemen. "Oh, Arthur," she greeted her husband, grateful for someone else to talk to. "Mrs. Barclay and Mrs. Falwell have been discussing their efforts on behalf of the poor children of their parishes."

"Most commendable," Mr. Dodgson said faintly.

"Yes, indeed, but we must be off," Dr. Doyle said abruptly. "We have to find—"

"Oh, of course." Touie blushed. "Perhaps you had better take me back to our lodgings, then, before you continue your search."

"Oh, what are you looking for?" asked the younger Miss Falwell. "Is it a treasure hunt?"

"Of a sort," Mr. Dodgson said. "But it is a hidden treasure."

Mr. Barclay looked worried. "Charles," he said, drawing his friend out into the hallway, while Dr. Doyle and his wife were assisted into their evening wraps, "you are not planning to search for that child tonight?"

"I must," Mr. Dodgson said, clutching his friend's arm as much for physical support as moral.

"Do not let that Dr. Doyle lead you into danger with his ambition to make a name for himself," Mr. Barclay warned. "And I shall wait up for you."

"Thank you, Henry." Mr. Dodgson took his hat and walked after his protégés. "I only hope that we shall find the child quickly, and that she is not harmed in the process."

Mr. Barclay followed the two of them down the path to Trafalgar Street, and let his butler find a cab on the Grand Parade while his dinner guests waited indoors.

"Charles, I still think you should let the police handle this matter," he said, finally.

"I would, if I had more confidence in their ability," Mr. Dodgson

140

countered. "Dr. Doyle seems to think that we may find some answers to our questions on Church Street. As soon as we have seen Mrs. Doyle safely to their lodgings, we shall make those inquiries. And then, Henry, we may be able to rouse the police to do their duty!"

CHAPTER 18

﷽

That Saturday night in Brighton was perfect for seekers of diversion. In spite of the sea breeze that was beginning to wreathe the beaches and Esplanade with mist, the weather held fair enough so that strollers would not be inconvenienced. The Theatre Royal was showing Mr. Henry Irving that night, in his renowned production of *Hamlet*. There was a full bill at the Music Hall, including Mr. George Grossmith (on loan from the D'Oyly Carte Company, one night only). Buskers, street musicians, and Punch and Judy all were out in full force, since they depended on a clear Saturday night to "make the nut," and pay for the following week's food and board, not to mention gin, beer, and rum.

Even more than the performers, the women (and a few young men) who strutted along Church Street were hoping for a good haul on Saturday. Weekdays might be dreary; Sunday was impossible. Friday gave promise, but Saturday was the time for a woman to take in a week's income—and Heaven help her if she did not, for no one else would!

Those Brighton streetwalkers who operated along the Queen's Road, that well-traveled route from the railway station to the more fashionable haunts of the Esplanade and Marine Parade, were subject to some annoyance from the constabulary. A girl could not actually stand on the Queen's Road, but had to be in a doorway or window. Church Street, which led from Queen's Road to North Street, was a narrow, cobbled street lined with two-story houses, most of which had flyblown signs in the windows advertising ROOMS TO LET. No one ever let the rooms for more than an hour at a time, and none of the letters of rooms ever considered taking in an unsolicited boarder. Taverns filled the ground floors of those houses, where young (and not-so-young) men could find a glass of ale, or something stronger. Behind the counters of the bars stood stout middle-aged persons of either sex, who were all too willing to recommend a friendly, clean, and willing young woman to a gentleman who offered a half-crown (or sometimes less) for the information.

Church Street was gaslit, but the lamplighters made sure to be well away before the night settled in. Under the lamps strolled women, young and old, full-fleshed and scrawny, with hair that varied in shade from the palest of blond to the darkest of jet (with some assistance from the new chemical dyes hawked in the back pages of the newspapers). Their charms were displayed in second-hand finery, culled from the leavings of ladies' maids, who could no longer be seen in their mistress's once-fashionable attire. Low-cut chemises revealed bosoms that were never used for suckling purposes; ankles were barely hidden by flounced petticoats; waists were cinched in by bodices and corsets to impossible dimensions.

To the sight of all this pulchritude were added the sounds of soprano and alto voices, calling, cajoling, enticing, promising the passerby "a good time, ducky," or "a jolly go," with no mention of the probable aftereffects: robbery, shame, or a dose of clap.

Church Street was patrolled by two constables, one at each end of the road, whose main function appeared to be to keep the women in their place, away from the higher-class tarts on the Esplanade. They studiously ignored the men who strolled along the road, while the men pretended they were only out to take the air (redolent with cheap perfume and gin). Gentlemen in evening dress, city chaps in suits, country fellows in shirts and waistcoats, soldiers in red coats and sailors in dress blues, all came to Church Street, looking for companionship, or its nearest equivalent.

To this salubrious locale came Dr. Doyle, with a shrinking Mr. Dodgson at his side. They were left off at the Music Hall by a cabby who gave them a knowing wink. "I can be back in an hour," the cabby promised. "That should do for the old gent. As for you, young feller, you might want to go a little longer!"

"One hour will do very well," Dr. Doyle said. "Remain at this location, and there will be a crown in it for you."

"Good enough," the cabby said, with a flourish of his whip. He joined the queue at the Music Hall end of Church Street.

Dr. Doyle and Mr. Dodgson were left to the tender mercies of the police constable, who carefully looked across the street as they peered around the corner to survey the territory. The elderly scholar eyed the scene with evident distaste.

"I do not think I can do this, Dr. Doyle," he confessed.

"It's not a pleasant sight," Dr. Doyle agreed. "Those poor women, forced into a life of shame."

"And those men!" Mr. Dodgson shuddered. "Open depravity! No, Dr. Doyle, I must reconsider our plan of action. Perhaps you should go ahead of me. Heavens!" He peered into the street, now beginning to be wreathed in mist. "I believe I recognize that man!"

"I sincerely hope no one of our acquaintance is here!" Dr. Doyle said fervently.

"What would people think if I were to be seen in such a . . . a disgraceful location?" Mr. Dodgson fussed. "No, no, I must not be here. You will have to continue your researches by yourself, Dr. Doyle. At least, as a young man, and a medical man at that, you have some excuse for your presence. Only the worst inferences will be drawn if I . . . Oh, dear me!" Mr. Dodgson tried to pull his hat over his face as he scanned the street ahead of him.

"What is it?"

"Is that not Mr. Kinsale? I thought we left him in London."

"What?" Dr. Doyle poked his head around the corner, then ducked back. "I do believe you are right, Mr. Dodgson. I suppose it is not surprising, given his reputation, that Roaring Ned Kinsale should patronize these, um, women, but his presence in Brighton is unusual. I was under the impression that his interests lay in London."

"Whatever shall we do? If he recognizes us . . . "

"He appears to be questioning some of those women."

Indeed, Ned Kinsale, in well-cut but carelessly worn evening dress, was chatting with two girls, whose age could have been anything from fifteen to fifty under their heavy cosmetics.

Doyle and Dodgson crept nearer, hoping to catch some of the dialogue.

"Pretty girls like you shouldn't be out on the streets this late at night," Kinsale chaffed them.

"And were you planning to put us to bed, then?" The one with the red hair leaned against him, leaving streaks of powder across his white shirtfront.

"And if I was, where would we go?"

"Just across the street, love. I've got a nice little room."

"Ah, but suppose you're not the one I'm looking for?" Kinsale's voice eased into the Irish brogue.

The girl pouted. "I'm sure I can make you happy, sir."

"Perhaps. But I'm looking for someone special, someone with red hair."

The girl laughed and teased him with the red curl that escaped over her shoulders.

"He wants hair that don't come out of a bottle," the other girl sniped. "True carrots is hard to find, sir."

"I hear there's one place . . . a house." Kinsale's voice dropped. "Just the sort of place a pretty pair like you might find work in. Somewhere where the girls are"—he leered—"girls."

The redhead shrugged. "I don't know nothing about a place like that," she said. Behind her, a tall man in a black velveteen jacket worn over a red silk shirt, open at the neck and tied round with a black scarf, materialized.

"Here, yer lordship, stop wasting the girl's time. Take the offer, or find someone else!"

Kinsale tipped his top hat and smiled winningly. "I'm in the market for red hair tonight, but not yours, m'dear," he said. "But here's a shilling for your time." He tipped the girls, waved at the pimp, and strolled on.

The older girl glanced at her pimp, then ran after Kinsale. "If it's real young you're lookin' for," she whispered hurriedly, "I've got a sister, works a flash place in King Street. Ask for Miss 'armon and say Gertie's sister sent yer." She laughed loudly and sashayed back to her post. Kinsale looked thoughtful as he continued his promenade.

Behind him, Mr. Dodgson told Dr. Doyle, "I cannot do this. I must return to the Rectory at once. I leave this part of the search to you, sir."

"Mr. Dodgson," Dr. Doyle urged him on, "I thought we had agreed on this course of action. We must question these young women and find out where Miss Marbury might have been taken."

Mr. Dodgson turned and faced his young companion, his face set in lines of extreme displeasure. "No, Dr. Doyle," he said firmly. *"You* agreed. You have dragged me hither and yon, from here to London and back, you have subjected me to a pointless chase, you have permitted me to be assaulted—"

Dr. Doyle's mustache bristled with indignation. "It was you, sir, who wished to go to London, not I! As for the assault upon your person, if you will recall, it was none of my doing, and I fought those bully-boys, even to the possible detriment to my own character!"

Mr. Dodgson was not listening. " . . . And now this . . . this scene of debauchery! Dr. Doyle, you and I must part company, now! I shall return to our cab, and drive to the Rectory of St. Peter's, where I shall be secure. As for you, sir, you may do as you will!" He turned his back on the sordid scene.

Dr. Doyle gazed at his erstwhile mentor sorrowfully. "I had thought better of you, Mr. Dodgson," he said at last. "Several times you have sworn that you would find that child, no matter what the cost. Now you cannot face a few disreputable women. I shall take you back to your safe haven of respectability, sir, and let the police do their job. Never mind what will happen to Miss Marbury in the meanwhile, not to mention the fact that the killer of that poor

nurserymaid will go scot-free. Perhaps I overestimated your forti-
tude, sir."

Mr. Dodgson marched resolutely onward. Dr. Doyle followed
him back to the Music Hall, where cabs were lining up, waiting for
patrons of the raucous arts to emerge from the Theatre Royal, some
to make their selection of the female wares along Church Street, others to proceed down the hill to the more respectable quarter of
Brighton.

The helpful cabby was still there. "That was a quick'un," he commented, as he tapped his horse with the whip.

"We . . . changed our minds," Dr. Doyle said. "Back to St. Peter's,
if you please."

Behind them, Ned Kinsale watched their retreat and grinned gleefully. So, young Doyle and the old codger were on the trail, were
they? Well, if they had heard him, let them make the most of it. His
other friends were waiting for him at the far end of the street. Better
that he be thought a libertine, Kinsale thought. The lads would not
appreciate any police interference with their plans.

He reread the handbill that had been shoved into his hands on the
Queen's Road. A Grand Protestation Meeting, was it? How apt that
the frequenters of Church Street should be informed of the event.
Perhaps the lads could make a protest of their own!

He turned down one of the small streets that ran between Church
Street and North Street. His friends would be waiting for news from
London, and he had quite a lot of it to give them.

Mr. Dodgson sat in huffy silence as the cab trotted back to St.
Peter's Church. Dr. Doyle regarded him sorrowfully.

"I thought you meant it when you said you would do anything for
that child," the young Scotsman said finally.

"There are limits, young man." Mr. Dodgson closed his eyes, as
if to blot out the scene he had just been forced to witness.

Mr. Dodgson emerged from his cab and marched into the Rectory
without another word to Dr. Doyle.

"Where to now, sir?" the cabby asked.

"Duke Street," Dr. Doyle said, with a disappointed sigh. "I may

147

have to do this myself, but not tonight." At least, he thought, Touie would be there, and she would understand.

The meeting at the Rectory had progressed considerably. Mr. Barclay's parlor was now full of excited clergymen, of various sects and sizes. He nearly missed Mr. Dodgson's entrance.

"Charles!" Mr. Barclay bustled out of the parlor, before Mr. Dodgson could escape his attentions. "You must—Why, whatever is the matter? You do not look at all well."

"I am not well, Henry. With your permission, I shall retire. I have a great deal to think about. It has been an eventful day."

Mr. Dodgson was led to one of the upstairs bedrooms by the butler, who provided him with the amenities of the house: a pitcher of drinking water and a glass, and a plate of water biscuits. Once alone, with the lamp properly lit, he could remove his collar and cravat and crawl into his nightwear, which had been laid out for him.

What should he do? he wondered, as he prepared for bed. As was his custom, he bowed his head in prayer. No answer came from on high. He shook his head, puzzled. "It does not make sense," he said aloud. "Why?"

Mr. Dodgson tried to think clearly, ignoring the hubbub downstairs. All things have a logic, even in madness, he decided. I will have to consider the events in their proper order, and all will be made clear.

As he closed his eyes, he wondered whether he had been too hasty. Dr. Doyle was not a bad chap. He was, after all, Dicky Doyle's nephew. Perhaps tomorrow would bring a better understanding.

In the lodging house in Duke Street, Dr. Doyle and his bride were also preparing for bed. Mrs. Keene had provided them with a brass bedstead of impressive size, fitted out with a sturdy mattress, down pillows, and linen sheets. Touie modestly hid behind a screen to complete her toilette, while Dr. Doyle removed his clothes and hung them neatly on the spindle-backed chair in one corner of the room.

He related the events of the evening, omitting such details as the appearance of Mr. Kinsale among the Soiled Doves.

"Mr. Dodgson would not continue with me," he said. "Why couldn't he have even tried?"

"Mr. Dodgson is not as robust as you," Touie consoled him, emerging from behind the screen and sliding between the sheets. "And, Arthur, he is a gentleman of rather . . . restricted . . . upbringing. You have knocked about the world a bit, after all."

Dr. Doyle smirked, slid in beside his bride, and blew out the candle. "I only hope the child will not be harmed because we did not find her in time."

"Oh, Arthur," Touie breathed. "You will surely save her!"

After which, there were no more words to say.

CHAPTER 19

King Street was one of the short connecting streets between Church and North streets. Only a few hundred yards lay between the trollops who plied their trade on the streets and the young persons who inhabited Miss Harmon's establishment, and those few hundred yards made all the difference. At Miss Harmon's, there were no overt displays of female charms, no garish cosmetics, no blatant calls or raucous ribaldry. Instead, Miss Harmon cultivated an ambiance of gentility. The parlor was furnished with comfortable chairs, and decorated with reproductions of Mr. Landseer's paintings. The very young employees were instructed in deportment that would not shock or disgust potential clients.

"Sit up straight, Helen," Miss Harmon ordered, as she arranged herself on her chair, ready for the early customers. She had changed her flowered day dress for a gray silk gown with a demi-train, embellished with jet beads. Her hair was piled high on her head, held in place with combs and hairpins. Only a light dusting of pale powder enhanced her face. Miss Harmon could have joined any of the select parties being held in Brighton at the Albemarle or Grand hotels, and no one would have known that she had started life in a stationer's shop in Oxford High Street.

"When are the punters coming?" Gertie asked, glancing at the clock over the mantlepiece.

"You must not use vulgar terms," Miss Harmon corrected her.

"But my sister says the gentlemen like a bit of fun," Gertie objected. "She says they like it when a girl talks flash. Makes 'em feel devilish."

"Perhaps, if you want to remain in Church Street for the rest of your life," Miss Harmon said severely. "But if you want to get on, you must learn to speak as the gentlemen speak. Rude talk and coarse behavior will not get you to London."

"London?" Gertie breathed. London was the crowning achievement of Miss Harmon's girls. To be chosen for the London house was to be assured of wealth beyond the dreams of the streetwalkers on Church Street. Only the very best girls, the most popular with the gentlemen, would go to London when the Brighton season was over. So said Miss Harmon, and she had not deceived any of her girls yet.

Miss Harmon looked over her charges, the six most promising young women she could cull from the byways of Brighton. Victoria, called Vicky, at fourteen, was a dark beauty. Gertie, plump and blond, was the favorite of the gentlemen, who liked what they called "meat on the bones." Susanne, who looked delicate, with pale brown hair that was midway between Gertie's gold and Helen's auburn, was probably the most intelligent of the lot; Miss Harmon would have to watch her, or she'd be up to nasty tricks like blackmail in a year or two. Lizzie and Deb were the youngest; their parents were ready to swear they were twelve, but Miss Harmon suspected otherwise. No matter; for a few pounds, the two girls were signed over to her, and they would be within the legal limit soon enough. Helen, the rowdy redhead, was most likely to be at the bottom of any mischief the girls might be brewing. It was Helen who had noticed the man being drawn out of the water that morning.

Miss Harmon had turned them away, lest they recognize Old Keeble. She was fairly certain that no one had seen him bring Alicia Marbury into the house the day before; the girls were supposed to be in their rooms, resting at that hour. She did not know whether anyone but Kitty knew there was one more little girl in the house, but it never hurt to be cautious.

Miss Harmon settled her brood around her in the parlor, on small chairs and ottomans, arranged to make the girls look even younger than they were. Mrs. J. had been careful to skirt the law; if twelve was the legal age of consent, then none of the girls was to be any younger—but that did not mean they could not look younger. Genteel suggestions had been made in certain hotels, and responses had been received. No one would be admitted to the house on King Street who was not known or, at least, could acknowledge that he had been sent by one of her own people.

The doorbell rang. The girls sat up, alert, ready for business. Mrs. Gurney, massive in her best black silk gown and white cap, answered the call.

"Mr. Carstairs," Madam announced. The eminent town councilor beamed on the company.

"I just dropped by a little early tonight," he explained. "The Reverend Mr. Barclay has requested that I join him at a meeting to plan the protestation rally on Monday, so I may be delayed in my usual round. However, I did want to see you were all well. How are we all today? And especially my little Vicky?" He winked broadly at his favorite, who dropped her eyes modestly in response.

"Protestation rally?" Miss Harmon asked sharply.

"To move Parliament to vote on Lord Richard Marbury's Bill. Our good Rector is quite wrought up about it. I shall, of course, have to attend the meeting, but I shall come by later, for my usual, er, chat."

"Of course, Mr. Carstairs," Miss Harmon said, with a smile that never reached her eyes. "It was good of you to let us know that your visit would be delayed. We might have worried, otherwise."

Mr. Carstairs stepped back into the hall. Miss Harmon followed him. "This protestation meeting—I heard something about it, but I had no idea the plans were already set," she said breathlessly.

"I believe the notices are being printed even as we speak, and some persons have been hired to hand them out tomorrow. Members of the clergy have all promised to preach on the subject at their respective services. What a to-do about nothing at all! It's these articles in the *Pall Mall Gazette*, getting people worked up. Of course, Mr. Stead and his ilk are not referring to an establishment like this one, quiet and respectable. I shall return later, when I have finished my discussions with Mr. Barclay and his committee."

The councilor took his hat from the Madam, who opened the door and handed him down the three stairs to the street, where his carriage was waiting.

Three doors down, Inspectors Wright and MacRae watched as the good citizen drove away. "And that's Carstairs," Wright informed MacRae bitterly.

"Likes 'em young, does he?" MacRae observed.

"So they say. I have also heard it said that he encouraged this arrangement so that he could indulge in his habit without having to go to Church Street," Wright said. "It wouldn't do for a town councilor to be seen there, would it?"

"So he gets word to someone else to set up shop." MacRae sounded disgusted. "And what odds he's going to be right up there on the platform on Monday, looking like butter wouldn't melt in his mouth."

Wright nodded. "No takers. Well, MacRae? Can you bring it off?"

MacRae settled his spectacles firmly on his nose. "I can mention a name or two. That might get me inside."

"What then? You won't . . . "

"Finish with one of the little darlings? Certainly not! But I will take a look around."

"I've got a warrant from Justice Rayburn, on the strength of young Corrigan's locket," Wright said, patting his breast pocket. "But I don't want to give our game away just yet. See what you can learn first, MacRae."

The London man squared his shoulders and marched up the three steps to the door. The Madam opened it, her vast bustle effectively blocking entrance.

"Yes?" Madam's voice was as forbidding as her frown.

"Good evening. I was told by a friend in London that I could find—ah—entertainment of a particular sort at this address," MacRae ventured.

"And what friend might that be?" Madam asked.

"I cannot recall, but you might ask Miss Harmon if a friend of Mrs. J. would be welcome," MacRae said meaningfully, with a heavy Glasgow burr.

"I'll see if you're known." Madam left MacRae outside while she disappeared into the house.

Inspector Wright edged closer. The door opened once again.

"You're not expected, but . . . " Mrs. Gurney reluctantly stepped aside and let MacRae inside.

MacRae found himself in a small, unexpectedly cozy environment. He was shown into a parlor that might be a model for any bourgeois household: the lady of the house, Miss Harmon, surrounded by her daughters, all clad in the finest of white drawers and camisoles under sheer negligées, sitting on a chintz-covered chair beside the fireplace (even in Brighton, a small fire was necessary).

Miss Harmon looked up from her book as he entered. "How do you do," she said, a smile lurking in her eyes. "I do not believe we have met before, Inspector MacRae."

"I beg your pardon?" MacRae blinked behind his spectacles.

"It is Inspector MacRae, is it not? Of Scotland Yard?"

"I admit that is my name, but . . . "

"You don't know how I know?" She laughed merrily. "Oh, Inspector, you are a notable person, and all notable persons are noted." She shrugged. "Now, can I offer you any . . . refreshment?" She nodded at the girls, who giggled back.

MacRae's face reddened. "I believe I have . . . "

"Made a mistake? You certainly have!" Miss Harmon rose. There was no merriment in her eyes now. "Whatever you came for, you had better leave, unless you have a warrant."

"I do not, but Inspector Wright of the Brighton Constabulary does." MacRae said. There was no need for subterfuge now. "He has reason to believe that a child is being held here against her will."

"Indeed?" Miss Harmon's voice rose with her eyebrows. "Do

summon your minions, Inspector. You may search this place from top to bottom, if you like. I assure you, all the young ladies here are present and accounted for, and are here at their own request. Is that not so?"

She turned to the girls, who nodded gravely.

MacRae's thin lips formed a line of distaste.

Mrs. Gurney leered at him. "You may not remember me, Inspector MacRae, but I remember you. Scotland Yard's come down in the world if they've sent you all this way chasing runaway girls!" She poked her head out into the street and yelled out, "You can come in, coppers! Yer man's been rumbled!"

Inspector Wright marched into the parlor and glared at Inspector MacRae. The London man could only shrug in annoyance.

Miss Harmon examined the legal document handed to her carefully. "You may search my premises, Inspector, but as I told your friend here, I have nothing to hide. Although," she added, as she led the two policemen up the front stairs to the bedrooms, "I do not understand why you have chosen to honor me with this visit."

"Acting on information received," Inspector Wright stated.

"Received? From whom?" Miss Harmon asked sharply.

"One of our constables found an article of jewelry that belongs to a young lady who has been reported as missing," Inspector Wright admitted.

"And you thought it might have come from my house? How very odd," Miss Harmon said. Her eyes were chips of green ice in the gaslight.

The two men marched up and down the hall, peering into the dainty bedrooms. They stood at the end of the hall, stared at the painted cupids on the wall panel, and shrugged.

Inspector Wright took one more look at the hallway. There was something indefinably wrong about that hall, but he could not make it out just then. He stroked his mustache. It would come to him. It always did.

For the time being, he could only march back down to the parlor and bow to the head of the household.

"Miss Harmon, I must apologize for the disturbance. We will have to pursue our search elsewhere. Inspector MacRae, will you come with me?"

The London man had no choice. He bowed briefly to the ladies and followed Wright out the door. The street echoed to the boom as the door swung shut behind them.

Once outside, MacRae turned on Wright. "What did you think you were doing?" MacRae hissed. "Telling her we had the locket?"

"I hoped to jar her into admitting something," Wright said.

"If that child is in that house, she's well hid," MacRae grumbled. "And we've no chance of finding her now."

"Once they know we're on their trail, they'll try to move her," Wright said. "And then we'll nab 'em."

"And in the meanwhile?"

"I've got a constable down the street, watching the place. Whoever goes in or out, we'll know. Meanwhile, you and I can repair to the tavern at the end of the street—"

"Not while on duty!" MacRae snapped out.

"—where we can have some tea and wait out the evening," Wright went on smoothly. "The barman'll serve us cider, if you like. It'll be easier waiting there than lurking about here."

MacRae shook his head. "By what I've seen, we may have a very long wait."

CHAPTER 20

M adge Gurney and Julia Harmon watched from behind the peephole in the front door as the policemen walked across the road and down King Street. The Madam said nothing until they had turned around the corner and were out of sight. Then she turned to Miss Harmon, her face growing purple with wrath.

"Kitty," she breathed. "She must 'ave talked to that young copper on the beat. That little bitch!"

"You mean our missy upstairs?" Miss Harmon nodded. "Kitty would never have thought of doing such a thing on her own. I told you not to let them be alone together. That girl has her father's silver tongue and her mother's blarney."

"Wot about the Lunnon man? I knew 'im as soon as I saw 'im, but 'ow did did yer know?"

"I was warned. The Guv'nor got to me in time." Miss Harmon smiled, then looked down the hall toward the kitchen door. "But we can't have our kitchen help going to the local coppers. Bring her upstairs."

" 'Ere?" Madam looked around the parlor.

"No. Up to the other room. The one where we put the naughty girls." Miss Harmon's eyes had narrowed to green slits.

From her place in the parlor, Victoria heard the words and felt a tremor of fear. She knew better than to arouse Miss Harmon's wrath. She herself had never been so foolish as to draw down that anger, but there were those who had, and they were not so pretty when Miss Harmon was finished with them.

Miss Harmon still stood in the hall, at the foot of the stairs. Victoria swallowed hard and quavered out, "We done nothing—that is, we didn't do anything . . . "

"I know you didn't," Miss Harmon said. She struggled visibly to maintain her icy composure. "This is something quite different. Kitty did wrong. She must be punished."

"What did she do, Miss Harmon?" piped up Gertie.

"She peached to the coppers," Helen hissed.

"What have I told you about using vulgar cant?" Force of habit took over. Miss Harmon smoothed her hair with one shaking hand. "Victoria, if any gentlemen come, give them tea and make them comfortable. I will be occupied for a few minutes."

Victoria sat up very straight, conscious of the honor that was being accorded her. As the head girl, she would be responsible for the smooth running of the establishment until the return of its mistress. Unconsciously imitating Miss Harmon, she took her place on the sacred armchair, while the rest of the girls shivered inwardly. None of them would have approached a policeman on their own, and none of them would do so now.

The Madam descended to the kitchen, where Kitty was dutifully scouring the last of the cooking pans and preparing the kettle for morning's ablutions.

One look at Madam's furious face told Kitty that her plot had succeeded, perhaps beyond her imagining. Before she could dart out of the kitchen and through the areaway, Madam's huge hands were on her, hauling her out and dragging her up the stairs to where Miss Harmon sat in her office, like the magistrate, handing down judgment.

"So, Kitty," Miss Harmon said, finally, as Kitty writhed in

Madam's hands. "You were disobedient. You talked to our new guest this afternoon."

"I didn't say nuffin'," Kitty quavered.

"I dare say you didn't. She did the talking." Miss Harmon's breath came in gasps. "She told you lies, Kitty. She told you she would be your friend if you would help her. Didn't she?" Miss Harmon caught Kitty by the chin and stared into her eyes. "Didn't she?"

"She . . . she said as 'ow she was some Nob's little girl," Kitty said.

"And you believed her? I suppose she told you she would take you to London if you helped her? And make you a *lady?*"

"No, Miss Harmon, I mean, she said Lunnon, but not the lady part."

"And she gave you something to show to the constable?" Miss Harmon went on.

"A chain, wiv a locket," Kitty sniveled.

"Well, the police have been and gone. They did not find her. And they will not find her, because she is going away, far away to France, and she will never be seen again. She is not going to help you, you foolish child. No one will ever help you. You have been very naughty, and naughty children are whipped!" Miss Harmon's face twisted in a spasm of hatred.

"No! No, Miss Harmon! I won't do it again!"

"I'm sure you won't. We have given you a good place here, Kitty. Many little girls from The Lanes would be glad to have a warm fire to sleep by, and good food to eat, but you have been ungrateful. You have betrayed our trust, and that is a dreadful fault. You have done badly, and bad girls are punished. Madam?"

The Madam took up the oil lamp and opened a cubbyhole in the panels over Miss Harmon's ornate desk, from which she withdrew a limber riding crop and a length of twine. Then she led the way as Miss Harmon pulled Kitty up the stairs. The girls downstairs shuddered as Kitty's shrieks were heard throughout the house. She was dragged up the stairs, through the secret door, into the attic where Alicia waited, shivering in her drawers and camisole.

This time Madam Gurney was taking no chances. She rattled the door first, then flung it open before Alicia could spring. Alicia ran right into Miss Harmon's waiting arms. Miss Harmon held the girl tightly while the Madam set down the lamp, took the cord, and bound Kitty's hands hard to one of the ominous hooks set into the wall.

Miss Harmon grabbed Alicia's curls and pinioned her head so that she could not turn away. "Watch!" Miss Harmon hissed, holding Alicia's head steady. "This is what happens to naughty children! I can't hurt you, can't mark your pretty white skin, little Miss Marbury, because the French gentlemen don't like it, but I can mark up this friend of yours, and you will watch!"

"No, I won't!" Alicia screamed. She struggled in Miss Harmon's arms, her red hair flying about her. The older woman was jerked back and forth as she tried to hold her down. Madam Gurney wasted no time watching the catfight. Instead she produced the riding crop from her capacious skirts and gave it a few practice whisks.

"Close the door," Miss Harmon ordered. "Too much noise there!"

The padding around the doorjamb muffled the sounds of battle. Alicia thrashed helplessly in Miss Harmon's iron grip. Kitty wailed piteously as Madam laid on the strokes against her shoulders, leaving angry red welts. Only when Kitty's screams had become muffled sobs and Alicia stopped kicking did Miss Harmon and Mrs. Gurney cease their efforts. Alicia was flung to the floor, and Kitty hung by her wrists. Both girls were sobbing, one in fury, the other in pain.

"Bring 'er down?" Madam asked.

Miss Harmon shook her head and gathered up her auburn hair, which had come undone in her struggle. "Too late. The gentlemen are coming in. Leave them be. They aren't going anywhere . . . not tonight."

The Madam laughed nastily and picked up the lamp. "Sweet dreams," she commented, laughing coarsely.

The door closed, and Alicia could hear the key being turned in the lock. The two girls were left alone together in the dark room, lit dimly by the reflection of the gaslights from the street coming through the round window.

Alicia was the first to move. She edged carefully over to Kitty.

"I'm so sorry," she said through her tears. She fumbled at the cord, trying to undo the knots. "You went to the policeman, and they hurt you, and it's my fault. I'm so sorry." Her fingers picked at the cord.

"I could'a' kep' quiet," Kitty said.

"You could have," Alicia agreed. "It's all right, though. Maybe, if you could lift your hands, I could get these knots out."

Kitty stretched out, stifling a yelp of pain. Alicia felt the cords give.

"That fat woman thought I couldn't get out, but I will," she muttered. "Bertram once tied me up at Waltham and left me in the Haunted Tower, but I got out anyway."

A burning hatred began to grow within her. Her O'Connell ancestors would have recognized the sensation at once: a deep-seated rage against injustice that would not be satisfied until the perpetrators were brought to book and all hurts were avenged.

With one last effort, Alicia managed to free her friend. Kitty dropped to the floor and lay quietly. Alicia began to feel about on the floor.

"Wot's that yer doin'?" Kitty asked.

"When Miss Harmon was fighting with me, I think her back hair came down," Alicia said. "I thought I heard some hairpins fall out. In the story I read in *The Boy's Own Paper*, Prince Frederick was imprisoned by his evil, usurping uncle in a tower, and he got out by picking the lock of his prison. If I can find a hairpin, I can pick the lock, and get downstairs and find a dress, and then I can get out and get you to a doctor, and . . . "

"Miss Harmon said you told lies," Kitty sniffled.

"Miss Harmon tells lies herself," Alicia maintained stoutly. "She said that nasty old man was Mr. Dodgson, and I don't think my papa would have sent me to a person who smells bad and brings me to this place." Alicia scratched about under the bed. Her fingers clutched her prize. "Got it!" she crowed. "Now all I have to do is straighten it . . . "

Kitty resumed her original thought. "Miss 'Armon ain't lyin' about France. There's a French comes 'ere sometimes, an' girls go wiv 'im."

"But I do not wish to go to France!" Alicia cried out. "I've only just started with Mam'zelle! I don't know any French!"

"Don't matter to 'im," Kitty said. "Miss, if you could 'elp me, I could get up on the bed."

Alicia braced herself as Kitty pulled up from the floor. The two girls lurched across the room and fell onto the bed together.

"I have the hairpin, and I'm going to get us out of here—you and me—and then we'll see who tells lies!" Alicia said breathlessly.

She felt her way across the floor and over to the door. She had never picked a lock before, but she had never failed to do exactly what she said she would do. In the dim light from the window, she set about her task. One way or another, she was going to get out of this prison!

It took somewhat longer than she had anticipated.

The story in *The Boy's Own Paper* had made it seem quite simple: One found a long, sharp metal object (say, a hairpin) and inserted it into the lock. Then one turned, juggled, jiggled, and presto—freedom!

In actuality, Alicia discovered, hairpins were not the all-purpose tool they had been advertised. Miss Harmon's hairpin was of the easily bent, narrow sort, perfect for holding up fine-spun hair, not particularly good as a lockpick. Working mostly by touch was frustrating, and starlight was inadequate to the occasion, she decided, as she tried to peer through the keyhole. What she really needed was a lamp . . . and a proper lockpick . . . and some supper. Alicia had never before been really cold or hungry. Now she was both, and she did not care for the sensation.

Kitty had managed to fall asleep on the bed. Alicia heard her snuffles and snores. Well, she thought, I shall have to rescue both of us. Papa always said the lower orders needed guidance; here was the proof. Kitty had put herself in Alicia's hands and it was up to Alicia to take care of her.

Alicia applied herself once again to her task. With or without light, cold or warm, hungry or fed, Alicia Marbury was not going to remain in any room where she did not wish to be!

There was a sudden *click* and the doorknob moved under her

hand. The door opened, revealing the narrow stairs that led to yet another closed door. Alicia cast a glance at the sleeping Kitty, then thought hard.

Kitty had alerted the police. That meant they were looking for her. So far, so good, but she could not go running about the streets of a strange place in her drawers and camisole. Nor could she get help for Kitty if she was taken up as a lunatic (the lunatic in the story in *The Boy's Own Paper* ran about in her shift) and clapped into the Asylum (another favorite prison in her favorite clandestine publication). Clearly, the most important thing she could do right now was to get decent clothing, so that she could remove herself and Kitty from this place as soon as there was light enough to see by. Then, properly dressed and identified, she could wreak her vengeance on those who had imprisoned her. It sounded like a good plan, and Alicia crept down the stairs to attack the secret door and put it into action.

On the other side of the door, business was brisk at Miss Harmon's. Several eminent and respectable gentlemen had presented themselves, given Miss Harmon their bona fides, and been allowed to escort the young ladies upstairs. The Madam pocketed the bills and coins discreetly, while Miss Harmon dispensed tea and biscuits in the parlor. The atmosphere was almost homelike; none of the vulgarity of Church Street here. None of these girls could possibly be harboring a vile disease, or hiding a blackmailing pimp in a cupboard. Any of the gentlemen who had ideas of disturbing the tranquility of the atmosphere were quickly deterred by Madge Gurney, who was as muscular as any male bouncer, and twice as terrifying. Miss Harmon's was safe, clean, and reasonably priced. What more could a seeker of very green fruit wish?

By the time Alicia had mastered the lock of the secret panel, it was nearly midnight. Every one of the bedrooms was occupied, and there were several gentlemen down in the parlor who had either completed their mission or were waiting their turn.

Alicia saw a tall girl leave one bedroom, just as a plump, fair one went into another with a stout man in evening clothes. The empty bedroom seemed to be the obvious place to begin her search for clothing, even though the dark girl was a good two inches taller than she. At least she could find something to cover Kitty with in the bedroom.

With that, Alicia eased out of the secret door and tiptoed into the hall. Before she could reach the empty bedroom, she heard footsteps. Someone coming! She grabbed for the nearest door, opened it, and stared, appalled.

She saw a bed, and on the bed lay the blond girl, with a fat man on top of her, his huge buttocks moving up and down, while he grunted and panted and wheezed. The blond girl's eyes were closed; her face looked blank, as if she were imagining something quite far away from what was happening to her.

Alicia could not even scream. She gazed at the sight, horrified yet fascinated. The blond girl's eyes opened and caught hers. "Go away," the blond girl mouthed. The man didn't seem to know anything. His attention was entirely on what he was doing to the girl.

He let out a high-pitched squeal. Alicia echoed it.

The man was jolted out of his self-induced trance. He heaved himself off the blond girl, so that Alicia could view his entire frontal display: red face, white shirtfront, bulging bare belly, and something damp dangling below. She backed out of the doorway, looking for a means of escape. Back down the hall, to the attic? Unthinkable! There were the stairs—she forgot her clothing, or lack of it. In a mad panic, she darted down the stair, still shrieking with horror at what she had just seen.

The cozy mood of Miss Harmon's parlor was shattered by her entrance. The waiting gentlemen were startled out of their wits by this howling creature with red hair flying in all directions, scampering about in her drawers and camisole. Miss Harmon nearly dropped a teacup. The doors upstairs opened as Gertie, Lizzie, and Susanne and their partners for the moment emerged to see what was going on. In the parlor, Helen and Deb started to giggle nervously as the gentlemen rose and sought the door.

Alicia was totally unaware of the disturbance she was causing. She grabbed the closest girl, who happened to be Victoria, and yelled, "There's a man upstairs—"

164

"I know," Vicky said, trying to evade Alicia's thrashing arms.

"He made noises!"

"It's all right, that's the way they do." Victoria had no idea who this creature was, but she was adept at soothing the new girls into accepting the nasty things that went with the fine clothes and good food at Miss Harmon's.

"But . . . " Alicia screamed again. Mrs. Gurney appeared in the doorway of the parlor.

"Wot? *How* . . . ?" She took in the sight of Alicia on the loose and Miss Harmon petrified and made the decision: "Get 'er!"

Helen whooped happily and gave chase, with Deb right behind her. Lizzie dodged around Madam, getting tangled up in the large woman's larger bustle, while two gentlemen edged around them to get out of what had become a madhouse.

Alicia darted around the room, looking for a way out, clambering over chairs and sofa, upsetting the tea tray in her flight. Helen hopped after her. Gertie took in the scene, then launched herself after the runaway who had interrupted her best customer. Alicia evaded both of them by careening off the small table that held the prize aspidistra in the front window. The plant crashed to the floor, sending potting soil in all directions over the Oriental carpet. Two gentlemen who had just arrived suddenly decided to find their amusement elsewhere and departed before anyone could convince them otherwise.

By this time, Vicky and Miss Harmon had recovered their senses. Vicky joined Madam at the door to the parlor, while Miss Harmon followed the last of the gentlemen to the front door, murmuring something about a minor disturbance, and how this did not happen often. She returned to the fray, her face set in grim lines of utter rage and bafflement.

Alicia spied an opening and headed for the parlor door. The other girls were on top of her like a pack of hyenas, clawing and scratching. Madam Gurney's massive form blocked the doorway. Alicia found herself engulfed in black silk and red flannel.

The Madam shook the other girls off Alicia and held her by one arm, while Miss Harmon shut the door behind the last of the night's customers. King Street was now empty, except for two constables trying to look inconspicuous.

The word would get out. There would be no more business tonight. She turned back to Alicia.

"Upstairs," Miss Harmon gasped. The Madam grimly hauled Alicia back up the stairs, through the hall, up the secret stair and into the attic room. This time she tied her firmly to the bedpost, and shook Kitty awake.

"Downstairs, you!" Madam snarled. "Your mate just destroyed the parlor. There's work for yer to do, and it's 'er fault!" Kitty was dragged off to clean the parlor, leaving Alicia breathless, alone, and more frightened than she had ever been in her short life.

The parlor was in a shambles. Teacups had been overturned and smashed, and shards of china littered the figured carpet, mingling with the dregs of the tealeaves and remains of biscuits. The chairs and ottoman had been overturned in the chase. The aspidistra lay in the ruins of its pot. The girls were hysterical, alternating between curiosity at the new arrival and panic at her wild appearance.

Miss Harmon shouted, "Quiet!"

The hubbub died down.

"That was . . . a new girl," she said, trying to maintain her usual icy calm. Her voice betrayed her, several tones higher than her familiar alto purr. "She is not used to our ways, yet."

"She will be," Helen giggled.

"They're all gone," Mrs. Gurney reported. "And there's coppers outside, taking down names."

Miss Harmon smoothed her hair with a trembling hand. "I shall speak to the constables," she said. "Girls, you may retire. Madge, put out the lights. We are not open for any more business."

"After that ruckus, we'll be lucky to be open at all," the Madam grumbled. A knock at the door proved her wrong.

Madam opened it, reluctantly prepared to deny entry. On the steps were Inspectors Wright and MacRae. "What do you want?" Madam asked truculently.

"We received a complaint," Inspector Wright said smoothly.

"There was some sort of disturbance." He tried to edge his way in.

Madam blocked their way. Miss Harmon behind her said, "One of my young guests had a nightmare, no more. I shall see to it that she does not eat Welsh Rarebit before retiring. Is there anything else, Inspector?"

"I suppose not. Good night, Miss Harmon." The two policemen moved away. Madam slammed the door shut behind them.

The girls straggled up to their bedrooms, still excited by their adventure. Miss Harmon stood in the ruins of her parlor, breathing deeply, struggling visibly to maintain her composure.

Madge came back into the parlor and surveyed the damage. "Give her back," she stated. "This whole venture was a mistake, from the minute the Guv'nor came up with it. Give 'er back, and no questions asked."

Miss Harmon's eyes narrowed to slits. "No," she said.

The Madam shook her head sorrowfully. "Mrs. J. won't like losing the business."

"It's not a matter of business now," Miss Harmon said. "I've gone too far to stop."

"It's not 'er pa, is it?" Madge asked shrewdly. 'Cause if it is, I say, that girl's more trouble than she's worth. Send 'er back to 'er pa—and good riddance!"

"Never!" Miss Harmon declared. "Monsieur LeBrun comes on Monday, and she goes with him."

With that, she stalked out, leaving Madam Gurney to turn down the gaslights and shake her head at the perversity of the modern generation.

CHAPTER 21

Sunday dawned, with its grim reminder that the pleasantest of
British weekends was liable to be dampened. The evening mist
of Saturday had settled into a deadly gray drizzle that shrouded
Brighton's fanciful architecture in wisps of fog and discouraged all
but the hardiest from venturing out onto the Esplanade.

The only diversion permitted on a Sunday morning in Brighton
was religion. Just as Friday and Saturday had been devoted to every
form of secular pleasure, so now visitors to Brighton could take their
pick of spiritual refreshment. Church of England, Church of Rome,
various dissenting sects were all ready to provide the antidote to the
previous evening's gaiety with a good dose of piety. The miserable
weather only added to the agreeable sensation of martyrdom for
those who sought their release from worldly cares in the environs of
holy ground.

Among those hardy souls abroad before the fashionable hour of
eleven o'clock in the morning was Mr. Dodgson, who marched down
the Queen's Road to Dr. Doyle's lodgings with purposeful strides.
He had already been to the early service in St. Peter's, conducted not
by the Reverend Mr. Barclay but by one of his visiting guests. There

he had prayed for guidance, and, as always, his Maker had not failed him. He was refreshed, physically and mentally, and ready to resume his quest.

To this end, Mr. Dodgson knocked at Mrs. Keene's door and demanded to see Dr. Doyle.

The landlady led Mr. Dodgson to the back dining room, where Dr. Doyle was at breakfast in his shirtsleeves, with Touie across the table from him in her tartan traveling dress.

Dr. Doyle got up hastily, still holding his teacup. "Mr. Dodgson! I am surprised . . . " he began.

Touie was more gracious. "Do sit down, Mr. Dodgson, and have some more tea."

" 'I've had nothing yet, so I can't take more,' " Mr. Dodgson quoted from one of his more celebrated scenes. "But I thank you, Mrs. Doyle. Doctor, I owe you an apology. I can only say in my defense that last night I was—"

"—No, no, sir, it was my fault. I had not made allowances for your age and condition," Dr. Doyle stammered, rushing to set out a chair for his visitor. "I should never have insisted that you accompany me to that . . . "

"No, Dr. Doyle, it is I who was pusillanimous. There is no other word for it. My courage quite deserted me."

"Gentlemen," Touie said sweetly, but firmly, "please sit down. Arthur, you did take Mr. Dodgson to a most disreputable street, where he might have been subject to all sorts of indignities. As for you, Mr. Dodgson, perhaps you were too vehement with Arthur, who, after all, is trying to help you find that child. Now, can I give you a cup of tea?"

The two men looked sheepishly at each other, then sat down and allowed Touie to pour for them.

"I came immediately after the early service," Mr. Dodgson said. "Of course, I will be glad to accompany you to the later one." He looked expectantly at his two young friends.

Touie looked at her teacup. It was for Dr. Doyle to explain: "I'm afraid Touie and I are not churchgoers, sir."

"Oh my, yes. You will, of course, go to the Romish church."

"I was brought up as a Catholic," Dr. Doyle admitted. "But over the years, I've had grave doubts, Mr. Dodgson. Let us say, my faith has been tested severely. But this is not why you came to us, is it? Simply to patch up a quarrel between what are, after all, mere acquaintances? As you so rightly told me last night," he added.

Mr. Dodgson inclined his head gravely. "Quite right, Dr. Doyle. I have spent some time going over this problem, or rather, problems. You and I have been pursuing one half of the equation, the disappearance of Miss Marbury. The death of the nurserymaid, Mary Ann, is, presumably, connected to that. So is the death of the actor, Keeble. It is this aspect of the case that I wish to follow today. And I assume you will wish to accompany me. In fact," he added shyly, "I may need your support, if we encounter any more persons such as those who accosted us yesterday."

Dr. Doyle buttered a piece of toast and munched on it. "I don't see where that will lead us."

Mr. Dodgson's voice took on the singsong quality of a teacher instructing a particularly dense pupil. "What do we know of the man who left his marks on Keeble?" he asked rhetorically.

"How do you know it was a man?" Touie put in.

"Keeble was of my own height and build, and I am not as short as I may seem," Mr. Dodgson said. "Unless she is a veritable giantess, I doubt that a woman could have lifted him over the railings of the Chain Pier, which have been built quite high enough to prevent such accidents from occurring. Also, the button was one used in male attire. I realize that some women have taken to wearing manly waistcoats when engaged in sports such as riding or bicycling, but neither horse nor bicycle was on the pier that night. If so, it would most certainly have drawn notice."

"So," Dr. Doyle said, warming to the task, "we are looking for a man, probably of average height or higher."

"Oh, taller than average," Mr. Dodgson corrected him. "And strong in the arms and upper body, to lift Keeble over the railings."

"Wearing a brown suit," Dr. Doyle added. "The button was brown, not blue or black. And if the man were in evening clothes, there would not be a button at all, but a white stud from his evening dress."

"Very good," Mr. Dodgson said approvingly.

"What's more," Dr. Doyle added, "we know that he is a gentleman, or at least, not a mechanic or farmer."

Mr. Dodgson raised an eyebrow in interrogation.

"The dents on his collar," Dr. Doyle explained. "They did not show any discoloration. A person who worked with his hands would have left a stain or smudge, as a farmer would have earth on his hands, or a blacksmith would have ashes."

"Aha!" Mr. Dodgson said with a decisive nod. "So: We have a tall gentleman, in a brown suit, on the Chain Pier at approximately nine o'clock of a Friday night."

"Nine?" Touie asked.

"I have consulted a chart as to the tides. According to our friends at the police station, the body was able to drift onto the shingle because it was thrown over at the low tide. If the tide were going out, the body would have been swept out to sea, and Keeble would simply have been one of those unfortunate persons who disappear, never to be seen again."

"Did you know the man?" Touie asked sympathetically.

"I have seen him on the Esplanade," Mr. Dodgson said. "I also may have seen him play in London. I enjoy the theater," he confessed.

Dr. Doyle set down his cup. "So, how do you propose to find his killer? Assuming, as we are, that the man did not merely stumble into the sea fully dressed, clutching a button."

Mr. Dodgson leaned earnestly over the table. "Dr. Doyle, I have come here with the purpose of requesting that you join me in this endeavor. I am, perhaps, not as fit as I once was, and a younger man might be better equipped to run about after villains."

Dr. Doyle smiled under his mustache. "Indeed, sir, I was thinking that I could not make head nor tail of this nonsense, and that I would have to rely on the police to finish the business for us."

"Hm! The police!" Mr. Dodgson sniffed. "They persist in regarding both these deaths as unconnected accidents. I do not believe that these two deaths are either accidents or unconnected with Miss Marbury's disappearance, and I am going to prove it—with your strong arm to assist me."

"Not another stroll down Church Street," Dr. Doyle warned him.

"Not at all. You and I, Dr. Doyle, must go out to the Esplanade and find Keeble's friends, the members of his troupe. I dare say they are having some sort of memorial for him, as is the custom of such people. We must question them and find out who, if anyone, contacted Keeble. He was supposed to have been performing that night. It follows that one of the troupe might have seen the person who owns that button."

"But who was that someone?" Dr. Doyle was on his feet, looking for his coat and deerstalker cap.

"I have considered that, too," Mr. Dodgson said. "Someone must have hired him to impersonate me."

"And you suspect that this mysterious someone then fought with him and threw him over the rails to the sea below . . . "

"Where he drowned, fuddled by drink," Mr. Dodgson finished for him. "If Keeble recognized something particular about his employer . . . "

"And tried to blackmail him . . . " Dr. Doyle took up the thread again.

"It is very possible." Mr. Dodgson looked favorably upon his new student. "Now we must ascertain if any of the troupe saw Keeble in conversation with a gentleman, in a brown suit, on the pier on Friday night."

"And then what?" Dr. Doyle looked about him for his deerstalker. Touie handed it to him fondly.

"You need not worry about me, Arthur," she said. "I shall remain here and write some letters. Just find that little girl, and bring her back here safely."

"Of course, my dear," Dr. Doyle said, pressing her hand to his lips.

"And do be careful," Touie called out, as the pair left the lodgings and turned their steps to the seafront.

172

The Esplanade was virtually deserted. The wind whipped the waves into curls of white foam that broke over the pebbled beach with a hiss and a roar. The hotels had put up canvas awnings to shield the verandas from the rain that would wreak havoc with rattan furniture or satin upholstery. The band shell was deserted; no musician would risk harm either to his instrument or his person on such a morning.

The only person in sight was a stout man in a Mackintosh coat with a pile of handbills in a sack slung around his shoulder, who looked as if he wished he were anywhere but on the Esplanade in the rain at nine in the morning of a Sunday, when anyone with any sense was in bed, at breakfast, or in church.

Mr. Dodgson crossed the King's Road resolutely, and descended gingerly down the slippery wooden stairs to the shingle below. To Dr. Doyle's surprise, the elderly scholar moved carefully down the beach, peering under the arches of the underpinning of the Esplanade.

"Good morning," Mr. Dodgson called out to someone under the piers.

"Hello." Dr. Doyle nearly stumbled on the stones in his haste to keep up with his companion.

Mr. Dodgson had found friends, three girls and a boy, ages between eight and ten, as far as Dr. Doyle could judge. The children were dressed in patched cast-offs, but they seemed cheerful, with none of the pinched look of the habitually hungry.

"It is a morning for ducks," Mr. Dodgson remarked. "I see you have found a dry spot. May I join you?"

"Suit yourself." The boy appeared to be the spokesperson for the group.

Mr. Dodgson drew the bag of sweets from his pocket. "I have heard," he said, "that lemon drops are a sovereign remedy for damp. Because they are so dry, you see," he explained.

"Dunno about that," the tallest girl said, taking the offered sweet.

"A pity about the rain," Mr. Dodgson said.

"Ay," the boy agreed.

"No punters out," Dr. Doyle put in. The children ignored him.

Mr. Dodgson smiled at the youngest girl. "I have seen you on the pier," he said. "You do acrobatics."

The girl smiled, revealing a gap where her two front teeth were missing. Then she bent backwards, flipped onto her hands, and circled Mr. Dodgson, her skirts hanging about her ears and her red drawers outstandingly visible. She flipped back onto her feet and took a bow.

Mr. Dodgson applauded. "Very clever, my dear. I do hope you continue to improve yourself. Girls are often able to get work in the circus, even in London."

"Ah," said the middle girl, wisely. "Lunnon. Pa says when the Brighton season's over, we may try our hand at Lunnon."

Dr. Doyle fidgeted. Why did the man take so long to get to the point?

Mr. Dodgson had taken the silk handkerchief from his pocket and was tying it into various shapes, to the delight of the children.

"You should do that on the pier," the boy observed. "You'd make a nice penny from that."

"Oh, dear me, no," Mr. Dodgson said. "I just like to amuse children. I could never be a professional, like, oh—let me see? Who does those tricks on the pier?"

"Old Keeble used to," the smallest girl piped up. "But he's dead. They found him on the beach yesterday."

"Drunk," the boy said succinctly. "My ma says it's drink as does you, every time. Made my pa sign the Pledge when the Salvationists came 'round."

"My pa says that's all rot," the middle girl stated. "He likes his pint, but he don't go off like Old Keeble and blue the lot."

"I believe I knew Old Keeble," Mr. Dodgson observed. "Wasn't he with the Bailey Boys?"

The oldest girl laughed heartily. "Not Old Keeble! You're thinking of the Jokers. They're down by the Chain Pier every night."

"Indeed." Mr. Dodgson put away the candy and the handkerchief. "I wonder, would they be performing today?"

"In this slop?" The boy was scornful. "They'll be down the beach, along with my pa and the rest of 'em, giving the old boy a good sendoff."

"Would you direct me to the place? As a patron of the art of busking, I would like to pay my respects."

"Come on, then. We only came out to get out of the way." The boy led Mr. Dodgson and the rest back along the beach toward the Chain Pier.

To Dr. Doyle's surprise, the children ducked under the shorings of the Esplanade, to a sort of cave that had been left when the construction had been completed.

Here, only a step away from the fashionable world, a makeshift tavern had been set up, where the Sabbath laws were cheerfully being broken by a crowd of actors, singers, acrobats, jugglers, and comic players. A rough plank table held bottles of beer and stronger stimulants, together with an assortment of glasses and mismatched mugs for dispensing of same. A short, balding man with enormous ears and a snaggle-toothed grin served the liquor, spicing his talk with a series of anecdotes. There was a dead silence as the company realized that a stranger was in their midst.

"Someone wants to pay respects to Old Keeble," the boy announced, in the sudden hush that descended at the sight of Mr. Dodgson and Dr. Doyle.

The trumpet player of Keeble's troupe stared at the tall, stooping scholar and his tweed-clad companion. "Dang me, for a minute there I thought you was him come back to haunt us!"

"Dear me," Mr. Dodgson said. "I had no idea the resemblance was so . . . so marked."

"Sit down, sir, and 'ave a pint on Old Keeble," the trumpeter said. "I'm the Joker, Joker Jim, you can call me." He slapped a measure of beer in front of Mr. Dodgson, who picked it up and set it down without tasting it.

"Old Keeble seems to have come into money," Mr. Dodgson observed.

"We found nine quid in his pockets," Billy, the comic genius of the troupe, said. "What better way of spending it than on a right

175

blowout? He can't use it where he's gone." There was a general laugh at that.

"Nine pounds? A veritable fortune," Mr. Dodgson said. "You must be doing quite well, for such a sum to come to him."

Joker Jim sat down at the table across from Mr. Dodgson. "Now that's the odd thing," he said, twisting his rubbery features into a grimace of perplexity. "We were doing well enough, but I did wonder about that nine quid. Y'see, Old Keeble had been talking on and on about his being on the stage, and how we didn't really appreciate his genius. And how there was some Nob who did, and were we going to be surprised some day."

"Any idea who this Nob was?" Dr. Doyle could not suppress himself any longer. Joker Jim shrugged.

"No idea. Old Keeble was getting past it," he said. "I thought I saw him on the pier, just before our turn Friday. Hey, Billy!" Billy squeezed out of the crowd. "Didn't you tell me you saw Old Keeble Friday night?"

"I did," Billy agreed. "Talking to some gent, he was, up on the pier."

"A gentleman?" Dr. Doyle pounced on the phrase. "Then, I suppose, this gentleman was in evening clothes."

"You mean soup-and-fish? B'iled shirt and tailcoat?" Billy shook his head. "Nay, 'e wore a sack suit."

"Brown?" Dr. Doyle hinted.

"Couldn't tell the color. But 'e sounded like a gent, all smooth and polished. Careful in 'is speech, like."

"Then you could hear what they were saying?" Mr. Dodgson leaned forward.

"Not the words, exactly," Billy said ruefully. "But I could 'ear they was angry."

"I don't suppose you could perform that scene," Mr. Dodgson said wistfully. "I have seen you, down at the pier. You have a gift, young man, a most interesting gift." He turned to Dr. Doyle. "This young man can mimic any voice, once heard. Very clever."

Billy's narrow chest puffed out slightly under the weight of public approval. "It was like this." He sprang up on the table, enacting first the old actor, then the Nob. "Keeble was against the rails, and the gent, he was in front of him."

"Did you see him go over?" Dr. Doyle asked eagerly.

"Nay. Jimmy called me over, and we were on."

"Did you hear any of the quarrel?" Mr. Dodgson continued.

Billy shook his head. "But if I know Old Keeble, he was putting the bite on the gent. That was his way; he owed all of us, one way or another."

"That's why we're making him pay for drinks now," Joker Jim said with a laugh. The rest of the company roared their agreement.

Mr. Dodgson produced some coins from his waistcoat pocket and lay them on the table. "I wish to offer my condolences on the loss of so valuable a member of your troupe," he said politely. Joker Jim snatched up one of the coins skillfully, tossed it in the air, and caught it.

"And you're a right one," he said. "Not like that other lot that come in here. We wouldn't have a word with them! Bloody Peelers!"

"Indeed." Mr. Dodgson rose, touched his hat, and moved toward the door. "One more thing: Mr. . . . Billy? Would you recognize this gentleman if you were to encounter him again?"

"You mean, could I point him out? D'ye think he's the one did for Old Keeble?"

"It is very likely," Dr. Doyle told him.

Joker looked around the room. "We take care of our own, sir."

"I'm sure you do," Mr. Dodgson said. "But, in the event, would you assist me in apprehending this . . . this murderer?"

"You mean catch him?" Joker looked around again. "It would do the Peelers in the eye, wouldn't it?"

"They have not been very assiduous in pursuing his killer," Mr. Dodgson observed.

"He means . . . " Dr. Doyle began.

"I know. Old Keeble was just some washed-up old rummy of an actor, not worth the bothering about," Joker Jim said bitterly.

"He was being used in a shameful plot to abduct a child," Mr. Dodgson declared. "He was chosen for his accidental resemblance to myself. For this reason, if for no other, I have sworn to find the man who hired him. If any of you can recall anything—if you have ever seen the man before—try to remember, please?"

He looked about the room. Billy frowned. Then the smallest girl, the child from the beach, said, "I saw Old Keeble with a Nob, once."

"Where?" Dr. Doyle pounced on her.

"On the pier. In front of the Grand Hotel. And there was a lady with him, a lady with red hair."

A woman in a gaudy red bodice and short striped skirt slapped the child resoundingly. "Betty, don't never let me see you with that woman, never!"

"But I didn't say nothing to her!" Betty wailed.

"Don't you even get close enough to look at her, nor her girls!" Betty's protector gave her a shake to punctuate the lesson. "We may be low, but we're not"—she looked at Mr. Dodgson's faintly ecclesiastical dress and paused—"not that low."

Mr. Dodgson sat down again. "My dear Miss Betty," he said, beckoning the child forward. Her mother kept a wary eye on him.

"This is most interesting," Mr. Dodgson said. "This woman, with the red hair. You know her?"

"Know of her," Betty's protector corrected him. "And I wouldn't have nothing to do with her, not for all the tea in China, nor all the gold in the Mint. I think better of myself than to sell my girls to that . . . that . . ."

Mr. Dodgson nodded. "Most commendable, ma'am. This woman—does she have a name?"

Another woman, tall and slender in blue velvet skirt and violet bodice, said, "Harmon. Miss Julia Harmon, she calls herself. And she may parade herself on the pier, but we know what she is, and what her girls are, and none of us would dirty our lips with her name, not in public." The rest of the performers nodded agreement.

"But there are some women who would," Mr. Dodgson murmured.

"Not in the profession," the woman in the blue skirt said indignantly. "As for that place of hers in King Street." She closed her mouth over her opinion, but her eyes spoke eloquently for her.

Mr. Dodgson rose again. He added more coins to the small pile on the table. "Thank you all," he said gently. "You have been extremely helpful. Master Billy," he added, "may I call upon you, if need be? I am beginning to have the inklings of an idea as to the identity of this miscreant, but I may want you to make the final identification."

Joker Jim scooped up the coins before the rest of the company could get to them.

"You're on, Guv'nor," he promised. "Just send word right here, and we're yours for the night."

Mr. Dodgson and Dr. Doyle left the buskers to their wake, and climbed back up to the world of the Esplanade. The drizzle had co-agulated into a definite rain now, sweeping across the pavement in sheets, driven by the wind.

"And what did all that signify?" Dr. Doyle demanded.

Mr. Dodgson smiled at him. "That there is a house in King Street where a respectable woman will not permit her daughters to be seen," he said. "I believe we may now approach the police with what we have discovered. If Miss Marbury is still in Brighton, the likelihood is that she is being kept in that house."

179

CHAPTER 22

Through the rain Mr. Dodgson and Dr. Doyle plodded to John Street, where the constables on the day shift were marching down the steps, off to do their duty directing the carriages in and out of the roads leading to the major religious edifices. It would never do for the visitors to St. Peter's, or St. Michael's, or the venerable St. Nicholas Church to be trapped in traffic, and so miss the most important part of the Sunday morning ritual: the display of one's finery for the delectation and envy of other visitors to Brighton. The constabulary had been provided with new Mackintosh overcoats as protection against the elements. Dr. Doyle began to wish that he had taken similar precautions.

Mr. Dodgson, on the other hand, seemed to be impervious to either cold or damp. He strode resolutely onward, past the disconsolate man on the Esplanade vainly waving his handbills and hoarsely announcing the "Great Protestation Meeting tomorrow night"; past the winkle sellers in their booths, staring blankly at the downpour; past the well-dressed ladies and gentlemen who were being handed into their carriages for the requisite appearance at the eleven o'clock service at St. Peter's Church.

180

Dr. Doyle followed his mentor as they tramped across the Marine Parade, up the hill, and into the side street that led to the police station.

"I thought we were going to King Street," he puffed out, as soon as he caught up with the indefatigable Mr. Dodgson.

"We are," Mr. Dodgson told him. "However, we are not going without some sort of reinforcements. I shall give the police one last chance to do their duty, before we have to do it for them."

He settled his top hat more firmly on his head and braved the winds once more, being blown up the steps to the police station.

Once inside, it was Sergeant Hartley who recognized the pair. "Back again, eh?" he greeted them.

"As you see," Dr. Doyle said, shaking the rain off his hat.

"No more corpses for you to anatomize," Hartley said. "The gal and the old busker're remanded until the Coroner's inquest. That long drink of water what calls himself Upshaw's been and gone, made a mort of fuss about getting the gal back to her own village in Derbyshire."

"Ah, yes. I had wondered about our Mr. Upshaw," Mr. Dodgson said. "Do you know when he came for that poor girl?"

Hartley scratched his head. "Don't see what business it is of yours."

"I only wondered if he were still in Brighton," Mr. Dodgson mused. "You see, his employer, Lord Richard Marbury, is expected in Brighton for the protestation rally tomorrow, and I thought Mr. Upshaw might still be about, so that my friend, Mr. Barclay, might consult with him about the, um . . . the . . . "

"Arrangements," Dr. Doyle put in. "Seating, police protection, that sort of thing."

Mr. Dodgson smiled benignly at Sergeant Hartley. The sergeant shrugged. "I can go and find out," he offered.

"No matter, no matter," Mr. Dodgson murmured. "We really wished to speak to your Inspector Wright. Is he about?"

"I'll see." Hartley stamped up the stairs to Inspector Wright's private office, where the Brighton and London police were sharing a late morning cup of tea.

Wright had donned his Sunday black suit, appropriate for his mood this gloomy morning. MacRae was still in his checked suit, with a clean shirt and collar and a grim expression on his face. Neither of the two men was pleased with the previous night's activities and their aftermath.

Wright was almost grateful when Sergeant Hartley interrupted them.

"May I have a word, sir?" Hartley asked,.

"You're having it," Wright said. "What is it, Hartley?"

"It's that precious pair again," Hartley announced, in tones of vast exasperation. "Dodgson and Doyle."

Inspector Wright sighed. Last night's debacle had yielded the names of several gentlemen of impeccable reputation, most of whom were visitors to Brighton and most of whom would kick up all sorts of row if their peccadillos were made public. Somewhere around midnight the constables on watch had come to him with the news that there had been some sort of fuss inside the house, but all was quiet by the time Inspector Wright could muster his troops. He and MacRae had not been allowed into the house. The door had been slammed unceremoniously and contemptuously in his face.

He had no desire for another bout with Miss Harmon until and unless he was on thoroughly firm legal ground. As it was, neither he nor Inspector MacRae could make an arrest on any charge under the present laws. It was not a crime to patronize a brothel and the borough of Brighton was not about to antagonize its most influential visitors by dragging them into the Magistrate's Court on such specious evidence.

Once the disturbance had died down and the lights were put out, the house on King Street was quiet. There was no reason for anyone to remain watching the place. Inspector Wright had accompanied Inspector MacRae to his modest lodgings and gone back to his own little flat, a two-room suite over a barber shop in North Street.

Wright had had plans for this weekend, which did not include either protestation meetings or searches for missing children. All those plans were now cast aside, thanks to little Miss Marbury and her sanctimonious parent. He scowled at Hartley, stroked his mustache, and watched MacRae drinking his tea.

Inspector MacRae had not revised his opinion of Brighton or its constabulary. He put Wright down as a time-server, a sucker-up to the higher-ups and a squasher of the lowly. The Harmon woman had been warned, and the most logical suspects were right there in the John Street Police Station. MacRae wondered how long it would take to find the missing child, and when he could get back to London, where he knew which of his comrades was on the take, and for how much.

MacRae was as soured as Wright on the amateurs who were taking over his case. Dodgson he put down as a meddling old codger, and Doyle was one of those nuisances who thought they knew more than the police about how to conduct an investigation into a crime. And now here they were again, barging in where they were neither wanted nor needed.

"What's on their minds?" Wright asked with a grimace.

"They said, the protestation meeting," Hartley stated.

Inspector MacRae shook his head. "Not the Edinburgh man," he said flatly. "A shilling says they're still on the trail of that girl."

Inspector Wright sat down again, a hint of a smile lurking under his mustache. "Bring them up, Sergeant," he ordered.

MacRae leaned forward. "What are you up to, Wright?"

Wright tapped the side of his nose and leaned back in his chair. When Mr. Dodgson arrived, with Dr. Doyle behind him, Inspector Wright rose and indicated that Mr. Dodgson should take the only unoccupied seat in the office.

"I have information," the scholar stated, once these amenities had been satisfied. "I have discovered . . . "

"That there is a house in King Street, an establishment run by a Miss Julia Harmon," Inspector Wright finished for him.

"Then you know about this . . . this establishment?" Mr. Dodgson's eager expression turned to one of peevish exasperation.

"Oh, come now, Mr. Dodgson, we're not as slow as they make us out in the newspapers. Of course we knew about it. In fact, we've had the place under observation for some time."

"And?" Mr. Dodgson leaned forward.

"And, except for a large number of male callers, there is nothing we can charge the inhabitants of that house with," Inspector Wright said.

Dr. Doyle broke in: "Surely, there are borough ordinances about running a, well, disorderly house?"

"Trouble is, the house wasn't disorderly," Inspector Wright said with a sigh. "No trouble, not a peep out of anyone in the street. We can't just go into a private house without cause. An Englishman's home . . ."

" . . . is his castle. I know the old saw," Dr. Doyle said.

Mr. Dodgson frowned. "I see your dilemma," he said finally. "However, suppose a private person, such as myself, were to swear out a complaint against the inhabitants of the establishment?"

"You'd have to have good cause," Inspector Wright said gloomily.

"Ah. Suppose, for the sake of argument, that I were to discover that a child was being held there against her will?"

"If you can find her, you'll do better than we did," MacRae put in. "We were in that house and searched it from top to bottom."

"Including the kitchens?" Dr. Doyle asked.

"And the upper story," Inspector Wright said.

"Most interesting," Mr. Dodgson murmured to himself.

"You aren't planning a visit to that house yourself, are you?" MacRae asked. "Because the lady of the house is a very knowing one. She was onto me before I even set foot in the door."

Mr. Dodgson frowned slightly. "Now, there you surprise me," he commented. "Dr. Doyle and myself were followed from the railway station and pursued through the streets, then accosted in front of this very building and warned off, as the sporting men have it. When, I wonder, did Miss Harmon discover that a representative of Scotland Yard was in Brighton?"

"Had to have been between the time we arrived and eight o'clock last night," MacRae said.

"And who told her?" Dr. Doyle asked pugnaciously. "There must be a spy among your men, Inspector. According to the *Pall Mall Gazette*, Mrs. Jeffries and her ilk have minions in every police station, providing them with information, letting them know when raids are planned."

"Dr. Doyle!" Inspector Wright stood up in righteous wrath. "How dare you imply that my men are in the pay of criminal elements!"

"I can think of no other way that Inspector MacRae's presence should be known to Miss Harmon," Dr. Doyle insisted. "No one else knew who or what he was, except the police, and not many of them, either."

"Not necessarily," MacRae said, anxious to clear his colleague's good name. "There was you, and that Upshaw fellow, and Lord Richard and that Kinsale chap—any one of them could have sent a telegram ahead, alerting the Harmon woman."

"She could even be on the telephone," Mr. Dodgson put in.

Wright glanced at MacRae. "I didn't see one," MacRae said.

"I don't think that part of Brighton is electrified," Wright commented.

"And both Mr. Kinsale and Mr. Upshaw are at this moment in Brighton," Mr. Dodgson said, returning to the subject at hand. "Harmon . . . Harmon . . . I do believe I know the name. I knew a man named Harmon in Oxford." Mr. Dodgson's eyes were fixed on a vision only he could see. "Gentlemen," he said suddenly, "I propose to pay a call on my old acquaintance, Miss Julia Harmon, this afternoon, after Divine Service."

Inspectors Wright and MacRae stared at him. The Brighton man found his voice first. "You're mad as a March Hare, sir! Why should she let you in at all?"

Mr. Dodgson smiled sweetly. "I knew her father, not to call on, of course, but as a tradesman. I shall tell her that I have heard she is now residing in this vicinity and wish to leave a card. After which, I shall insert myself into the house and discover where Miss Marbury is being held."

"And you think you can do this?" MacRae's expression clearly showed that he doubted Mr. Dodgson's ability to tie his own shoelaces, let alone find a missing child in a house already searched by the police.

"I have promised my friend Mr. Barclay that I would read the lesson at today's service, and there will be dinner afterwards," Mr. Dodgson said. "I can meet with you gentlemen after the service and after dinner, let us say, at two o'clock this afternoon? And then we shall find Miss Marbury."

Mr. Dodgson rose, bowed, and marched back out into the rain. Inspector MacRae looked at his countryman as if to say, It's us Scots against these mad Englishmen. Inspector Wright shook his head.

"I only hope he knows what he's doing."

Dr. Doyle smiled under his mustache. "I'm beginning to think he's sharper than any of us. I can't wait to tell all this to Touie!"

CHAPTER 23

By borough ordinance, all places of refreshment or recreation were closed on Sunday until noon. The sole source of recreation being spiritual, all of Brighton, both resident and transient, took itself to church. Even those visitors whose religious affiliations were vague at best suddenly decided to attend Divine Service at one of the edifices available.

The old town had boasted but one parish church, the venerable St. Nicholas, dedicated to the patron saint of sailors, as well it should in a town whose economic mainstay was the sea. As the town had grown, new churches were added to the roster: the pseudo-Gothic splendor of St. Peter's, the more pedestrian red brick of St. Michael's, and the utilitarian stonework of St. Anselm's. The Society of Friends had built their meetinghouse in The Lanes, where General Booth's Army of Salvation had taken refuge as well. There was even a small set of rooms in one of the old houses behind the Royal Pavilion where various gentlemen of the Hebrew persuasion met daily for prayers and study. In short, Brighton was as eager to provide its visitors with this as with any other diversion.

On this rainy Sunday, with all other places of recreation closed, the fashionable world hied to St. Peter's in carriages or cabs; the less fashionable (and less worldly) walked to the nearest church or chapel (depending on their inclination). Gentlemen wore their severe Sunday suits or frock coats, with high hats or bowlers. Their female counterparts forsook the flowery for the formal, and black silk, black linen, and black bombazine were the order of the day. Hats were the only extravagance, exploiting the flowers of the field and the birds of the air to stunning effect. Only the unmarried daughters of the respectable burgesses of Brighton and their even more respectable guests could do pastels: peach, cornflower blue, pale straw, or ivory lace. Necks and arms, bared for the evening, were modestly covered during the church services, no matter how warm the temperature within.

Today, there was no danger of heat stroke. Most of the congregants were perfectly happy to don shawls, coats, and jackets against the penetrating chill. Whether stone or brick, the churches seemed to shudder with the damp.

The Reverend Mr. Barclay, as the most eminent divine in residence, took the pulpit at St. Peter's Church. He looked out at the congregation, and wondered if they were prepared for his sermon. He had tried to be careful, but there was no getting around his topic. Sin was rampant in Brighton, and Sin must be cast out!

Behind him, Mr. Dodgson followed the service carefully. He stepped up to the lectern at the appropriate moment, conscious of his tendency to stammer in moments of stress. He must speak slowly and carefully, lest he subject not only himself but his host to ridicule.

" . . . And Jesus said, 'Suffer the little children to come unto me, for theirs is the Kingdom of Heaven,' " Mr. Dodgson pronounced. Was it not the very text he had quoted in his letter of protest to the Prime Minister? Was it right, or even proper, to expose the ills of society to the pillars of society? And in the house of God? "Here endeth the lesson."

Mr. Dodgson sat down, still troubled. His friend, Barclay, was a good, honest servant of the Church. He would not defame the Lord's house with evil.

That settled, Mr. Dodgson considered the problem before him as

188

the Divine Service continued around him. He spoke the responses automatically, as he had done for over fifty years. He had the service memorized; he tended to let his mind wander at times. He barely heard the choir as they vigorously attacked "The Heavens Declare the Glory of God" with more panache than finesse.

What bothered him about the whole business, he decided, as Mr. Barclay ponderously took the pulpit and cleared his throat, was the timing of it. Why should Miss Marbury have been abducted in August, when the offensive articles began in July? Who knew that Inspector MacRae was from Scotland Yard, and how could Miss Harmon be notified about it between three and eight o'clock of a Saturday afternoon? Did Miss Harmon have the telephone? And who, of all the possible suspects, could have killed Old Keeble?

Mr. Barclay's voice rambled on. " . . . And, my friends, you may ask me whether it is the place of the Church to lower itself to the level of the persons writing in the public Press. Why, you may ask, should we, who are among the righteous, be concerned with those who are sinners? Women whose very lives are a disgrace and a blot upon the face of this fair city? But I remind you of the words of Our Lord: 'Let him who is without sin cast the first stone.'

"There are those among us, I regret to say, who are all too willing to look the other way, to let Sin run rampant when it puts silver into their pockets. But I tell you, my friends, that in this case, the left hand does not know what the right hand is doing."

"Of course!" Mr. Dodgson said aloud. The deacon on his right stared at him. Mr. Dodgson's eyes shone with a new light. "That must be it!" he told himself. "I must inform Dr. Doyle, and the police." He started to rise. The deacon seated next to him shot him an astonished look of warning. Mr. Dodgson came to his senses and sank back into his chair as the Reverend Barclay reached his conclusion:

" . . . And so, my friends, I urge all of you to attend the protestation meeting tomorrow at six o'clock in the evening, to make your voices heard, and to join in the universal condemnation of these dreadful evils! And let us say, Amen!"

"Amen!" Mr. Dodgson agreed.

"And now," Mr. Barclay said, "let us all sing."

Mr. Dodgson was jolted back to reality by a rustling of feet. He stood with the rest, his reedy voice adding to the chorus.

" 'Abide with me, fast comes the Eventide,' " he sang. Not particularly appropriate for a morning service, he thought. " 'Help of the helpless, Oh, Abide with me.' " Who was more helpless than Alicia Marbury, locked in some cellar or attic. Now, he thought, why did I think of an attic? I do wish I had told Dr. Doyle to reconnoiter for me.

Mr. Dodgson managed to get through the rest of the service in a fever of expectation. He had it, or at least, he knew what had happened. But who—or rather, *which*? That was the problem. He wondered where Dr. Doyle was, then wrenched his mind back to the matter at hand. God first, then Miss Marbury.

Dr. Doyle had taken his wife onto the Esplanade for a stroll. The rain was winding down, becoming a thin drizzle that gave a peculiar sheen to the struts of the Chain Pier, and shimmered on the pebbles of the beach.

Dr. Doyle stared at the waves and then glanced at his faithful bride. "I haven't been very kind to you, Touie," he said apologetically. "This was supposed to be our honeymoon, and I've spent most of it with Mr. Dodgson."

Touie patted his arm and smiled into his face. "Oh, Arthur, you must know that I will support you, whatever you do," she said. "And that poor child."

"Yes, of course," Dr. Doyle said. "According to the police, she is most likely being held in a house on King Street. Mr. Dodgson thinks he can get in there."

"Mr. Dodgson?" Touie suppressed a giggle. "I'm sorry, Arthur, but after last night's adventure, I am most surprised that Mr. Dodgson would go anywhere near such an . . . an establishment."

"He may have some acquaintance—that is, the name of the, um, proprietress is familiar to him," Dr. Doyle said.

"How odd!"

The Chain Pier was before them, glittering in the distilled light. Dr. Doyle and his wife turned their steps onto the pier, where the high tide was lapping at the struts. For a moment, they stood in silence.

"I really should take a look at the place," Dr. Doyle said. "Just to stroll past, you know. King Street isn't far, across the King's Road and across from North Street, where the shops are. But, if you prefer, we can stay on the Marine Parade and watch the people coming down from St. Peter's. It is supposed to be quite a sight, all the riders and carriages."

"I would like to see more of the town," Touie said calmly. "But it might not be a good idea to show too much interest in that particular house. If, as you say, the police have already been there, the people who run that, um, place, may have been alerted. You would not like to put the child into danger, Arthur."

Dr. Doyle nodded. "You are right, as always, Touie," he said. "We shall stroll by, like ordinary people, and not take any particular notice of it. And then we shall go back to our lodgings and have dinner. Mr. Dodgson has asked me to accompany him this afternoon. Touie," he said suddenly. "Do you suppose he might . . . oh, it's too much to ask, but . . . "

"Yes, dear, I think he might read your new novel," Touie said. "Now, Arthur, you must show me this famous house on King Street. I am most curious to see what all the bother is about."

Together they crossed back onto the King's Road, and trudged up the hill, skirting the area known as The Lanes, to North Street, where the famous domes of the Brighton Pavilion dominated the sky.

Behind the railings that kept the curious at bay, workmen were beginning to construct a platform.

"Hello!" Dr. Doyle called out. "What's that for?"

"Protestation meeting tomorra," one of the workers said, punctuating it with a spit. "All sorts coming down for it. I hear General Booth is putting in an appearance. And Lord Richard Marbury."

"Really!" Touie exclaimed. "Arthur, we shall have to attend. I cannot go home without seeing Lord Richard Marbury. Why should you keep all your adventures to yourself?"

"Of course, my dear," Dr. Doyle said. "Perhaps Mr. Barclay will get us good seats. It should be quite a show!"

191

From the Royal Pavilion, North Street ran east to west, across the town. Dr. Doyle and his wife paraded slowly across the street, noting the many shops, now boarded up, closed for the Sabbath rest enjoined upon their owners by borough ordinance. King Street was one of the cross streets between North and Church streets. Dr. Doyle suddenly realized where he and Mr. Dodgson had been the night before.

"So close!" he groaned. "We might have found her last night, if only . . . "

"Hush, Arthur!" Touie patted his arm consolingly. "How could you have known, in the dark? Is that the place? That small house, across the street? It looks quite ordinary."

By day, the green house, jammed between the two shuttered shops, looked as if it were sleeping, waiting for afternoon callers. Dr. Doyle glanced at the house with its gabled facade.

"I shall be able to direct Mr. Dodgson to it," he said. "But I have no idea whether he will be able to get inside. And if he does, what will come of it?"

"Mr. Dodgson will not fail you again," Touie promised, as they wandered back to North Street and the Pavilion.

They joined the exodus from the churches that wended its way across the broad expanse of North Street and onto the Grand Parade, that boulevard that led from the Esplanade to St. Peter's Church. The bells rang out; Divine Service had been read. With souls refreshed, the congregation poured into the watery sunlight.

It would be a relatively fine afternoon. Dr. Doyle spotted Mr. Dodgson on the steps of St. Peter's. He was pulled back by his wife.

"Mr. Dodgson will come for us, to our lodgings," she told him firmly. "I would very much like to have my dinner at Muttons, and have more turtle soup. You haven't spent much of this honeymoon with me, Arthur Doyle, but you will at least grant me Sunday dinner."

CHAPTER 24

T he drizzle had given way to scattered clouds, with a hint of blue sky, when Mr. Dodgson, fortified by the Reverend Mr. Barclay's Sunday mutton, ventured into King Street, attired for Sunday calls in his best black frock coat, white shirt, striped trousers and waistcoat, and top hat, his hands, as always, encased in gray cotton gloves. Apparently unmindful of the presence of Dr. Doyle behind him, and completely ignoring the two inspectors at the North Street end of King Street, he sauntered along, carefully noting the number of each shop. When he got to the mysterious green house, he stopped and stood back. Then he continued up the steps, the very picture of innocence, and knocked on the door

The atmosphere within the house was somber. The parlor had been reassembled after Alicia's wild rampage, but the chairs were not in their usual places. The aspidistra was gone, and the small table before the front window looked ridiculously bare, almost undressed, without it. The lace curtains that discreetly hid the interior of the parlor from the casual passersby were askew, leaving a gap through which the street could be seen

The girls were subdued, reminded of their possible fate by the events of the previous night. None of them wanted to believe it, but they knew that the little girl in the drawers and camisole might have been one of them, meant to be shipped to France instead of being toasted in London. They had been told that such would be the destination of any girl so foolish as to disobey Miss Harmon and Mrs. Gurney. Now they sat, sewing in the parlor, dressed in demure frocks of pale blue and pink and yellow, while Miss Harmon read aloud, just as any other family would do on a Sunday afternoon; just as families all over England were doing.

Miss Harmon herself was upset. The sight of Old Keeble had shaken her more than she liked to admit, even to herself. The Guv-'nor was not stable; he was clearly removing anyone who could identify him to the police. A note from Sergeant Barrow had told her about the dismembered body of the young person who had been identified as the servant accompanying Miss Alicia Marbury. She herself might be next! True, the Guv'nor had warned her about that interfering Inspector from Scotland Yard, but that was no assurance that he would not turn on her later. Miss Harmon sat in the parlor and tried to read the new novel by Mr. Trollope to her girls, who sat and listened and stitched away at their mending, and tried not to think about Kitty and the new girl in the attic.

A knock at the door made them all alert. Gentlemen did not usually come to the house on King Street this early of a Sunday afternoon; they waited until nightfall, when their whereabouts would not be noticed.

Mrs. Gurney, roused from her postprandial nap, lumbered slowly to answer the door. Her eyes opened wide as she realized who had come to call. She hustled back to the parlor, her broad face flushed with her exertions. "It's *him!*" she gasped out. Miss Harmon put down her book.

"Who?"

Mrs. Gurney gestured violently. Miss Harmon sighed, and joined her in the hall, where the conversation continued in agitated whispers.

"It's that feller what looks like Old Keeble!"

Miss Harmon allowed a small crease to mar the perfection of her forehead. "Mr. Dodgson? Here?"

"Looks just like Old Keeble," Mrs. Gurney repeated. "What do I do?"

Miss Harmon smiled, not pleasantly. "I can only assume those two policemen told him about this place. Well, it is high time the old fool learned a few things not taught in mathematics classes at Christ Church College. Let him in. Show him into the parlor. Then take that chit down the stairs, and get her to the docks. Keep her there until LeBrun shows up, and get her off to France."

"But . . . "

"She can wear Kitty's dress and apron. No one will look twice at another girl on the docks."

"But 'er 'air . . . "

"Covered by Kitty's cap and bonnet. Now, let Mr. Dodgson in, Madge. We must not keep my father's old acquaintance . . . waiting." Miss Harmon walked back into the parlor, as Mrs. Gurney let their surprising visitor into the house. "Girls, I have a great treat for you," she announced cheerfully, as Mr. Dodgson was shown into the parlor. "This is Mr. Dodgson, a very old friend of my father's, who has come to pay us a call."

Mr. Dodgson bowed to the girls, who stared back at him. Victoria looked up from her sewing and assessed the elderly scholar. "Ten minutes, and he's out," she said dismissively. The other girls giggled.

Mr. Dodgson flushed but stood his ground. He bowed slightly to Miss Harmon and smiled at the girls, who simpered in reply.

"Do forgive me, Miss Harmon," he said. "I had not known you were residing in Brighton, or I would not have been so long in paying you a call. You may not remember me . . . "

"Oh, but I do, Mr. Dodgson," Miss Harmon said. "Do sit down, sir. You were one of my dear father's favorite customers."

"Ah . . . yes." Mr. Dodgson handed his hat to the Madam and sat gingerly in the chair that had been placed for him, its back to the parlor door. Behind him, Madam bustled up the stairs as quietly as she could, dragging Kitty with her. Mr. Dodgson heard the tread of her feet, and counted one, then two flights of stairs. But he had only seen one, leading up to the private reaches of this extremely peculiar establishment.

Upstairs, in the attic, Alicia's determination was beginning to wear thin. After the Great Escape, Miss Harmon and Mrs. Gurney had taken no more chances. Alicia had been tied to one of the bedposts, and there she had to stay, in spite of her plaintive cries, with odiferous results to the bedding. She had not been fed. Her hair was a tangled mop of auburn snarls instead of neat curls. Her drawers and chemise were grimy from the contact with the floor and her two wild attempts at escape had left her limp with exhaustion. She perked up when she heard footsteps.

Madam thrust Kitty into the attic room. "Git that pinney off," she ordered. "And you, missy, you're goin' fer a boat ride."

"I won't go to France!" Alicia declared.

"You'll go where you're taken!" Madam said sternly.

Alicia looked at Kitty's shoulders, still bearing the marks of her last beating. "Very well," she said sulkily. Kitty eased out of her coarse brown dress and checked apron, and helped Alicia on with them.

"There's summon in the house," Kitty whispered. "Looks like the old geezer brung you in."

"It's Mr. Dodgson!" Alicia whispered back. "The real one, the one who knows my papa. Please, please, Kitty, help me just one more time? Try to make some noise—tell them where I'm going!"

"No talking there!" Madam grated out. "Now, missy, you come with me, and no more shenanigans or your friend gets worse than last night!"

With Kitty's drab dress draped about her slender frame, Alicia was hauled down the secret stairs and into the hall, then pulled down the back staircase that led directly to the kitchens.

Mr. Dodgson, meanwhile, was acutely uncomfortable. He had never paid a social call on a "tradesman," particularly not one of this trade, and he wasn't sure that he would ever do so again. The girls were far too knowing in their glances, while Miss Harmon's smile never reached as far as her eyes.

"And how is your father?" Mr. Dodgson asked. "After his . . . removal . . . from Oxford, we lost track of him."

"My father is dead," Miss Harmon said bleakly. "He suffered from heart trouble."

"I am sorry to hear that," Mr. Dodgson said. "I rather enjoyed our, um, acquaintanceship."

"Yes," Miss Harmon purred. "As I recall, he considered you one of his most loyal customers. He even asked that you take my photograph."

"Did he?" Mr. Dodgson closed his eyes, apparently in thought. He cocked his head. He could have sworn someone was clumping down the stairs. "Ah, yes. That was some time ago. I was quite interested in photography then."

"You said you preferred not to take me," Miss Harmon reminded him. "I was quite disappointed. It was considered an honor to be photographed by Mr. Dodgson."

"Ah, but you see, I only took little girls when their mothers were present," Mr. Dodgson explained. "As your mama was deceased, it was out of the question."

There—he was certain of it! Someone had just gone down another flight of stairs!

"It has been most interesting, meeting you again, Miss Harmon." Mr. Dodgson rose and looked about him for his hat and gloves. "I must not keep you, and your—guests."

"I have friends, who permit me to take their daughters in charge for the summer," Miss Harmon explained.

"Indeed?" Mr. Dodgson wandered into the hall. The door that led to the nether regions was swinging gently on its hinges, as if someone had just shoved it mightily, in a tearing hurry to get downstairs. "This is a charming residence, Miss Harmon. A trifle out of place, but charming." Above him he thought he could hear some kind of noise. "Dear me," he said, with a worried frown, "you appear to have some sort of, ah, vermin, in the building. You must get a cat."

"I assure you, Mr. Dodgson, this house is quite free of any rats or mice," Miss Harmon said, holding out his hat.

Mr. Dodgson shook his head. "There is definitely something quite wrong here," he told her. "If you will permit me?" He mounted the stairs before she could stop him.

"Mr. Dodgson, those are the private rooms, used by my visitors."

Miss Harmon's cry literally fell on deaf ears. Mr. Dodgson headed straight for the blank wall at the end of the hall. "Odd," he murmured. "When I observed this house from the street, it appeared to have three stories, not two. I deduce an attic—My, my, my!" He tapped on the wall. "There seems to be a hollow here. Miss Harmon, there is someone trapped behind this wall!" From behind the wall came a muffled thumping sound, as if someone was moving around, or even bouncing on a bedframe.

"I have no idea . . . " Miss Harmon began.

Mr. Dodgson's mild expression hardened into that of a stern teacher, intent on beating some knowledge into his unruly students. "I think you do, ma'am. Be so kind as to unlock this door, or I will summon Inspector Wright of the Brighton Constabulary to do it for me. He is waiting outside, for my command."

"You're bluffing!"

"I never tell lies, Miss Harmon. If you or your confederate will look out the door, you will see several constables, ready to do their duty."

Miss Harmon shot him a look of hatred and produced the tiny key that fit into the hole in the wainscoting. Beyond the steep stairs lay another door, and behind that—Mr. Dodgson pressed on, followed by the entire entourage. Miss Harmon's girls had heard about the Secret Room. Now their worst fears were revealed to be true!

Mr. Dodgson felt vindicated. He had deduced such a room existed and here it was—but this was most assuredly not Miss Marbury. Instead, he saw a bony child tied to the bed with rough twine, a handkerchief tied between her jaws to prevent her crying out, clad in her scanty drawers and nothing else.

"This," Miss Harmon stated, "is our kitchen maid. She was disobedient, and she was punished for it, as you have seen. Now, Mr. Dodgson, if you have finished with disrupting my domestic arrangements." She turned and began to push the group down the stairs, back into the hall.

"Miss Marbury was here," he whispered.

Miss Harmon looked triumphantly at him. "Prove it!"

Mr. Dodgson stooped and picked up a long strand of reddish hair. "I shall ask my friend Dr. Doyle to examine this under a microscope," he stated. "I do believe he is able to distinguish hairs from a particular head."

"This girl actually tried to strike me," Miss Harmon countered. "Those hairs could be mine."

"We shall see," Mr. Dodgson said. He looked at Kitty. "That child should not be left here," he added severely. "Let her get back to her duties. She has obviously been punished enough, no matter what her crime."

"If you say so, Mr. Dodgson," Miss Harmon gave in. "Girls, you get downstairs. I shall untie Kitty, and she will never do it again, will you?"

Kitty shook her head, tears forming in her eyes. Miss Harmon released her gag, then her hands, so that she could attempt to cover her scrawny nudity.

"I'm sorry, Miss 'armon," Kitty whispered. Her voice grew louder as she went on: "I won't never peach to the coppers again. I won't never tell 'em that a Nob's little girl's been 'ere and is on 'er way to France right now. I won't never do that again!" She ended on a gleeful shout.

Miss Harmon's hand descended, only to be caught by Mr. Dodgson. "That is enough, Miss Harmon," Mr. Dodgson told her. He averted his face from Kitty while she scrambled off the bed. "Make yourself decent, child, and tell Inspector Wright exactly what you told me. He is undoubtedly downstairs at this very moment."

"You've nothing to hold me on," Miss Harmon hissed, as Mr. Dodgson thrust her down the stairs and into the waiting arms of the law.

"Abduction of a minor, for one," Mr. Dodgson said. "Mistreatment of another minor. Maintaining a disorderly house."

"And what is that? I'll appear in the Magistrate's Court, pay a fine, serve a few weeks in jail," she shot back. "And who's to look after these girls while I'm gone?"

"I will!" trumpeted the woman in the hall. Resplendent in purple velvet, a hatful of ostrich plumes nodding over her broad face, diamonds winking in her ears, Mrs. Jeffries herself had come to Brighton.

CHAPTER 25

Mrs. Jeffries swept into the room like a dreadnought, followed by a large man in a striped blazer and straw hat, a small man in a checked suit of dittoes and a derby hat, and Inspectors Wright and MacRae, who was followed in their turn by Constable Corrigan and Sergeant Hartley. All of them stopped and stared at Miss Harmon, who was descending the stairs with as much aplomb as was possible with one's back hair coming down, and Mr. Dodgson at her heels, shepherding the shivering Kitty.

"You've made a right pig's ear of this, my girl," Mrs. Jeffries scolded her subordinate. Then she noticed the elderly gentleman behind the girls. "Who the hell are you? And what are you doing here? Business hours ain't till five of a Sunday. Even the Lord rested on the Sabbath, and so do my girls."

Mr. Dodgson winced at the profanity, wriggled through the bevy of girls, and produced his calling card. "I am Mr. Dodgson, of Oxford," he explained. "Had Miss Julia Harmon not dragged me into this matter, I would be in Eastbourne at this minute. As it is, I believe Miss Alicia Marbury is still in grave danger."

"Who?" Mrs. Jeffries asked blandly.

"Miss Alicia Marbury. The daughter of Lord Richard Marbury, the man you threatened yesterday morning, in my hearing," Mr. Dodgson persisted.

"Never heard of her. What I'm here for," Mrs. Jeffries stated, "is to see what's been going on in my house while I've been, um, away."

"Away? You mean, in jail," MacRae snickered.

"Wherever I've been, it's no concern of yours," Mrs. Jeffries snapped. "Harry, bring in my bags. Julia, I can see you've got a lot to tell me. Policemen in the house!" She sniffed audibly at the sight of Sergeant Hartley.

"First, I must warn you, Miss Julia Harmon," Inspector Wright stepped forward, his voice taking on the official cadence. "You are charged with the abduction of Miss Alicia Marbury, for immoral purposes."

"On whose authority?" Miss Harmon had recovered her icy demeanor.

"On information received by Mr. Dodgson and Dr. Doyle," Wright continued. "You may consult with your solicitor."

"I can't call him on a Sunday," Miss Harmon demurred.

"I can," Mrs. Jeffries put in. "Garthwaite, do your duty."

Mr. Garthwaite, the man in the checked suit, dutifully announced that he would act for Miss Julia Harmon, on the advice of her employer, Mrs. Martha Jeffries.

"Now, let's get comfy in the parlor," Mrs. Jeffries said, leading the way. "Girls, you get out. I want to talk to these, ah, gentlemen."

Victoria sighed. "Where should we go, then?"

"Take a walk on the street. Get out into the sun. Madge Gurney can go with you. Where's Madge Gurney?"

Mr. Dodgson peered through the gap in the curtains. "If you mean the large female who took my hat . . . I do believe that is she, going down the street!" Mr. Dodgson spied two figures heading toward Norwich Street: a large, black-clad woman and a child in a brown dress and gingham apron.

From his post in the areaway behind the dustbins, young Dr. Doyle sprang out. The black-clad woman was clearly leaving the house with a child in tow; the logical conclusion must be that the child in question was Miss Alicia Marbury. "Hi, you! Stop at once!"

Mrs. Gurney had no intention of stopping. She strode down the street, dragging Alicia behind her, with Dr. Doyle in pursuit.

Constable Corrigan, stationed at the door of the establishment, saw Dr. Doyle off after the large woman and the small child He glanced over his shoulder, then decided that this was the time for initiative. He bounded down the steps after Doyle, who ran after Alicia, who trotted breathlessly after Mrs. Gurney, unable to cry out.

The passersby stared at the odd procession: Madge, hauling Alicia by the arm, followed by Dr. Doyle, followed by Constable Corrigan, all walking, then trotting, then loping along, until they reached the end of King Street, crossed Norwich Street, and found themselves facing a brick wall.

"They're going into The Lanes!" Corrigan called out. Doyle nodded to show that he had heard, and the two of them raced after the two females, who had ducked into an alleyway and down a set of steps set into the pavement that led to a section of twisting ways that marked the boundaries of the old village of Brighthelmstone.

Here the houses leaned crazily against each other, their front doors giving directly onto the cobbled streets that wound in and out in a tangled maze. Vile-smelling puddles of ooze pooled in the streets between the cobbles. Women lurked in the doorways, watching the children who capered along the narrow walkways. Men were in short supply, being out on the beaches or out at sea.

"Coppers behind me. Want to take me kid," Madge wheezed out to the watching women in the doorways.

No more need be said. The women knew without asking that the coppers were to be foiled, by any means necessary. Alicia could not cry out in her own defense.

She pulled and twisted in Madge Gurney's iron grip. The hem of Kitty's gingham apron was unraveling. Alicia recalled another of her favorite stories, and began to unravel the apron even further. She would not give up yet!

The women in The Lanes began to edge out into the street. The children ran across the cobbles, shrieking and laughing, further delaying the pursuit.

"We've lost 'em," Doyle panted out, as they reached a fork where three of the narrow alleys split off.

"Which way?" Corrigan asked Doyle, between gasps. "They could be anywheres in this muddle."

"Don't you know your own town?" Doyle asked, scanning the streets for some indication of who had passed there recently, a footprint or a mark on the stones.

"No one goes into The Lanes who doesn't have to," Corrigan told him.

"Look!" Doyle pointed to one cobbled street. "The child's clever. She's leaving us a trail." Bits of colored thread were scattered along the street, floating in the puddles that were the only memento of the morning's rain.

Together, Doyle and Corrigan followed the trail, around the clusters of stone cottages and barrows of shelfish, through streets barely wide enough for Mrs. Gurney to pass through.

Suddenly, there was a break in the gloom. The Lanes gave onto Marine Parade, filled with after-dinner strollers, taking advantage of the afternoon sun.

Mrs. Gurney was forced to halt by the press of the carriages, filled with more legitimate seekers after fortune and fame. Doyle and Corrigan were within reach of Alicia, when the Madam saw an opportunity to cross the road.

Alicia, by this time, had caught her breath. She looked back, recognized the familiar blue jacket of the constabulary, and gave vent to her feelings at the top of her lungs.

"No, no, I won't! I won't go! I won't go!" she yelled, pulling the Madam back onto the pavement.

"You'll go where you're told!" Mrs. Gurney retorted.

"I won't! I won't!" Alicia had more or less given up on temper tantrums; Nanny Marsh was not moved by them, and Mary Ann had jollied her out of them by reminding her that a great girl of ten could get what she wanted in better ways than by crying like a baby. However, the knack had never quite left her. Alicia decided that if ever there was a time to throw a temper tantrum, this was it.

Accordingly, she proceeded to jerk back and forth until the

Madam had to let her go before she herself was pulled down into the street. She then stamped, kicked, shrieked, and generally carried on, to the utter discomfiture of Mrs. Gurney and the shocked disapproval of the decorous Mamas and Papas in the carriages that passed slowly along the Steine, leading down to the Esplanade.

It was Constable Corrigan who stopped the hullabaloo with his official voice: "Here, here, what's all this?"

Mrs. Gurney took a deep breath. "This here is my niece," she explained. "She's to go to service, and she's being a little fool about it."

"That's a lie!" Alicia shouted. "This is a bad woman, and she put me in the attic and this is *not* my dress, and they want to take me to France!"

Madge Gurney reached for Alicia again. Dr. Doyle interposed himself between the girl and her captor.

"Dear me," he said with great concern. "This child looks quite ill. I am a doctor, Dr. Doyle, of Portsmouth, and I assure you, ma'am . . . or should I say madam?"

Mrs. Gurney blanched and shut her mouth tight. She quickly considered her options: She could fight or run or give up. Under the circumstances, the third option was the most prudent. She glared at Constable Corrigan, but made no further move.

Dr. Doyle squatted down, to put himself at Alicia's level. "Miss Marbury?" he said, "I am a friend of Mr. Dodgson's. I saw your father yesterday, and he is coming for you today. This is Constable Corrigan, and he and I will take you back to Mr. Dodgson. Will you come with us?"

Alicia looked up at Mrs. Gurney. "What about her?" she asked. "She beat Kitty. Kitty is my friend, and she tried to help me."

"She did help you," Dr. Doyle said, standing up and taking Alicia by the hand. "And now, Constable, you may do your duty. Perhaps a night in the lockup will convince this woman to cooperate with the police."

Corrigan saluted, and marched back up the hill with Mrs. Gurney, presumably to John Street Police Station. Dr. Doyle hailed a cab and bundled Alicia into it. "King Street," he ordered.

The situation in King Street was at a stalemate when Dr. Doyle arrived with his charge. Victoria and the girls were clustered around the steps, while Sergeant Hartley stood guard over them. Indoors, Miss Harmon sat on the sofa between Inspectors Wright and MacRae, while Mrs. Jeffries, having removed her hat, took the armchair with regal disdain. Mr. Dodgson had been installed on the straight chair by the door. No one was speaking to anyone.

Dr. Doyle was let into the house by Sergeant Hartley. "Miss Alicia Marbury," he announced, as he brought her into the parlor.

Mr. Dodgson stood up and offered the child his hand. She took it gravely, and eyed him carefully before taking the chair to which he ceremoniously handed her.

"Are you the *real* Mr. Dodgson?" she inquired finally.

"None other," he assured her. "I taught your papa when he was in the House."

"But he goes to the House every day," Alicia protested.

"I should have said, when he was at Christ Church."

"Then you should say what you mean."

"But I do—that is, I mean what I say," Mr. Dodgson said.

"It's not the same thing," Alicia observed.

"Never mind all that," Inspector Wright broke into the pointless dialogue. "Little girl"—he caught himself—"Miss Alicia Marbury, can you state that you were abducted by this woman?"

Alicia frowned. "She didn't do it herself," she admitted. "But she kept me locked up in the attic, and she beat Kitty for helping me, and she told the fat woman to send me to France."

Mrs. Jeffries's face grew grimmer and grimmer at this recitation. "Julia," she declared, "what have you been up to?"

Miss Harmon glared at her mentor, and said nothing.

"That'll do," Wright said, with satisfaction. "Miss Harmon, you'll come with me. Magistrate sits in the morning, and we'll see what he has to say about stealing children and locking them in attics."

"And beating Kitty, and making girls do nasty things with fat old men," Alicia added.

"Eh?" Wright stared at Alicia.

"Yes, I saw a horrid old man on top of a girl, and he made nasty noises—"

"Oh dear, dear," murmured Mr. Dodgson. "This is most unfortunate. I don't know what her father will say. I had so hoped that the sordid realities would be kept from her."

Mrs. Jeffries stood up. "If Julia's been so foolish as to kidnap a child off the street, then I wash my hands of her. And if you think for one minute that I'd permit such a one in a house of mine, then you're far off. Every one of my girls is there because she wants to be. Isn't that right, girls?" She turned to the girls, who nodded, some more vigorously than others. "You see?" She nodded triumphantly at Inspector Wright.

"This abduction was not, as you seem to think, a casual affair," Mr. Dodgson said earnestly. "I was deliberately brought into it. An actor was found to impersonate me!"

"And where is he?" Mrs. Jeffries demanded.

"Alas, the poor fellow is dead."

Mrs. Jeffries snorted. "Hah! Then someone went to a great deal of trouble, and all for nothing. If Miss Marbury was taken to influence her pa into holding off on his famous Bill . . . "

"For someone who claims to know nothing about it, you know a great deal," Inspector MacRae said.

"Like I said, *if* that was so, it didn't work," Mrs. Jeffries declared. "Look at this!" She spread out a copy of the *Pall Mall Gazette* to display the bold leader: "Marbury to Speak at Brighton Rally."

Miss Harmon's pale face flushed and her green eyes flashed, but she held her head high. "It was you who told us to find some way of stopping him," she snapped out. "You and the Guv'nor."

Mrs. Jeffries glared at her subordinate. "So you cooked up this scheme between you?" She turned on Miss Harmon. "And you said he'd give in! Bah! You've let your heart rule your head, my girl, and you can take the consequences. Revenge is all very well, but it mustn't get in the way of business. Well, Inspector, take her away!"

"Miss Julia Harmon," it was now Inspector MacRae's turn, "I charge you with conspiracy in the murder of Mary Ann Parry and William Keeble."

Mr. Dodgson shook his head. "Oh no, Inspector," he said gently. "You must not do that. Miss Julia Harmon may have abducted Miss

Marbury and intended to send her to a procurer from France, as charged, but she did not kill either of those two people. Someone else did that."

"And I suppose you know who did?" Inspector MacRae's voice dripped sarcasm.

"Not quite. It is one of two persons, but I cannot prove which—at least, not yet. I have a witness, who saw Mr. Keeble on the pier with someone he describes as 'a gent.' I dare say I shall know by tomorrow. In the meanwhile, Miss Marbury, I think we shall take you to my dear friends, the Barclays, who will be very glad to see you."

"And what about the rest of these poor children?" Dr. Doyle asked, in real concern.

"Oh, you needn't trouble yourself, sir. I'll see to them," Mrs. Jeffries assured him.

Inspector Wright's eyes narrowed. "Are you intending to remain in Brighton?" he asked.

"And why not? It's my house. I hold the lease. Julia Harmon was only acting for me. I think I'll take the air, see the sights, walk on the Esplanade, and keep the company of these charming girls Julia's been educating. And I hear there's going to be some doings tomorrow night."

"The protestation meeting?" Mr. Dodgson frowned. "Surely, ma'am, you're not attending?"

Mrs. Jeffries smiled broadly. "I wouldn't miss it for the world!"

CHAPTER 26

It was a triumphant procession that marched from King Street to Church Street, across Church Street, up the hill and around the churchyard to the Rectory of St. Peter's on that Sunday afternoon. Mr. Dodgson and Dr. Doyle led the way, with Alicia Marbury between them. Kitty was between Inspectors Wright and MacRae, clad in her "other dress," an even more hideous and baggy garment than the one that covered Alicia. Behind them, Sergeant Hartley and Constable Corrigan lent a military air to the proceedings.

They crossed the Grand Parade just as the Reverend Mr. Barclay emerged from the Evensong service. Only the most assiduous of churchgoers would forsake the afternoon sun for worship, not when the holiday weekend was drawing to its close, so Alicia Marbury's disastrous attire and her choice of companion were observed by just a handful of local parishioners.

Mr. Barclay noticed the assemblage first, as he was crossing the churchyard, on his way to a well-earned tea. "Good Heavens!" he exclaimed, and went to alert his wife and her guest. Mrs. Doyle had insisted on being present when Miss Marbury should arrive, an event she decided would occur within an hour of her husband's visit to King Street.

"They've found her!" Mr. Barclay announced, before the butler had time to do the formalities.

Mrs. Doyle sprang up and ran for the door. "I knew Arthur would do it!"

"And Mr. Dodgson," Reverend Barclay reminded her. "But—oh dear, who is that other child?"

The group was welcomed in, even before they could knock at the door. Under the eyes of the butler, the two inspectors, Mr. Dodgson and Dr. Doyle, and the two children were ushered into the parlor, leaving Sergeant Hartley and Constable Corrigan to guard the front door.

Alicia spotted the tea table first. She felt faint. It had been a very long time since she had eaten anything, and then it had been bread and cheese. Only her ingrained good manners prevented her from falling upon the sandwiches in a way that would have shocked even her Waltham cousins (who were known for voracious appetites). Instead, she curtsied politely to the most senior and imposing lady in the room, who happened to be Mrs. Barclay.

Mrs. Barclay examined the child, and exclaimed, "My dear child, what are you wearing!"

"This is Kitty's dress," Alicia explained. "And this is Kitty." She drew the shrinking slavey forward. "She's my friend." That was all the information Alicia needed; Mrs. Barclay looked at Mr. Dodgson for further elucidation.

"This is the young person who served as menial in that, um, establishment, and assisted us in locating and apprehending the abductors," Mr. Dodgson told her. "Miss Marbury has taken a fancy to her, and wishes that she be suitably rewarded."

"I see," Mrs. Barclay said, eyeing the not-very-attractive Kitty with distaste.

"Hello, Touie!" Dr. Doyle greeted his wife. "Have you been here long?"

"You told me you were bringing the child here, so I decided to come and see her when she arrived. Is this the little girl?" Touie knelt down to greet Alicia.

"I'm not a little girl," Alicia maintained stoutly.

"Indeed not," Dr. Doyle agreed. "You are a heroine!"

"I'm hungry," Alicia added. "All I've had is bread and cheese, and porridge, but I didn't eat that. I threw it at that fat woman, and she made me wash pots."

"Then you must have something to eat, at once," Touie told her. "Mrs. Barclay, could something be done for these children? Perhaps your cook could prepare a small tea?"

"And Kitty must have some, too," Alicia insisted. "Because she helped me, and they hit her with a riding whip."

Mrs. Barclay's face turned rigid. "My dear child," she said, "you must not discuss that place, ever. It must have been a dreadful experience, but it is all behind you now, thanks to Inspector Wright and Inspector MacRae."

"And Mr. Dodgson," Dr. Doyle added.

The Rector had by this time removed his ceremonial gown and donned his black jacket. "Gentlemen," he announced, "I believe tea is being served."

"And Peters, take this child to the kitchen, and feed her," Mrs. Barclay ordered. "Miss Alicia will have her tea here."

"Oh, but Kitty must stay with me," Alicia said, clinging to Kitty's hand. "Because she is my friend."

"I'll go to the kitchen, miss," Kitty said timidly, looking at the overpowering grandeur of the Rectory parlor, filled with large dark furniture and the scowling portraits of previous rectors of St. Peter's.

"No, you must sit here with me," Alicia said firmly. "Then we will tell the policemen all about that horrid place, and they will arrest all of them and take them to jail!" Alicia nodded fiercely.

Mrs. Barclay had ordered a selection of sandwiches and cakes to sustain her husband and whichever of the worshippers cared to partake after Evensong. Now she proceeded to take her place at the tea table. She nodded to Touie, who handed cups to Mr. Dodgson and Dr. Doyle, then hesitated when it came to the two inspectors. Did

211

one offer tea to the police? Touie did not know, and Mrs. Barclay did not indicate whether she should include them in the company or not.

Finally, she asked Inspector Wright, "Will you have a cup of tea, Inspector?"

Inspector MacRae adjusted his spectacles, Wright stroked his mustache in embarrassment. "We're still on duty," Inspector MacRae reminded his audience. "We're not finished yet."

"But you have the wretched Harmon woman in custody," Mr. Dodgson said, accepting a teacup from Touie.

"That we do," Wright said. "But the only charge against her now is that of running a, hem, disorderly house. Which, as the law now stands, is not a crime but a misdemeanor. We cannot hold Miss Harmon if no further charges are brought against her."

"And the housekeeper, or whatever she is?" Dr. Doyle asked.

"According to her story, she was acting under orders of Miss Harmon. She'll be let go," Inspector Wright told them apologetically.

"Do you mean, you can't put her in jail for what she did?" Alicia asked, through a mouthful of egg-and-watercress sandwich.

"Not according to the law," Inspector Wright explained to her.

Alicia's face took on a decidedly mulish look. "But she kept me in the attic, and beat Kitty, and took away my dress and . . ."

"Yes, she did, I am sure," Inspector MacRae said. "And there were other things." His voice faded under Mrs. Barclay's basilisk stare. "Not very nice things," he went on.

"There was a great, fat man, and he was on top of . . ."

"You must be quite tired after all that running about," Touie said, before any more indiscretions popped out of Alicia's mouth. "And that dress." She turned to Mr. Dodgson. "Whatever became of Miss Marbury's clothes?"

"Oh dear me," Mr. Dodgson said in confusion. "As I recall, I told the porter at the station to send them on to my lodgings in Eastbourne."

"Well, she can't go about dressed like that," Touie decided. "Mrs. Barclay, last night you were discussing your work for charity. Do you collect clothes for the indigent, as we do in Portsmouth?"

Mrs. Barclay considered. "I believe there is some such collection."

"In that case," Touie went on, "could you find some sort of dress for Miss Marbury, and one for her, um, attendant?"

Mrs. Barclay looked dubious. "Such clothes would hardly be suitable."

"Suitability is neither here nor there under the circumstances," Touie reminded her. "Miss Alicia cannot continue to wear that dreadful smock. Whatever you can give her may serve until Miss Marbury's parents arrive, or until we can fetch her trunks back from Eastbourne."

Mrs. Barclay nodded. "You are quite right, Mrs. Doyle. We do have some garments laid aside, some of which may be suitable for Miss Marbury."

"And Kitty, too," Alicia insisted.

"And her companion," Mrs. Barclay went on. "And perhaps we could prevail upon my dresser to prepare a bath."

"My thoughts exactly," Touie said. "Miss Alicia, are you quite finished with your tea? Because if you are, you may go upstairs, and we will find you something to wear."

Mrs. Barclay rang the bell. A pair of housemaids entered. "Take these two girls upstairs and wash them," Mrs. Barclay ordered. "And Jane, you may go into the church and find something in the clothes-basket for them to wear."

Kitty, who had been speechless up to now, let out a shriek. "Wash? All over?"

"It's not all that bad," Alicia soothed her. "Rather fun. You'll see. Nanny Marsh says that cleanliness is next to godliness. When you get to London, you will take a bath every week. We have water laid on."

Kitty, properly awed, allowed herself to be removed by the maids, while Alicia followed her up the stairs, still chattering. Inspector Wright breathed audibly in relief.

"That's a very outspoken young lady," he observed.

"Quite like her papa," Mr. Dodgson agreed. "Has anyone sent word to him yet that Miss Marbury has been found?"

"We've got the telephone at the station," Inspector Wright said proudly. "I sent a constable to inform the station, who will inform

213

Scotland Yard, who will send a messenger to Lord Richard Marbury."

"Well, that job's done," Inspector MacRae said.

"But there is still the matter of the deaths of the maid, Mary Ann, and the actor, Keeble." Mr. Dodgson took a sandwich from the plate and munched meditatively.

"It would be useful to have evidence," Inspector Wright said.

"If you need more evidence of Miss Harmon's complicity in the abduction plot, you will find the paper similar to the one used to write the ransom note in her desk. It reeks of the scent she uses."

"Thank you, Mr. Dodgson." Inspector Wright made a note in his book, then turned to his colleague from London.

"Not so fast," MacRae said. "If Miss Harmon didn't do in that nurserymaid and the old fellow, who did? And why?"

"Oh, the why is obvious. Almost elementary," Mr. Dodgson said. "Mary Ann recognized the murderer, who was supposed to be elsewhere. Old Keeble also recognized him, tried to extort money from him, and was removed from the scene for his pains."

Dr. Doyle had ingested several sandwiches and a cup of tea. He now tried to follow Mr. Dodgson's reasoning.

"So: our murderer is a man, tall enough to heave Keeble over the Chain Pier railings, in a brown suit, missing a button off his waistcoat, who was in Brighton on Friday night, but wasn't supposed to be?"

"Could be anyone!" Inspector MacRae scoffed.

"Add to that," Mr. Dodgson continued, "that he had to have had access to Lord Richard Marbury's typewriting machine, he had to have known that Miss Marbury was to come to me, and he had to have some acquaintance with me and my, um, habits."

"That narrows it down a bit," Inspector MacRae agreed.

"Yes, it does. Unfortunately, the description matches two persons connected with this case. I cannot accuse an innocent man," Mr. Dodgson said firmly. "Inspector MacRae, will you be able to prolong your visit to Brighton by one more day? There is someone who witnessed a meeting between Keeble and the man who probably killed him on the night in question."

"A witness? And why hasn't he come forward, then?" Inspector MacRae asked fiercely.

"Because he has the greatest dislike for, um, Peelers," Mr. Dodgson said. "If I can persuade him to give his evidence, we may be able to trap this man before he kills again. He is quite desperate now, and may strike at any time."

"A madman?" Touie gasped out.

"No, far worse. A desperate man. He will do anything—anything!—to keep Lord Richard Marbury from getting the Criminal Amendment Bill passed. It is his livelihood, you see, that is at stake."

"Good Heavens!" Reverend Barclay gasped.

"And his self-esteem," Mr. Dodgson went on, serenely eating a sandwich. "A man may do almost anything to preserve his own opinion of himself."

Dr. Doyle stood up. "Gentlemen," he announced, "I have spent a good deal of this weekend on this business, but it is, after all, my honeymoon. I said I would see Miss Marbury found, and I have. Now, if you will excuse me, I shall take my wife to Muttons for one last bowl of turtle soup before we go back to Portsmouth. My practice, such as it is, awaits me."

Mr. Dodgson smiled suddenly. "But the adventure is not yet over, Dr. Doyle. Would you not like to see the story through to its final chapter?"

Dr. Doyle glanced at his wife. "Of course, but . . . "

Mr. Dodgson nodded. "Henry," he turned to his friend, the Rector, "can you arrange to have tickets sent to Dr. Doyle and his wife, for seating at the protestation meeting tomorrow night?"

"Of course, but—"

"And Inspector MacRae," Mr. Dodgson smiled at the Scotland Yard representative. "You can, of course, obtain further leave?"

"You're not trying to pull one of those fancy scenes, the kind in detective stories?" MacRae asked suspiciously.

"Oh no," Mr. Dodgson said. "But I am going to try to convince the witness to make a positive identification that will solve your problem, and mine, to both our satisfactions."

"In that case, sir, I will remain in Brighton one more day," MacRae said.

Inspector Wright straightened his jacket and nodded to the assemblage. "I thank you for your information," he told Mr. Dodgson. "Abduction is a serious crime, and if, as you say, we find the same paper, with the same scent, as that ransom note, then we've got enough to send Miss Harmon off to Pentonville for a few years."

"And then what?" Dr. Doyle asked sharply.

"And by then, with the Lord's help—" Reverend Barclay began.

"And Lord Richard Marbury's help—" Mr. Dodgson added.

"By then, as I say, the Criminal Amendment Bill will be passed, and there will be less opportunity for the likes of Miss Harmon to flourish," the Rector finished.

"Amen to that," Dr. Doyle said. He crooked his arm. "Touie, shall we stroll?"

Before they could take their leave, the butler announced: "Lord Richard Marbury and Lady Patricia Marbury."

"I have come in answer to your telegram," Lord Richard explained, advancing on the Rector as the most obvious representative of the Church of England in sight.

"My telegram?" the Rector looked confused.

"Inviting me to attend your meeting," Lord Richard said.

"Oh, that telegram!" The Rector beamed at his honored guest speaker. "There was some slight difficulty, but I am so relieved that you are here. There is to be a meeting here at the Rectory tonight to complete the plans for the protestation meeting."

"Then you did not get the message from Scotland Yard?" Inspector Wright interrupted the Rector's effusions.

"Message? What message?" Now it was Lord Richard's turn to be confused. "I received a telegram from Mr. Barclay yesterday, summoning me to speak at this protestation meeting. My wife and I left London shortly after noon. If there was any other message, I never got it."

Mr. Dodgson cleared his throat. "Miss Alicia Marbury has been found," he announced.

The announcement was unnecessary. "I heard Papa!" Alicia

bounded into the parlor, clad in a serviceable but plain dress of nautical cut and decoration, her red hair still tangled but her spirits unquenched.

"Alicia! My baby!" Lady Pat enveloped her child in her arms.

"Mama! I have had such adventures!"

"But you are quite all right now?" Lady Pat turned to Dr. Doyle, who smiled benignly.

"As you can see, my lady, the child is none the worse physically for her escapade."

"Thank God for that," the girl's mother said fervently. "Now, Alicia, dear, we have brought Nanny Marsh with us. She is putting our rooms at the hotel to rights, but as soon as we can, we shall take you to her. She will take good care of you."

"Where is Mary Ann?" Alicia asked.

Lady Pat looked about her in confusion. Mr. Dodgson took Alicia by the hand.

"Your attendant, Mary Ann, met with . . . an accident," he said gently.

"They killed her to get me!" Alicia cried out. "Oh, they are wicked, wicked people, and I hope you put them all in jail!"

"We shall do that, my dear," Mr. Dodgson said, patting her hand. "Now, you must go back upstairs. Mrs. Barclay's maid will give you and Kitty a good supper, and then you will go with your mama and papa to the hotel?" He looked about him for confirmation of these plans.

"Perhaps the child could remain here at the Rectory," Lady Pat suggested. "I can send Nanny Marsh to care for her. The hotel is no place for a child."

"And Kitty must stay with me," Alicia insisted.

"Kitty?" Lady Pat inquired.

"The menial at the, um, establishment. She was very helpful in retrieving your daughter," Mr. Dodgson told her.

"She was my friend," Alicia stated. "And I promised her she could come to London with us, and be my maid. And a Waltham never goes back on his word. Isn't that so, Papa?"

Lord Richard smiled down at his daughter. "Quite right, Alicia.

Your Kitty may take Mary Ann's place, at least until we get back to London. Nanny Marsh will show her what to do. Now, say good night, and go back to your room, Alicia. We have a great deal of work to do."

Alicia curtsied politely to the grownups and turned to go. Suddenly she turned back. "Papa, are you going to be at the big meeting tomorrow?"

"Yes, my dear, but . . . "

"Everyone is talking about it," Alicia said. "Mama, may I hear Papa speak?"

Lady Pat looked at her husband. Lord Richard shrugged. "It will be a very long meeting, Alicia. It may not be very amusing, rather like sitting through several church sermons. You are not always very calm during the sermons at church."

"But I would like to hear you thrash those awful people, Papa," Alicia insisted. "And I want Kitty to be there, too."

"Very well, Alicia, if you wish to be there, I will have Nanny Marsh bring you." Lord Richard sighed.

Alicia smiled sweetly and left the parlor. She had an idea of her own, that would make this protestation meeting into something exciting. Hadn't that woman in the purple dress said that she would be there? Well, if the police could not put Miss and Madam in jail, she, Alicia Marbury, would let everyone know how awful they were, and then they'd be sorry they put her into an attic and beat her friend!

CHAPTER 27

Sunday night in Brighton was a time of packing up the pieces of one's holiday. The pretty seashells and seaweed did not look quite so pretty, and would soon be discarded. The bathing dresses would have to be scrubbed and well rinsed to remove the miniscule bits of sand and shell embedded in the heavy wool or coarse cotton. Sunburned faces would be anointed with lotion. Another weekend gone; another week of work to be faced on Monday morning.

On this particular Sunday night, however, all Brighton hummed with anticipation. Word had got out that Lord Richard Marbury had come to Brighton, with the express purpose of speaking at the protestation meeting. Immediately, what had been a target for vulgar jokes and speculation became an event.

Once it was known that Lord Richard would, indeed, speak at the protestation meeting, the telegraph office found itself inundated with vital messages flashing back and forth between London and Brighton, and between Brighton and most of the British Isles. Members of Parliament sent their names to the committee, demanding a space on the platform. The Borough Council issued permits for enterprising businessmen to set up booths for serving hot and cold foods on the grounds of the Royal Pavilion. An equally enterprising businessman cornered the market on seating, providing chairs at three shillings each for the front five rows, one shilling after that.

By eight o'clock, the Old Ship had the air of a military headquarters, with aides running back and forth between the Rectory and the hotel. The Reverend Mr. Barclay and his clerical colleagues had recruited as many of their parishioners as they could to serve as messengers between the printers's shops, the carpenters' shops, and Lord Richard's suite. The hotel staff was summoned to minister to the urgent needs of their noted guest; trays of sandwiches, fruit, and cakes were prepared and sent up at intervals, to be ingested by the aforesaid aides and minions of the forces of decency.

Mr. Dodgson found himself caught up in the furor in spite of himself. He was pressed into service in the Rectory parlor, to oversee the production of the the printed program, which had to be revised every time another dignitary sent word he was going to attend and wished to say a few words (undoubtedly a great many words by the time said dignitary was finished).

With the most recent revision in hand, he went with Mr. Barclay to the Old Ship, that venerable hostelry on the Esplanade, where Lord Richard and Lady Pat had bespoken a two-room suite for themselves, plus rooms for their servants. Here, like a spider in a web, Lord Richard sat, with the ever faithful Upshaw in attendance. He looked up in distraction as Mr. Dodgson and Mr. Barclay entered the suite.

"Lord Richard," Mr. Dodgson began.

"Is that the program? Good!" Lord Richard scanned it, then waved it in the direction of Upshaw.

The lanky secretary seemed to spring from the ground instead of from his position behind the door, at one of the small tables set there by the management for the purpose of holding a tray of refreshment. The tray had been removed, and the inevitable pile of paper that accompanied Mr. Upshaw now took its place.

"Upshaw, go to the Albemarle. Sir Thomas Conym is there. You must have him read this, and get back to me with his reply."

"Yes, Lord Richard." Upshaw looked more harried than usual.

"The . . . the persons from the Press are demanding an interview," he said. "And Lady Patricia wishes to know if she should send Mrs. Marsh to the Rectory in a cab, or have her walk there?"

"For heavens sake!" Lord Richard threw down his pen in exasperation. "Tell her to do what she thinks best. At least Alicia is safe at the Rectory."

"Shocking! That she should have been kidnapped at all," Upshaw sputtered. "How providential that she was found before the protestation meeting."

"Providence had nothing to do with it," Lord Richard said testily. "It was Mr. Dodgson, and his friend, that doctor chap."

"Doyle," Mr. Dodgson provided the name. "Please, Lord Richard, a moment of your time."

A knock at the door brought another telegram. "Aha! Rector, you will be pleased to hear that Dr. Sullivan himself will lead your choir. He is coming down tomorrow, taking time from his rehearsals for the new opera at the Savoy to run your choristers through their paces."

Mr. Barclay's face flushed with pleasure. "I must let my choirmaster know immediately!"

"And be sure to put it into the program," Mr. Upshaw added.

"Oh dear, oh dear," fussed Mr. Dodgson. "Will no one listen to me?"

Apparently, no one would.

"Lord Richard, I *must* speak with you—in private!" Mr. Dodgson tried to convey the urgency of the situation, but Lord Richard was firing off some more orders to Upshaw.

"This program must go to the printers first thing tomorrow morning. We must have them before the protestation meeting begins!"

"Yes, Lord Richard. I shall see to it." Upshaw busied himself with his papers again.

Lord Richard turned and found Mr. Dodgson in front of him. "If you please, Mr. Dodgson," he said peevishly. "You have done your part. You found Alicia . . . "

"But that is not the end of it!" Mr. Dodgson said firmly. "Lord Richard, consider, I beg you! The people who abducted your daughter may take even more forceful methods to stop you from achieving your goal."

"What?" Lord Richard stopped in mid-stride. "You are being melodramatic, Mr. Dodgson. This is not America, and these people, as you call them, are not anarchists. They are merely criminals, and like most criminals, they are cowards at heart."

"I fear one of them is known to you," Mr. Dodgson said. "I did not mean to bring it out in this public place—but the woman who ran the, um, establishment where your daughter was found was Julia Harmon."

Lord Richard stood still for a moment, breathing hard. Then he said, "I am sorry to hear it, but it makes no difference to me. My campaign goes on."

"But . . ."

Lord Richard took Mr. Dodgson by the arm and began to lead him to the door. "Sir, you have done all that can be expected of you. I thank you for it, but you must not trouble yourself further."

"At least let me take Miss Alicia in hand tomorrow morning," Mr. Dodgson pleaded. "Another attempt may be made to secure her."

"By all means, entertain Alicia," Lord Richard said. "It is what I asked you to do, after all. Good evening, Mr. Dodgson, and thank you for all you have done."

Mr. Dodgson was gently but firmly thrust out of the room.

"This won't do," Mr. Dodgson said to himself. "I cannot think in this confusion. I will go and find some quiet spot, where I can consider what to do next."

He pottered down the corridor, brushing past Mr. Edward Kinsale on his way into the suite.

"Hello, Dodgson," Kinsale said with a leer. "Had enough of the ladies?"

Mr. Dodgson ignored the leer. "Miss Marbury has been found," he told Kinsale. "But I am not satisfied. There is more to this matter than mere abduction of a child, although that is bad enough. I wonder, sir, whether any man could be so callous and cruel as to pretend to assist in an enterprise while doing his best to destroy it."

Kinsale's normal easy smile faded. "If you mean me, sir, I suggest you think again. I don't like what Ricky's doing, but I'd never try to undermine him."

"I sincerely hope not," Mr. Dodgson said. "But I tell you in confidence, someone is attempting to destroy Lord Richard Marbury. I would not like to think it was someone related to him, by marriage or by blood."

With that, Mr. Dodgson touched his hat and proceeded down the stairs to the lobby of the hotel, where a number of shabby-looking men in loud-checked suits, striped shirts, and battered hats were demanding attention.

"Are you anyone?" one of them demanded of Mr. Dodgson.

"Oh no," Mr. Dodgson said. "I am no one of any importance. Good evening, gentlemen."

He left the Press behind, and strolled out onto the Old Steine. The night wind blew off the Channel. The lights were going out on the West Pier. Mr. Dodgson wondered briefly if he was doing the right thing by continuing to pursue the killer of Mary Ann and Old Keeble. Was it his business to do so? He could let the matter drop, let their deaths remain mysterious accidents, and go back to Eastbourne—but then someone would be free, perhaps to kill again!

No, Mr. Dodgson thought, as he turned back up the hill toward the Rectory, I am with young Dr. Doyle in this matter. I must see it through to the end.

CHAPTER 28

Monday in Brighton was not, as a rule, the most cheerful of days, even when it did not rain. The Sunday punters had left, filling the late trains that would take them back to their flats or cottages or villas, back to the weekday world of shop or office or farm, in city or town or village. Sailors had to return to their ships, soldiers to their encampments. The only ones left were those who had the wherewithal to remain for the rest of the week and those who actually lived in the town of Brighton, the citizens whose particular interest was to serve the visitors.

On this Monday, however, Brighton had a feverish air of expectancy. Everyone who could manage to coax an extra day's worth of holiday time from recalcitrant employers did. Some of the excuses handed in on the Tuesday would be worthy of inclusion in *The Times.* Aged relations were ruthlessly sacrificed, obscure diseases contracted, accidents manufactured to such an extent that there might well have been a run on Lloyds. No one wanted to miss the protestation meeting, which was rapidly growing in scope, far beyond the modest bounds suggested by the Reverend Mr. Barclay and his colleagues. Among the speakers announced by the newest handbills were General William Booth of the Salvation Army, who had come with his famous petition, and the editor of the *Pall Mall Gazette*, Mr. W. T. Stead himself. With those two on hand, there were sure to be vocal fireworks!

Even the weather cooperated. Sunday's drizzle had totally dissipated, and the sun shone fair enough for picnics to be set up in the grounds of the Pavilion, which had been opened by the Borough Council for the purpose. Vendors of ices and sweet drinks appeared, followed by the purveyors of spicier fare. When the gates to the grounds were opened, it was all the constables could do to keep the throng at bay.

While the populace spread themselves out on the grass, the organizers of the event met in what had been the private sitting room of the Prince Regent to arrange the order of speakers. It was a touchy matter, involving the balancing of social and political precedence with musical considerations. The Reverend Mr. Barclay was not in favor of hymns at public meetings, whereas General Booth and Mr. Branwell (of the Methodist Chapel) felt that music added to the spirit of the occasion. Lord Richard's speech was, of course, to be the highlight of the event, and must be positioned accordingly, not so early that people would miss it, but not so late that some of the audience would have left. General Booth wanted a table set up for signatures on his petition; the more he had, the more influence he could bring when he offered it up to Parliament, as he fully intended to do.

The Lord Mayor of Brighton and his councilors had to have their say. Mr. Carstairs, in particular, was determined not to offend any of the fun-loving visitors to Brighton by implying that any of them came to this town in search of illicit, um, entertainment. He deplored the necessity for such a public airing of private linen in the first place, but since the protestation meeting was scheduled, let it be done with as much decorum as possible.

Mr. Barclay favored Mr. Carstairs with an icy stare. He had every reason to suspect Mr. Carstairs of being the mysterious person seen by Alicia Marbury in her nocturnal ramblings at Miss Harmon's, but he could hardly accuse him at this planning meeting. Mr. Barclay privately decided not to accept another invitation to dine with Mr.

Carstairs, unless he could absolutely not avoid it. In the meanwhile, there was the order of speeches to be determined, and yet another printing of the program, which had already driven three printers to distraction.

Mr. Dodgson was conspicuous by his absence. He was, that Monday morning, watching the Punch and Judy show with Miss Alicia Marbury and her maid, Kitty Beggs, on the West Pier. He had spent the night at the Rectory, but excused himself from the exertions of the planning committee with a shy smile.

"It is most important that Miss Alicia should be entertained, and distracted from her recent sordid experiences," Mr. Dodgson said softly, when his friend tried to urge him to attend the planning committee meeting.

"But you must," Mr. Barclay complained, as they sat down to breakfast in the sunny room just off the dining room.

"My business is done," Mr. Dodgson said. "Ah, good morning, Lord Richard. I trust your rooms at the Old Ship were comfortable."

Lord Richard Marbury did not wait to be announced, but marched into the Rectory breakfast room with the butler at his heels. "My dear Rector," he said. "May I use your study for my work? The Old Ship is impossibly crowded, and the rooms they have assigned to my wife and myself are not suitable for the preparation of such an important speech."

"Of course," Mr. Barclay said, scrambling up from his place at the table. "You must allow me to show you upstairs. Mr. Dodgson has very kindly offered to take Miss Alicia on the pier this morning."

"After all," Mr. Dodgson reminded him, "you did send Miss Alicia to me."

"Oh yes, of course." Lord Richard clearly had other things on his mind besides his errant daughter. "Upshaw—Where is Upshaw?" he asked petulantly, looking behind him.

"Here, sir." Upshaw stepped into the breakfast room. "I have just been to the telegraph office. I felt it incumbent upon me to inform Mr. and Mrs. Parry—that is, Mary Ann's family—of her untimely passing."

"We must send them something," Lord Richard said absently. "See to it, Upshaw."

"Unfortunately, the Coroner will not release the, um, remains until after the inquest tomorrow," Upshaw told him. "The funeral will be as soon after that as we can move her to Waltham. I have taken the liberty of ordering a spray of flowers, with the sentiment, 'Well done, thou good and faithful servant.'"

"Most appropriate," Lord Richard said. He thrust a pack of papers at his secretary. "Now, Upshaw, I want you to go to the Albemarle and the Grand Hotel, where these people are staying, and see they get these. Then get over to the Pavilion and make sure the platform is steady. It would never do to have the speaker's platform collapse."

"Certainly not, sir." Upshaw cast a glance at Mr. Dodgson, who was quietly buttering his toast.

"And then, you may come here and help me prepare my text," Lord Richard went on, as he mounted the stairs to Mr. Barclay's attic study.

Mr. Dodgson now had much to consider as he watched the puppets whack each other about. Alicia laughed gleefully at the Policeman and clapped heartily when the Devil took Mr. Punch off at the end of the show.

"That's what should happen to that Miss and Madam," Alicia said viciously.

"I believe Miss Harmon will be sent to the assizes for trial," Mr. Dodgson told her. "But you should not dwell on what happened to you, my dear. They were all very unpleasant people, but you are safe now."

Alicia frowned. "I am safe," she said, "but what about Kitty?" She looked at her friend, who sat entranced by the puppets. "If I hadn't been there, she would still be washing nasty pots and being beaten."

"There are many little girls who are not as well cared for as you," Mr. Dodgson said gently. "Your papa and his friends are trying very hard to help them. This is what the protestation meeting is all about."

227

"That's why I want to go," Alicia said, with a decided nod. "That fat woman in the purple dress said she was going to be there. Will she, do you think?"

Mr. Dodgson sighed. "I expect she will."

"Even if she is going to be thrashed?"

"I expect she will find it amusing." Mr. Dodgson shook his head sadly.

Alicia considered the odd behavior of grownups. Then she looked at Mr. Dodgson. "You are not amused, are you?"

"No, my dear, I am not. I find all this very, very sad."

Alicia put her arms around the scholar's neck and hugged him briefly. "You were very brave, to come and find me," she said. "Thank you. Now, may we walk on the beach? And may I take off my shoes and stockings, and paddle?"

Mr. Dodgson smiled at her, his mind relieved. She was, after all, still a child. Her sordid experiences in Miss Harmon's house had not spoiled her essential nature. "Of course," he told her. "Kitty will hold your shoes and stockings, and you may paddle."

The elderly man and the two children descended the stairs and walked carefully on the pebbles that led to the gently lapping waves. Three little girls capered out from the arches beneath the Esplanade to join them.

"Hello!" It was Betty, the young gymnast who had led him to the house on King Street.

"Good morning," Mr. Dodgson greeted her. "A much better day, today. This is Alicia, and Kitty." He made the necessary introductions.

Betty turned a cartwheel. Alicia's eyes widened. "Can you do anything else?" she asked.

"Watch me!" Betty turned upside down on her hands, flipped back onto her feet, and stood, hands on hips, waiting for more applause.

"Where is your friend, Bouncing Billy?" Mr. Dodgson asked. "I would like to speak to him."

"The Jolly Jokers is working the tip over to the Pavilion," Betty informed him. "Big crowd for the protestation meeting."

"My papa's speaking at it," Alicia said proudly.

"Well, my pa's going to be playing in the band," Betty capped her. "He's got a solo!"

"Show me how to do a cartwheel?" Alicia coaxed her latest acquaintance.

Mr. Dodgson watched as the three girls careened over the pebbles. He was not sure that Lady Pat would approve of the company her daughter was keeping, but Mr. Dodgson was not alarmed. After all, artists must have a certain licence.

It was only when the noon gun sounded that Mr. Dodgson called Alicia away from the water, and led her back up the hill to the Rectory. She was taken in hand by Nanny Marsh, who exclaimed over the state of her borrowed clothing, and declared that she must rest after her luncheon.

"Henry," Mr. Dodgson found his friend closeted with Lord Richard and the ecclesiastical committee in the dining room. "I must ask a favor of you."

"Whatever you like, Charles, but can you not wait until . . . "

"This is most vital, Henry. I would like you to place Lady Patricia Marbury and her daughter in the front rank in the Visitors' Seats at the protestation meeting this evening."

Lord Richard looked up from his notes. "Eh? Pat and Alicia in the front? I don't know about that. Pat might not like to be so . . . so prominent. She's always been keen to help me, of course, but she's not like Jenny Churchill—thank God!" he added. "And Alicia, well, what if she falls asleep? I thought it might be better to keep her in the back."

"Miss Alicia gave me the impression that she wished to see you speak," Mr. Dodgson said.

"Then she shall have her wish," Mr. Barclay said heartily. "I shall leave word that Miss Alicia and Lady Patricia are to have seats in the very front of the Visitors' Section. And you, Charles, are you still determined to shun the limelight?"

"I have other plans," Mr. Dodgson said with a smile. "But I shall most assuredly be there. By the bye," he asked, as he turned to go, "is Mr. Edward Kinsale scheduled to speak?"

"Ned? I didn't ask him, knowing his feelings on the subject." Lord Richard frowned. "Now that you mention it, I thought I saw him at the hotel."

"Oh yes, I observed him here myself on Saturday," Mr. Dodgson said. "I thought it odd at the time, but perhaps he is here to support Lady Patricia in this difficult time. Perhaps you can send Mr. Upshaw to find him, Lord Richard, and see that he is given a seat in the Visitors' Section. I am sure he would come, if he were invited."

"Charles," Mr. Barclay asked, eyeing his old friend suspiciously, "what are you up to?"

"The end of the story, of course," Mr. Dodgson said, and went down the stairs and out of the Rectory, to stroll through the growing crowds and admire the outrageous architecture of the Pavilion.

CHAPTER 29

The Royal Pavilion was the chief attraction of Brighton. Its bulbous towers loomed over the surrounding cottages. None of the blocks of houses built to accommodate the Prince Regent's courtiers was allowed to overshadow this enormous tribute to Chinoiserie that had begun life as a simple farmhouse. Having bought the building to enjoy the rustic life, the Prince Regent proceeded to expand and elaborate it, until the modest farmhouse disappeared under a welter of vaguely Oriental ornamentation, inside and out.

The Prince Regent's garish extravagance was not to the taste of the Prince Consort, and what Albert disliked, Victoria loathed. Since the Pavilion had been sold, the building had been used for everything from a concert hall to a banqueting hall to a paying teashop. The public was allowed to traipse all over the parquet floors on which the feet of royalty had trod. The figured wallpapers and gaudy paintings had been allowed to disintegrate to the point where there had been mutterings about removing the entire structure as a blight and an eyesore.

The artistic clique was ignored. No one intended to do such a foolish thing! The Royal Pavilion was the very symbol of Brighton, appearing on everything from painted china to souvenir shells. No one left Brighton without some replica of the Royal Pavilion tucked away in their luggage.

The Pavilion had originally been built on a small farm that lay just outside the village of Brighthelmstone. As the building expanded, the farm became a small park; when the town engulfed the Pavilion, the park became a playground, fenced in decorously to keep the vulgar at a reasonably safe distance, but opened to the public on such occasions as the protestation meeting on this August evening.

The day had progressed, with rainclouds no more than a wisp or two in the sky at dusk. As the handbills had been passed around, so had word-of-mouth. The protestation meeting looked to be a good show, and a free one, and as such, it drew not only the transient residents of Brighton but the permanent ones as well.

By six o'clock on the Monday evening, the population of the Pavilion lawn had swelled to include visitors and residents of Brighton as well as those of the surrounding towns. The Brighton Constabulary had had to pull every officer in to control the crowds. The refined visitors of Hove clamored for seating, to hear the shocking revelations promised by the *Pall Mall Gazette*. Mr. Dodgson's friends from Eastbourne were there, as were the members of Dr. Doyle's Portsmouth Literary and Scientific Society. As many members of Parliament were spending their holidays on the south coast of England, they insisted on attending, and were to be massed in evening dress on the platform, their wives and daughters to be seated below them on the small wooden chairs provided by the borough of Brighton. Tucked away beside the platform were the gentlemen of the Press: *The Times, The Evening Standard, The Globe, The Manchester Guardian*, and, of course, the *Pall Mall Gazette*, whose editor in-chief, the redoubtable W. T. Stead, sat defiantly on the platform with the illustrious speakers. Inspector Wright stood at one end of the Press Section, and Inspector MacRae glared at the crowd at the other end.

No fog marred the evening; only a light breeze coming off the water lent a chill to the atmosphere that would undoubtedly be chased away by the fiery rhetoric to come. Light was provided, not only by the gaslights of the park, but by torches, firmly embedded in the ground.

The paid seats were filling up nicely, with only one rank, in the very front, vacant. When asked, all the usher could say was that those were "reserved." By whom? The usher could not say.

Around the seats, those who could not or would not spare a shilling stood, waiting for the speakers. Until the meeting began, they were willing to watch whoever else was on hand to entertain them. The Jolly Jokers did especially well, following brisk patter with brisker acrobatics and a trumpet flourish or two. One by one the dignitaries filed into the park from the Pavilion itself. There was a hum of expectation in the air.

The crowd was by now ready for anything. The buskers had been at their work, rallying the crowd with parodies of popular songs. The Salvation Army's brass band had rent the air with renditions of hymns, enthusiastically sung by those who knew the words and hummed by those who didn't.

The program, as finally revised and printed, listed the speakers in the order of their importance, with General William Booth vying for prominence with Lord Richard Marbury. The famous petition rested on a table to one side of the platform, with the general's staunch wife, Catherine, a famous speaker in her own right, in charge of collecting the signatures of anyone who wished to add their name to the list of those who supported the Criminal Amendment Bill.

There was a roar of appreciation as the diminutive and dapper Dr. Sullivan took the podium and the choir of St. Peter's Church filed through the gate that led from the lower regions of the Pavilion to the lawn, to await the rising of the baton. The Salvation Army's trumpet-and-tuba band joined forces with the Brighton Orchestral Society, and the crowd roared out

> Onward, Christian soldiers,
> Marching as to War,
> With the cross of Jesus
> Going on before!

The protestation meeting had officially begun.

The dignitaries were seated on the platform (which did not give way under the collective advoirdupois, although it did sag a bit). Those who were knowledgeable applauded Lord Richard Marbury as he mounted the platform, his fair hair drooping over one eye. There was another massive roar at the sight of General Booth, in his quasi-military uniform, his white beard and haggard face giving him the look of an Old Testament prophet who had somehow been transported to Sandhurst.

The ladies were seated with great ceremony on the chairs below the platform. Lady Patricia Marbury and her delicate-looking daughter took their places beside Mrs. Barclay and the wife of the Lord Mayor, their pale dresses making a spot of color agains the unrelieved black and brown of the older ladies. Behind them, Mrs. Doyle, in her tartan traveling suit, sat with Kitty and Nanny Marsh. Mr. Dodgson remained with those standing behind the seated ladies, while Dr. Doyle, having greeted his Portsmouth friends and placed his wife among the honored guests, joined his mentor.

"Dr. Doyle," Mr. Dodgson said, as the Salvation Army band ceased its exertions momentarily, "I would like you to find our athletic young friend, Billy, and bring him here to me. We may have need of him before the night is over."

There was a murmur as the Reverend Mr. Barclay stood up, a sheaf of papers in his hand, to pronounce the Invocation that would begin the protestation with a prayer. The gentlemen of the Press readied themselves.

Then, just as Mr. Barclay was about to announce the first speaker, the crowd began to roar again, this time with laughter. Mrs. Jeffries, in her favorite purple (this time, satin, trimmed lavishly with ivory lace), marched down the aisle leading her girls, all in their finest white dresses. With enormous dignity they filed into the very first rank of seats that had been reserved for them by Someone (who? no one could say), and sat down, the pictures of innocent maidenhood, ready to be instructed.

Behind them, those who knew who they were began to laugh. Those who did not know who they were were soon informed. The

Reverend Mr. Barclay felt the situation was getting away from him. He turned to the dignitaries behind him for support.

It came from General Booth. The famous revivalist had dealt with the likes of Mrs. Jeffries before. In a stentorian voice, he announced, "Let us pray, my friends!"

"Pray for yourself, you old fraud!" someone called out.

"We are here to denounce Sin!" the General thundered out.

"Speak for yourself!" From another section of the audience, catcalls and boos echoed the sentiment.

"I will speak for those who cannot speak for themselves! I speak for the homeless, the poor, the despairing, the men and women destroyed by the Demon of Drink."

The constables standing behind the crowd moved forward, trying to pinpoint the direction of the roughnecks who were bent on disrupting the orderly procedure of the meeting. They inched through the throng, batons at the ready.

Inspector Wright stood next to the platform, trying to keep his eyes on the constables and their sergeants. Someone had gone to a great deal of trouble to disrupt this meeting, and Inspector Wright was not going to let that happen.

General Booth had permitted the Lord Mayor of Brighton to join him in controlling the crowd. The Mayor welcomed the crowd in appropriately rotund phrases, punctuated by more catcalls from the back of the crowd. Mrs. Jeffries smiled benignly through it all.

There was a spatter of applause as the Mayor sat down. Then, in the lull as the Reverend Mr. Barclay fumbled with his notes, a shrill voice rang out:

"That girl is wearing my dress!"

All eyes turned to the child who had stood up and was pointing directly at Mrs. Jeffries and her brood.

"Alicia!" Her mother pulled her down.

Alicia had other ideas. She jumped up again and shouted, "That girl is wearing my dress! They took it away from me, and they gave it to her! She is not to wear my dress!"

"What . . . who . . . " The dignitaries on the platform muttered and mumbled among themselves. The gentlemen of the Press pricked up their ears and began to scribble on their pads. Here was indeed a revelation, one that would make the *Pall Mall Gazette* look pallid by comparison.

Alicia advanced upon Mrs. Jeffries and pointed to Helen. "That girl is wearing my dress," she repeated.

"That's a lie!" Helen spat out, before Mrs. Jeffries could stop her.

"You live in that house, where they do nasty things . . . "

By now the crowd was craning to see what was going on. Lord Richard Marbury took the podium. "Please, this is my daughter, Alicia. Alicia," he called to her, "you must sit down now."

"But that girl . . . " Alicia repeated stubbornly.

"Yes. She is wearing your dress." Lord Richard glanced at his wife, who stared back blankly. "Because"—he took a deep breath—"Because, ladies and gentlemen, because my own child, my little Alicia, was abducted in this very place, and very nearly forced into unspeakable acts. Were it not for the vigilance of the Brighton Constabulary, and particularly Inspector Wright, who stands here with me, she might even now be taken abroad, to who knows what fate? My friends, good people, shall we permit this? If my own child is not safe, whose child is? I urge you, sign the petition! I shall accompany General Booth to Westminster tomorrow, and present the will of the people to Parliament!"

The catcallers were shouted down by the forces of moral rectitude. A queue began to form in front of General Booth's table.

From his place behind the Visitors' Section, Mr. Dodgson nodded to Bouncing Billy. "Now, young man," he said. "Do you see anyone here like the gentleman who accosted Old Keeble on the pier?"

Billy looked at the crowd. "Hard to say," he said, with a shrug and a glance at Inspector MacRae, who had moved to join Mr. Dodgson.

The Scotland Yard man glared at him through his spectacles. "You listen to me," he said severely. "This man has caused the deaths of two people that we know of. One of 'em was a friend of yours. Now, look again!"

Billy eyed the crowd. The constables were still standing by, batons at the ready, but the noisy disruption had been stifled. Now the speeches were mere background as the queue formed in proper British fashion.

"Hello!" Billy moved forward, with Mr. Dodgson and Inspector MacRae behind him.

"Who is it?" MacRae urged him onward.

Billy moved ahead, to the Visitors' Section. Lord Richard had left the platform, to console his wife, who was in tears. Alicia had been swept away by Nanny Marsh, and was now at the edge of the crowd. Ned Kinsale had stepped out of the mob, to hand Alicia into the carriage that awaited her. Geoffrey Upshaw was hovering around the Marbury family, waiting to bring Lord Richard back to the public eye.

"That's him!" Billy pointed at the Marbury contingent.

Inspector MacRae strode ahead of Billy and Mr. Dodgson. Ned Kinsale stared at Mr. Dodgson, taking in the sight of the trio, frowning in puzzlement.

Geoffrey Upshaw looked wildly about him and bounded away, scattering ladies in bustles, gentlemen in frock coats, and children in smocks as he ran.

Constable Corrigan had been stationed behind the Visitors' Section. He took off after Upshaw, leaving Kinsale to the tender attentions of Inspector MacRae.

"I've got you now, me lad!" MacRae gloated. "Member of Parliament or no, you won't play your tricks again! You and your Fenian friends will think twice before you disrupt public meetings!"

While MacRae held on to Kinsale, Upshaw ran blindly through picnics and parties, leaving a chorus of outrage behind him, while Corrigan pounded along behind. Dr. Doyle wasted no time in running after Upshaw, but headed for the gate to the grounds, the nearest outlet to the street. If Upshaw got to it, he could vanish into the crowds on the Steine.

Upshaw loped around the park, to the gate. Dr. Doyle was already there, ready to stop him.

"Not so fast, Mr. Upshaw," Dr. Doyle grated out.

Upshaw was not too winded to struggle in the young doctor's

arms. The two men wrestled back and forth until Constable Corrigan reached them, gasping for breath, but still able to wheeze out, "Mr. Geoffrey Upshaw, you are under arrest, in the name of the Queen!"

With Upshaw subdued, they marched back to the Marbury carriage, where Ned Kinsale was held firmly by Inspector MacRae.

Inspector MacRae stepped forward. "Mr. Edward Kinsale," he intoned, "I arrest you . . ."

"Oh no, Inspector," Mr. Dodgson corrected him. "Mr. Edward Kinsale has been imprudent, but he is not a murderer."

Kinsale wrenched himself away from MacRae and brushed himself off. "Thank you for that."

"The one who killed Mary Ann and Old Keeble was Mr. Geoffrey Upshaw. And I believe that the rest of this business should be conducted somewhere more private. Inspectors, you may do your duty. Lord Richard, I will see you later in the Rectory of St. Peter's. As for you," he turned to Alicia, "you are a very naughty little girl."

Alicia grinned back at him. "But I got those nasty people, didn't I?"

"You most certainly did," Mr. Dodgson told her. "Now, you will let us take care of this unfortunate man, and I shall tell you all about it later."

"Is that a promise?"

Mr. Dodgson nodded solemnly.

"Then I will go back to the Rectory," Alicia stated.

Geoffrey Upshaw had been brought over to Inspector Wright, who eyed him dispassionately. "Geoffrey Upshaw, I arrest you on the charge of murder of Mary Ann Parry and William Keeble. You are warned that anything you say—"

"Murder? No! It was an accident!" Upshaw gabbled. "I didn't mean to do it. Truly, I didn't mean to . . ."

"—may be taken down in evidence and used against you." Inspector Wright finished his rubric. "Sergeant, take him away."

Lord Richard Marbury watched his secretary, the loyal Upshaw, being taken into custody. "What is going on here?" he demanded.

"Sorry, sir," Inspector MacRae said, "but Mr. Upshaw will be detained for a while."

"He was responsible for the deaths of Mary Ann and the actor, Keeble," Mr. Dodgson told Lord Richard. "And if you will meet me at St. Peter's Rectory, I can explain how. As for why." He sighed. "That is for the police to discover."

Upshaw looked at Lord Richard, then over at Mrs. Jeffries, who pointedly stared at General Booth, who was holding forth at great length and with unbelievable volume. Seeing no aid in either quarter, Upshaw's expression turned to a snarl.

"Why? Ask him! I was there to do his bidding. Go here, Upshaw! Do this, Upshaw! Learn the typewriter, book my railway tickets, find me a cab, Upshaw! And for the pittance he paid me? How was I supposed to maintain myself as a gentleman? I got a better offer, a much better offer, and I took it! Why not?"

Lord Richard gazed at his secretary with the look of one who has just had the breath beaten out of him. "But I thought you were with me in this?"

"You'll never win, Marbury," Upshaw spat out.

Lord Richard's spine stiffened. "Possibly not. But I must continue to fight," he said.

"Then you're a damned fool!"

Constable Corrigan led the cursing man out of the park and across the Grand Parade to the John Street Police Station, there to await the Magistrate's Court and the Coroner's inquest in the morning.

Dr. Doyle handed his wife into the carriage with Lady Pat and Alicia, then turned to Mr. Dodgson. "And what of Mr. Kinsale?"

That individual had regained his poise and his Irish charm. He now grinned at Mr. Dodgson. "I'll be at the Rectory, too. Pat needs someone to hold her hand—and I would like to know how you hit on Upshaw."

Mr. Dodgson looked severely at Kinsale. "I did not hit on him, as you put it. I used reason and logic, and the answer was there before me. I shall see you at the Rectory."

He strode off into the night. Behind him, St. Peter's Choir rendered Handel's "Hallelujah!" with evangelical fervor.

Inspector Wright and Inspector MacRae looked at each other. "I'd like to know how the old boy reasoned it out, myself," Inspector MacRae said at last.

"No matter," Inspector Wright said. "We've got a confession, and that's all the Coroner will need. This whole business will be cleared up by tomorrow, and everyone can go home."

CHAPTER 30

I t was nearly midnight by the time the Rector was able to leave the protestation meeting. He arrived at the front parlor of the Rectory, his face shining with the light of righteousness. Lord Richard Marbury loped in his wake, almost shamefaced in his triumph, with Inspectors MacRae and Wright bringing up the rear, having seen Mr. Geoffrey Upshaw settled in a cell at the John Street Police Station, not two doors down from the one in which Miss Julia Harmon was housed.

They found Lady Pat and her brother in the parlor with Dr. Doyle and Mr. Dodgson, while Mrs. Barclay and Mrs. Doyle oversaw the preparations for a cold supper in the dining room. Bread and butter, slices of cold ham and mutton, biscuits and cakes, tea and sherry awaited the ravenous fighters for the cause of Virtue.

Alicia had protested vigorously, but had been put to bed by the staunch Nanny Marsh, with Kitty by her side. The ex-slavey actually looked quite presentable in her neat new gown, with her straggling hair safely confined under a prim cap.

"And you will come tomorrow, and tell me everything," Alicia instructed Mr. Dodgson, as she was led up the stairs.

"I promise," said Mr. Dodgson.

Now Mr. Barclay and his wife led the parade into the dining room, where Lord Richard wasted no time, but attacked the collation with a single-minded ferocity that said volumes for his attitude. Upshaw was forgotten in the press of events.

"We have collected over five hundred more names!" Lord Richard announced, as he took the seat offered him by Mr. Barclay. "To-morrow, General Booth will present his petition in person, to Parliament! During the last week he has spoken in four different cities, and collected over six thousand names, including the ones added tonight. We must prevail now!"

"Richard!" Lady Pat exclaimed. "Aren't you at all interested in what is going to happen to poor Mr. Upshaw?"

"Poor Upshaw indeed!" Lord Richard huffed. "The man was a traitor, a snake in the grass, working against me all the time. He said he was trying to locate the members of Parliament at their various holiday homes, but now I find that his attempts consisted of railway journeys that led nowhere! What was he thinking of? To deceive me, to deceive us all—an employee of mine!"

"But he was not," Mr. Dodgson said.

"Eh?" Lord Richard eyed his old tutor.

Mr. Dodgson turned to Inspector MacRae. "I believe you will find that Mr. Upshaw is one of those persons mentioned in the *Pall Mall Gazette*, suborned by Mrs. Jeffries, and paid to obtain information concerning the members of Parliament. Did you never wonder why this Bill has failed in passing so often?"

"No!" Lord Richard gasped. "I cannot believe that those who sit with me . . . should be . . . " He choked over his tea.

All eyes turned to Mr. Dodgson, who had seated himself in a corner, as if to hide from the light of public gaze. Now, however, he rose, in full professorial mode, to instruct the ignorant.

"Indeed, Lord Richard, it is an unhappy fact that every person has some small peccadillo, a skeleton in the closet, so to speak. It was Mr. Upshaw's task to discover any such skeletons and pass on the information to Mrs. Jeffries."

"But—why did he involve you?" Lady Pat asked.

"Ah, yes. That was the beginning and the ending, was it not? For Mr. Upshaw did not know me at all. It must have given him a nasty start when he realized who it was sharing his railway carriage."

"But if Mr. Upshaw did not know you, who did?" Dr. Doyle asked, still confused.

"Ah, that was Miss Harmon's contribution to the plot," Mr. Dodgson said. "As you pointed out, there seemed to be two persons involved in this business. One knew of the Marbury household; the other knew of me, and my connection with Lord Richard. One was a cautious, careful planner; the other was impetuous, and easily panicked. It was the impetuous one who suggested that Miss Alicia might be used as a lever to pry Lord Richard's support away from the Criminal Amendment Bill; it was the cautious one who decided how this could be accomplished.

"When the Criminal Amendment Bill was given its previous readings, no particular notice had been taken of it by the general public. This time, however, the articles in the *Pall Mall Gazette* were inflaming public opinion. Between Mr. Stead's articles and Lord Richard's zeal, there was every likelihood that the Bill might actually be passed. Mrs. Jeffries was in jail, serving her sentence, and could not restrain her subordinates, Mr. Upshaw and Miss Harmon. Between them, they took advantage of Miss Alicia's change of holiday plans to attempt to influence you, Lord Richard.

"The articles appeared beginning on the fourth of July, the very time that Lord Richard attended the boat races at Oxford and met me there. I imagine that gave Mr. Upshaw the idea of suggesting that Miss Alicia be sent to me—that, and my resemblance to the actor, Keeble, or rather, his to me.

"It might have been Miss Harmon who continued the plot, with the aim of having personal revenge upon you, Lord Richard, for, ah, past slights.

"Now, who knew Lord Richard's personal history? Not Geoffrey Upshaw."

"Of course not!" Lord Richard snorted at the very idea.

"But Miss Julia Harmon did," Mr. Dodgson continued. "She has a passionate nature, Lord Richard, and the emotion she once felt for you turned to hatred. I apologize, Lady Patricia, if I bring up such matters."

"I told Pat all about it before we were married," Lord Richard said. "All water under the bridge now."

"Quite," Mr. Dodgson shot him a glance, as if to silence a student who kept interrupting the class. "I suspect Mr. Upshaw met Miss Harmon through their mutual connection with Mrs. Jeffries. Inspector MacRae will undoubtedly find evidence of such a meeting once he gets back to London."

"You take a good deal for granted, Mr. Dodgson," MacRae gritted out.

"Logic demands that the evidence is there. There will be witnesses," Mr. Dodgson said serenely.

"So, Miss Harmon planned the kidnapping, and Upshaw organized it," Dr. Doyle summed up. "It was he, then, who used the typewriting machine to send you to Brighton Station at the wrong time."

"Exactly. And while it was Miss Harmon who discovered Keeble, it was Upshaw who paid him, with money given him by Mrs. Jeffries. And there, I believe, the stage was set for disaster.

"You see, Miss Julia Harmon had not seen either me or Lord Richard in several years. She should have known that he would never permit personal emotions to interfere with his public duty. Mr. Upshaw did not know me at all, except as a rather foolish old man who wrote a tale for children. He thought that, having missed finding Miss Marbury, I would then remove myself back to Eastbourne and forget the matter completely.

"He was wrong, on both counts!" Mr. Dodgson looked almost fierce.

"But how did you know it was Mr. Upshaw?" Lady Pat asked.

"I didn't, not at first. It could have been either of two men who fulfilled Dr. Doyle's particulars." Mr. Dodgson said, looking at his prize pupil, who smiled modestly at the company assembled in the parlor. "I must thank you, Dr. Doyle, for your invaluable assistance in this affair. Your astute observations gave me the first clues."

Dr. Doyle turned brick-red with embarrassment and pride. "I was only applying what Dr. Bell taught," he began.

"No, no," Mr. Dodgson said. "It was you, sir, who located the machine on which the note had been typewritten. It was you who pointed out the dents on Keeble's collar, which led to the conclusion that his death was no accident, and it was you who noticed that the button in Keeble's hand was brown, just the color of the ones on Upshaw's waistcoat. Most of all, it was you who suggested to me that there might be two hands at work in this business. Although your sermon, Henry, gave me the final clue."

"Eh?" Mr. Barclay sputtered over a bite of his sandwich. "I had nothing to do with it!"

"Oh, but you did," Mr. Dodgson assured him. "When you spoke of the left hand not knowing what the right hand was doing, I realized that all through this weekend, messages kept going astray. First the one to me, to meet Miss Marbury; then the ransom note, then the summons to the police."

"Coincidence," scoffed Inspector Wright.

"Hardly," Mr. Dodgson said. "All these messages passed through one particular person's hands."

"So, you applied logic to the matter, eh?" Dr. Doyle said.

"Precisely. Once I realized there were two persons involved, I could reassess the evidence. Unfortunately, the evidence pointed to both Mr. Upshaw and Mr. Kinsale."

"What!" Kinsale was on his feet, outraged.

"I had to take all the evidence into account," Mr. Dodgson continued tranquilly. "After all, sir, you would not give your whereabouts on the Friday night in question; you are familiar with the Marbury household; you had a button off your waistcoat; and I did see you in Brighton on Saturday night.

"Given the very public nature of Keeble's death, I felt there must have been a witness to the crime. Therefore, Dr. Doyle and I questioned the children on the beach, and found a performer who had seen Mr. Keeble and Miss Harmon together. That gave me one point of reference. Then I had to find someone who was a member of the

Marbury household, with access to the typewriting machine, missing a button off his waistcoat, who was in Brighton on Friday night. Either Mr. Upshaw or Mr. Kinsale could have been the killer, but I had to eliminate Mr. Kinsale because he could not have sent all the messages back and forth."

"Couldn't he?" MacRae gritted out.

"The time, sir, the time!" Mr. Dodgson cried out. "Someone had to alert Mrs. Jeffries that we were on the trail of Miss Marbury's abductors, before we boarded the train back to Brighton, for Dr. Doyle and I were followed from the station. Mr. Kinsale had not the time to do that, but Mr. Upshaw was gone from the house for at least half an hour. On the other hand, Inspector MacRae was not accosted until he attempted to gain admittance to Miss Harmon's establishment. Clearly, she was warned after he arrived in Brighton, but not before!"

"Then, who sent the false telegram to me, announcing Lord Richard's appearance at the protestation meeting?" Mr. Barclay asked in confusion.

"That, I believe, was the work of Miss Julia Harmon. The left hand, as it were, not telling the right hand what it was doing. Mr. Upshaw only wished to continue in his vain pursuit of the sums disbursed to him by Mrs. Jeffries. Miss Julia Harmon, on the other hand, had a much more sinister plan in mind."

"But—Upshaw wasn't in Brighton on Friday," Lord Richard began.

"Oh, but he was, "Mr. Dodgson said. "He came dashing to the train on Saturday morning, when Dr. Doyle and I were leaving, at eight-thirty-five in the morning. I suspect this is what occurred:

"Mr. Upshaw, who was supposedly in Margate or Torquay, came to Brighton quite early on Friday afternoon, to oversee Keeble's abduction of Miss Alicia, and to satisfy himself that all was well. Unfortunately, Mary Ann Parry noticed him at the station, and accosted him. In his haste to get away from her, he pushed her into the wheel of the oncoming engine, with dreadful results.

"Upshaw must have begun to reconsider his part in the proceedings, but by that time it was too late to withdraw. He was supposed to meet Keeble on the Chain Pier. Keeble was the go-between, who would hand him the ransom note, which would be written by Miss Harmon. Presumably, Mr. Upshaw would have produced the note the following day, with some specious explanation.

"However, two events occurred to throw him off this schedule. Keeble demanded more money, leading to a quarrel, which led, in turn, to Keeble being thrown from the pier.

"The second distracting event was my involvement, together with Dr. Doyle. The story was undoubtedly supposed to be that Upshaw found the ransom note on the doorstep. Of course, with both Dr. Doyle and myself watching, he could not possibly say that, so he said that it had been placed into his pocket by one of the persons in the crowd."

"But no one came near us," Dr. Doyle put in.

"Precisely," Mr. Dodgson said. "But what made me look very closely at Mr. Upshaw was his eagerness to remove his employer from public life. Mr. Upshaw was at great pains to tell us that he had not been in London for a week. How then could he be prepared to write the draft of Lord Richard's resignation speech?"

Inspector MacRae glared at Ned Kinsale. "And what about our Irishman?"

"Oh, Mr. Kinsale's indiscretion is political, not personal," Mr. Dodgson said tranquilly. "I suspect his meeting on Friday night was with the followers of certain Irish societies, some of whom are not friendly to England."

Lady Pat tut-tutted at her brother, who grinned and shrugged.

"At least I stand acquitted of kidnapping and murder," he said.

"And what about Upshaw?" Dr. Doyle insisted.

"Ah, yes, Mr. Upshaw. I noticed how very eager he was to accompany us to Brighton, yet, once the unfortunate Mary Ann was identified, he vanished from sight. He must have notified Miss Harmon about the arrival of Inspector MacRae."

"And left me looking a pretty fool," MacRae said bitterly.

"It was Miss Harmon, however, who decided to send Miss Alicia to France," Mr. Dodgson continued. "It was she who precipitated her own downfall, in her determination to destroy your character, Lord Richard."

"And so you found Billy, and got the confession out of Upshaw," MacRae said. "We may need more than that to finish the job."

"I leave it to the police to find the evidence of his involvement with Mrs. Jeffries. There will have to be witnesses, possibly bank drafts or memoranda of payments, which will come to light. It is quite elementary, really."

"Bravo!" crowed Dr. Doyle. "So, all's well that ends well, eh? Miss Alicia is back in the bosom of her family, and your Bill will certainly go through, Lord Richard. That precious pair will stand their trial, and good riddance to them! Well, Touie, we must be going. I thank you, Mr. Dodgson, for letting us hear the end of the story."

"Of course," Mr. Dodgson said graciously. "I could not let you go without satisfying your curiosity."

"And what of you, Mr. Dodgson?" Dr. Doyle asked, as he and his wife prepared to leave.

"I shall attend the Coroner's inquest tomorrow, and give my evidence, if I am so requested. Then I think I shall return to Eastbourne. I must finish my new book. If you will excuse me, Henry, Mrs. Barclay, I think I shall retire now."

"And I shall return to the Old Ship," Lord Richard said, rising and holding out a hand to his wife.

"You'll be needed at the Coroner's inquest tomorrow, too," Inspector MacRae reminded him.

"And then?"

"And then it will all be over," Mr. Dodgson said.

Lady Pat looked anxiously up at her husband and then at Mr. Dodgson. "Will it ever be over?" she asked.

CHAPTER 31

Tuesday seemed like an anticlimax after the startling revelations of the Great Protestation Meeting. The visitors who had extended their stays now had to depart, to make way for another influx of holidaymakers. The good people of Brighton had to return to their fishing boats, shops, taverns, and lodging houses. No one was particularly interested in attending the Coroner's inquest on an obscure nurserymaid and a broken-down actor, even though it was rumored that the nurserymaid had belonged to the household of Lord Richard Marbury and the actor might have been involved in the kidnapping of his daughter.

Dr. and Mrs. Doyle accompanied Mr. Dodgson to the inquest that morning, where the verdict was handed down that Mr. William Keeble had met his death at the hands of Mr. Geoffrey Upshaw as a result of a quarrel. No mention was made of the sensational abduction and subsequent return of Miss Alicia Marbury, much to the disgust of the assorted representatives of the Press, who had been hoping for a juicy scandal. Instead, Mr. Geoffrey Upshaw had admitted to his crime, and was remanded into the custody of the Brighton Constabulary, until the assizes.

As for the unfortunate Mary Ann, the Coroner deemed hers a "death by misadventure," and let it go at that. Upshaw went to his cell insisting, "It was an accident . . . an accident!"

Miss Julia Harmon was not called as a witness in Geoffrey Upshaw's case. Her meeting with the magistrate was to take place later in the day, and she retained her icy calm in the face of both the constables and their female warders, brought in for the purpose of watching over the weekend's crops of pickpockets and prostitutes.

Lord Richard Marbury and his lovely wife had been called to give evidence as to the movements of Mary Ann Parry. That done, they were free to leave Brighton, or, at least, as free as the ever vigilant Press would let them be.

Lord Richard Marbury addressed the Press, in the person of Mr. W. T. Stead himself, the august editor of the *Pall Mall Gazette*. The two men met briefly in the anteroom of the Criminal Court, as Upshaw was led away, still protesting.

"I beg of you," Lord Richard said earnestly, "consider my daughter's future. It can do no good to display her across the pages of the public newspapers. You have quite enough copy as it is. Let her go, sir. Rest assured, the Bill will pass this time."

"Then there is no truth to the rumor that you are going to resign?" Stead asked.

"Certainly not." Lord Richard pushed the errant lock of hair off his forehead. "You may inform your readers—and your colleagues—that I will remain at my post to the end!"

The Press were not to know of the meeting between Lord Richard Marbury and Miss Julia Harmon before her appearance in the Magistrate's Court.

"I have to see her," Lord Richard told his wife, as they watched Upshaw being led away.

"Richard," Lady Pat began. Then she gave a sigh. "You should not see her."

"There are certain matters . . . " He could not look at his wife.

"The child," she finished for him. "Do you really suppose she would use that against you? It must never come out."

"It is bound to come out," Lord Richard said stiffly. "Pat, do you recall what I said about the American president last year?"

Lady Pat frowned. "I'm sure I don't know anything about American politics," she said. "American presidents all seem to be backwoods lawyers or motheaten generals."

"Mr. Cleveland is an honorable man," Lord Richard said stiffly. "I especially recall his campaign. Someone had uncovered an old scandal—something about fathering a child on a woman not his wife. I was struck by his response: 'Sir, I have cared for my bastard. Can you say the same?' "

"Richard!" Lady Pat cried out.

"I have not done my duty by Julia Harmon," Lord Richard stated. "I must find out about that child."

He was shown into the grim room used for interviewing prisoners, where a stout matron stood guard. Julia sat on a wooden stool, waiting for him. Her elegant gray gown had been replaced by a coarse prison smock, but her red hair was neatly arranged in its usual chignon, and her face betrayed nothing as Lord Richard approached her.

There was an awkward silence as the old lovers eyed each other. Then Lord Richard asked the question. "Where is the child, Julia?"

"You should have asked that fifteen years ago," Miss Harmon spat out.

"I could not," Lord Richard said softly. "But I ask it now. Where is the child?"

"You don't even know or care if it was a boy or a girl," Julia said bitterly. "Your son is in Canada, with my cousins."

"Does he know?"

"Who his father is? No. They took him with them when they emigrated. I believe he is a strapping young farmer. That is all you need to know." She shut her mouth and refused to look at him.

"And you will not let me help you?"

"I have friends who will take care of my legal expenses, if that is what you mean," she said. "You made it clear enough that you wanted nothing more to do with me the day you left Oxford."

"But—"

"But what? How did I find my way to Mrs. Jeffries's door? That, Richard, is a long and not particularly pretty story. Not something for one of Mr. Dodgson's little fairy books. Let us say, I saw an opportunity when it came, and let it go at that."

"And when did you decide to take Alicia?"

Julia laughed. "Oh, that was Geoffrey's idea, not mine. However, I do wish Mr. Dodgson were not quite so persistent. Alicia would have done quite well in France—for a while."

Lord Richard shook his head. "And I nearly married you. I can only wish you a speedy trial. Good-bye, Julia."

He turned his back on her and left. He was badly shaken in his own esteem. How could he have worked with a man for two years and not even known him? Should he resign his seat? No! Lord Richard's head went up, and his back stiffened. He would not resign. If Waltham wished to be rid of him, they must vote him out.

Lord Richard Marbury returned to his wife. "Let us go," he said. "There is still time for me to get to London and attend the evening session of the House."

They left the law courts and followed the crowds to Brighton Railway Station.

Dr. Doyle and his wife were in the waiting room, with Mr. Dodgson and Mr. Barclay, when the Marbury party arrived.

"So all's well that ends well, eh, Mr. Dodgson?" Dr. Doyle said. "I must say, it's been instructive, working with you, sir."

"Indeed." Mr. Dodgson let his hand be enthusiastically shaken by his impetuous young friend.

"And you must come visit us in Portsmouth, should you ever find yourself there," Touie added.

"Were I to find myself in Portsmouth, I should have to visit you, for I would be quite lost otherwise," Mr. Dodgson quipped.

Dr. Doyle scratched at his mustache in embarrassment. "There is one other thing."

Mr. Dodgson looked at him in mild perplexity.

"As you know, I've been doing some writing of my own."

"So you have said."

"And I have begun work on a novel."

"But I am not a literary man," Mr. Dodgson protested.

"I would value your opinion, all the same."

The conversation was interrupted by a veritable procession charging down the platform: Lord Richard and Lady Pat Marbury, Miss Alicia Marbury and their suite, which consisted of Lord Richard's valet and Lady Pat's maid, Nanny Marsh, and the newly washed and much-improved Kitty, her homely face radiant with the promise before her of a better life in the metropolis.

"Ah, Mr. Dodgson!" Lord Richard hailed them. "Dr. Doyle! I am glad I caught you before you left. I wanted to thank you for all you've done for me and for my family."

Mr. Dodgson waved a gray-gloved hand modestly. "Once I was brought into the business, I could not rest until I had set the matter right," he said. "It was Dr. Doyle here who kept me at it, so to speak."

Alicia tugged at Mr. Dodgson's coat, to pull him down to her level. "What will happen to Mr. Upshaw?" she asked.

"That is up to the jury and the judge," Mr. Dodgson explained. "He will be tried in the Autumn Assizes. If they find him guilty of murder—"

"Off with his head!" Alicia quoted, with great satisfaction.

"We hang murderers now, dear," her mother murmured. "But you should not think of such things."

"And what about Miss Harmon? What will happen to her?" Alicia persisted.

"You should not think—" her mother began.

"My dear Lady Patricia," Mr. Dodgson protested. "Miss Alicia does think, and thinks quite well. Miss Harmon will also be tried, for assisting Mr. Upshaw and for . . . other things."

"But not for kidnapping me? Why not?" Alicia's eyes grew bright with anger. "She should be punished for what she did, not just to me but to Kitty, too. Kitty is my maid now," she confided to Mr. Dodgson. "Nanny Marsh is showing her how she should go on. I promised her that she should come to London with me, and a Waltham always keeps his promises."

Mr. Dodgson patted her hand and stood up again. "If Miss Alicia wishes to come to me next year, I will be delighted to have her," he told her parents. "And this time there will be no confusion about the arrival of the trains."

Lord Richard glanced at his wife, then down at Alicia. "With all respect, Mr. Dodgson, I think we shall continue to send Alicia to my brother at Waltham for her holidays. However, you may call on us when you are in London."

"Papa," Alicia piped up, "will I be expected to give evidence against Miss Harmon?"

"Certainly not!" Lady Pat exclaimed. "You should not have spoken out last night, at the meeting."

"Why not? It made the police arrest Mr. Upshaw, didn't it? And it made all those people sign General Booth's paper," Alicia pointed out.

"Yes, it did, but ladies do not speak in public," Lady Pat said firmly.

"But Mrs. Churchill does. I heard you say that Lady Randolph Churchill goes and speaks for Lord Randolph."

"Lady Randolph Churchill is an American," Lady Pat said. "They are—independent."

Alicia considered this. "Then when I am older, I shall be an American, and be independent," she decided. "And I shall listen to Papa speak in Parliament."

Her proud father beamed down at her. "I only wish you could stand," he said wistfully.

"Why can't I?"

"Because you are a lady, and ladies do not stand for Parliament. Ladies do not vote," her mother told her. "Now, Alicia, say your good-byes to Mr. Dodgson, and run along with Nanny Marsh."

Alicia regarded her mother and father with clear blue eyes. "Yes, Mama," she said, with a dutiful curtsey. "Good-bye, Mr. Dodgson. Thank you for everything you have done." She reached up and drew him down to her level again, planted a kiss on his cheek, and whispered, "But some day I shall speak out, and I shall stand for Parliament!"

Nanny Marsh took her politically inclined charge in hand and marched her off to the train, leaving the grownups to make their farewells.

Dr. Doyle shook his head, half in amazement, half in amusement. "That is a young lady who will do what she has a mind to," he declared.

"Yes, she is a very determined person," Mr. Dodgson said.

"Well, then," Dr. Doyle began. The shriek of a whistle and his wife's urgent pull on his coat reminded him that his train was about to depart. "Mr. Dodgson, would you do me the honor of reading my manuscript?"

"You may send it to me at Eastbourne," Mr. Dodgson said. "But the opinion you will get will be that of Mr. Dodgson, Lecturer in Mathematics, and not that of Mr. Lewis Carroll."

"Arthur!" Touie's voice urged him.

"That is all I ask." Dr. Doyle waved, and was gone.

Mr. Dodgson turned to his friend Henry, who had stood silent during the conversation with the Marbury contingent.

"Surely you are not going to keep up the acquaintanceship with that young man?" Henry protested, as he led his friend to the train that would bring him back to his Eastbourne lodgings.

"I don't see what harm it could do to encourage him in his literary leanings."

"He's not . . . quite . . . "

"Henry! Young Dr. Doyle is, perhaps, a bit enthusiastic."

"He's a pushing young particle, to quote Mr. Gilbert's play," the Rector fumed. "A Scot, and a practicing physician, not a consultant."

"But he will send me his manuscripts," Mr. Dodgson said, with a smile. "And I will read them and give some advice, which he may or may not take. Yes, I shall correspond with him. After all," he gave his friend the clinching argument, "he *is* Dicky Doyle's nephew, you know."

AFTERWARD

L ord Richard Marbury lost his seat in Parliament when the Liberal Party lost the General Election in November of 1885. He was returned to Parliament twice more. During the interims, he wrote tracts and spoke against the white slave trade and other abuses of children. He died in 1901, of a heart attack brought on by overwork.

Lady Pat remained in the Grosvenor Square house with her daughter, Alicia, until the zeppelin attacks during World War I sent her back to Kinsale in 1916. She died there in 1921.

Edward Kinsale retained his Parliamentary seat through several elections, largely on the strength of his commitment to Irish Self-Rule. He was knighted by Edward VII in 1905, and died the following year in a hunting accident.

Miss Alicia Marbury endured a tempestuous season or two as a debutante. She received several offers of marriage, but accepted none of them, to the great despair of her mother. (It was thought that she had given her heart to her cousin, Captain Lord Bertram Marbury, who was killed in South Africa relieving Mafeking.) Instead, she became a member of several organizations devoted to bettering social conditions, swearing that she would continue her father's work. She came into her own in 1914, when she organized women's labor forces in factories, and used her social connections to improve working conditions for women everywhere. She was made a Dame of the British Empire in 1920. She never married, but continued her charitable work until her death in the Blitz in 1941.

Kitty remained with Alicia Marbury during her debutante years. She married one of the footmen from Waltham Castle (said footman then became Dame Alicia Marbury's butler and general factotum). She and Alicia cast the first votes by women in Waltham Village. Her son, Alexander, holds the seat for Waltham, for the Conservative Party.

Geoffrey Upshaw and Julia Harmon were tried and convicted of conspiracy in the death of William Keeble. Geoffrey Upshaw was sentenced to ten years in Dartmoor Prison, where he died of pneumonia brought on by the unhealthy climate and conditions in the prison. Julia Harmon served her term at Pentonville Prison for Women; when she was discharged, she joined her family in Canada, where she died during the Spanish influenza epidemic of 1919.

No mention was ever made in the Press of the abduction and subsequent return of Miss Alicia Marbury.

Mr. Dodgson went back to Eastbourne and resumed his regular round of writing, occasional lectures, and study at Oxford.

Dr. Arthur Conan Doyle returned to Portsmouth, where he practiced medicine and wrote sensational fiction for popular magazines.

Mr. Dodgson and Dr. Doyle were to meet several times more— but that, as they say, is another story.

AUTHOR'S NOTE

The events of July and August of 1885 are a matter of public record. The series of sensational articles in the *Pall Mall Gazette* appeared; the Reverend Mr. Charles Lutwidge Dodgson wrote a letter to Lord Salisbury, the Prime Minister, and another which was published, both decrying the articles; protest meetings were held across England; and General William Booth collected over five thousand signatures to a petition, which he presented at Westminster.

The Criminal Amendment Bill passed, by the barest of majorities, on August 29, 1885. Among other things, it raised the age of consent for girls from twelve to sixteen years of age, made pandering a criminal offense punishable by imprisonment, and decreed prison sentences for sexual acts between males.

Mrs. Martha Jeffries was a noted Madam. Her various houses of prostitution were patronized by the most noble and notable gentlemen. Her release from a brief prison sentence occurred as described. She died in her bed, at an advanced age. Her funeral was attended by many of her most faithful patrons.

Dr. Doyle and Mr. Dodgson actually never met. This story is an exercise in "what if."

ABOUT THE AUTHOR

Roberta Rogow has been writing since she could hold a pen. Her stories have appeared in several anthologies of Sherlock Holmes pastiches, as well as in the *Merovingen Nights* anthologies. This is her first novel.

Roberta has been an avid science fiction fan for the last twenty-five years, attending Star Trek conventions, singing her own parodies, and playing her guitar. She has honed her writing skills in "fanzines," underground publications devoted to Star Trek, Star Wars, and other television shows and movies.

When she is not writing, Roberta is the children's librarian at the New Jersey Union Public Library. She lives in Fair Lawn, New Jersey, with her husband of thirty-five years, Murray Rogow, a freelance publicity and public relations writer.